MEDIA, FEMINISM, CULTURAL STUDIES

I0682025

The Sacred Cinema of Andrei Tarkovsky
by Jeremy Mark Robinson

Jean-Luc Godard: The Passion of Cinema / Le Passion de Cinéma
by Jeremy Mark Robinson

Liv Tyler
by Thomas A. Christie

Stepping Forward: Essays, Lectures and Interviews
by Wolfgang Iser

Wild Zones: Pornography, Art and Feminism
by Kelly Ives

'Cosmo Woman': The World of Women's Magazines
by Oliver Whitehorne

The Cinema of Richard Linklater
by Thomas A. Christie

Walerian Borowczyk
by Jeremy Mark Robinson

Andrea Dworkin
by Jeremy Mark Robinson

Cixous, Irigaray, Kristeva: The Jouissance of French Feminism
by Kelly Ives

Julia Kristeva: Art, Love, Melancholy, Philosophy, Semiotics
by Kelly Ives

Luce Irigaray: Lips, Kissing, and the Politics of Sexual Difference
by Kelly Ives

Helene Cixous I Love You: The Jouissance of Writing
by Kelly Ives

Sex in Art: Pornography and Pleasure in Painting and Sculpture
by Cassidy Hughes

The Erotic Object: Sexuality in Sculpture From Prehistory to the Present Day
by Susan Quinnell

Women in Pop Music
by Helen Challis

Detonation Britain: Nuclear War in the UK
by Jeremy Mark Robinson

J.R.R. TOLKIEN
POCKET GUIDE

Jeremy Mark Robinson

Crescent Moon

Crescent Moon Publishing
P.O. Box 1312,
Maidstone, Kent
ME14 5XU, Great Britain
www.crmoon.com

First published 2010. Second edition 2013.
© Jeremy Mark Robinson 2010, 2013.

Printed and bound in the U.S.A.
Set in Helvetica Neue Condensed 9 on 11pt.
Designed by Radiance Graphics.

British Library Cataloguing in Publication data available for this title.

ISBN-13 9781861713780 (Hbk)
ISBN-13 9781861714763 (Pbk)

CONTENTS

ACKNOWLEDGEMENTS

To the authors and publishers quoted, including Allen & Unwin, Unwin Hyman, HarperCollins, Ballantine Books, Macmillan, Virgin, Tolkien Society, Mitchell Beazley, Pavilion, Wallflower Press, Courage Books, Junction Books, Abacus, and Oxford University Press.

Picture credits:
New Line Productions, Inc. The Lord of the Rings, and the names of the characters, events, items and places therein, are trademarks of The Saul Zaentz Company d/b/a Tolkien Enterprises under license to New Line Productions, Inc.

Getty Images. Hulton Archive. Houghton Mifflin. Allen & Unwin. Unwin Hyman. HarperCollins. X-Box.

Every effort has been made to contact copyright owners of the illustrations. No copyright infringement is intended. We welcome enquiries about any copyright issues for future editions of this book.

ABBREVIATIONS

FR	*The Fellowship of the Ring*
HME	*The History of Middle-earth*
L	*The Letters of J.R.R. Tolkien*
LR	*The Lord of the Rings*
MC	*The Monster and the Critics and Other Essays*
RK	*The Return of the King*
S	*The Silmarllion*
TL	*Tree and Leaf*
TT	*The Two Towers*
Sib	*Peter Jackson* by Brian Sibley

FA	First Age
SA	Second Age
TA	Third Age

Tolkien in Oxford, above, and at Merton College, 1955, below.

Above © Houghton Mifflin.
Below: © Hulton Archive/ Getty Images

Portraits of J.R.R. Tolkien - in 1916 (above left), in younger days (above), in Oxford (below), and Tolkien's friend C.S. Lewis (below left)

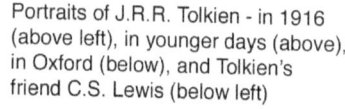

INTRODUCTION

For me, J.R.R. Tolkien is an astonishing writer, but not the most brilliant as a stylist (Rainer Maria Rilke, Francesco Petrarch and D.H. Lawrence beat him there), not the greatest writer of letters and diaries (John Cowper Powys, André Gide and Henry Miller trump him there), or the creator of the most intriguing and compelling characters (William Shakespeare and Thomas Hardy effortlessly top him there), or the most accomplished creator of battles and action (Homer and Mary Renault surpass him there), or a writer with the most profound things to say about being alive (Sir Thomas Browne and Chuang-tzu outshine Tolkien there), or the most fascinating writer in terms of his personal life (Arthur Rimbaud and Lord Byron beat him in that respect). And most any poet is a more enchanting poet than Tolkien.

J.R.R. Tolkien's Middle-earth writings are among the high water-marks in fantasy and heroic romance, yes, but for me the *Earthsea* books of Ursula Le Guin, for instance, are more profound in terms of philosophical and spiritual statements, and far better written as prose and poetry.

But there is something compelling about John Ronald Reuel Tolkien and his fictions – principally, his three most well-known works, *The Hobbit* (1937), *The Lord of the Rings* (1954-55) and *The Silmarillion* (1977), which this study concentrates on much more than his lesser-known books (such as *Leaf By Niggle*, or *The Adventures of Tom Bombadil*). One thing is certain, Tolkien's books have become a cultural phenomenon in the contemporary era, with the 2001-2003 Hollywood film versions of *The Lord of the Rings* further enhancing Tolkien's global reach.

Philip Toynbee declared, in 1961, that J.R.R. Tolkien's 'childish books had passed into a merciful oblivion', a wonderful statement, just a teeeeeensy bit inaccurate. In 1997, *The Lord of the Rings* was voted the top book of the 20th century by readers in a British bookstore's poll (Waterstone's bookstore). 104 out of 105 stores and 25,000 readers put *The Lord of the Rings* at the top (*1984* by George Orwell was second).

The results of the poll angered many lit'ry critics in Blighty. Howard Jacobson, Mark Lawson, Bob Inglis, Germaine Greer and Susan Jeffreys were among those irritated by *Lord of the Rings'* success among readers. The *Daily Telegraph* readers' poll came up with the same results. The Folio Society also ran a poll (of 50,000 members), and Middle-earth was top again (*Pride and Prejudice* was second and *David Copperfield* was third).

It was J.R.R. Tolkien's incredible *popularity* that annoyed some critics and journos. Writers are nothing if not bitchy and envious of other people's success, and British journalists have a long tradition of knocking down anyone who's successful. So the popularity of *The Lord* served to underline many of the prejudices of the literary establishment and media in the U.K.:

(1) That people who liked J.R.R. Tolkien were geeks, anoraks, sci-fi nuts, college students, hippies, and so on.

(2) That J.R.R. Tolkien's fiction was juvenile, reactionary, sexist, racist, pro-militaristic, etc.

(3) And it was badly written, simplistic, stereotypical, and so on.

(4) And it was in the fantasy genre, which was automatically deemed as lightweight, as 'escapist', as fit only for adolescent boys. And so on and on.

❈

Around 100 million copies of *The Lord of the Rings* had been sold by the end of the twentieth century, and 60 million copies of *The Hobbit,* with sales of around 3 million per year of the two books combined. Readers just love reading J.R.R. Tolkien's books. It's that simple. You can't force people to buy books or go see movies; there's isn't a magic formula (or ruling ring) to hypnotize readers and consumers (if there was, it'd be worth billions). And the Tolkien phenomenon began with *readers.* Back in 1937, 1954 and 1955, the publishers Allen & Unwin did their bit, of course, with reviews, blurbs, advertizing and so on, promoting *The Hobbit* and *The Lord of the Rings,* but it was readers who first started the phenomenon that has become truly global.

J.R.R. Tolkien's influence on literature has been considerable, too, and not just in the realm of fantasy, sci-fi, fairy tales and related genres. As fantasy author Terry Brooks said, Tolkien 'was the premier fantasy writer of the last century, and all of us writing today owe him a huge debt.' No other writer W.H. Auden reckoned had 'created an imaginary world and a feigned history in such detail' (in A. Becker, 45). Colin Wilson agreed that only a few writers have concocted a total universe, and that Tolkien's was very impressive. Tolkien's mythological writings may be the 'largest body of invented mythology in the history of literature', according to David Day (12). Invented, that is, by one person. It's also 'certainly the most complex and detailed invented world in all literature' (13).

A massive Tolkien industry has been around for decades: the 2001-2003 *Lord of the Rings* films have simply added to that. The Tolkien industry consists of (among other things): Tolkien societies in many countries, Tolkien fan newsletters, Tolkien merchandize catalogues, Tolkien websites, decorative porcelain plates, fantasy posters, Middle-earth maps, calendars, *Lord of the Rings* plastic figures (Mithril Miniatures, Harlequin, and movie tie-ins), music and songs based on Tolkien's writing,

Tolkien's verse set to music, Middle-earth puzzles, fan fiction, Middle-earth poems, playing cards, Middle-earth games and activity packs, diaries, a *Hobbit* birthday book, Frodo necklaces, Gandalf pendants, replica swords, replica jewellery (including the golden ring, of course), telephone cards, Kinder Surprise chocolate egg figures, role-playing games (MERP, METW), *Lord of the Rings* stickers, postcards, fridge magnets, and Middle-earth stationary. Plus Tolkien fan conferences, seminars and symposia and Tolkien art exhibitions. Then there are myriad editions of Tolkien's books: limited editions, collector's editions, boxed editions, anniversary editions, pop-up books, cartoon books, etc.

Among the books dedicated to the world of J.R.R. Tolkien's fiction are: dictionaries of Elvish, guides to Tolkien's invented languages, guides and atlases to Middle-earth, Tolkien bestiaries, teachers' guides to Tolkien, Middle-earth quiz books, Tolkien books of days, books of fantasy art, spin-off books, and spoofs (*Bored of the Rings*). Radio versions of *The Lord of the Rings* and *The Hobbit* (on CD, tape, I-Pod, etc), audio books (read by the author, or by actors), film versions (on video, DVD, etc), and stage productions.

The combination of music and J.R.R. Tolkien includes rock bands with Tolkienesque names (*thousands* of them), acts singing about Tolkienesque subjects (Led Zeppelin, Rush, Genesis), and the many singers, songwriters and acts who interpreted the verses in Tolkien's books.

If that isn't an industry gathered around a writer's work, I don't know what is. Also, it existed quite healthily prior to the 2001-03 movies (before the 2001-03 films J.R.R. Tolkien's books had sold in their millions). And it only occurs to a very, very writers (in Great Britain, the Brontës, D.H. Lawrence, Thomas Hardy, Charles Dickens, etc).

❊

This is a much shortened and reworked edition of my 2008 book on J.R.R. Tolkien. That book was long (812 pages) and dense: this *Pocket Guide* aims to deliver a more concise account of Tolkien and his works (as well as correcting the text). For a pocket guide to the *Lord of the Movies* movies, please see the companion book to this volume. The book is intended to be dipped into, rather than read straight through.

Amounts in British pounds (£) have been converted to U.S. dollars ($) at the rate of 1:1.6. Some of the spelling I use is deliberately eccentric.

Jeremy Mark Robinson
Kent, England, 2012

chápter 1

J.R.R. TOLKIEN'S BIOGRAPHY

I am in fact a *Hobbit* (in all but size). I like gardens, trees and unmechanized farmlands; I smoke a pipe, and like good plain food (unrefrigerated), but detest French cooking; I like, and even dare to wear in these dull days, ornamental waistcoats. I am fond of mushrooms (out of a field); have a very simple sense of humour (which even my appreciative critics find tiresome); I go to bed late and get up late (when possible). I do not travel much. I love Wales (what is left of it, when mines, and the even most ghastly seaside resorts, have done their worst), and specially the Welsh language.

J.R.R. Tolkien (*Letters*, 289)

As there are many biographies available, I will just mention a few aspects of J.R.R. Tolkien's life here. Tolkien wasn't keen on the kind of criticism that uses an author's life to interpret their works. Tolkien disliked the tendency of critics to look to an author's biography or personality to throw light on what was essentially a narrative art whose goal was enjoyment (L, 414). (And the opposite: to study the fiction to gain insights into the writer). I agree with him, and try to avoid it (though sometimes it's irresistible).

J.R.R. Tolkien was born in Bloemfontein, Africa, on January 3, 1892, and died in Bournemouth, England, on August 28, 1973. Some people (university friends) called him 'Tollers', to school friends he was John Ronald. His colleagues at Oxford called him J.R.R.T. or Professor Tolkien. He was Ronald to his wife, parents and relatives.

One of the most significant events in J.R.R. Tolkien's life was the early deaths of his parents: his father, Arthur, died in South Africa in 1896. His mother, Mabel, moved back to England in 1895 (sailing on the *S.S. Guelph* via Suez), with her two sons, Ronald and Hilary. Mabel Tolkien died aged 34 in 1904. Tolkien was deeply affected by her death. (Mabel had grown up in Evesham, Worcestershire, in a religious family, and had worked with missionaries in Africa. Tolkien's love of trees, flowers and the natural world was partly inspired by his mother's encouragement. Mabel also liked parades, festivals, and pageantry, which Tolkien enjoyed). For Michael White, Tolkien may have retreated emotionally into his mythological fantasy world following his mother's death; it was a realm where he was in control. And it was a distinctly non-Christian, non-Catholic world.

In England, the Tolkiens settled in and around Birmingham, the industrial centre of England. Birmingham was heavily industrial at that time – a contemporary version of Mordor, a 'Black Country', but Tolkien also enjoyed the museums, the libraries, the parks, and the friends he had at school.

At first, the Tolkiens first lived in Sarehole, a mainly rural region which made a deep and lasting impression on the young Tolkien, but after that they lived closer in to Birmingham: in the suburbs of Mosely, then King's Heath, and Rednal, and then (in 1902) to Edgbaston. Rednal was a hamlet on the edge of Worcestershire (the Tolkiens lived in a cottage in 1904, in the grounds of the country house built by Cardinal Newman for the Oratory clergy. It was an idyllic time for Tolkien). Tolkien loved the countryside around Sarehole: 'I loved it with an intensity of love that was a kind of nostalgia reversed', he recalled, and spoke warmly of the mill, the lake, the sand pit, the flowery dell, the village, the stream, and the country lanes. (Tolkien said he was always aware that it couldn't last, though: 'behind all this hobbit stuff lay a sense of insecurity. I always knew it would go away, and it did').

The Tolkien boys continued to be shifted around Birmingham after Mabel's death: they lived with an aunt (Beatrice) for a while, changed schools from King Edward's to St Philip's (then back again), and moved to Stirling Street and to Duchess Road in Edgbaston. So although Tolkien spent the first three years of his life in South Africa, and what appeared to be an idyllic four years at Sarehole Mill, he was in many respects a Birmingham boy, spending the bulk of his formative years in the industrial city – from 1900 (when he was 8) until he went up to Oxford in 1911 (he had failed to get into Oxford the first time, failing the entrance exam in 1909).

J.R.R. Tolkien walked to school from Sarehole, four miles there and back. His mother undertook his education for some time (helping him to gain the scholarship to King Edward VI School in Birmingham in 1900); he also spent some time at St Philip's grammar school. At St Philip's, Tolkien was influenced by the English teacher George Bowerton, who had a dislike of what he regarded as imported words in the English language (particular those coming from French. He disliked French cooking, needless to say).

In 1911 J.R.R. Tolkien went up to Oxford to study English at Exeter College, graduating in 1915. Tolkien was annoyed that he had performed badly in the Moderns (languages) exam in Easter, 1913, gaining a second class honours (partly because there weren't any lecturers at the time in Anglo-Saxon).

OXFORD AND THE MIDLANDS.

Apart from his tenure at Leeds University and a few years in the late 1960s in Poole in Dorset, J.R.R. Tolkien lived in Oxford (Tolkien came to live in rooms at Merton College, at 21, Merton Lane, in the last years of his life). In terms of place, Oxford is at the centre of Tolkien's life (as for travelling, Tolkien said he hadn't done much, apart from Wales, Scotland, Ireland, France and Belgium [L, 219]). He received many invitations to go overseas when he became a famous author, but rarely accepted them. He took holidays in ordinary places, and didn't travel outside Britain for the central portion of his life.1

Travel and new experiences weren't important to J.R.R. Tolkien as a writer, because he already had plenty of experiences to be going on with in order for him to write books like *The Lord of the Rings*. As he explained in a letter, *The Lord of the Rings* had been gestating in his mind for years, and its roots went back to his early years (with linguistics playing a large role).

'I am a West-midlander by blood, and took to early West-midland Middle English as to a known tongue as soon as I set eyes on it', J.R.R. Tolkien wrote to the poet W.H. Auden.2 For Tolkien, it seemed that Oxford was part of the Midlands, the central region of England, not, as some people who live in and around Oxford see it, as a town on the Northern reaches of London and the South of England. It's an important distinction (albeit a provincial one) that Tolkien's Oxford wasn't part of a commuter belt which encompassed Surrey, Sussex, Kent, Essex, Hertfordshire and so on, that Oxford didn't orbit around London, but was really part of another region, the central area of England that Tolkien regarded as his heartland, that became the inspiration for the Shire. (Oxford, a place of learning since mediæval times, would be the equivalent of Rivendell).

J.R.R. Tolkien loved the sea, but didn't visit it often; he liked the Mountains, but didn't go there very much. He had always wanted to visit Iceland, but didn't. Travel appealed to him, but it wasn't essential. As his biographer Humphrey Carpenter put it 'gradually one forms the idea that he did not altogether care very much where he was' (1995, 129).

At Oxford, J.R.R. Tolkien worked on the *Oxford English Dictionary*, and was Rawlinson and Bosworth Professor of Anglo-Saxon (1925-45) and Merton Professor of English Language and Literature (1945-59). At Leeds University he was Reader and Professor of English Language (1920-25). He also received honorary degrees from Oxford, Nottingham, Dublin and Edinburgh universities. Tolkien's field of study as an academic was Old English (between 700 and 1100 AD) and Middle English (1100 to 1500 AD).

Eric Gordon, an English lecturer at Leeds, was an important work colleague for J.R.R. Tolkien. They formed a Viking Club together at Leeds, and collaborated on books (including Tolkien's edition of *Sir Gawain and the Green Knight*). Tolkien also produced a *Middle English Vocabulary*, an edition of *Ancrene Wisse*, a study of *Beowulf*, and other studies.

At the Oxford Union, Tolkien put forward motions such as 'the house deplores the success of the Norman Conquest'. The Norman Conquest of Britain caused Tolkien as much grief as if it had happened in his lifetime, Humphrey Carpenter observed (134).

Oxford student life for J.R.R. Tolkien included mandatory Oxford activities such as punting on the Cherwell, watching the boat races on the Thames, sport matches, and visiting pubs (such as the Swains and the George). Tolkien also played baseball in Christ Church Meadow, cricket behind Ruskin College, visited the cinema, saw Gilbert & Sullivan operas, and tramped and cycled around the Oxfordshire countryside.3

There are many clubs at Oxford University; in J.R.R. Tolkien's time they included the Uffizi Society, the Essay Club, the Dialectical Society, the Stapledon, the Charon Club and the Wodehouse Society. With friends such as Nevill Coghill, Hugo Dyson, Helen MacMillan Buckhurst, R.M. Dawkins and George Gordon, Tolkien formed the Coalbiters, a group that was devoted to Old Icelandic and the myths and legends of Northern Europe. Gathering once a week for dinner, the group would read translations they'd made from Icelandic texts.

In Oxford, J.R.R. Tolkien lived in Northmoor Road for 21 years (from 1926 to 1947). The family lived at no. 22 first, then moved to no. 20 (which had been Oxford publisher Basil Blackwell's house). In 1947, they moved to Manor Road, in 1950 to Holywell Street, and in 1953 to Sandfield Road in Headington (Tolkien used the garage as his study). In 1968, the Tolkiens moved to Poole in Dorset, with Tolkien returning to Oxford for the last two years of his life (he looked after at Merton by Charles and Mavis Carr, and took to chatting with Mavis in Welsh, her native tongue. He was, Mavis Carr recalled, excellent at speaking Welsh).4

J.R.R. Tolkien eked out supplementary income by marking exam papers – for universities (including Oxford), and also for secondary schools (the School Certificate). The job meant visiting many universities throughout Britain, including Ireland (Tolkien chose to work as an examiner in Irish colleges after WW2). He did that extra work for years, and said it was very 'boring', 'agony'. I've marked exams papers: it's *sooooo* boring.

CATHOLICISM.

J.R.R. Tolkien spoke of himself as a Christian, a Roman Catholic, and *The Lord of the Rings* as a 'Christian' work. Tolkien's Catholic background shouldn't be under-estimated; it stemmed in large part from his mother's religiosity (she was received into Catholicism in 1900, and chose where to live partly because of the proximity to Catholic churches such as the Oratory in Birmingham. Mabel's patriotism was another influence on the young Tolkien). In Edgbaston, the Oratory was an important part of Tolkien's younger life; he would spend much time there, with his brother Hilary: helping out with morning mass with Father Morgan, and after school having tea there. Morgan's significance in Tolkien's childhood shouldn't be under-estimated too, especially after his mother's death. Mabel's conversion to Catholicism led to her family severing ties with her; her father John Suffield rejected her (he was a strict Methodist), and her brother-in-law, Walter Incledon, withdrew his financial assistance, which he had given since Tolkien's father's death.

According to his first biographer (Humphrey Carpenter), J.R.R. Tolkien went to Mass (often at St Aloysius, or in Headington) every day. 'His committment to Christianity and in particular to the Catholic Church was total', Carpenter claimed (133). Tolkien undertook confession often. George Sayers called Tolkien 'a very strict Roman Catholic. He was very orthodox and old-fashioned'.5 It was an emotional, not a rational, relationship that Tolkien had with Catholicism (and it was linked with his mother). His wife Edith moved away from Catholicism, and wasn't an active church-goer like her husband. Tolkien's son John became a Catholic priest.

In *The Lord of the Rings,* the narrator writes that the fellowship leave Rivendell on 'a cold grey day near the end of December'. In the chronology in the appendices of *The Return of the King*, it is no less than one of the most significant dates in the Christian calendar: Christmas Day. And the overthrow of Sauron occurs on March 25: Good Friday.

Protestant and Anglican Christianity (the dominant forms of Christian religion in Britain) doesn't celebrate the Annunciation (or other festivals linked to the Virgin Mary, such as the Assumption on August 15, or the Madonna's birthday, on September 8). But Catholicism does.

EDITH BRATT.

The significance of Edith Mary Bratt (1889-1971, born in Gloucestershire) in J.R.R. Tolkien's life was huge: from the first time he saw her, when he was sixteen and she was nineteen, she seems to have been the only really important woman in his life (apart from his beloved mother. Maybe Tolkien had affairs, but they haven't come out in biographies yet). Tolkien had been moved around different households following the death of his mother, and had met Edith Bratt when she was a lodger at Mrs Faulkner's house at 37, Duchess Road in Birmingham. As Tolkien put it to his son Christopher after Edith's death: 'she was (and knew she was) my Lúthien'.6

What comes across in biographies of J.R.R. Tolkien is how much Tolkien loved her, how much she meant to him. Tolkien was prepared to wait three years, until he was 21, in order to marry Edith – because his guardian, Father Francis Morgan, had forbidden him to see her or contact her until he came of age (she went to Cheltenham, to live with a solicitor and his wife). As Humphrey Carpenter put it in 1977, a more rebellious youth might have gone against Father Morgan, but Tolkien didn't. He abided by the decision (he hadn't been able to resist meeting Edith on a number of occasions, though. Unfortunately, news eventually reached Father Morgan via friends and cooks, and his guardian sternly forbade Tolkien to see Edith). Tolkien married Edith in March, 1916, in the leave he had before going to the front.

They did argue, though, and get on each other's nerves. And J.R.R. Tolkien probably found it hard to adjust to married life – he'd spent a lot of time amongst men, at Oxford, and with his T.C.B.S. friends. The journalistic way of linking everything in an author's real life to their fiction is too easy, too pat, but it's tempting to make connections between Tolkien and Bratt's relationship and that of Arwen and Aragorn in *The Lord of the Rings:* both couples shared a short time together but much longer apart; and Tolkien had travelled around quite a bit. There was also a prohibition put on them (by Tolkien's guardian, Father Morgan), which corresponds with Elrond's provisos (it was as if Tolkien had to prove to Morgan that he was worthy of Bratt, as Aragorn did to Elrond about Arwen).

TOLKIEN'S LATER LIFE.

The second half of J.R.R. Tolkien's life could appear dull from the outside: after Leeds, he returned to Oxford, where he lived for most of his life (apart from a brief spell in Bournemouth). The Tolkiens moved to Bournemouth and Poole from Oxford, on the South coast, late in life, prompted partly by Edith, who had enjoyed visiting the Miramar hotel in Bournemouth (Bournemouth was a favourite spot on the South coast for retired folk).

The Tolkiens stayed in the centre of Bournemouth, up in the West Cliff area (at 19, Lakeside Road, near Branksome Dene Chine), which had a Catholic church and a friendly doctor nearby, as well as the sea. Tolkien was also free of being bothered by fans there, as the phone number and address were kept secret. The Tolkiens were one of thousands of older people who still come to seaside towns like Bournemouth, Bognor and Eastbourne in their retirement.

J.R.R. Tolkien received a C.B.E. in 1972, and honorary doctorates from universities (including Oxford). Tolkien didn't spend lavishly when he became a millionaire in the late 1960s. His spending was modest, running to expensive clothes and dining out. The Tolkiens went on a Mediterranean cruise in 1966. Money was put into trust funds for his children and successors.

HOMOSEXUALITY.

Critics who want to see homosexual relationships underneath J.R.R. Tolkien's life and writing can find plenty of examples to illustrate gay subtexts: Tolkien attended single sex schools, and Oxford was largely all-male, as was his experience in the war fighting alongside his companions. Throughout his life, Tolkien seemed to prefer male company. In *The Lord of the Rings*, critics have drawn attention not only to Frodo and Sam, but to Frodo being threatened by men who want to take the ring from him, and to the friendships of Pippin with older men (Gandalf, Denethor, Beregrond), as well as Merry. Pippin also sleeps out under the stars with Frodo (Pippin and Merry may be the prime candidates for a gay couple in Tolkien's fiction, rather than Frodo and Sam). Marion Zimmer Bradley likened the friendship of Sam and Frodo to the idealized friendships between David and Jonathan, or Achilles and Patrocles (although many critics see Achilles and Patrocles as lovers).

C.S. LEWIS AND THE INKLINGS.

The Inklings and J.R.R. Tolkien's fellow writers and artists have been discussed in many books, so that need not be explored in detail here. C.S. Lewis's significance, for Tolkien and the creation of his Middle-earth legends, was not in the sense of a literary influence, but as someone who encouraged him. Indeed, without Lewis there might have been no *The Lord of the Rings*, Tolkien admitted:

> He was for long my only audience. Only from him did I ever get the idea that my 'stuff' could be more than a private hobby. But for his interest and unceasing eagerness for more I should never have brought *The Lord of the Rings* to a conclusion. (L, 362)

Occasionally Lewis would be angry when J.R.R. Tolkien wouldn't accept his suggestions for improvements to the texts he read loud at the Inklings' meetings. Although Lewis once remarked that Tolkien was 'uninfluenceable!', Tolkien said he did try and take on board suggestions and improve his writing (C. Plimmer, 1968). But it also appeared that he simply ignored suggestions, and continued in his own way. But, clearly, Clive Lewis, Charles Williams and the Inklings were hugely important for Tolkien and the development of his stories.

J.R.R. Tolkien was reluctant at first to have *The Hobbit* published – maybe because he feared the ridicule of his colleagues at Oxford University, maybe because he didn't want his book to be rejected by publishers, maybe he was distracted by working on *Beowulf* in the mid-Thirties, or maybe he didn't want the attention publishing a children's book might bring.

Some of J.R.R. Tolkien's friends were surprised that he had published

The Hobbit, and quietly derided it. As Michael White commented, 'the tone of many dons has always been one of mockery towards almost everything they encounter' (155), and at Oxford University rivalry and derision were commonplace.

C.S. Lewis (1898-1965), known to friends as 'Jack', had read Classics and then Greats at Oxford; he also studied at Malvern College. Lewis was editor of *Isis* (the university magazine). By the time of the Inklings meetings, Lewis was one of the significant intellectual and social presences at Oxford. Tolkien disliked Lewis's *Narnia* books for a no. of reasons; one was that Lewis wrote the books so fast, and it took Tolkien such a long time to bring a story up to the standard he wanted for publication; he didn't like the *Narnia* story itself, or the many errors and inconsistencies he found in it. Maybe it was also that Lewis had encroached upon very similar mythological and fantastical territory, and Tolkien perhaps saw Lewis as a rival. He certainly disliked it when readers and critics put *The Lord* beside *The Lion, the Witch and the Wardrobe.* (There's a humorous scene in Norman Stone's BBC docu-drama on C.S. Lewis where Lewis reads some of his *Narnia* book at an Inklings pub meeting and Tolkien replies that 'it won't do!' It wasn't the thing to have a faun in the same story as witches and talking lions),

I would also make a strong case, in terms of influence, for the significance of J.R.R. Tolkien's children, in particular Christopher Tolkien (born 1924) and Michael Tolkien (1920-1984) (Tolkien's other children were Priscilla, born 1929, and John, 1917-2001). Tolkien often wrote to them and discussed his ideas and writings at length. And Christopher Tolkien became the most important person in the Tolkien industry after the professor's death ('I am the person most likely to know what it was about', Tolkien's son said). It was Christopher Tolkien who took up the mountain of papers on Middle-earth that Tolkien left behind at his death. He was also working with Humphrey Carpenter on the first official biography. Tolkien's son followed him into academia, studying the same subject (Anglo-Saxon) at the same university (he also smoked pipes like his father). In 1975, Christopher Tolkien moved to France, resigning from his post at University College (where he remained). Ironically, Tolkien's son may have published more of Tolkien's writings than Tolkien did himself in his lifetime.

TOLKIEN THE LECTURER.

J.R.R. Tolkien's lectures at Oxford were often held at the Examination Schools in the High, and also at Pembroke College. Among Tolkien's lectures were the compulsory courses on Mediæval Literature. There was something of the performer in Tolkien (perhaps every lecturer has to be something of a performer). Tolkien certainly enjoyed the aspects of teaching which involved reading from Middle Ages texts, or reading his fiction aloud to the Inklings, or recording himself reading in Elvish. Tolkien had appeared in plays at school, and gave speeches at the clubs he founded.

Students have recorded how J.R.R. Tolkien could transform the lecture room into a mediæval mead hall, but others (such as Nevill Coghill) said you had to sit in the front row, otherwise you wouldn't really understand what the professor was saying. In conversation, Tolkien often talked rapidly, and sometimes quietly, or with his pipe glued to his mouth (William Cater called Tolkien's pipe-smoking 'a pyrotechnic display in aid of Bryant and May'). Tolkien tended to flit from one idea to another, assuming a scholarly range of learning in his listeners.

And in lectures, his delivery was like rapid machine gun fire, as Coghill recalled. Some students said J.R.R. Tolkien's lectures were 'very often difficult to understand', and that Tolkien was 'really in many ways an appalling lecturer'.[7] Sometimes Tolkien would wander off the point, and 'occasionally speak extemporaneously on whatever interested him at the moment'.

Even so, J.R.R. Tolkien's lectures were often crowded – Tolkien was popular even before he became a celebrity author. If Tolkien were lecturing nowadays, no doubt Olympic stadiums would be required to fit in the thousands of fans who would love to hear the author of *The Lord of the Rings* talk (J.K. Rowling has a similarly enormous following, and has given readings to thousands of *Harry Potter* fans).

CHILDREN.

Maybe *The Hobbit* began life with stories read to J.R.R. Tolkien's children, as some critics have claimed (and sometimes Tolkien did too), but *The Lord of the Rings* wasn't: that was read to Tolkien's contemporaries, the Inklings, learned academics, not children.[8] However, the seeds of some of Tolkien's works came out of the act of telling stories to his child: *Roverandom* was a children's book about a dog named Rover and his adventures which grew out of the tales that Tolkien told his children.

A character like Tom Bombadil also had a link with J.R.R. Tolkien's children. *The Adventures of Tom Bombadil* was a book of Tolkien's poetic tales about Bombadil, and characters such as Goldberry, Old Man Willow, the Barrow-wight, and a band of badgers.

J.R.R. Tolkien was one of many critics who regarded fairy tales as not written for children at all, but for adults. The link between fairy tales and children was modern and wrong, Tolkien maintained. One of his reasons for writing his own fairy stories (his term for *The Lord of the Rings* and other Middle-earth legends) was to create a new version of a fairy tale for adults (*Letters*, 216). Tolkien was adamant: '[i]t was *not* written 'for children'' (although he acknowledged that parts of it might appear 'childish' [L, 310]). In February, 1950, 4 years before publication, Tolkien remarked: 'I have produced a monster: an immensely long, complex, rather bitter, and very terrifying romance, quite unfit for children' (L, 136). Tolkien was aware that children of about 10 years old were getting into his book, but commented 'I think it rather a pity, really. It was not written for them' (L, 249). *The Lord of the Rings* became famous for attracting readers (invariably male) around the 10-13 year-old mark. So many readers and fans of the book have confessed they became absorbed by Middle-earth at that age. Eating up *The Lord of the Rings* in adolescence went along with other anorak or geeky behaviour, like *Star Wars*, *Star Trek*, *James Bond*, superheroes, comics, skateboards and computer games.

F.J. Harvey Darton's *Children's Books in England* is quoted in Martin Sutton's *The Sin-Complex: A Critical Study of English Versions of the Grimms' Kinder- und Hausmärchen in the Nineteenth Century*, to show what Sutton means by 'sin-complex' in relation to fairy tales:

> The fear or dislike of fairy-tales, in fact, was not and is not dependent to a marked extent on the feeling of any one period. It is a habit of the mind which has often been dominant in the history of children's books without much aid from contemporary circumstances. It is a manifestation, in England, of a deep-rooted sin-complex. It involves the belief that anything fantastic on the one hand, or anything primitive on the other, is inherently noxious, or at least so void of good as to be actively dangerous.

TOLKIEN THE WRITER.

Someone once said 'Lewis published too much and Tolkien too little'. The amount of J.R.R. Tolkien's published work is far, far less than many other authors. Tolkien wasn't lazy or unmotivated when it came to writing, but he could be, like so many writers, easily distracted. He tended to put off some of the writing chores that needed to be addressed, like so many writers. Instead, he'd write letters, or concentrate on the details of his Middle-earth writings. And there were always plenty of other things to preoccupy him – his family life, his home life, his friends, his academic workload, and so on (by the time of the war, Tolkien was the senior professor in the English department, which added further responsibilities). There was also depression. Tolkien mused in a letter:

> I suppose the major English vice is *sloth*. And it is to sloth, as much or as more than to natural virtue, that we owe our escape from the overt violences of other countries. In the fierce modern world, indeed, sloth does begin almost to look like a virtue. (L, 55)

As a writer, J.R.R. Tolkien acknowledged he had a tendency of avoiding what had to be done, of being distracted. All of the tendencies Tolkien exhibited in the writing of *The Lord of the Rings* are very familiar to any artist: the need to be totally immersed in the world he'd created, his explorations of new ideas and alternatives before arriving at solutions, his obsessive attention to detail, his perfectionism, his dissatisfaction with previous drafts, and the countless distractions from the work. Like other artists, Tolkien had a habit of complaining about endless diversions which took him away from writing. With regard to *The Silmarillion*, though, as the years passed, it was clear that there were deeper reasons for Tolkien's inability to complete the text so it was satisfactory for publication than everyday distractions.

Daniel Grotta described J.R.R. Tolkien the writer thus:

> Tolkien was a disorganized writer, an incorrigible procrastinator, a slow worker, and one who created his own distractions. When trying to write, he often doodled and drew, or worked on Elvish languages, or practiced calligraphy... He also looked forward to visits by friends or family as an excuse to interrupt and put aside his work. (11)

J.R.R. Tolkien acknowledged that he was very particular in his writing: 'I'm a pedant; everything has to be worked out', he confessed. Tolkien's sense of detail and pattern extends through *The Lord of the Rings*, down to the exact day and dates for every event, the phases of the moon, the times of sunrise and sunset, the weather, the changing seasons, etc. The patterns of light and dark, day and night, exactly what the weather was like on a certain day, are important in *The Lord of the Rings* (N. Isaac, 1968, 7). Thus, *The Lord of the Rings* was abandoned from time to time, with Tolkien taking up a new idea. There were gaps of years when nothing was added to the novel.

It's important to remember that when J.R.R. Tolkien began creating his Middle-earth mythology, there was no publisher in place, no contract, no advance. It was purely a personal endeavour, to be enjoyed by Tolkien and his close friends.

Humphrey Carpenter suggested that J.R.R. Tolkien didn't finish *The Silmarillion* because he wanted to continue to live, imaginatively, in his sub-created world. Perhaps Tolkien felt that when he stopped writing about his invented world it would cease to possess its magic, or its hold over him. So he kept working over the stories again and again, to keep them alive.

The mythology and the poetry in J.R.R. Tolkien's writing was slowly over-taken by the philosophy and theology, Christopher Tolkien said, so that Tolkien was more concerned with explaining how things worked in his secondary fantasy world, rather than creating new stories or writing new poems.[9]

In his later years, J.R.R. Tolkien was still contemplating his Middle-earth writings. As Christopher Tolkien explained in *Morgoth's Ring*, Tolkien was still concerned with issues such as the fall of mankind, the orcs' origins, the decay and immortality of the elves, the problem of reincarnation, the myth of light, the nature of Arda, and the significance of Morgoth himself (HME, 10, viii).

If you consider the whole of the *History of Middle-earth* volumes, you see J.R.R. Tolkien going over the same stories again and again. Maybe the hunger for creating fresh stories wasn't as strong as in his youth, but Tolkien was still imaginatively engrossed in his Middle-earth *legendarium*. It's just that he was more interested in explaining how it all worked, and in exploring the details and intricacies of his fantasy world, than in adding new tales.

That's in opposition to the tendencies of advanced capitalist societies, which prefer to add more and more to the mix: *more* books, *more* sequels, *more* movies, *more* computer games, *more* cartoons, *more* comics. What many people would have preferred would have been *more* of *The Lord of the Rings, more* of *The Hobbit,* and *more* of *The Silmarillion* (and Tolkien's publishers would have liked that, too. A second tome of the order of *The Lord of the Rings* appearing in, say, 1971, would've promised zillions of green). But instead of pursuing Aragorn and Arwen into the Fourth Age, or following the hobbits and the Shire into obscurity, or exploring in depth what Gandalf was up to between *The Hobbit* and *The Lord of the Rings,* Tolkien preferred to investigate Elvish calendars, or go back over the *Quenta Silmarillion* yet again, or ruminate once more on the fate of Atlantis-Númenor.

WORLD WAR ONE.

J.R.R. Tolkien didn't write much in the trenches of World War One. It's a poetic image, but the truth was it was very difficult to write in those conditions.

> That's all spoof [Tolkien asserted]; You might scribble something on the back on an envelope and shove it in your pocket, but that's all. You couldn't write... You'd be crouching down among the flies and filth.[10]

The war deeply affected J.R.R. Tolkien; he spent a long time convalescing after his experience in the war. He was moved around, and Edith was too – Tolkien was ill, not continually, but for a good deal of two years.

Geoffrey Smith and Christopher Wiseman were friends from J.R.R. Tolkien's youth who also fought in the First World War. According to Michael White, Tolkien had been deeply moved by Geoffrey Smith's last letter to him, written a few days before Smith was killed in the war (83). In the letter, Smith discussed their friend and fellow T.C.B.S. member Christopher Wiseman's death, also in combat, and said that the surviving members of the T.C.B.S. should do something worthwhile, and not let the flame of the Tea Club, Barrovian Society die. Smith's letter, and his death soon after, helped inspire Tolkien to begin creating his Middle-earth legends.

For Roger Sale, J.R.R. Tolkien withdrew from modern life following his experiences in the war. But it was also impossible to deny his place in the 20th century, that he was part of modern life. 'Yet during the long years of his withdrawal, his imagination was coming to terms with the inescapable fact that he is a modern man and not an elf or an ent', remarked Sale.13

LANGUAGE.

J.R.R. Tolkien could chant in Elvish, sing in Gothic, and recite poetry in Icelandic. According to Clive Lewis, Tolkien 'had been inside language': he hadn't just studied it, he was also an inventor of languages. Tolkien knew a number of languages, including Old English/ Anglo-Saxon, Middle English dialects, German, Dutch, Spanish, French, Italian, Old Icelandic/ Norse, modern Danish, Norwegian, Swedish, Finnish, Russian, and modern and mediæval Welsh. It's worth recalling that Tolkien was a student of spoken and living languages, as well as the written word. Languages for him were living things, not just dead languages found in dusty old books.

NORTHERN SOUL.

The Northern spirit of Europe was very precious to J.R.R. Tolkien, as a letter written in the dark days of World War Two attested: Tolkien attacked 'that ruddy little ignoramus Adolf Hitler' for the way he was

> Ruining, perverting, misapplying, and making forever accursed, that noble northern spirit, a supreme contribution to Europe, which I have ever loved, and tried to present in its true light. Nowhere, incidentally, was it nobler than in England, nor more early sanctified and Christianized... (L, 55-56)

'Germanic' was J.R.R. Tolkien's umbrella term for the Northern European culture of pre-mediæval era, and it included England and Scandinavia (L, 55), while 'Classical' culture was that of ancient Southern Europe.

TOLKIEN'S POLITICS.

Even a cursory browse of J.R.R. Tolkien's Middle-earth writings indicate that his politics were fundamentally conservative, royalist, patriotic, pro-military, and traditionalist. He described his politics as leaning towards ''unconstitutional' Monarchy' or philosophical Anarchy (L, 63). He wasn't a liberal, or even pro-democracy ('I am not a 'democrat'').

Jack Zipes remarked in *Breaking the Spell: Radical Theories of Folk and Fairy Tales*:

> In my opinion, the essential quality of all great fantasy works is linked to their capacity to subvert accepted standards and to provoke readers to re-think their state of being and the institutions that determine the nature of *existence*. (2002a, 230)

Maybe, but for J.R.R. Tolkien there's a strong component of desire for the past, a consuming nostalgia for things ancient, and for home comforts – a fire, good food, a pipe, beer and good company. One doesn't immediately think of Tolkien as a *subversive* writer.

By their nature, heroic romance and mythological forms of literature are conservative. Although Tolkien was writing in the modern era, he was opposed to modernism. Like the other Inklings, Tolkien espoused a pre-modernist culture, the opposite of an élitist, intellectualized European *avant garde* (embodied in the work of James Joyce, Marcel Proust, T.S. Eliot and Antonin Artaud). The Inklings' pre-modernism was classicist, mediæval and Renaissance (and not only pre-Reformation or Enlightenment, but pre-Renaissance). Tolkien also sidestepped the whole liberal (libertarian) project. Tolkien went even further back than the Renaissance or the Middle Ages, to the 'Dark Ages' and Anglo-Saxon era. John Wain defined the Inklings as '[p]olitically conservative, not to say reactionary; in religion, Anglo- or Roman Catholic; in art, frankly hostile to any manifestation of the "modern spirit"'.[11]

For Jack Lewis, the break between the pre-modern and the modern epochs occurred around the middle of the 19th century. But Lewis saw the break primarily in religious and philosophical terms, not socio-economic. For Lewis, the break was between a Judaeo-Christian and Classical belief system and the modern, post-Christian world. Belief was the key for Lewis: the difference, he said, between a pagan and a Christian was far less than between a pagan or Christian and a post-Christian ('pagan' here didn't mean non-Christian or heretic, but Classical). Lewis and Tolkien exalted the values of the Old West, that is, the Judaeo-Christian world and the Classical, Mediterranean cultures of Europe and the Near East. (The Christian proseletyzers among the Inklings became known as the 'Oxford Christians'; but they were by no means the first Christian thinkers and writers at large in Oxford).

THE MYTHOLOGY.

The first of John Ronald Reuel Tolkien's Middle-earth stories to be written down was "The Fall of Gondolin", composed in 1917 when Tolkien was in hospital at Great Haywood. A second major story in *The Book of Lost Tales* ("The Children of Húrin") was written while Tolkien was convalescing in Hull. It concerned the ill-fated hero Túrin (the elements in the Túrin story of Kullervo in the *Kalevala*, and European mediæval heroes like Siegfried and Beowulf, are easy to spot). The third of the early stories (the three are also called the 'Great Tales') had a huge significance for Tolkien – Beren and Lúthien. The three 'Great Tales' allowed for a fuller expression, Tolkien thought, and could also exist separately.

One of the first expressions of J.R.R. Tolkien's grand mythology was the poem he wrote ('The Voyage of Earendel the Evening Star'), which had been inspired by the line *Eala Earendel engla beorhtast!* in Cynewulf's *Crist*. Humphrey Carpenter said that Tolkien was more like a historian chronicling real historical events, than a novelist writing a work of fiction (1995, 12).

Later, J.R.R. Tolkien developed some of the tales into poems: one of his favourite poetic forms was the Anglo-Saxon half-line, with its alliterations rather than rimes. He used that *Beowulf* form for the story of Túrin. The tale of the doomed lovers Lúthien and Beren was composed in rhyming couplets (and entitled *The Lay of Leithian*).

Of his mythology, J.R.R. Tolkien said it was dedicated 'to England; to my country'. It was meant to crystallize the clear, cool air and climate of Britain and North-Western Europe, something Celtic, not Italy or the Aegean or the East. It was intended to be 'for the more adult mind of a land long steeped in poetry'.[12]

ELVES.

Humphrey Carpenter likened J.R.R. Tolkien's elves to humans rather than fairies or the elves of 'Goblin Feet' and traditional fairy tales – specifically, to humans before the Fall, people in Eden, in a time before sin (1995, 100). 'Sister Songs' (by Francis Thompson) and Edith's liking of 'little elfin people' may have been influences on Tolkien alongside the fairies and elves of fairy tales.

J.R.R. Tolkien's elves are poets, writers, craftsmen, painters – in a word, they're artists. They are immortal and so '[o]ld age, disease, and death do not bring their work to an end while it is still unfinished or imperfect. They are therefore the ideal of every artist', commented Humphrey Carpenter (1995, 101).

DISLIKES.

J.R.R. Tolkien's well-known railing against industrialization derived partly from seeing the places he loved – Sarehole, Warwickshire, Oxford – being overrun by industry and suburbanization. 'The country in which I lived in childhood was being shabbily destroyed before I was ten, in days when motor-cars were rare objects', Tolkien complained in the Foreword to *The Lord of the Rings* (FR, 13).

Industrialization was bad enough when it was happening the world over, but it was especially distressing for J.R.R. Tolkien when it overwhelmed his childhood haunts. In the 1960s, Tolkien wrote a satire on the car industry overtaking Oxford in *The Bovadium Fragments*.

As well as his dislike of cars, J.R.R. Tolkien also mistrusted modern technology like televisions, washing machines and dishwashers – the Tolkiens didn't have those sorts of electrical appliances in their house. The Tolkiens had a radio, but Tolkien didn't listen to it much. (Tolkien did drive a car, in the 1930s, but was famously a reckless and dangerous driver. He would drive on through signals, crying 'charge 'em and they scatter!').

J.R.R. Tolkien's other dislikes included journalists, psychotherapy and psychology, and many of the illustrations chosen by publishers for his books. As with the actors in the 1956 BBC radio adaption of *The Lord of the Rings*, Tolkien often felt he could do better at illustration himself. Some of Tolkien's dislikes seemed to be a little extreme: Miguel de Cervantes, Tolkien declared, 'was a weed-killer to romance', and Dante Alighieri was 'full of spite and malice. I don't care for petty relations with petty people in petty cities'.13 Tolkien took a dim view of publishers, too; they didn't market and distribute his books properly, he felt.

J.R.R. Tolkien's negative view of France may have been linked to his disastrous experience in 1913 when he was looking after two Mexican boys on a trip. They visited Paris and Brittany. Two aunts joined them for the trip, but in Dinard a car crashed carrying the elder of the aunts and she died.

HOBBITS.

There's a perfect expression of J.R.R. Tolkien's hobbit politics in the 1944 British film *This Happy Breed* (based on Noel Coward's play), where Robert Newton (the central character) defines the British as a nation of gardeners, quiet, different, with their own way of doing things. *This Happy Breed* encapsulates the middle class hobbitish way of life: the cups of tea, the cigars and slippers, a little alcohol now and then, a bit of gardening on a Saturday, the conservatism and nationalism, going to war to fight for one's country, the distrust of foreign ideologies like communism and fascism, and so on.

J.R.R. Tolkien's description in an early draft of the foreword to *The Lord of the Rings* can easily be applied to the author himself: hobbits 'like to have books full of things they already know set out fair and square with no contradictions' (HME, VI, 313).

TOLKIEN IN THE MEDIA.

J.R.R. Tolkien didn't make many appearances in the popular media – not like some writers today who seem to be everywhere, doing the rounds of TV and radio chat shows, magazine and newspaper interviews. Tolkien was protective of his privacy, and rarely disclosed intimate details about himself. He was suspicious of outsiders. He certainly did not like becoming a cult author at all.

The 1968 BBC documentary (directed by Leslie Megahey) attempted the standard television exploration of the man through the work (and vice versa). So J.R.R. Tolkien 'was made to attend a firework show' (at the Dragon School in Oxford), because Gandalf used fireworks, even though they had little to do with Tolkien or *The Lord of the Rings* (L, 390). Tolkien was interviewed, and also shown wandering around Merton College. As Tolkien put it, 'they appeared completely confused between ME and my story' (L, 390); and 33 years later, when the Hollywood versions of *The Lord of the Rings* hit the screen in the early 2000s, the same simplistic confusions between author and artwork occurred.

In Worcestershire in the early 1950s, before *The Lord of the Rings* was published, while visiting George Sayer, who taught at Malvern College, J.R.R. Tolkien made some recordings of readings (including some singing) from *The Lord of the Rings* and *The Hobbit*, which were released on vinyl in 1975 (as *J.R.R. Tolkien Reads and Sings His 'The Hobbit' and 'The Fellowship of the Ring'*).

Donald Swann released an album of songs inspired by J.R.R. Tolkien's fiction and poetry, *The Road Goes Ever On and On*. Swann (best known for being part of the musical duo Flanders and Swann) set Tolkien's poems to music, including 'The Road Goes Ever On and On', 'I Sit Beside the Fire and Think' and 'In Western Lands'. At the Tolkiens' golden wedding anniversary celebration at Merton College in Oxford in 1966, Swann performed the song cycle. Tolkien responded to the compliment with 'the words are not worthy of the music'.

J.R.R. Tolkien sold the film rights to *The Lord of the Rings*, according to Daniel Grotta, for 'a "very high" price'. Other critics have said that Tolkien virtually gave them away. Amounts of $10,000-20,000 have been suggested. In the light of how much the *Lord of the Rings* franchise was worth by the time of the 2001-03 movies of *Rings*, those amounts were indeed tiny.

In the years following the publication of *The Lord of the Rings*, some of the effects of Tolkienania were bizarre: a man complained to Tolkien that his wife had fallen in love with Aragorn! The schoolboy who played Frodo in a school play in Cheltenham could not come out of the character for a month afterwards. Famous people wrote to Tolkien, including Hollywood stars.

THE TOLKIEN ESTATE.

The Tolkien estate at his death was valued at £144,159 ($230,654; much of the money that Tolkien had made, to avoid the high taxes of Blighty, had been given away – to charities, friends and relatives). It was estimated that *The Lord of the Rings* had earned Tolkien about four million dollars while he was alive. Tolkien left bequests to individuals, £500 ($800) to Trinity College, £1,000 ($1,600) to the Birmingham Oratory, but most of the literary estate went to his children and their offspring.

J.R.R. Tolkien recognized in his son Christopher an important reader of his Middle-earth stories. For a long time, Christopher was one of the few people who knew about them in detail (along with C.S. Lewis and the Inklings). Tolkien and his son Christopher were similar personalities too, Tolkien said. It was fitting, then, that Christopher Tolkien would become the keeper of the flame of his father's writing and estate after his father's death.

A biographer of J.R.R. Tolkien, Michael White, has lamented that the Tolkien estate has been so protective of Tolkien's reputation, carefully controlling how Tolkien is represented, and not encouraging any alternative or more intimate portraits. There's little, White complains, about Tolkien's personal demons in his published letters, or details of his private life, his marriage to Edith, or his friendships with the Inklings (2002, 5).

HarperCollins' publishing director David Brawn said that the three surviving children of J.R.R. Tolkien didn't want anything to do with the films made by Hollywood in 2001-2003. 'If they had their way, I don't think there would be a film at all'. They avoided publicity and were 'incredibly difficult' to deal with, according to HarperCollins. While Christopher wrote at length on Tolkien in his editions of his father's works, Priscilla and John maintained a constant silence (Priscilla and John lived in Oxford, and Christopher in France). Tolkien's grandson, Adam (son of Christopher), was a little more congenial, though, and appeared in the media).

THE FANS.

'Many young Americans are involved in the stories in a way that I am not', J.R.R. Tolkien once remarked. It's very common for writers and artists to move on to the next book or project after completing one, and not spend any more time than necessary in revisiting their work. *Making the work is the thing*. It's nice if people read it and enjoy it, but the writer or artist is already deep into the next project. Tolkien could easily separate himself from his books. They were stories that were written to entertain audiences, but that didn't mean the author himself spent days immersed in his old books.

Tolkien societies were founded in the 1960s, in the U.S.A. and Britain at first; there was an underground magazine called *Gandalf's Garden*, a nightclub called Middle-earth, and students were taking up the world of Tolkien big time (at Warwick University, the ring road was renamed 'Tolkien Road'). Around 3 million copies of *LOTR* had been sold globally by the end of 1968. (Some of Tolkien's fans were obsessive, to put it mildly, and some claimed to have interpreted Tolkien and his work correctly, rather like St Paul and other followers of Christ.)

In the letters you see J.R.R. Tolkien responding to numerous enquiries from readers about Tom Bombadil, or the Valar, or hobbits, or elves, or the Third Age of Middle-earth. Tolkien knew from the 100s of letters sent to his publishers that readers had been fascinated by the history and legend in the appendices to *The Lord of the Rings*. Tolkien called the appendices to *The Lord of the Rings* 'straight teenage stuff' that would appeal to the young. True. But Tolkien himself loved that kind of teenage stuff, and spent months putting it together, correlating dates and genealogies, restructuring calendars, inventing names and the like. In fact, it was all too easy for Tolkien to become deeply embroiled in that kind of 'teenage stuff', struggling to get it absolutely right. (It's one of the reasons he couldn't get *The Silmarillion* finished during his lifetime).

J.R.R. Tolkien further pondered on why *The Lord of the Rings* seemed to be received so literally or realistically by readers: maybe it was the degree of detail and information in the book, the background of history, lore, legend, chronology, geography and language which he had crammed in there (L, 210). When *The Lord of the Rings* was published, in the mid-1950s, some readers started clamouring for more information about this richly detailed fantasy world. But Tolkien recognized that if further background information were to be provided, it would have to be precisely and properly presented (L, 210). Indulging in this kind of fantasy material, Tolkien realized, required a certain amount of leisure time (again, relating reading to a middle-class lifestyle which has time for such pursuits).

NOTES: TOLKIEN BIOGRAPHY

1. H. Carpenter, 1995, 129.
2. Quoted in H. Carpenter, 1995, 137.
3. D. Grotta, 1991, 42.
4. In D. Grotta, 151.
5. In Kilby, 194.
6. H. Carpenter, 1995, 105.
7. C. & D. Plimmer, *Daily Telegraph*, Mch 22, 1968.
8. D. Grotta, 171.
9. In A. Becker, 92.
10. In D. Grotta, 57.
11. In D. Grotta, 59.
12. J. Wain, in C. Duriez, 2000, 5.
13. H. Carpenter, 1995, 97f.
14. In D. Grotta, 77-79.

chapter 2

SOURCES AND INFLUENCES

SOME LITERARY SOURCES

The Lord of the Rings combines elements of the fairy tale, fantasy, epic, mythology, mediæval (and Arthurian) romance and *chanson de geste*. The influences on *The Lord of the Rings*, and Tolkien's works, are many, and include William Shakespeare, the *Bible*, Greek mythology, and the well-known Tolkien passions for Germanic, Finnish, Icelandic, Anglo-Saxon and other Northern European texts and traditions (the *Elder Edda*, the *Kalevala*, the *Mabinogion, Beowulf, Sir Gawain and the Green Knight*, the *Völsunga-saga*, Arthurian legend, Sigurd, etc.) The 'nameless North' was always Tolkien's favourite as a land of mythical tales – above stories of pirates, little girls called Alice, Native Americans, and Arthur and Merlin. It was the North of Sigurd, 'the prince of all dragons' (NC, 135).

If one had to put it somewhere on a critical list, C.S Lewis said *The Lord of the Rings* should lie between *The Odyssey* (which would be at the top) and Edgar Wallace at the bottom.1 For Robert Giddings, part of the success of *The Lord of the Rings* was Tolkien's creative ability to mix together a host of literary sources which the reader half-remembered, 'to manipulate our memories of the classics'.2 Thus, when he wanted to evoke a rural idyll for the Shire, Tolkien orchestrated elements from literature going back from the Edwardians and Georgians, through the Victorians and Romantics, to the Renaissance and mediæval times, to construct a pastiche of glimpses of rural nostalgia (appealing to British suburbia). For the battle sequences, Tolkien reworked Shakespeare's history plays, Arthurian legend and Middle Age romances.

Robert Giddings and Elizabeth Holland have made lengthy, detailed and persuasive accounts of the influence of books such as the Allan Quatermain books (Rider Haggard), *Lorna Doone* (R.D. Blackmore), *The Wind in the Willows* (Kenneth Grahame), Alfred Tennyson's and Sir Thomas Malory's Arthurian poems, and *The Thirty-Nine Steps* (John Buchan) on J.R.R. Tolkien's *The Lord of the Rings*. Other influences included William Morris, John Milton, James Hilton, and adventure writers (discussed below).

For Giddings and Holland, *The Lord of the Rings* follows aspects of Haggard, Grahame, Buchan and Blackmore (among others) very closely. They cite the portrayal of characters such as Frodo and Aragorn as Mithraic, Christ-like saviour figures: Frodo as Christ, a deity like pagan gods Frey or Mithras, and Aragorn as the Sun King, or Theseus, Gandalf as Hermes, the messenger, and also Christ, a saviour. Or Frodo as Arthur, Aragorn as Henry V, and both as heroes such as Ulysses, or Grail knights like Sir Perceval or Sir Lancelot.

Robert Giddings and Elizabeth Holland claim that the opening and closing sections of *The Lord of the Rings* derive from themes in *The Thirty-Nine Steps* (for example, the Black Riders, the power behind them remaining unseen, the pursuit). Then follows riffs on *King Solomon's Mines* (Moria, Frodo's wound, the *mithril* mail shirt). The Lothlórien sequence draws on *Allan Quatermain* and *Lost Horizon* (by James Hilton), according to Giddings and Holland (in *Lost Horizon*, made into a classic film in 1937 by Frank Capra, a group of Westerners find themselves in Shangri-La, a paradisal Tibetan world; in *Allan Quatermain,* Sir Henry Curtis and his companions end up in an African lost world. Certainly the sheltered, mythical kingdoms in Tolkien's story, like Rivendell, Fangorn or Lórien, do resemble the lost worlds of adventure fiction). The scenes at Théoden's court at Edoras further mirror *King Solomon's Mines* and *The Princess and the Curdie,* as well as Alfred Tennyson's poem 'Lancelot and Elaine'. *Lorna Doone* provides inspiration for the subsequent section of Frodo and Sam alone on the wild moorland approaching Mordor (the landscape evokes the Exmoor of Blackmore's novel).

Giddings and Holland suggest further affinities: between the myth of Theseus and the Minotaur with Sam and Frodo in Shelob's lair, for example (a dark labyrinth, a monster, magical aids (Ariadne's thread, Galadriel's phial), the motif of spinning and weaving).[3] The end of *The Lord of the Rings* draws again on *King Solomon's Mines* (the king's journey), *The Thirty-Nine Steps* (Frodo's adventures) and *Lorna Doone* (lost on the moors). The scouring of the Shire evokes *The Wind in the Willows* again (invaders, stoats and weasels, from the Wild Wood, take over the animal heroes' homes; Rat, Mole, Badger and Toad join forces to drive out the enemy). Other possible influences discovered by Giddings and Holland include Shakespeare's *Henry V* (in the battle scenes, Aragorn's characterization, etc), and Ernest Thompson Seton's animal books (such as *Lives of the Hunted King*).

ANDREW LANG. Andrew Lang (1844-1912) was another inspiration for J.R.R. Tolkien (Lang produced anthologies of fairy tales which Tolkien often referred to). A favourite book of Tolkien's childhood was Lang's *Red Fairy Book.* Lang crops up in Tolkien's own writings about his influences, and is particularly important in relation to encouraging Tolkien's first responses to fairy tales.

ROMANTICISM. Another influence on the Inklings was German Romanticism: Owen Barfield was indebted to Novalis (1772-1801), the wonderful mystical German poet, as was George MacDonald (another important influence on the Inklings). MacDonald (1824-95), the Scottish fantasist, was a significant influence on both J.R.R. Tolkien and C.S. Lewis (although Tolkien was ambivalent towards MacDonald, and played down MacDonald's influence). A theorist and writer, MacDonald's concepts of fantasy contributed to the views on fiction of Tolkien and Lewis. Mac-Donald's works included *Phantastes* (1858), *Lilith* (1895), *Bannerman's Boyhood* and the *Curdie* children's stories: *The Princess and the Goblin* (1872) and *The Princess and Curdie* (1882), whose goblins are precursors of those in *The Hobbit*. Lewis Carroll and John Ruskin were among MacDonald's literary friends.

LORD DUNSANY. British poet Lord Dunsany (1978-1957) may also have influenced J.R.R. Tolkien: Dunsany wrote of goblins in *The Hoard of the Gibbelins*, elves in *The King of Elfland's Daughter*, and spider gods in *The Distressing Tale of Thangobrind the Jeweller*. Walter Scott (1771-1832) is another influence, perhaps, with his Waverley novels, and *Ivanhoe*.

FENIMORE COOPER. *The Last of the Mohicans*, Fenimore Cooper's (1789-1851) classic adventure novel, may be another influence (in the bows and arrows, the canoes, the forests, the plains and horse-lords, the elves and Aragorn as hunters and trackers).[4]

WILLIAM MORRIS. William Morris (1834-96) was another inspiration for J.R.R. Tolkien (there are correspondences between Morris's *Roots of the Mountains*, 1889, and *The Hobbit*, for instance).[5] Morris had written a book (*The Earthly Paradise*) in which a mariner sails to a strange land and hears stories, which helped to inspire Tolkien's early stories of the voyager Eriol/ Elf-friend.

CELTICISM. Ronald Tolkien didn't love everything Celtic automatically (as one might imagine, from reading *The Lord of the Rings,* which seems steeped in Celtic culture – or is it that artists' visualizations of Tolkien's mythos have mined the Celtic world, and coloured the way it's received?). Although he loved the Welsh language, for instance, Tolkien found Gaelic 'wholly alien' (L, 219). Other linguistic aversions included French (for Tolkien, if he didn't like the language of a country, it put him off the whole place).

One might conclude, from a cursory look at J.R.R. Tolkien's output of mythological, pre-mediæval tales of heroes, quests and fabulous beasts, that the author was part of the Celtic revival, the late Victorian and early 20th century culture found in the work of W.B. Yeats, William Morris, Burne-Jones, Dante Gabriel Rossetti, the Pre-Raphaelites and others.

Smith of Wootton Major might have been published in the *Yellow Book* with illustration by Aubrey Beardsley, Colin Wilson thought (1974).

In fact, Tolkien distanced himself from Celtic art. For him, the Celts were colourful, but fundamentally insane (L, 26). Even so, Celtic culture found its way into Tolkien's Middle-earth mythology – by way of the Welsh and Irish language, for example.

E.A. WYKE-SMITH. E.A. Wyke-Smith's *The Marvellous Land of Sergs* (1927) was another influence (Tolkien acknowledged its influence on *The Hobbit*).

HILAIRE BELLOC. Hilaire Belloc (1870-1953) was another influence, according to Colin Wilson (1974), in particular Belloc's travel book *Path To Rome* (1902), a walk from Switzerland to Rome. Jeffrey Farnol and his *The Broad Highway* (1901) is another possible influence, for Wilson.

The Lord of the Rings was as significant for Colin Wilson as 20th century classics such as *Remembrance of Things Past* or *The Waste Land*. Wilson (1974) put the book in the European Romantic tradition, a book that took the same themes as Goethe's *Faust*, E.T.A. Hoffmann, Hermann Hesse's *Steppenwolf* or De L'Isle Adam's *Axel*.

C.S. Lewis compared *The Lord of the Rings* to Ludovico Aristo (which J.R.R. Tolkien resented), Naomi Mitchison to Malory, Richard Hughes to *The Faerie Queene*, and Louise Halle to the *Odyssey* and *Faust*.

G.K. CHESTERTON. G.K. Chesterton (1874-1936) was another influence that critics have drawn attention to. As well as Chesterton, Colin Wilson also cited W.B. Yeats (1865-1939), who also wrote about fairies, and regarded them symbolically.

JOHN MILTON. John Milton (1608-74) and *Paradise Lost* has been cited by many commentators as an inspiration for the theology of J.R.R. Tolkien's Middle-earth writings (particularly Milton's depiction of the Fall).

ALFRED TENNYSON. The farewell at the Grey Havens recalls Alfred Tennyson's poetic account of the death of King Arthur (the sailing of Frodo into the West in J.R.R. Tolkien's book, of Arthur to Lyonnesse in Tennyson). Earlier, Frodo has to give up the magical ring, which has to go back to its place of origin, like Excalibur in the lake at the end of Tennyson's poem and Malory's (1405-71) *Le Morte d'Arthur* (Tolkien loved Malory's Arthurian poem). Sailing West also recalls burials at sea in Scandinavian and Germanic culture, as well as clichés such as sailing into the sunset, sailing into the unknown and sailing into legend.

H.G. WELLS. The landscape at Mount Doom recalls the desolation caused by the battles between humans and Martians in H.G. Wells' (1866-1946) *War of the Worlds*. The orcs and crossbred creatures manufactured by the enemy recall the hybrids genetically manipulated in Wells' *The Island of Dr Moreau*.

J.R.R. Tolkien said he read modern fantasy – Isaac Asimov, Mary

Renault (her novels on Theseus), and E.R. Eddison (L, 377). That's important to remember – that Tolkien wasn't an aloof Oxford don writing in an ivory tower, separated not only from 'real life' (he was a family man with four kids), but from contemporary literature. Being a teacher would have kept Tolkien in contact with young people – and, through them, popular culture of all kinds. (Mary Renault (1905-83), a former student of Tolkien's, created in her novels set in ancient Greece detailed worlds that were as impressive, characters that were far richer, and battles and action that far outstripped Tolkien's. Renault was also a far greater prose stylist, and a deeper thinker).

S.R. CROCKETT. J.R.R. Tolkien's creatures and characters were culled from many sources. The hobbits and ents and one or two other creatures were 'original', but all the rest were not. Tolkien acknowledged that the warg attack in *The Hobbit* came from S.R. Crockett's (1860-1914) *The Black Douglas*, which had 'deeply impressed' Tolkien in his school days (*Letters*, no. 306). The term *warg* was Anglo-Saxon for wild wolves.

EDWARDIAN WHIMSY. The wistful nature mysticism of Edwardian fantasies, with their very English woodland settings (such as in *The Wind in the Willows* or *Peter Pan*), resemble J.R.R. Tolkien's fiction – especially *The Hobbit* and the early chapters of *The Lord of the Rings*. And Tom Bombadil, a chthonic spirit of the Old Forest, recalls the nature god Pan. Of a theatrical production of *Peter Pan*, Tolkien wrote in 1910: 'indescribable, but I shall never forget it as long as I live'.[6]

The Wind in the Willows, a favourite of Edwardian/ Georgian whimsy since it was published in 1908, has been cited as another influence: *The Lord of the Rings* has multiple affinities with Kenneth Grahame's (1859-1932) children's fantasy classic (for instance, the Wild Wood, and the Piper at the Gates of Dawn sequence, which chimes with Frodo and the hobbits encountering elves in *Book One*).[7]

PUBLIC SCHOOL. One critic compared the structure of *The Lord of the Rings* with that of a public school (interesting for a comparison with the *Harry Potter* books): Gandalf as headmaster, Aragorn as head boy, Gimli, Faramir and Legolas as house captains for the dwarf, man and elf houses, hobbits as prefects, and the accompanying rituals, ceremonies and punishments of the public school system.[8]

SPY AND CONSPIRACY FICTION. *The Lord of the Rings* reworks the conspiracy plot, and the invasion plot (not only during WW2), which fed on national paranoia, fear and distrust, rival nations, the build-up of weaponry, and the threat of war.

Robert Giddings linked the plot of *The Lord of the Rings* to the spy stories which flourished between the wars (*The Secret Agent, The Spy In Black, The Lady Vanishes, The 39 Steps, The Man Who Knew Too Much* and *Dark Journey*) and throughout the Second World War (*Casablanca*,

Continental Agent, Sherlock Holmes, Across the Pacific, Berlin Correspondent), continuing into the nuclear paranoia of the Cold War era (*The Third Man, James Bond, The Manchurian Candidate, The Avengers, The Professionals, The Man From U.N.C.L.E., Torn Curtain*, etc).

NOTES: SOME LITERARY SOURCES

1. C.S. Lewis, in H. Carpenter, 1978, 145.
2. R. Giddings, 1983, 10.
3. R. Giddings, 1981, 117. T
4. T. Shippey, 1982, 223.
5. *The Annotated Hobbit*, 204.
6. Tolkien, quoted in K. McLeish, op. cit., 130.
7. K. McLeish, "The Rippingest Yarn of All", in R. Giddings, 1983, 126.
8. R. Giddings, in R. Giddings, 1983, 8.

THE INKLINGS

John Ronald Reuel Tolkien was a member of a number of literary clubs, launching some himself. At Leeds University, Tolkien founded the Viking Club with a colleague, formed 'to drink large quantities of beer, read sagas and sing'.[1]

At Oxford University, J.R.R. Tolkien formed the Coalbiters with C.S. Lewis, a group which convened for reading Icelandic sagas. This club merged with the Inklings. The Inklings were very much a part of Oxford's university culture (with its professorships, lectures, intellectual talk, literary societies and largely masculine bias). They used to meet in Lewis's rooms at Magdalen College (often on Thursdays), or at the Eagle and Child (which they called 'The Baby and Bird') pub in St Giles on Tuesdays (later on Mondays, and sometimes at Tolkien's rooms at Merton College.)

The core Inklings were J.R.R. Tolkien, Lewis, Charles Williams, and Owen Barfield (they were fictionalized in Tolkien's unfinished "The Notion Club Papers"). Others writers associated with the Inklings included children's author Roger Lancelyn Green, H.D. 'Hugo' Dyson, Nevill Coghill, Commander Jim Dundas-Grant, Adam Fox, Colin Hardie, Humphrey Harvard, Gervase Matthews, R.B. McCallum, C.E. 'Tom' Stevens, Charles Wrenn, J.A.W. Bennt, Lord David Cecil, Major W.H. 'Warnie' Lewis (Lewis's brother), the poets Roy Campbell and John Wain, and Tolkien's son Christopher. (It was strictly a men only club – Dorothy Sayers wasn't allowed to join).

The time scale of the Inklings meetings runs from 1933 to 1963 (when Lewis died). Typical subjects of conversation were religion, theology, politics, æsthetics, art, literature, poetry and Oxford University gossip. And of course, one of the chief things the Inklings did was to read out from their own work and receive criticism from the group (the first public audience for *The Lord of the Rings* was this group of Oxford dons).

The values of the Inklings can be summarized as: conservative (or reactionary) in politics; Christian (Anglican or Roman Catholic) in religion; anti- and pre-modernist in art (pro-mediæval and Renaissance); Anglo-Saxon, Germanic and Northern European in linguistics; classicist and 'Dark Age' in mythology; romantic and utopian in philosophy (Lewis's 'joy', Tolkien's eucatastrophe or happy ending); with romantic, idealized notions of love and marriage.

The fiction of the Inklings can be classed as 'Christian fantasy'. Other examples of Christian fantasy might include the *Divine Comedy,* Middle-English religious poetry, the Grail and Arthurian romances of the mediæval era, *Dr Faustus* (by Kit Marlowe), *The Faerie Queene* (Edmund Spenser), Metaphysical poets such as John Donne, Thomas Traherne and Henry Vaughan, *Paradise Lost* (John Milton), *The Pilgrim's Progress* (John Bunyan), and George MacDonald's fiction. (Behind the Christian romant-icism of Lewis, Williams and Tolkien, R.J. Reilly commented, stood G.K. Chesterton, and behind Chesterton, George MacDonald, and going back further, Samuel Taylor Coleridge.[2])

For J.R.R. Tolkien, fantasy was 'not a lower but a higher form of Art, indeed the most nearly pure form, and so (when achieved) the most potent' (MC, 139). If fantasy meant 'escape', what's so bad with 'escape'? Tolkien mused.

J.R.R. Tolkien himself was suspicious of classifying writers. He certainly wouldn't like to be categorized (as he often is) as a 'fantasy writer':

> Affixing 'labels' to writers, living or dead, is an inept procedure, in any circumstances: a childish amusement of small minds: and very 'deadening', since at best it over-emphasizes what is common to a selected group of writers, and distracts attention from what is *individual* (and not classifiable) in each of them... (L, 414)

With C.S. Lewis and J.R.R. Tolkien so popular among global readers, the Inklings may have had more influence in popular culture than the Algonquin writers in New York, the Paris of Ernest Hemingway and Gertrude Stein, the 1930s of Christopher Isherwood and W.H. Auden, or the Bloomsbury Group (N. Isaacs, 130).

Lewis praised *The Lord of the Rings* when he read it in typescript for the first time: its sense of sub-creation and inventiveness, 'as if from inexhaustible resources', greatly impressed Lewis. As did its *gravitas*. And Lewis was among the first of many commentators who remarked upon the endless series of obstacles and set-backs that Tolkien piles upon his heroes before they win through:

all victories of hope deferred and the merciless piling up of odds against the heroes are near to being too painful. And the long *coda* after the eucatastrophe, whether you intended it or not, has the effect of reminding us that victory is as transitory as conflict... [3]

Lewis it seems would have preferred a happier ending, or an ending which guaranteed a longer-lasting joy.

J.R.R. Tolkien acknowledged Clive Lewis as an important influence on *The Lord of the Rings* – not least in encouraging him to continue with it (L, 303). Tolkien recognized parts of himself in the character of Ransom that C.S. Lewis had included in his science fiction novels. However, Tolkien never got on with Lewis's *Narnia* books. He didn't like them, and that may have contributed towards the two friends growing apart a little. [4]

Christopher Tolkien has become by far the most important figure in the Tolkien literary cult, after Tolkien himself. Tolkien junior contributed immensely to his father's literary legacy, editing most of the significant works after Tolkien's death in 1973. But even when Tolkien was in the midst of writing *The Lord of the Rings*, his son Christopher was crucial: Tolkien wrote to Christopher in November, 1944: 'I chiefly want to hear what you think, as for a long time now I have written with you most in mind' (L, 103). Although many critics have cited the influence of C.S. Lewis and the Inklings on Tolkien's Middle-earth legends, one shouldn't under-estimate Christopher Tolkien (who was also one of the Inklings), as well as Tolkien's wife Edith.

NOTES: THE INKLINGS

1. H. Carpenter, 1977, 105.
2. N. Reynolds, *Daily Telegraph*, Jan 20, 1997.
3. In H. Carpenter, 1995, 207-8.
4. In H. Carpenter, 1995, 204.

MYTHOLOGY

Some of the written sources for J.R.R. Tolkien's kind of heroic romance and mythological fiction include: James G. Frazer, Robert Graves, Joseph Campbell, C.G. Jung, Robert Briffault, Sigmund Freud, and Jessie Weston. Some of Tolkien's contemporaries, such as T.S. Eliot and W.B. Yeats, used some of those writers' works as inspirations.

There isn't space here to go into the many links between ancient and mediæval mythologies and literature of the 20th century. Greek mythology and Homer in James Joyce's *Ulysses*, for instance, or John Cowper Powys's visionary incorporation of the Grail myths and Arthurian legends in *A Glastonbury Romance, Wolf Solent* and *Porius*.

For instance, Frodo's journey can be regarded as a mythic descent and return, a sacrifice, death and resurrection (Frodo seeming to die is a recurring motif in *The Lord of the Rings*, as with the hero in mythology). James G. Frazer wrote about the death and resurrection of the hero in *The Golden Bough*, which relates to the Grail myth of the maimed king and the wasteland (*The Golden Bough* also contains masses of research on tree worship and tree cults, which chimes with J.R.R. Tolkien's passionate tree culture, which informs so much of his work). Mircea Eliade and Joseph Campbell developed Frazer's anthropological research, combining it with C.G. Jung's psychoanalysis.

You only have to pick up Robert Graves' *The White Goddess*, or Joseph Campbell's *Masks of God* series, or anything by Mircea Eliade or Carl Jung, to have an instant way in to this rich field. No doubt J.R.R. Tolkien would disagree with many of the conclusions and views of some of these writers; he disliked Graves, and found psychology dubious. But he was employing many of the same materials, the same motifs, the same archetypes, the same characters, and the same situations. Tolkien wouldn't use the same terminology of psychology, anthropology, literature, mythology and so on, but he was exploring much the same mythic territory.

BEOWULF

Beowulf (8th-11th centuries) was a key source for John Ronald Reuel Tolkien, of course (L, 31), and Tolkien's project was to produce a modern (though not modern*ist*) *Beowulf*, an updating of *Beowulf* which would keep intact the pre-mediæval aspects of the tale which had made it so important. *Beowulf* was significant, Tolkien explained in "*Beowulf*: The Monsters and the Critics", because it fused the Christian and the pagan, the Christian and the Northern European, the old and the new. (Beowulf = 'bees' wolf' (i.e., bear). Tolkien used it for his character Beorn.)

One wonders if J.R.R. Tolkien had to choose just one Northern European myth or legend or tale, above any others, it might well be *Beowulf* (though the competition with *Sir Gawain*, the *Kalevala*, the *Volsunga Saga*, the *Elder Edda* and the *Niebelungenleid* is fierce for Tolkien's affection. These were tales which were very dear to Tolkien's heart).

The dragon sequence in *The Hobbit* derives partly from *Beowulf*, where a thief steals treasure from a dragon's hoard; the Golden Hall of the Rohirrim is modelled on King Hrothgar's hall Herot; the culture of Rohan recalls that of *Beowulf*; the name Frodo comes from Froda, the chief bard.

The Rohirrim clearly derive from Old English and Anglo-Saxon culture (T. Shippey, 1982, 93f). Their language and names are Old English. Tom Shippey identifies the 'Mark' of Rohan with Mercia, the Anglo-Saxon name for the English Midlands. So the riders of Rohan have a special significance for Tolkien, as they are the Anglo-Saxons of Tolkien's homeland in Mercia. (Another source for the Rohirrim may be the Langobards, a Germanic tribe also known as the Lombards, who moved into Northern Italy).

NORTHERN EUROPEAN LEGENDS: THE *NIEBELUNGENLEID*, THE *KALEVALA*, *THE ELDER EDDA* AND THE *VOLSUNGA SAGA*

One of the motivations for creating Middle-earth and its stories for Ronald Tolkien was to make his own version of the Finnish saga *Kalevala;* the *Kalevala*, for Tolkien, was 'the original germ of *The Silmarllion*'. Tolkien's first attempts at writing Middle-earth legends date back to 1912 (L, 215). There are many affinities between Tolkien's Middle-earth and the *Kalevala*, ranging from names such as Ilmatar and Ilúvatar, Ilmo and Ulmo, to the Finnish style of the Elvish Quenya language, and the magical object of the *Kalevala*, the *sampo,* and the *silmarili* (the *sampo* was interpreted variously as the Golden Fleece, an allegory for the sky, a fertility object, a pillar idol from Lappland, etc.)

In *The Hobbit*, J.R.R. Tolkien drew on the Icelandic/ Old Norse *Elder Edda* (*c.* 1270s) and *Vafarúnismaál* (*c.* 1200): the *Fáfnismál* (*c.* 1270s) for the conversation with Smaug; the *Skirismál* for the orcs and Misty Mountain; the *Voluspá* (*c.* 1270s) for the names of the dwarves (in the *Prose Edda* are Thorin, Dwalin, Balin, Kíli, Fíli, Bofur, Bombur, Bifu, Dori, Nori, Ori, Oin, Glóin, Thráin, Thrór, Dáin and Nain).[1]

Another influence on *The Lord of the Rings* cited by critics was Richard Wagner (1813-83) – the *Ring* cycle (1876), the Northern mythology (the *Nieblungenlied*, Sigurd the dragon-slayer) – but J.R.R. Tolkien disliked Wagner's treatment of *Der Ring des Niebelungen* (even though the subject matter was dear to him). 'Both rings were round, and there the resemblance ceased', Tolkien asserted.[2] But the links continued to be made by critics and fans between Tolkien and Wagner. For David Day, *The Lord of the Rings* was 'certainly an attempt by Tolkien to reclaim the ring as a symbol of 'that noble northern spirit' which had fallen into such disrepute in Germany' (2001, 179). Day reckoned that Tolkien was motivated in part to rewrite the European ring quest tradition, to reclaim and renew it.

The influences of the great German mediæval *Nibelungenleid* are easy to discern on J.R.R. Tolkien's fiction. Magical swords, Siegfried the dragon slayer, the magical properties of dragon's blood, cursed hoards of treasure, betrayals and deceptions, cloaks of invisibility, warrior-queens like Brunhild who are subdued, it's all very familiar stuff.

The German mediæval *Nibelungenleid* ('Lay of the Downfall of the Niebelung dynasty'), written around 1200, was itself a version of the Scandinavian *Volsunga* saga, which Tolkien also drew on. The Norse *Volsunga* saga (late 13th century) is earthier, more archaic, with more magic and magical creatures, while the *Nibelungenleid*, being a product of the 13th century, is more courtly and refined (and Christianized). But the characters in the *Volsunga* saga – Sigurd, Gunnar, Gudrun, Brynhild, Hogni – are clearly Siegfried, Gunther, Kriemhild, Brunhild and Hagen.

Both the *Volsunga* saga and the *Nibelungenleid* are about the cataclysmic events of the fifth and sixth centuries in Northern Europe, the era of the decline of the Roman Empire, warring communities, the overthrow of the Burgundian society, and figures such as Dietrich von Berne (Theodoric the Goth), Charlemagne, and Attila the Hun.

The heroes Sigurd/ Siegfried, King Arthur and Aragorn have many similarities, as David Day pointed out: all are orphans, raised in secret, of noble blood, the last of their line, and are in danger of being assassinated. All fall in love with beautiful maidens, but have to win through many obstacles before they wed (each woman has a tragic future: Brynhilde commits suicide, Guinevere becomes a nun, and Arwen becomes mortal),

The broken sword as heirloom in *The Lord of the Rings* comes in part from the *Volsunga Saga*: Sigurd's sword was broken by Odin and he can't reclaim his kingdom until the sword is reforged. As well as the *Volsunga Saga*, the magical sword in *Rings* also draws on Arthurian legend.

The Lord of the Rings follows mediæval romance in opening with a feast where magic or strangeness is introduced, as well as the hero and the quest. (The party at the start of *The Hobbit* has affinities with the fiction of Edith Nesbit and Enid Blyton for Colin Wilson [1974]).

The dwarf Alberich or Andvari in Norse and German mediæval stories is a potent figure – clever, sinister, powerful, he's part-smith, part-guardian (of the ring and treasure), part-wizard and part-god. He becomes Alferich, Elbeghast and Laurin in other tales, and Auberon or Oberon in English literature (Oberon In *A Midsummer Night's Dream*).

David Day (2001) has suggested another link with the *Nieblungenleid*: the four-way romantic grouping of Aragorn, Arwen, Éowyn and Faramir: Brunhild falls in love with Siegfried, though he's betrothed to Kriemhild (Faramir doesn't quite fit in as a Hagen or Gunther figure, though, and Arwen's not scheming like Kreinhild). In the *Nieblungenleid*, Brunhild is eventually tamed by marriage to Gunther, and Éowyn the shield-maiden, after her heroic exploits on the battlefield, marries Faramir and becomes dedicated to more peaceful pastimes.

The Northern European deity Odin is an ancestor of J.R.R. Tolkien's gods, including Sauron and Gandalf: he was a ring lord, carried a staff, travelled in disguises, and was the trickster, mystic, shaman, poet and magician king of the gods.[3] Manwë also resembles Odin – he has the same stern, grey-bearded countenance, is giant-high, and wears a cloak. Like Sauron, Odin becomes one-eyed. (In Celtic mythology, the king Balor has a deformed eye which is kept shut because it can wither and destroy what it looks at). Gandalf recalls the Norse god Odin in his use of magical powers, runes, and chants.

NOTES: NORTHERN EUROPEAN LEGENDS

1. T. Shippey, 1982, 221; D. Day, 2001, 32.
2. H. Carpenter, 1977, 202.
3. D. Day, 2001, 31, 37.

ATLANTIS AND NÚMENOR, AND GREEK MYTHOLOGY

Some critics saw the Valar in J.R.R. Tolkien's mythology as Norse or Scandinavian gods, but they are closer in many ways to Greek deities. There are significant influences of Classical and Greek mythology in Tolkien's Middle-earth project, as well as Northern European mythology. The myth of Atlantis, for example, lies behind the notion of the West (L, 303), the Land of the Valar, and the Great Isle of Westernesse, inhabited by god-like beings, and unreachable by mere mortals. (Tolkien said he used to have a recurring dream about the great wave that swamped Atlantis, even into adulthood). Tolkien even gives Númenor a name like Atlantis: in Eldarin, it is called 'Atalantë' (S, 281). For Tolkien, Númenor was 'in the middle of the Atlantic'. In other words, it was Atlantis.

J.R.R. Tolkien's fascination with Atlantis goes right back to his earliest Middle-earth writings. When he was writing the 'Silmarillion' myths and legends, he was also working on a book called *Númenor*, but abandoned it when it became 'too grim' (D. Grotta, 45).

It's not just the Atlantis myth that Tolkien employs, though: he also drew on the island of Avalon, the 'apple island' of Arthurian legend, resting place of King Arthur, and the Holy Grail, and also identified variously with Glastonbury, with the Celtic otherworld, a land of glass, and a looking glass world (HME, VI, 215). (Tolkien had started an epic poem on King Arthur which he hadn't finished). Then there's Lyonnesse, a sunken kingdom of legend supposedly lying off Cornwall, which had fascinated Thomas Hardy. And magical kingdoms or cities which have sunk beneath the waves occur in many legends.

The Blessed Realm in the West obviously evokes Paradise in the Old

Testament, which, after the fall of Númenor, becomes a lost Eden, a memory of a paradisal land which can never be recovered by mere mortals. The lost paradise is a very common motif in world mythology.

The word 'Numemore' was not related to 'numen', Tolkien explained, but meant 'Westernesse' in Elvish (L, 151).

> N[umenor] is my personal alteration of the Atlantis myth and/ or tradition, and accommodation of it to my general mythology. Of all the mythical and 'archetypal' images this is the one most deeply seated in my imagination, and for many years I had a recurrent Atlantis dream of the stupendous and ineluctable wave advancing from the Sea or over the land, sometimes dark, sometimes dark and sunlit. (L, 361)

At one time J.R.R. Tolkien had attempted to write a time-travel book about a man going back in time to the drowning of Atlantis [L, 347]).

Further correspondences with Greek myth: Manwë recalls Zeus, the stern, bearded patriarch, Ulmo resembles Poseidon, god of the sea, Mandos, lord of the dead, recalls Hades, Yavanna resembles Demeter, Aulë is a version of the smith Hephaestos, Oromë the hunter looks back to Orion, and Tulkas recalls Hercules.

Another link with Greek mythology is Elrond and Elros, who recall the twins Castor and Pollux, a mortal man and an immortal god (the twins are united in the heavens by Zeus, as stars, and Elrond and Elros's father Eärendil becomes a star).

The black sails in the Greek myth of Theseus are consciously evoked in the black sails of the pirates' ships on the River Anduin. King Minos sees the black sails from a cliff as Theseus returns and kills himself, believing that all is lost. In *The Lord of the Rings,* Denethor sees the black sails of the Corsairs and imagines the worst. Both leaders turn out to be wrong.

ANCIENT EGYPT

There's quite a bit of ancient Egypt in the Middle-earth tales too. The Númenóreans of Gondor, for example, are

> proud, peculiar, and archaic, and I think are best pictured in (say) Egyptian terms. In many ways they resembled 'Egyptians' – the love of, and power to construct, the gigantic and massive. And in their great interest in ancestry and in tombs. (L, 281)

It's in Númenor that the cult of the dead begins on a wide scale in Middle-earth's history (prior to that, humans have accepted their mortality, in general). But in Númenor, despite being blessed by the Valar with extended lifespans, the Númenóreans become obsessed with death. Thus begins the construction of colossal tombs, and the delaying of death by any means (they only succeed in discovering embalming bodies, but not prolonging life [S, 266]). The line of kings of Númenor (when they are ruling Númenor in the Second Age) recall the kingships of ancient Egypt, and even their names recall ancient pharaohs (Ar-Pharazôn, Ar-Adûnakhôr, Ar-Zimraphel).

The architecture of the Númenóreans is colossal, like ancient Egyptian architecture: an architecture that advertizes political power, a sense of empire and imperial majesty, a proto-fascistic architecture. When Sauron's temple is constructed, for instance, it's an enormous circular building with a black dome and walls fifty feet thick, recalling the Pantheon in Rome, or the designs that Albert Speer produced for Adolf Hitler. When the Dark Lord arrives in Númenor for the first time (in 3262 of the Second Age) he is startled by the immensity and magnificence of the architecture:

> Sauron passed over the sea and looked upon the land of Númenor, and on the city of Armenelos in its days of glory, and he was astounded; but his heart within was filled the more with envy and hate. (S, 271)

In another aspect the Númenóreans resemble ancient Egyptian culture: incest. Echoing the brother-sister marriages of ancient Egyptian pharaohs, Ar-Pharazôn marries his cousin, Tar-Míriel (Ar-Zimraphael) (S, 269). This unlawful union occurs at the end of the rule of the Númenórean kings, recalling Cleopatra and her brother Ptolemy, at the end of the line of Egyptian pharaohs.

Ar-Pharazôn also resembles the Roman emperors and the Egyptian pharaohs in being a greedy, ambitious king with a consuming lust for power. He takes Tar-Míriel as his wife because she is the heir of Tar-Palantir (his father, Gimilkhâd's brother); he then usurps the throne.

In *The Lost Road*, Alboin muses on the people that lived on the Western shores of Europe before the time of the Romans and the Carthagians, in Portugal, Ireland, Spain and Britain (note the absence of the French). 'I wonder what the man thought who was the first to see the western sea', Alboin wonders (HME, 5, 39). Alboin seems to prefer a non-Latin or pre-Latin culture, and the Atlantic (the Western sea) rather than the Mediterranean sea.

ARTHURIAN LEGENDS

Although he was clearly inspired by the Arthurian legends, J.R.R. Tolkien found them 'too lavish, and fantastical, incoherent and repetitive' (the people who don't like Tolkien might describe his own fiction in the same way!). He did, though, compose one piece of Arthuriana, a poem, 'The Fall of Arthur', which dealt with the final years of the story of King Arthur.

Arthurian literature also, J.R.R. Tolkien insisted, was a too explicit manifestation of Christian religion: myth and fairy tale should not have such religious or moral material on the uppermost levels, in the Primary World of its fiction. Rather, it should be buried underneath. Tolkien went on to explain that his project in creating Middle-earth was to rejuvenate the heroic romance and fairy tale traditions of Britain, to create tales and legends which would be written for and about Britain:

> ...once upon a time... I have a mind to make a body of more or less connected legend, ranging from the large and cosmogonic, to the level of romantic fairy-story – the larger founded on the lesser in contact with the earth, the lesser drawing splendour from the vast back-cloths – which I could dedicate simply to: to England; to my country. It should possess the tone and quality that I desired, somewhat cool and clear, be redolent of our 'air' (the clime and soil of the North West, meaning Britain and the hither parts of Europe: not Italy or the Aegean, still less the East), and, while possessing (if I could achieve it) the fair elusive beauty that some call Celtic (though it is rarely found in genuine ancient Celtic things), it should be 'high', purged of the gross, and fit for the more adult mind of a land long now steeped in poetry. (L, 144-5)

For David Day, 'there can be no doubt that the novel's bittersweet ending is consciously modelled on the tales of Arthur's death' (2001, 68). And at the end of *The Lord of the Rings*, it's the humble hobbit Frodo, not Aragorn the almost superhuman Arthurian hero, who sails away like King Arthur into the West.

Some critics railed against interpretations of J.R.R. Tolkien and Middle-earth (such as illustrators, or films such as the 2001-03 productions) that were (too) mediæval. For these critics, Tolkien's fiction was not 'mediæval', but set in an older, pre-Middle Age, perhaps a Dark Age world. But Tolkien employs a range of historical periods in Middle-earth. Much of the linguistic sources were pre-mediæval (Anglo-Saxon, Old English, Welsh, Germanic, Icelandic, Finnish) and much of the culture was from the Dark Ages. Some of the mythology of Middle-earth was older – going back to the myths of Atlantis and Greek mythology.

Though J.R.R. Tolkien disliked Arthurian literature, his Middle-earth fictions inevitably became associated with it (the kings, knights, ladies, quests, magic, wizards and courtly ideals – even though Tolkien insisted that his story 'does not deal with a period of 'Courtly Love' and its pretences; but with a culture more primitive (sc. less corrupt) and nobler' [L, 324]). Referring to Charles Williams, Tolkien said he 'actively disliked his Arthurian-Byzantine mythology' (L, 349).

But plenty of J.R.R. Tolkien's Middle-earth fiction is 'mediæval', and Tolkien drew on mediæval traditions of the romance (he had translated *Sir Gawain and the Green Knight*). There's plenty of Arthurian and mediæval tradition in the treatment of figures such as Aragorn and kings Théoden and Denethor. And the romances – Aragorn-Arwen and the unrequited Aragorn-Éowyn relationship – draw on mediæval courtly love (Éowyn as an Elaine figure, for instance). Tolkien, though, further refined and Christianized Aragorn as King Arthur, making him more moralistic and upstanding (and the Arthurian legends were Christianized throughout their development, arising in pagan Europe, but acquiring Christian aspects as time passed).

Moving closer to the present time, there are Renaissance and Reformation influences in J.R.R. Tolkien's Middle-earth books. Much of the hobbit's culture is 18th and 19th century (the social structure of Hobbiton, food and pastimes, etc). Although Tolkien went back to heroic romances of the Middle Ages and earlier (such as *Beowulf*), he often called his fictions fairy stories. Folk and fairy tales are often ancient, but they weren't collated extensively until the work of the Grimm brothers, Charles Perrault and others in the 18th and 19th centuries, and didn't become widely known (or read) until that time. Thus, although Tolkien drew on folk tales and mythology going back millennia, the influence of 18th and 19th century culture and literature on his Middle-earth *legendarium* is very great.

Ronald Tolkien was adamant in describing *The Lord of the Rings* as a 'heroic romance', not a 'novel' (L, 414). It wasn't meant to be a novel, Tolkien said in a letter, a book about the state of the nation, or about English society. It was intended to be an older and distinctive form of literature. (Implicit in this comment is Tolkien's desire that *The Lord of the Rings* not be treated in the same critical terms as a novel, and put into the same literary category, or be judged in the same way by critics, as William Faulkner, Virginia Woolf, André Gide or William Golding). In the same letter, Tolkien took a dim view of critics and pundits who wanted to 'label' writers, or put them into categories.

OTHER MEDIAEVAL CORRESPONDENCES

There are numerous correspondences between Northern European mythologies and J.R.R. Tolkien's myths. The Valar (originally the Ainur) lived in
Aman, while Norse gods, the Aesir and Vanir, live in Asgard, a realm across
the rainbow bridge. The slain go to the Hall of Valhalla in Asgard in Norse
myth, while in Tolkien's mythology they go to the Hall of Mandos. They wait
there until the day of judgement (called Ragnarok by the Vikings).

However, J.R.R. Tolkien adds many modern elements. For instance,
the notion that 'power corrupts', a modern concept that isn't found in the
Northern European myths.

Other mediæval texts, apart from J.R.R. Tolkien favourites such as
Beowulf, The Pearl, Sir Orfeo and *Sir Gawain and the Green Knight*, that
may have influenced Tolkien's fiction included La3amon's *Brut*, an
Arthurian epic, *Mandeville's Travels*, written *c.* 1375, and Marie de
France's *Lais*.

The *Ancrene Riwle* or *Ancrene Wisse*, written *c.* 1225 in Herefordshire, was another favourite Tolkien mediæval text (he published an article
on it in 1929). The *Ancrene Wisse* was an instructional text for a group of
anchorites (religious hermits), probably based in Tolkien's beloved West
Midlands.

Sir Gawain and the Green Knight was one of J.R.R. Tolkien's choice
mediæval narratives. In his essay on the poem, he calls it 'the best
conceived and shaped narrative poem of the Fourteenth Century, indeed of
the Middle Ages, in English' (MC, 105). Only Geoffrey Chaucer's *Troilus
and Criseyde* rivalled it, though Chaucer's poem was no 'wiser or more
perceptive, and certainly less noble' (ibid.).

Wayland the Smith is another source for Tolkien, the Saxon hero and
craftsman. The mediæval legend is linked to the landscape of the White
Horse and Wayland's Smithy, not far from Oxford. Wayland the Smith hints
at magical craftsmen in Tolkien's *legendarium* like Sauron, Fëanor,
Celebrimbor and Telchar, who forged the magical rings, jewels and
weapons. Wayland the Smith was the maker ot Siegfried's sword Balmung,
and Charlemagne's Joyeuse sword (and also the Saxon hero Walter of
Aquitaine, and Witig in the *Wilkina Saga*).

Aragorn also had links with King Charlemagne, with the unification of
the North and South realms of Middle-earth, Arnor and Gondor, being
related by J.R.R. Tolkien to the foundation of the Holy Roman Empire by
Charlemagne. (Tolkien had spoken of the Holy Roman Empire, and also as
Gondor as a kind of Byzantium, connecting the North and South of Middle-
earth with the East (Byzantium) and West (Rome) of the Roman Empire).
Like the Roman Empire in Byzantium, Gondor is assailed by hordes from
the East (the Easterlings in Tolkien, the Teutonic tribes in history).

J.R.R. TOLKIEN AND WILLIAM SHAKESPEARE

Although J.R.R. Tolkien was severely critical of William Shakespeare's influence on subsequent English literature, he was not averse to enlarging upon the Bard's plays when it suited him (he uses speeches from *Henry V*, for example).

There are numerous correspondences between J.R.R. Tolkien and William Shakespeare. Both grew up in Warwickshire and the English Midlands, and used that landscape in their works. They both recognized the value of rural, village life. Both loved home comforts, and recognized the importance of 'home'. Both enjoyed good male company, and created many scenes featuring men smoking, drinking and talking together. Both valorized the past, and were fascinated by history (not only English history). Both reworked stories from the past – legends, myths and folk tales as well as historical and mythological tales. Both knew Greek and Roman history, and employed it in their writing. Both were adherents of storytelling, and loved a really good story. Both wrote stories on a grand, epic scale. Both writers loved big speeches, the noble and heroic form of writing. Both wrote at length about kings, princes, the divinity of royalty and kingship. Both were influenced by Catholicism. Both loved poetry, and regarded poetry as the highest form of literature. Both included many songs in their fictions. Both loved the oral culture of poetry and song.

J.R.R. Tolkien clearly draws on the themes of royalty, kingship, nobility and divinity that were such a large part of William Shakespeare's works. Shakespeare's kings are among his most accomplished creations: Richard, Henry, Lear, Macbeth. When it comes to writing about kings, Shakespeare has no equal. None. One of Shakespeare's obsessions was with the aristocracy, and with the divine nature of kingship. The idea of the throne, the crown and the king was a preoccupation for Shakespeare 'much more than to any other writer', as Orson Welles put it. For the Bard, 'a king was someone in a quite singular and separate tragic position' (59).[1] Many of Tolkien's kings – Aragorn most obviously – draw on Shakespeare's conception of the divine, noble and tragic nature of kingship (and the identification of king with notions of 'nation' and 'state').

Many of the J.R.R. Tolkien's heroes are nobility or royalty, from Galadriel, Legolas and Finrod Felagund, to Théoden, Elendil, Isildur and Aragorn. And while the hobbits appear to be everyday folk, with no royal and noble lineage, they are still high up in the social hierarchy. And in a 1944 letter Tolkien compared the relationship between Gollum and Sam to that between Ariel and Caliban in *The Tempest* (letter no. 64).

NOTES: TOLKIEN AND SHAKESPEARE

1. Orson Welles, in *Orson Welles: Interviews*.

Chapter 3

LANGUAGE, STYLE, HUMOUR

CRITICISMS OF J.R.R. TOLKIEN'S STYLE

J.R.R. Tolkien's writing style prefers solid metaphors and similes drawn from the natural world. Characters rushing by like the wind… Rohirrim spears like a thicket of trees … characters vanishing like a mist… the elves like starlight, with eyes of stars… Tolkien keeps his comparisons within the bounds of the Secondary World he has created. He is careful to keep the lid on 'modern' phrases and notions (although they creep in everywhere).

Sometimes J.R.R. Tolkien's narrator's comments upon the action can seem self-conscious and clumsy. Most of the time, Tolkien wants an invisible narrator, an observer who just happened to be there and witnessed the events. But sometimes Tolkien steps back and comments upon them. Most awkward of all, and most difficult for an audience to take, are the passages where the prose – lo! – behold! – gets all solemn and Biblical.

A few times J.R.R. Tolkien allows his narrator to pull the reader out of the illusion of the fictional world of Middle-earth. In Lothlórien, for example, Frodo and Sam remark that they felt as if they were 'inside' a song. Later, in the far less agreeable surroundings of Mordor's borders, they wonder whether their experiences will be the subject of stories for future generations.

At Cirith Ungol, Sam says, very self-consciously, '"why, to think of it, we're in the same tale still! It's going on. Don't the great tales never end?"' (TT, 403). That might be a comment on the length of *The Lord of the Rings* itself (*The Lord of the Rings* contains around 600,000 words, quite long compared to other heroic romances, or to fairy tales, which are typically two or three pages). Or on the author's long struggle to finish the thing. It's as if Tolkien is wondering to himself if his book will ever be completed.

In *The Hobbit* and to a lesser extent in *The Lord of the Rings*, there are asides from the author/ narrator to the reader. They are self-indulgences which J.R.R. Tolkien later excised (though not entirely). I like them; they're quaint and friendly, and remind the reader that they're reading a story, which's being told by someone. It fits in with Tolkien's notion of the whole of *The Lord of the Rings* and *The Hobbit* being written down as a record, by hobbits and others. It also makes those first chapters light-hearted, and not in the grand style of the rest of the book. Tolkien, when he re-read *The Lord of the Rings* 25 years after publication, remarked that the first book 'is really very different to the rest'.1

Another criticism of J.R.R. Tolkien's fiction would be that the characters tend to merge with one another, that Tolkien has only a few archetypes that he uses repeatedly, and that it's difficult to differentiate between them. Like his landscapes, the characters tend to double, triple and quadruple each other. There's one stolid, solemn warrior who's tempted and fails (Boromir) followed by one who's tempted by remains true (Aragorn), then there's another, this one a banished son (Éomer), and another banished son, who's also tempted (Faramir).

Critics of J.R.R. Tolkien's style pointed out his over-use of words such as 'suddenly' ('suddenly the lights went out'); the churchy, Biblical, ponderous prose in the later parts of *The Lord of the Rings* ('lo!', 'behold!'); inversions in dialogue; the portentous, unbelievable (and pretentious) dialogue; and the lack of humour. (Tolkien said he put in the 'thees' and 'thous' to indicate a more formal language.)

Let's face it, there's not a lot of humour in *The Lord of the Rings* or J.R.R. Tolkien's other Middle-earth writings. On the whole, Tolkien tends to play it straight – *very* straight. There are jokes, and some humour that's intentional, but not much. Often the humour is unintentional. There's a huge amount of carnage in *The Lord of the Rings*: it's the story of the wars of the ring, after all. But not much black or gallows humour.

J.R.R. Tolkien's prose style is very easy to parody (just look at film or TV adaptions). What humour there is tends to cluster around the hobbits; much of the humour also occurs in the early part of *The Lord of the Rings,* the last third of the novel being far more serious (some would say ponderous) in tone. There's a joke in the first line of *The Lord of the Rings* (about Bilbo's 'eleventy-first birthday' (which Derek Robinson likens to A.A. Milne, Lewis Carroll and T.H. White in tone [1983, 108]).)

For Burton Raffel, J.R.R. Tolkien's writing in fiction was too often generalized, vague; although it was visual, it wasn't really offering a rich portrait of a world. Raffel compared the prose style of Tolkien to D.H. Lawrence's, and found Lawrence's much more vivid, with 'complexities, complications, subtleties that Tolkien does not admit'. But Tolkien's prose style wouldn't work for D.H. Lawrence, and vice versa.2

Christopher Manlove, commenting upon the solemn exchanges between Treebeard, Celeborn and Galadriel at the close of *The Lord of the Rings,* when they talk about never meeting again, wrote:

The over-worked cadences, the droning, monotonous pitch, the sheer sense of hearts charged not with lead but gas, can offer only nervous sentimental indulgence or plain embarrassment to the reader' (1975, 189)

Philip Norman, interviewing J.R.R. Tolkien in 1967, remarked that the writer had a solid prose style ('an amalgam of Celtic bard and Fowler's *Modern English Usage*'). Tolkien's style may have its detractors, Norman averred, but 'an author who can create and sustain and make us revere a race of people resembling trees could never be failed by his style'. A 'workman-like' style was a common view of Tolkien's prose: a cross between something scriptural and that of a mediæval chronicler (recalling the writers who chronicle the events in the book itself – Bilbo and Frodo, and Sam).

The hobbits have a stolid, 'make do' camaraderie: they grumble occasionally, but basically put up with the hardships of the quest. Give them food, tobacco and a warm fire, and they're content. But there's not much joking amongst them or the Company. Considering how much time the fellowship spend with each other, there's very little ribbing, leg pulling, one-liners or wisecracks to lighten the leaden mood. All of the fellowship, and pretty much everyone they come into contact with, is serious, whether they're on the good or evil side (in a fairy tale, Tolkien insisted, 'one thing must not be made fun of, the magic itself' [MC, 114]).

Tom Bombadil is one of the few characters in *The Lord of the Rings* who's irrepressibly happy: with his capering and 'ring a ding dillo' dialogue he recalls the Trickster God of archaic mythology, the dancing shaman (and later incarnations, such as King Lear's fool or the mediæval court jester). One of the reasons some readers are turned off by Bombadil is perhaps because his high spirits and goofing off are out of place in the gloomy seriousness of most of the narrative (as well difficult to take in a super-cynical, postmodern age).

Boromir is dour and intense; Aragorn's even dourer and intenser (though he does allow himself one or two pops at people – usually at the hobbits Merry and Pippin). Gandalf, despite the twinkle in his eye which suggests mischievousness, is amongst the most severe characters in *The Lord of the Rings*. If he uses humour, it's usually to put down the hobbits with their foolishness or ceaseless questions ('fool of a Took!' – Pippin). If characters (Frodo or Bilbo, say) joke about the ring, Gandalf soon puts them right, and reminds them of the terrible importance of the matter. Gimli has the grouchiness and stubbornness of dwarves, but there's a little joshing between him and Legolas (often with the differences between their species as the subject).

The great and the good of Middle-earth – Elrond, Galadriel, Denethor, Théoden, Saruman – are never less than grave (though Denethor does veer into dark humour, and Saruman is, inevitably, sarcastic at times, like a nasty school teacher).3

As well as 'grim', one of J.R.R. Tolkien's oft-used terms, are 'doom' and 'fate'. 'Doom' and 'fate' were used in place of chance, luck and destiny. Tolkien's narrators talk about the 'doom of the elves', the 'doom of men', and the 'fate of Middle-earth'. A term such as *doom* comes from *dom* in Old English, which meant 'judgement' as well as 'bad fortune' ('judgement' as in *domdaeg*, 'Doom's Day', i.e., the Last Judgement or Judgement Day). Maybe it was luck or chance at work in the history of the ring, but Gandalf seems to prefer concepts such as fate or destiny.

The orcs have a stage hall/ vaudeville Mockney dialogue (culled from the Victorian/ Edwardian handbook of plebian slang), but their verbal interplay, despite its clunky stereotyping of the working class, at least has a healthy vigour about it. The orcs' digs at each other sound more like people who work together for long periods than the fellowship or other groups of the 'free peoples' (who are usually deferential and reverential). (Tolkien wrote that the orcs' language was 'actually more filthy and degraded than I have shown it', and if he'd converted it into English it would have been 'intolerably disgusting and to many readers hardly intelligible' [HME, 12, 42]. Well, of course it was: Tolkien wasn't going to put in swearing and 'bad language' in a heroic romance modelled along mediæval lines).

Increasingly through the narrative, the dialogue in *The Lord of the Rings* becomes pompous – and long-winded. J.R.R. Tolkien might have criticized William Shakespeare on all sorts of fronts, but Tolkien's dialogue sometimes rivals even the Bard's for unfettered prolixity. There are times in *The Lord of the Rings* (as in Shakespeare's plays) when characters will speak in terms of long strings of names and places ('son of… house of… heir of…'), where a simple 'yes' or 'no' would do. Characters also seldom interrupt each other; in their arguments, each character allows the other to finish (great for actors who like to hog scenes).

As well as sounding like *Revelations* ('and lo!') or a Catholic preacher admonishing his flock about hellfire and damnation on a Sunday morning, *The Lord of the Rings'* narrator also employs inversions to make things Sound More Impressive ('Edoras those courts are called').4

For John Bayley, *The Lord of the Rings* is 'fantastically badly written', because of its stylistic faults. Maybe, but it is also hugely loved, and read by millions.

'There is never much development in the episodes; you simply go on getting more of the same thing', Edmund Wilson moaned in his famous review, "Oo, Those Awful Orcs".5 'These characters who are no characters are involved in interminable adventures the poverty of invention displayed in which is, it seems to be, almost pathetic', Wilson went on. Tolkien has 'little skill at narrative and no instinct for literary form'. It *should* be really exciting and moving, Wilson maintained, but it wasn't. 'The wars are never dynamic; the ordeals give no sense of strain; the fair ladies would not stir a heartbeat; the horrors would not hurt a fly'.

Surprisingly, for a cunning linguist like Professor Tolkien, there's also not much wordplay and punning (according to Tolkien, one of the Inklings' pastimes was creating puns). Rather, all of Tolkien's inventive skills were brought to bear on the names, places and the languages (there are some in-jokes for philologists, though). Wordplay and punning tends to make readers aware of the act of construction of the text, and Tolkien wanted his fairy tale to be a 'romance', in the old style, rather than a modern 'novel'. Thus, modernist devices such as self-consciousness, self-reflexivity and *mise-en-âbyme* were scrupulously avoided. No extravagant Shakespearean insults either for Tolkien (though surely he could have invented some good ones).[6]

Humour also slows up a narrative, and enables the reader to step outside of it for a moment, or reminds the reader that they're reading a story. With his narrative driving onwards, unstoppable and relentless, Tolkien didn't want to slow things up with jokes. Maybe his intention was to write a serious tome; but *avoiding* humour doesn't automatically make something *more* 'serious'.

Also, humour can be (is) anti-authoritarian and subversive. It questions authority, codes and rules. J.R.R. Tolkien's Middle-earth was ruthlessly hierarchical, with the sites and levels of authority firmly in place. Authority could not be questioned, and as authority is one of the prime targets of humour, it had to go. The idea of one of the characters making fun of the patriarchal lines of leaders of Rohan, Gondor, the Dúnedan or the elves is unthinkable in *The Lord of the Rings* (unless they're one of the enemy). No character, except one or two of the baddies (Saruman, Wormtongue), ever questions authority. And no one ever speaks of Ilúvatar or the Valar in anything other than a deeply reverent tone.

It is assumed in *The Lord of the Rings* that the 'free peoples' will be able to govern themselves correctly, for the greater good and without corruption – simply because they are *not* the enemy. And the enemy is only ever assumed to want to destroy and corrupt everything. There's no suggestion that Sauron (or Morgoth) wanted to do anything other than rule the world and dominate everyone in it. *The Lord of the Rings* is reassuringly clear-cut, politically, ideologically, socially and morally. That must be part of the appeal for audiences: it's an escape into a fictional world where every moral choice, every political decision, is comfortably crystal clear.

1. In H. Carpenter, 1995, 196.

2. *The Lord of the Rings* is 'a very *good* book; indeed a very goody-goody book; and the goodness mounts up until I, for one, thirst for a sliver of redeeming vice, just one little taste of genuine bloody-mindedness' (D. Robinson, 1983, 116).

3. 'Parts of *The Lord of the Rings* sound like lines rejected from the draft script for *Monty Python and the Holy Grail* because they weren't quite pompous enough', Derek Robinson noted (1983, 122).

4. In A. Becker, 53.

5. Neil Isaacs has composed a list of some of the puns and jokes in *The Lord of the Rings,* but they're pretty obscure: 'the Town Hole' at Michel Delving, the S.-B.'s (Sackville-Bagginses) = sons-of-bitches; the name Halfast = half-assed'; a pun on the verb in Treebeard's line: 'there'll be the Lord of the Fields of Rohan, mark you!'; Goldberry's dialogue: 'I see you are an elf-friend; the light in your eyes and the ring in your voice tells it'. (In N. Isaacs, 10.)

WORDS AND NAMES

Ronald Tolkien was precious about his invented names, which he said he fussed over just as much as the poetry or other aspects of his Middle-earth mythology. Tolkien wished that names could be copyrighted – it piqued the novelist when an Aquastroll hydrofoil vessel was named 'Shadowfax' in 1964 (L, 349). For W.H. Auden, Tolkien's talent for naming 'surpasses any writer, living or dead, whom I have ever read'.[1] Tolkien's famous saying ran '[t]he 'stories' were made rather to provide a world for the languages rather than the reverse. The name comes first and the story follows' (L, 219). Creating Middle-earth, Tolkien said, 'was an effort to create a situation in which a common greeting would be *elen sila lúmenn' omentielmo*' (L, 264-5). Many critics have found that claim bogus.

Names in fairy tales are significant: fairies disappear when the name of Jesus or God is uttered; fairies are sometimes referred to by an alternative name, as their actual name can be unlucky (in Ireland they're called *sidhe*, the Good Folk, in Celtic lore they are the Hill Folk, in England and Germany they are the Kleine Volk or Little Folk); in many religions the name of (a) God is taboo; in Christianity names have a superstitious power – a child's name is not announced before baptism, as a protection against bad spirits or witches; new or second names are given to children and young adults at initiation rituals; the second or 'spiritual' birth (or rebirth) often requires a new name; some names can work magic, such as the *Open Sesame* of Ali Baba, or the ancient Hebrew *abracadabra*; in *Rumpelstiltskin* it is the name itself that destroys the dwarf (in English folk tales there is *Tom Tit Tot*, from East Anglia, while in Cornwall the Devil appears as Terry-top; in Scotland the name is Whuppity Stoorie; in Austria Kruzimugeli, in Spain Marie Kirikitou, and in Iceland Gilitrutt). (Names were so important to Sauron, he didn't allow anyone to use his own name, or write it, as Aragorn tells Legolas and Gimli (TT, 15), a common taboo in fairy tales.)

J.R.R. Tolkien preferred a solid Anglo-Saxon word or phrase to something more flowery, or self-conscious, or showy, which's why his prose style can sometimes appear plain and unadorned. Tolkien disliked over-using terms from Latin or romance languages, or prose that was trying too hard. Here's an example of an ultra plain style, from *The Treason of Isengard*:

> They came to the gates. The main gates were closed; but a small door was still open. Sentinels stood on either side, and at the opening stood an armed warder, gazing out into the gathering dusk. The Orcs were waiting for the messenger from Baraddur. (HME, 7, 337)

J.R.R. Tolkien does dazzle the reader with his names for places and people, and his vast Middle-earth back-story, but his prose style is actually often fairly straightforward. Tolkien isn't one of those writers who likes to show off how much they know about unusual words. (Not everyone was won over by Tolkien's prose style: C.L. Wrenn told Przemyslaw Morckowski: 'Tolkien is a genius! If only he wrote accordingly, what wonders could he accomplish'.2)

Plenty of critics drew comparisons between J.R.R. Tolkien's description of Mordor – with its mud, its squalor, its craters, its smoke, its stench, its armies crawling like ants, its all-pervading gloom – with the hellhole of the Great War, the trenches and battlefields of the Western Front. The Dead Marshes episode is really vivid in its prose.

The meaning of the name Mordor derives from 'mor' (dark, black), also found in Moria, Morgoth, Morgul, etc (another link with *Macbeth*: Mordor and Cawdor). 'Crack of doom' also comes from *Macbeth*. The alliteration of 'fail' and fall' in a conversation between Gandalf and Théoden may be an echo of *Macbeth*.3 And the only Shakespeare play with Anglo-Saxon characters is *Macbeth,* which would endear it to Tolkien. And Tom Shippey noted that the

> final and strongest influence of *Macbeth* on *The Lord of the Rings* is quite obviously in theme. If there is one moral in the interlacements of the latter it is that you must do your duty regardless of what you think is going to happen. This is exactly what Macbeth does not realise. (1982, 138)

The Witch-king is clearly meant to be a forerunner of a doomed former king – in particular, Macbeth (J.R.R. Tolkien emphasized the links between Angmar and Macbeth in a number of ways). Only someone not born of a woman can kill Macbeth, but Shakespeare's solution of someone born by cæsarean isn't quite as elegant or convincing, perhaps, as

Tolkien's answer of a woman dressed as a man (aided by a hobbit).

The *Macbeth* prophecy concerning the Witch-king has a different meaning in earlier drafts of *The Lord of the Rings:* instead of being defeated by someone of no woman born, he is, says Gandalf, 'to be overthrown by one who has never slain a man' (HME 8, 335). J.R.R. Tolkien was dismissive, though, of Shakespeare's play: '*Macbeth* is indeed a work by a playwright who ought, at least on this occasion, to have written a story, if he had the skill or patience for that art' (TL, 53).

While the names Morgoth and Sauron connote evil and all things nasty, names like Eärendil and Aelfwine are sweet Elvish. And Treebeard's name, as he tells the hobbits Merry and Pippin, is a story in itself: '"*my* name is like a story. Real names tell you the story of the things they belong to in my language' (TT, 80). A totally Tolkien concept.

Maybe 'hobbit' came from J.R.R. Tolkien combining the Anglo-Saxon terms *hol* (or hole) and *byta* (dweller), which would produce *holbyta* (which Théoden uses to define the hobbits). Hobbits are linked to rabbits in their dwelling in holes in the ground, their furry feet, and their behaviour, though Tolkien always denied the connection (even though it's in *The Hobbit*). The word 'hobbit' had appeared in *The Denham Tracts* (1895), the Folklore Society's dictionary of folklore. Douglas Parker likened the word "halfling' to 'half-fairy, half-man', i.e., a transition between the Third and Fourth Ages of Middle-earth, between the fantastical realm of fairies (elves) and that of humans.[4]

As well as names, J.R.R. Tolkien loved to add accents and other fiddly bits to words (the 'tehtar' or 'signs' above consonants). It wasn't 'Smeagol', it was 'Sméagol'. 'Gríma' not 'Grima'. 'Fëanor' not 'Feanor'. 'Númenórean' not 'Numenorean'. 'Nazgûl' not Nazgul'. One wonders if that wasn't just the philologist in Tolkien, but also the calligrapher and artist, who liked the look of words with accents or tehtar (and Tolkien had different systems of vowel markings for Quenya and Sindarin Elvish languages). Certainly when you see Tolkien's invented languages written down – the Cirth (or Dwarvish) runes, or Fëanor's Tengwar script – their elegant appeal is apparent.

So to typeset *The Lord of the Rings* extra keys were required for the accents. It took a careful attention to detail with its many unusual names and references. Then there were the maps.

NOTES: WORDS AND NAMES

1. W. Auden, in N. Isaacs, 51.
2. In D. Grotta, 124.
3. T. Shippey, 1982, 137.
4. D. Parker, "Hwaet We Holbytla", *Hudson Review*, 9, 1956.

LANGUAGES

As a schoolboy, J.R.R. Tolkien could easily converse in Latin and Greek (it was customary for debates at the Debating Society of King Edward's school to be conducted in Latin). Tolkien also spoke Anglo-Saxon, and Gothic. One of his first lectures, while at school, was entitled "The Modern Languages of Europe: Derivations and Capabilities". It was such a long lecture, the teacher stopped Tolkien before he could get to the capabilities of languages (it had taken three one-hour lessons to deliver the lecture).

For J.R.R. Tolkien, language was 'a natural product of our humanity... of our individuality' (MC, 190). Tolkien's lifelong passion for languages informs so much of his writing. Some critics have said that Tolkien's claim that he invented Middle-earth in order to have a place where his languages could be spoken shouldn't be taken too seriously. A philologist, Tolkien said people didn't believe him seriously when he claimed that the language came first.

As the narrator of *The Lost Road* puts it, Alboin 'liked the flavour of the older northern languages' (HME, 5, 39). It's a flavour or 'language-atmo-sphere' which still comes through in echoes, 'in odd words here and there', often common words (ib., 40). Language goes back in time, Alboin argues in *The Lost Road*, just as much as race or culture. As Michael Stanton pointed out, 'if one word – "Mellon" or "Friend" – can open the Doors of Moria, language itself is the passkey to the world of Middle-earth' (147).

For J.R.R. Tolkien, language was sacrosanct: 'I am a *pure* philologist. I like history, and am moved by it, but its finest moments for me are those in which it throws light on words and names!' (L, 264). He wrote at length on his beloved invented Elvish languages, *Quenya* (High-elven) and *Sindarin* (Grey-elven), as well the Common Speech (Westron), the Black Speech of the orcs, entish, and dwarvish. *The Lord of the Rings'* appendices included detailed descriptions of the pronunciation, history and written forms of Tolkien's languages. Sometimes Tolkien took his passion for names to extremes. At the beginning of *The Return of the King*, for instance, there's a sentence that runs: '[t]he king mounted his horse, Snowmane, and Merry sat beside him on his pony: Stybba was his name' (RK, 55).

The Welsh language was the source of inspiration for some of J.R.R. Tolkien's invented languages. Tolkien recalled that seeing Welsh on coal trucks as a child (during his first holiday in Wales with Father Morgan) impressed him greatly. Welsh, he said, 'always attracted me more than any other language'. In his essay on the Welsh language, Tolkien wrote: 'two things seem important: Welsh is of this soil, this island, the senior language of the men of Britain; and Welsh is beautiful' (MC, 189). Tolkien described his early encounter with the Welsh language:

But all the time there had been another call – bound to win in the end, though long baulked by sheer lack of opportunity. I heard it coming out of the west. It struck at me in the names on coal-trucks; and drawing nearer, it flickered past on station-signs, a flash of strange spelling and a hint of a language old and yet alive; even in an *adeiladwyd 1887*, ill-cut on a stone-slab, it pierced my linguistic heart. 'Late Modern' Welsh (bad Welsh to some). Nothing more than an 'it was built', though it marked the end of a long story from daub and wattle in some archaic village to a sombre chapel under the dark hills. (MC, 192)

J.R.R. Tolkien spoke of being enamoured of the sound of Welsh, just the sounds of the words, the names, the shapes of the words. But it wasn't a 'literary' or 'poetic' pleasure. 'It is simpler, deeper-rooted, and yet more immediate than the enjoyment of literature' (ib., 190).

To illustrate how much he loved the sound of Welsh, J.R.R. Tolkien cited the example of the sound of the words 'cellar door' in English as being particularly pleasurable, and said that in Welsh

for me *cellar doors* are extraordinarily frequent, and moving to the highest dimension, the words in which there is pleasure in the contemplation of the association of form and sense are abundant. (ib., 190-1)

In his essay on the Welsh language, J.R.R. Tolkien made an interesting point: the common belief is that the outerlying regions of the United Kingdom are the most 'Celtic' or 'Teutonic' or 'British' or 'Belgic' (the 'Celtic' fringe of Wales, Scotland, Ireland, Cornwall, etc). Tolkien suggests that the opposite may be true, that the South-East of England may have been the most 'Celtic', or 'British', or 'Belgic'. Tolkien reckoned that if Kent, Sussex, Surrey and Essex and other parts of South-East England are regarded now as the most 'English' (or 'Danish') parts of the U.K., they must also have once been the most 'Celtic', or 'British', or 'Belgic', because of their proximity to the Continent. The invaders, whether Celtic or Germanic, would have come to the South-East first. At the same time, the South-East would have been first area to be inhabited by Romans, and later cultures, such as Normans.

The very 'word-form', J.R.R. Tolkien explained in his lecture on new languages such as esperanto, can have an æsthetic pleasure like being entranced by 'the line of a hill, light and shade, or colour' (MC, 206).

William Graigie, a philologist and editor of the *Oxford English Dictionary* (which J.R.R. Tolkien later worked for), had helped to encourage Tolkien to invent his own languages. Craigie introduced Tolkien to Finnish and Icelandic.

J.R.R. Tolkien spoke of being fond of many languages – Old and Middle English or Anglo-Saxon is an obvious love, but also Welsh, Latin and Romance languages, Gothic, Spanish, Italian, Greek, Finnish and

Germanic (though he disliked French and Gaelic, and preferred Spanish to Italian). Discovering Finnish (in a grammar in Exeter College library) was like 'discovering a complete wine-cellar filled with bottles of an amazing wine of a kind and flavour never tasted before' (L, 214). The comparison between language and wine emphasizes the direct, physical (and sensual) pleasure that language gave Tolkien (French feminist philosophy would call it the *jouissance* of language, the sexuality of the text). Only Finnish, Tolkien confessed, gave him the most pleasure – along with Welsh (MC, 192).

Finnish partly inspired the first of J.R.R. Tolkien's major invented languages: *Quenya*, which was highly developed, with a vocabulary of 100s of words, by 1917. *Quenya* was the older of the Elvish languages, and was the primary among the Elvish languages that Tolkien invented. (Tolkien's invented languages grew and grew: to see how complex they became, have a look at the Tree of Tongues in *The History of Middle-earth* volumes, diagrams which depict a complicated interplay of languages and branches of Elvish tongues).

J.R.R. Tolkien likened Quenya, the language of the High Elves or Eldar, to Latin (he called it 'Elven-Latin'). Quenya, Tolkien explained, drew on Finnish, Greek and Latin languages. It was the language of lore, of the Noldor, of the elves who remained in Eldamar or Elvenhome. Sindarin, which drew on Welsh, was the language of the elves who stayed behind in Beleriand, the exiles from Eldamar, the elves who didn't travel to Eldamar.

French gave him less pleasure than most other languages, J.R.R. Tolkien admitted, but he fell in love with Greek, and Spanish (Spanish 'gave me strong pleasure, and still does – far more than any other Romance language' Tolkien said [MC, 191]). The encounter with Gothic languages was close to a life-changing event for Tolkien: 'Gothic was the first to take me by storm, to move my heart' as he put it in his essay "English and Welsh" (MC, 191).

Of course, J.R.R. Tolkien does show off in numerous ways – in his linguistic prowess, for example, or his knowledge of etymologies, or his knowledge of history, or fairy and folk tales, and his sometimes pedantic search for the source or root of words or ideas. And providing reams of background material (genealogies, dates, histories) at the back of *The Lord of the Rings* is a kind of showing off (as well as obsessiveness).

TOLKIEN'S POETRY

It's true that John Ronald Reuel Tolkien isn't an obvious candidate for an exquisite or ornate prose style. He is no modernist stream-of-consciousness stylist like James Joyce or Virginia Woolf, or as musically rhythmic and sensual as D.H. Lawrence, or earthy and poetic like Ursula K. Le Guin, or austerely spartan like Samuel Beckett, or delicate and intricate like V.S. Naipaul or Anaïs Nin.

J.R.R. Tolkien's poetry, too, is not going to offer competition for great poets like Friedrich Hölderlin, or Francesco Petrarch, or John Keats. Really, it's not even as accomplished as some of the low ranking troubadours and courtly love poets, and is nowhere near the achievement of mediæval poets such as Bernard de Ventadour, Giraut de Borneil, Arnaut Daniel, Bertran de Born, or England's own William Langland or Geoffrey Chaucer. As poetry, Tolkien's verse is not the equivalent, either, of the mediæval texts Tolkien admired (*Sir Gawain and the Green Knight*, for example, or *The Pearl*). Burton Raffel commented: 'I find almost all of Tolkien's verse embarrassingly bad', and the poetry in *The Lord of the Rings* has 'almost no independent literary merit'.[1]

But J.R.R. Tolkien's poetry was hugely significant for him, as it so often is for poets (Robert Graves spoke of his own poetry as a 'spiritual autobiography'. Graves refused to read Tolkien's books (although Graves's wife Beryl enjoyed them.)[2] For Tolkien, poetry could clearly express something personal, subtle, emotional, something that could only be expressed in a poetic form. It's no surprise, then, that his longest poem is *The Lay of Lúthien*, a poem about one of his favourite stories from his *legendarium*, the romance between Beren and Lúthien (which had personal links to his wife Edith).

And J.R.R. Tolkien's poetry, which is found throughout his work (in his essays as well as fiction), does serve an important function in his books. In *The Lord of the Rings*, for example, characters resort to poetry or songs when they're happy (the hobbits' drinking songs), or melancholy (Aragorn singing *The Lay of Lúthien*), or rejoicing (the eagle singing over Minas Tirith).

Not only are some of J.R.R. Tolkien's favourite characters writers (Bilbo, Frodo, Alboin), they are also poets (at some point or other in *The Lord of the Rings* and other books, many characters are also poets: Bilbo, Frodo, Sam, Gollum, Aragorn, Gandalf, etc). Three pages of *The Lord of the Rings*, for instance, are given over to Bilbo trying out his poem about Eärendil on an audience of elves at Rivendell (it's the longest piece of poetry in the book). It's a poem in the act of creation, and in the act of performance.

Note that many poems in J.R.R. Tolkien's fiction are not *written* and *read* by a single person, but are *performed*, for an audience. It's very much an oral tradition of poetry, in keeping with its roots in mediæval poetry. The poems and songs only come alive, in a way, when they are performed. Also, it's a poetic tradition where verses and songs are learnt by heart, and handed down through generations.

The verse J.R.R. Tolkien put into *The Lord of the Rings* was not decorative or for subjective expression, he claimed, but had a dramatic, narrative purpose. Music, singing and poetry is a principal element in the world of Middle-earth: not only do most of the key characters break out into verse throughout *The Lord of the Rings*, they also sing (some 55 songs and verses are listed in the index to *The Lord of the Rings*). Tom Bombadil and Goldberry communicate in singsong (and he saves the hobbits from Old Man Willow with a song); even when Bombadil communicates in straight dialogue, it scans like verse; Tom Shippey has analyzed Bombadil's speech in terms of poetry (1982, 81). The hobbits (and elves) entertain each other with songs; songs occur at pivotal narrative moments (Frodo's song of 'The Man in the Moon' in the *Prancing Pony*, Sam rallying himself with a song in Shelob's lair, and so on).

Sauron fights Finrod Felagund in song in *The Silmarillion*, Lúthien's song awakens Beren when he's imprisoned in Sauron's dungeons (like Sam's song to Frodo in Cirith Ungol), Lúthien's song destroys Sauron's tower, and Fingon finds out where Maedhros is hanging on Thangorodrim's mountains by singing. (While Tolkien provides some of the songs of Bombadil, Frodo, Bilbo and others in *The Lord of the Rings*, he refrains from writing the far more narratively important songs of Lúthien, Finrod, Sauron and Beren).

Although J.R.R. Tolkien disliked theatre and drama as an artform, he did enjoy readings (particularly poetry), and acting out classic texts – his own, and also Geoffrey Chaucer (Tolkien had played Chaucer in an Oxford 'Summer Diversion' in the late Thirties).

In his poetry, J.R.R. Tolkien employed the Anglo-Saxon alliterative half-line: this's an example from *The Lay of the Children of Húrin*:

the white arrows of the wheeling sun
gazed down gladly on green hollows (HME, 3, 60)

J.R.R. Tolkien also composed in simple rhyming couplets: *The Lay of Leithian* is composed in octosyllabic lines with end rimes. And, being a student of languages, he also liked to write poetry in Old English.

NOTES: TOLKIEN'S POETRY

1. In N. Isaacs, 229, 231.
2. M. Seymouth-Smith, *Robert Graves*, Paladin, London, 1987, 375.

J.R.R. TOLKIEN AND CHRISTIANITY

Tom Shippey noted that *The Lord of the Rings* was not exactly a Christian 'myth' or mythic in the Christian sense: Frodo 'is not sacrificed, is not the Son of God, and buys for his people only a limited, worldly and temporary happiness' (1982, 154). Frodo, one could argue, does come close to dying or being sacrificed, and J.R.R. Tolkien could have had Frodo falling into the abyss, as the only way he could destroy the ring, making his death a heroic sacrifice.

The problem then with making *The Lord of the Rings* a Christian myth is still that the new world order the destruction of the ring and the passing of Sauron bring about is distinctly secular, not sacred. It's an 'age of men', not a Biblical rebirth. Indeed, the drift is towards secularization as many of the truly magical or powerful beings in Middle-earth pass away over the sea (Galadriel, Elrond, Círdan, Gandalf). The spiritual power of the elves passes too, and the dwarves and ents will fade. There is a great battle (at Pelennor and the Morannon), but it's not the Last Battle out of the *Bible*, and Christ doesn't vanquish the Anti-Christ.

If Middle-earth is a Christian world without a Christ, it is full of Christian attributes. But it's not a perfect world – there is evil at large. J.R.R. Tolkien described the religious outlook of his Middle-earth as a 'monotheistic world of 'natural theology'' (L, 220).

Commentators compared the compendium of legends in *The Silmarillion* to the *Old Testament*: *The Silmarillion* begins, like the *Bible*, with a Creation myth and contains a multitude of stories, involving families, heroes, monsters, and magical acts. As in the *Bible*, there's the occasional intercession of the deity, the cunning schemes of the Devil, periods of exile from Paradise (Valinor), and people who prove themselves worthy of the Divine, or fall into sin, or turn away from God.

The *Valaquenta* follows the fall of man in the *Bible* pretty closely. Like the *Bible, The Silmarillion* could continue to enlarge upon its legends eternally (and Tolkien did just that, working on the material in *The Silmarillion* throughout his life so that, as with the *Bible*, some legends were rewritten a number of times). If *The Silmarillion* is the *Old Testament*, that would make *The Lord of the Rings* the *New Testament*: a messiah-figure (Frodo) comes to save the world. (The attributes of the saviour are shared between Frodo, Aragorn and Gandalf – and Sam too, some readers would claim).

Frodo has many affinities (like Aragorn) with Jesus. His journey echoes the Christian year: the Fellowship leave Rivendell on Christmas Day; Mordor falls on Good Friday, approximately, with the climactic events in Mordor occurring during Easter (it's actually March 25, a sacred day in the Christian calendar, being the day of the Annunciation of the Virgin as well as the Crucifixion). Frodo's torture by the orcs in the tower recalls Christ's Passion (he also has a wound in the chest and hand, and he's tended by Sam, like Christ with the Magdalene). The Frodo-Sam relation recalls Jesus and his disciples. (The scouring of the Shire has been linked to the war in heaven and the cleansing of the Temple by Jesus.)

Frodo's final act of crawling up the side of Mount Doom to deliver the ring to the fire recalls Christ at Golgotha, carrying the Cross to make the ultimate sacrifice. The comparisons between Frodo's experience of carrying the ring to Orodruin and the Stations of the Cross of Christian myth are easy to spot. And Sam carries Frodo, like Simon the Cyrenian carrying the Cross for Jesus.

For some critics, Frodo's suffering and sacrifice cannot be equated with Christ's; Cynthia McNew asserted that Christ's sacrifice was more profound than Frodo's (partly because at the end, it wasn't Frodo who destroyed the ring).[1]

With Aragorn as the prophecized saviour or messiah, Sauron becomes the Anti-Christ, a Lucifer who appears at the end of the world to do battle with the forces of good. If *The Lord of the Rings* is a Biblical or Christian narrative, Sauron could never win. Ever. The Anti-Christ, or Lucifer, or the Devil can never be victorious.

Another link between Aragorn and Christ is that they are descended of royal lines (David's descendant, and Isildur's heir). They both came out of obscurity; both were leaders of men; both toiled in the wilderness.

Galadriel obviously draws on the image and character of the Virgin Mary in Catholic art and theology, as J.R.R. Tolkien acknowledged (L, 407); she's humble, content to stand on one side rather than be a Queen, a decision made clear in the scene where Frodo offers her the ring (R. Purtill, 85). Tolkien was more sceptical, though, when some readers became more obscure in their inferences – such as linking *lembas* (waybread) with the Eucharist (L, 288).

When the eagle flies above Minas Tirith at the climax of *The Lord of the Rings* it sings in a very churchy, Biblical tone ('sing and be glad, all ye children of the West, I for your King has come again'). The allusions in the language are to the *Bible*, while 'the King', although it means Aragorn, has distinct Christian overtones (and Apocalyptic allusions, to the renewal of the world in *Revelations*).

The temptations that the ring represent have Christian models, including Christ in the wilderness being tempted by the Devil, and many Christian saints being tempted (such as St Anthony).

One of the paradoxes of J.R.R. Tolkien's Middle-earth fiction is that it is full of pagan characters, who, with their pagan beliefs and customs, seem difficult to square with Tolkien's own Christian (Catholic) beliefs. There were many aspects of pagans and paganism that Tolkien admired, but there plenty too that he disliked (the blood lust, the violence and cruelty). Tolkien called *The Lord of the Rings* a 'Christian' work, but of course it treads a path carefully between Christianity and paganism, between the sacred and the secular, as Tom Shippey noted:

> The care with which he maintained this position (highly artificial, though usually passed over without mention) is evident, with hindsight, on practically every page of *The Lord of the Rings*. (1982, 152)

J.R.R. Tolkien's Middle-earth world would be blasphemous and heretical to thousands of Christian scholars, theologians and saints from throughout history. For theologians such as Tertullian, Origen, St Augustine (Bishop of Hippo) and St Thomas Aquinas, and saints and mystics such as St Bernard of Clairvaux, St Teresa of Avila, St John of the Cross and St Catherine of Siena, the idea of a world with a pantheon of gods (and also one God), a world without churches, altars, religious rituals, services or sacraments like the Mass, a world with no authority above that of king, a world with wizards and magic and magic rings, a world with no heaven and no redemption, a world without Christ, would be heathen, pagan and heretical.

For Jack Zipes, J.R.R. Tolkien secularized his Middle-earth fictions in response to the changing world around him. It was a protest, Zipes reckoned, against the 'failings of institutionalized religion, the rise of atheism and communism, the threats of war and fascism, the reification of values and human relations under capitalism'(2002a, 165).

So J.R.R. Tolkien created Middle-earth in order to show how it was possible to 'recover' religion. So it was ironic that Tolkien elevated

> the small person, the Hobbit, to the position of God, that is, he stands at the center of the universe and is the humanistic source of all creation. God is absent from the Middle-earth. The spiritual world manifests itself through the actions of the redeemed small person. (ibid.)

For the denizens of Middle-earth, there is no salvation in the manner of Christianity, no rewards for living a good, sin-free life, no karmic after-life. The ontological split between elves and men, with their different fates, is also difficult to square with Christian theology (having two races or species, both conscious and both very similar, going to different places after death is problematic from a Christian mind-set). Tolkien toyed with the idea of reincarnation – for the elves – but rejected it after some thought. Reincarnation presents all sorts of narrative and metaphysical enigmas.

Classic Gustave Doré fairy tale illustrations, to Charles Perrault, 1867, including Puss In Boots, and Little Red Riding Hood.

Some book covers of J.R.R. Tolkien's works
(U.K. editions)

A tiny fraction of the merchandize and toys generated by J.R.R. Tolkien's books.

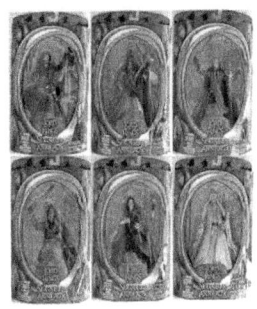

Oxford, where Tolkien lived for most of his adult life (above and left).

The Oxfordshire countryside (below. Photos: the author).

Oxford: Radciffe Camera and the Bodleian Library, on the right (above).
Merton Street (below). Tolkien lived at Merton College (on the left) in his final years.

Cháprer 4

MIDDLE-EARTH

John Ronald Reuel Tolkien's Middle-earth legends take place in a perpetual pre-mediæval period, somewhere between the Fall of the Roman Empire and the Norman Conquest. For thousands of years of the First, Second and Third Ages of Middle-earth nothing much changes, in the social and political systems, in the living conditions of castles, strongholds and villages, in the weaponry (swords, shields, spears, bows and arrows), the military tactics (battles on plains), and so on. Once Tolkien had set up his world – of elves (and later, men) living in Valinor and Beleriand with the ever-present threat from Morgoth – he let it run on for age after age. There is no sense of social or economic evolution, or notions of 'progress', and of any character desiring to improve the basic way of life.

Curiously, the engine that drives most of the change in Middle-earth comes from the enemies. J.R.R. Tolkien depicts these social changes in technological terms: Morgoth using a bastardized science to cross-breed elves and orcs, for example, or Sauron's Industrial Revolution of noisy, dirty, dehumanizing machines, of iron and steel, smoke and dust. Technological advances represent one of the most significant threats to the way of life of the 'free peoples' of Middle-earth: Tolkien always paints the science that Saruman and Sauron utilize in a negative light: it's pollution, noise, filth. The robotic mechanisms simulate 'real life' without having any of the qualities that make living things valuable or worthy. Both wizards, for instance, use the magic of fire sometimes: Gandalf to illuminate Moria with his staff, and Saruman to blow up the wall at Helm's Deep, but Gandalf's magic is 'good' and Saruman's is 'devilry'. But the fundamental objection to technological progress in Tolkien's fiction is that it seeks to emulate (or worse, replace) the creation of Ilúvatar or God.

J.R.R. Tolkien was fanatical about geography as well languages and names. Much of *The Lord of the Rings* concerns lengthy descriptive passages of landscapes. Sometimes the prose can achieve the level of nature poetry, putting Tolkien in the long line of British poets who wrote lovingly about the landscape (from Geoffrey Chaucer and William Langland through Will Shakespeare and Robert Herrick to the Romantics such as John Keats, William Wordsworth and Percy Bysshe Shelley). The early chapters of *The Lord* have a wistful, introspective melancholy about them: the hobbits set off, significantly, in early Autumn, mid-September. There are passages about the English Autumn, the season of bonfires, leaves, mushrooms, streams, hills and leave-takings. Tolkien is very strong on the bleaker places – Mordor, the Dead Marshes, the Emyn Muil, etc.

In his commentary on the *Athrabeth*, J.R.R. Tolkien described the kingdom of Arda as roughly equivalent to the Solar System. Something like a 'world' or 'Earth' wasn't quite big enough for the grand, cosmogonic design Tolkien wanted (HME, 10, 374). Middle-earth was just one part of Arda.

J.R.R. Tolkien saw the accounts of his Middle-earth mythology as deriving two stages away from the 'truth' of what actually happened. There is no 'true record' of the mythology, because it was disseminated first by the elves who wrote of the Valar and their dealings with the gods, and secondly via the accounts of humans (Númenóreans), supplemented by other histories and tales (HME, 10, 401-2).

Linking the creation of the sun and the moon with the light of the two trees of primordial Aman was, J.R.R. Tolkien acknowledged in 1958, 'astronomically absurd' (HME, 10, 370f). (But Tolkien also liked to try). A Maia, Arien, was chosen as the vessel of the sun. It was also tricky fusing a 'flat Earth' philosophy with a round Earth one, Tolkien noted, and working out how the light of the two trees operated (with issues such as rising and falling).

Why was the Earth round? It wuz the gods wot did it: when the men of Atalantë/ Númenor sailed on Valinor, the Valar 'globed the whole earth so that however far a man sailed he could never again reach the West, but came back to his starting-point', J.R.R. Tolkien wrote in *The Lost Road* (HME, 5, 12). The old lands were underneath the new ones.

J.R.R. Tolkien maintained that his Middle-earth creation was firmly based in this world, with the Third Age of Middle-earth leading up to the beginnings of human history. But it was also always only a tale, a piece of literature, and to be taken as such (L, 188). Tolkien said he gave *The Lord of the Rings* the appearance of being 'real history', and some readers were taking it that way, but the 'tale is after all in the ultimate analysis a tale, a piece of literature'.

Another of the attractions of J.R.R. Tolkien's fiction is that he constructed a world (Middle-earth) that was complete in itself: it was a closed world, blissfully self-sufficient, which the professor had mapped out in every detail ('he has anticipated every question and found an answer before you asked').[1] Robert Giddings compared Middle-earth with other closed systems, such as hospitals, schools, colleges and the army.[2] And this is what happens in Tolkien studies: ask any question about Middle-earth and the Tolkienites situated around the globe can answer it by consulting one of Tolkien's tomes. Tolkien himself is regarded as the god of his own Middle-earth – all enquiries are directed back to the writer himself, not to anything outside of Tolkien and his creation (not even to C.S. Lewis and the Inklings). Tolkien is seen as the ultimate authority in Middle-earth studies.

One of the curious omissions from J.R.R. Tolkien's Middle-earth are animals. There are birds (including giant eagles), fish, heroic horses, rabbits (called coneys), and plenty of nasty creatures like giant spiders, tentacled lake monsters and wargs. But as the fellowship travels through Middle-earth, there are far less encounters with the animals of Middle-earth than one might expect. If Middle-earth is partly based on Western Europe, travellers would be passing thousands of sheep, cattle, goats and pigs, as well as horses. But Tolkien opted to leave out many of the domestic farm animals of Europe. So one wonders what people ate in Middle-earth (the good guys tend to eat vegetarian food, while the orcs have nasty meat). Tolkien's Middle-earth writing isn't big on food (although hobbits are). Tolkien's narrators do describe food from time to time, but it usually seems to be vague.

J.R.R. Tolkien acknowledged that most everything in his Middle-earth legends had existed before, except perhaps 'the cats of Queen Berúthiel' (L, 228). (Those cats are enigmatically mentioned once in Tolkien's fiction, but never again).

The closer the hobbits travel to Mordor, the more realms become corrupt or ailing. Rivendell and Lórien are still intact and thriving (though conscious of it all having to end sometime and probably soon), but all is not right at Isengard, or Rohan, or Gondor. Rohan has an ailing king, and orcs on its borders. Some wonder if Rohan pays tribute to Mordor. Gondor is led by a steward who's being corrupted into despair by Sauron via the *palantír*. Minas Tirith has seen better days, and the population's dwindling (there aren't enough young people).

The geography of Middle-earth is conceived in broad strokes: the ocean lies to the West; a jagged coastline (but basically on a North-South line); there are mountain ranges in straight lines through Middle-earth, which often form boxes (Mordor, Hithlum); mountains dominate the North (the Iron Mountains, where the enemy lives); there are enormous tracts of forest (Doriath); secret kingdoms ringed by hills (Gondolin, Nargothrond, Dorthonion); and big rivers dissect Middle-earth, flowing from North to South.

The North is cold, dangerous, icy, dark, the South and East are hot and unknown (and desert), with the East as particularly evil, and the West is where everyone really wants to be (i.e., as close to the Blessed Realm as possible). Just as each Age in the history of Middle-earth replays earlier ones, and one villain replaces another (Sauron and Morgoth), so the topography of each period in Middle-earth's history echoes former periods. For example, in the First Age of Middle-earth, Beleriand, where most of the action takes place, locates the sea in the West and a line of mountains (the Ered Luin, or Blue Mountains) in the East; two large rivers flow North to South (Sirion in West Beleriand and Gelion in Ossiriand). The elves cluster around hidden or protected kingdoms and strongholds (Gondolin, Nargothrond, Menegroth, Brithombar).

In the Second Age, much of that land falls into the sea, but Middle-earth still looks similar: sea in the West, a ragged coastline (though with a large bay, Lune in the North and the bay of Befalas in the South), mountains in the East (the Hithaeglir or Misty Mountains), with great rivers (the Loudwater/ Greyflood, Baranduin and the Anduin) flowing North-South. Some mountain ranges are altered (the Blue Mountains are split apart by the Gulf of Lune, and part of the Ered Engrin, Morgoth's Iron Mountains, survive as the Grey Mountains). Again, there are enclaves of elfdoms: Rivendell, Mithlond, Wooded Realm, and Lothlórien. However, there is a new land, created by the Valar, in the West: Andor (Númenor or Westernesse). In the Third Age, after the downfall of Númenor and the Last Alliance), Middle-earth isn't much changed, but the seas are now 'bent', and Númenor is no more.

Christopher Tolkien remarked that Tolkien wanted to link up his own legends with those of Western cultures: the stories of time travellers from the 20th century going back into a multi-layered past would offer a way of connecting with all sorts of myths and legends. And they were all about living in Western Europe over the past few thousands years: 'all concerned with the stories and the dreams of people who dwelt by the coasts of the great Western Sea' (HME, 5, 98).

In his guide to the names in *The Lord of the Rings*, J.R.R. Tolkien said that Middle-earth was '[n]ot a special land, or world, or 'planet', as is too often supposed, though it is made plain in the prologue, text, and appendices that the story takes place on this earth and under skies in general the same as now visible'.[3]

Middle-earth is based on (or takes its starting-point as) Europe, J.R.R. Tolkien explained in a letter in 1967, with Middle-earth corresponding to North-western Europe and the Northern shores of the Mediterranean (L, 376). '*The Lord of the Rings* may be a 'fairy-story', but it takes place in the Northern hemisphere of this earth', Tolkien said in relation to the first attempt to film his book (L, 272). The term 'Middle-earth' was meant to refer to the real, historical world of Northern Europe (but the historical period was imaginary, Tolkien said [L, 239]). The geography of the land masses might have been changed, but it was definitely the Old World (L, 220).

But, J.R.R. Tolkien went on to explain, Middle-earth wasn't wholly

Northern European: '[i]f Hobbiton and Rivendell are taken (as intended) to be about the latitude of Oxford, then Minas Tirith, 600 miles south, is at about the latitude of Florence. The Mouths of Anduin and the ancient city of Pelargir are at about the latitude of ancient Troy' (ibid). That would make Hobbiton and The Shire where the West Midlands are (where I grew up), in particular the counties of Worcestershire, Warwickshire, Staffordshire, Shropshire and Herefordshire (Tolkien identified The Shire as 'more or less a Warwickshire village of about the period of the Diamond Jubilee', rather than North Oxford [L, 230] That is, the land of his own childhood).

Pursuing this fantasy geography would make Mordor about where the Balkans are (which J.R.R. Tolkien confirmed; on another occasion, Tolkien placed Mordor where the Mediterranean volcanic basin is, with Mount Doom corresponding to Mount Stromboli [K. Fonstad, 90]); the Misty Mountains are the Alps (though they remind me more of Welsh mountains); Mirkwood would be the Black Forest and the forests of Germany (Tolkien associated Mirkwood with ancient Germanic forests [L, 369]); the Anduin would be the River Rhine, and so on.

Putting Minas Tirith in the middle of Italy, around Florence, also fits in with *The Lord of the Rings*, which ends, as J.R.R. Tolkien explained, 'in what is far more like the re-establishment of an effective Holy Roman Empire with its seat in Rome than anything that would be devised by as 'Nordic'' (L, 376). (Tolkien disliked the French term 'Nordic', preferring 'Northern European').

When J.R.R. Tolkien visited Italy in the mid-1950s, he loved Venice, describing it in terms of his Secondary World: 'incredibly, elvishly lovely – to me like a dream of old Gondor, or Pelargir of the Númenórean Ships, before the return of the Shadow'.[4]

J.R.R. Tolkien confirmed that his Middle-earth was based on Northern Europe in many other ways. He referred to real places, regions and countries in terms of their Middle-earth names, in the same way that he talked about people (including himself) as hobbits, dwarves, elves or wizards.

One of the origins for the inspiration of the lengthy journey of the Company (the marches through a variety of landscapes, the camping and cooking, the resting and sleeping) is J.R.R. Tolkien's hiking holidays of his youth. In a letter to his son Michael, Tolkien discusses one such walking holiday of 1911, with its many adventures. Tolkien spoke lovingly of the spectacular peaks of the Alps: the Eiger, Mönch, Jungfrau and Silberhorn (L, 392). In referring to the Alps, Tolkien linked the real mountains with his fictional Misty Mountains ('the *Silberhorn* sharp against dark blue: the *Silvertine* (*Celebdil*) of my dreams' [ibid.). Tolkien illustrator John Howe said that Minas Tirith was 'easily recognisable to anyone who has been to Alsace'. An early draft of the foreword to *The Lord of the Rings* noted of the elves that they were 'much the most important people of those times', and that the

> lands in which they lived, changed though they now are, must have been more or less in the same place as the lands in which they still linger: the North-west of the old world. (HME, 6, 311)

Mordor is also called the 'Black Country' (HME, 6, 216), which had a particular resonance in Britain, because the area of the English Midlands surrounding Birmingham is also called the 'Black Country', due its massive industrialization. Indeed, the Black Country of the Midlands is still a vast area of factories, warehouses, terraced houses, a wasteland where towns merge into one another in endless, grey, dull suburbs. There are people who appreciate that kind of environment, but for me the Black Country is about the most depressing place in Britain.

The hobbits, like the 'English' or 'British' people, are not natives to their homeland: the hobbits came from between the Loudwater and Hoarwell rivers, as the 'English'/ 'British' came from Germany and Scandinavia. There were three tribes of hobbits (Stoors, Harfoots and Fallohides) like three tribes of the 'English'/ 'British' (Angles, Jutes and Saxons).

There are numerous other affinities between the hobbits and the 'English'/ 'British': the villages, the little counties and regions, the mayors, meetings, councils, Shiriffs, the small-mindedness, the petty squabbles and resentments, the beer and ale, the inns, the cups of tea, the pipes, the country houses, the little farms, the rural way of life, the Protestant work ethic, the timidity, the shyness, the quietness, the eccentricities, the mistrust of 'outsiders', the racism, the class system, the conservative values, and so on. Of course, it's a heavily idealized, nostalgic view of 'English'/ 'British' life that never existed in the first place.

Diana Wynne Jones related the landscape of the first chapters of *The Lord of the Rings* to Oxfordshire: the Upper Thames Valley, Wychwood, the Windrush and Evenlode rivers, the orchards and fields around Didcot, and prehistoric monuments such as the Rollright Stones, Seven Barrows and Wayland's Smithy. (The chalky ridges of Wiltshire and Dorset, further South of the Midlands, may also have inspired Tolkien: they are full of ancient structures, in particular Stonehenge, Avebury and hundreds of round barrows or burial mounds (there are many barrows on the Berkshire downs near Oxford). Tolkien describes the landscape of the Barrow-downs as chalky ridges). Tom Shippey has noted how Tolkien drew on English place-names, particularly those of the English Midlands, for The Shire: Tuckborough, Buckland, Nobouttle, etc (1982, 78).

WALES AND WELSH. Wales (and the Welsh language) was another influence on J.R.R. Tolkien's fiction ('I also find the Welsh language specially attractive' he wrote [L, 218-9]). Tolkien had visited Wales for two weeks following his mother's death. He loved it immediately.

THE MIDLANDS. The border country (also known as the Marches or Marcher lands), between England and Wales, is one of J.R.R. Tolkien's great loves and touchstones. He spoke of regarding his real roots as being in Worcestershire and the counties on the border with Wales; his mother was from Suffield, near Evesham, in South Worcestershire; she was buried in Bromsgrove, in East Worcestershire, in the Catholic church. Tolkien knew the Vale of Evesham, and the majestic Malvern Hills (apparently, the Hills were an inspiration for the mountains of Middle-earth, and he visited friends in Malvern). Tolkien's aunt (Jane) lived in a farm at Dormston in Worcestershire, which locals called Bag End.[5]

'I am a West-midlander by blood... I am indeed in English terms a West-midlander at home only in the counties upon the Welsh Marches', he admitted (L, 213, 218); 'any corner of [Worcestershire] (however fair or squalid) is in an indefinable way 'home' to me, as no other part of the world is' (L, 54). Although he was born in Bloemfontein in South Africa, Tolkien said he'd lived most of his life in Birmingham or Oxford, with 5 or 6 years in Leeds after the Great War. 'Though a Tolkien by name, I am a Suffield by tastes, talents and upbringing', he remarked. Tolkien reckoned that the Suffields, his maternal ancestors, had lived in and around Worcestershire for generations.

ATLANTIS/ AVALON/ ENGLAND

J.R.R. Tolkien related the island in the far West of Middle-earth, over the ocean, to the ancient British myths of Avalon, Westernesse and Lyonnese. The island, which is both Númenor and Valinor, was also identified with Britain itself. An example of Tolkien identifying the island far West of Middle-earth with Britain occurs in one of his notes for the story of *The Lord of the Rings*, in an early draft (late 1930s). Tolkien wrote: 'Elrond tells him [Bilbo] of an island. Britain? Far west where the elves still reign. Journey to the perilous isle' (HME, 6, 41). It's intriguing that, for Tolkien, the island(s) West of Middle-earth were, at various times:

(1) mythical realms such as Atlantis,
(2) the Avalon of Arthuriana legend,
(3) sunken kingdoms such as Lyonnese and Westernesse,
(4) also Britain itself.

(In *The Lost Road*, Eressëa is also called 'Avallon'). In the earliest *Silmarillion*, elves travel from Lúthien, J.R.R. Tolkien's name for Britain or England, to Valinor and Tol Eressëa (HME, 4, 39).

J.R.R. Tolkien sometimes called England/ Britain 'Lúthien', or 'Leithian', 'Leithien' or 'Luthany'. It must be significant that the most beloved elf in Tolkien's *legendarium*, Lúthien Tinúviel, was also his name for his homeland of Britain.

One of J.R.R. Tolkien's stories was entitled *Ælfwine of England*. Ælfwine means 'elf-friend', sometimes called Alboin, or Albinus, or Elwin, or Eriol, and linked to Alboin of Lombardic legend, and Ælfwine of *c*. 918 AD (Frodo and Aragorn were also called 'Elf-friend'. Tolkien had variations on the name of the mariner who travels to other lands and hears grand tales). In *The Lost Road*, the name Ælfwine is linked to King Alfred's grandson, who died in 937, and another Ælfwine who died at Maldon, who were part of 'the long line of Elf-friends' (HME, 5, 38).

It's enchanting to think of England as fairyland, a land where elves are still living. The journey in *The Lost Road* is symbolic, a time travel, sci-fi jaunt, as well as a 'real' one. Maybe Ælfwine dreamt it all: 'alone in the waters, hungry and athirst, he fell into a trance and was granted a vision of that isle as it once had been', Tolkien wrote in *The Lost Road* (HME, 5, 103).

In the earliest form of this narrative (known as *The Cottage of Lost Play*, written in 1915), Ælfwine/ Eriol sailed to an island, Tol Eressëa, which was not Atlantis or somewhere out in the middle Atlantic Ocean, but England itself. And the town or Kortirion or Koromas in the middle of Tol Eressëa, the ancient realm of the fairies, was Warwick in the Midlands, and other places in the story, such as the Land of Elms, was Warwickshire, and Tavrobel was Great Haywood in Staffordshire (there were links between *kor*- and *war*- etymologically [HME, 1, 24-25]). In later versions of the story, Ælfwine becomes an Englishman in the Anglo-Saxon era who sails over the Atlantic from England to Tol Eressëa. (The character of Ælfwine Verlyn Flieger says embodies 'some of [Tolkien's] most deeply rooted attitudes toward myth, language, history, and the participation of the unconscious in all these' [1997, 64-65]).

In one of the notes on Númenor, J.R.R. Tolkien toyed with the idea that the men of Númenor had flying ships (HME, 5, 22). Not as far-fetched as it sounds – there is quite a bit of aerial activity in Tolkien's *legendarium*: the winged steeds of the nazgûl, the spying birds, the giant eagles, the dragons, and Eärendil in his flying boat.

The ending of *The Lord of the Rings* recalls Arthur going to Avalon, and Viking and Anglo-Saxon burials at sea (how every fan of mediaeval Scandinavian, Icelandic, Germanic and British would like to go). Maybe Frodo does go to his death at the end of *Rings*; Saruman says it will be 'a grey ship, and full of ghosts' (RK, 317).

The High-Elves (the Eldar) had the promise made to them that they can leave Middle-earth when their struggles are over (L, 198). But the elves want to have things their own way: '[t]hey wanted to have their cake and eat it: to live in the mortal historical Middle-earth because they had become fond of it' (L, 197), so they weren't 'wholly good or in the right'.

NOTES: MIDDLE-EARTH

1. K. McLeish, "The Rippingest Yarn of All", in R. Giddings, 1983, 135.
2. In R. Giddings, 1983, 8.
3. J.R.R. Tolkien, in J. Lobdell, 189.
4. H. Carpenter, 1995, 225.
5. In *The Annotated Hobbit*, 24.

cḣä́pᴛєᴘ 5

THE SILMARILLION

The descriptions of J.R.R. Tolkien's Middle-earth included here are taken largely from *The Silmarillion*, published in 1977, and also from the many other versions of Middle-earth, its different histories and narratives, written by Tolkien over many years, from around 1914 up until his death in 1973. Thus the stories of the Valar, the Maiar and the many inhabitants of Middle-earth and the West (the elves, men, dwarves, ents, orcs, hobbits and many other creatures) are mainly drawn from those in *The Silmarillion*, as well as some of those in, say, *The Earliest 'Silmarillion'* or other texts published in *The History of Middle-earth* volumes.

THE STYLE OF *THE SILMARILLION*

The style of the stories in *The Silmarillion* varies considerably. Ronald Tolkien's versions of the *Book of Genesis*, his own creation myth for Middle-earth, the *Ainulindalë* and the *Valaquenta*, have a 'high' style that recalls the *Bible*. Many of the stories in the *Silmarillion* proper (the *Quenta Silmarillion*) develop that style, with churchy phrases ('and now there came another...', 'for it is said'), references to the deity out of the *Old Testament* ('why hast thou done this?'), and Biblical inversions ('but it availed him not').

For J.R.R. Tolkien, all of the *legendarium*, from its earliest events in the music of the Ainur and creation of Arda to the latest incidents of the early part of the Fourth Age of Middle-earth, was connected together. In his mind, at least. Whatever the literary modes were (poetry, tale, novel, sketch), and whichever draft taken from a long lifetime of writing, it was interlinked. That's one of the problems: it might have all fitted together neatly in Tolkien's mind, but getting that out into a satisfactory published form was something else. (The *Quenta Silmarillion* was one of the key documents in the *legendarium* which Tolkien had revised and annotated many times; it seemed impossible to get that text into a final, publishable form).

J.R.R. Tolkien used repetition, reflection and echo a great deal in his fiction. Events echo those of the past, or are variations on them, or reflect them ironically; characters are reincarnations of earlier heroes; the same thresholds are reached again and again. In the story of Beren and Lúthien, Tolkien's premier Middle-earth tale, there are the singing scenes, three woodland interludes, two fights with wolves, Beren is wounded three times, saves Lúthien from an arrow twice, Huan speaks thrice, and Lúthien pursues and rescues Beren twice.1

There are songs in *The Silmarillion*, as in J.R.R. Tolkien's other Middle-earth writing, but some of the songs in *The Silmarillion* which demand to be heard, Tolkien held back from writing. One of these is the song of Lúthien in front of Morgoth. What Lúthien actually sang to Morgoth, the most powerful villain in the history of Middle-earth, to make him change his mind, would surely be worth hearing. But Tolkien would not (could not?) provide those songs (nor the songs of Sauron, Beren and Finrod).

Exaggeration is one J.R.R. Tolkien's narrators' standard devices. Thus, Beleg is the best tracker and hunter ever in Middle-earth, or Lúthien is the most beautiful woman, and each battle is bigger, louder and more gruesome or tragic than the last. When people wear the silmaril they become more glorious than anyone else: when Lúthien wears the silmaril in the Nauglamír, she's 'the vision of greatest beauty and glory that has ever been outside the realm of Valinor' (S, 235), but when, after her death, it passes to Dior, 'he appeared as the fairest of all the children of the world, of threefold race: of the Edain, and of the Eldar, and of the Maiar of the Blessed Realm' (S, 236).

The *Quenta Silmarillion* was rewritten by J.R.R. Tolkien over the years a number of times; the revisions became 'exceedingly complex' as his son Christopher put it, as the professor sought to harmonize the different drafts and visions of his Secondary World. He never really succeeded at that, never quite managed to complete a coherent version which would satisfy the pedant and perfectionist in him. Instead, there are the different versions published in the *History of Middle-earth* volumes, one layer differing from another.

One of the delights of J.R.R. Tolkien's fiction is the way he blended existing world mythologies into his 'sub-creation' of Middle-earth's mythology, the way that the reader is offered glimpses or reminders of earlier mythologies: the incest of Túrin and Nienor, for example, recalling the Oedipal myth, while the incest of Ar-Pharazôn and Míriel recalls the Egyptian pharaohs Ptolemy and Cleopatra. The dragon-slaying of Túrin evokes the Scandinavian tale of Sigurd and Fafnir, while the tale of lost kings like Aragorn or shield-maidens like Éowyn or wizards like Gandalf echoes Arthurian literature. The stories of the Valar recall Mount Olympus,

Ilúvatar evokes stern father-gods such as Zeus and Jehovah, while Númenor replays the myth of Atlantis. Túrin was probably partly influenced by Kullervo in the *Kalevala*, a doomed, cursed hero. Names such as Ilmatar and Ilmo may have suggested Tolkien's Ilúvatar and Ulmo.

Some of the stories in *The Silmarillion* are compressed versions of much longer stories ("Of Tuor and the Fall of Gondolin"), while others, although quite substantial and lengthy (such as "Of Túrin Turambar"), still had the appearance of being shortened. Many of the tales are extant in a number of variations: the story of Beren and Lúthien, for instance, was rewritten by J.R.R. Tolkien as a very long poem. Other tales were translated into Old English. Some of the oldest Middle-earth tales were reworked many times (the stories of Túrin, Eärendil and Beren and Lúthien, for example).

The story of Tuor and the fall of Gondolin is one of J.R.R. Tolkien's most action-packed narratives. In a mere six pages, Tolkien describes sea voyages, gods appearing to mortals, strange meetings, a journey to a hidden city, gods' curses, a romance, a massive seige and battle, a secret escape, an ambush, fights with balrogs, another appearance by the god of the sea (this time to the gods in Valinor, Tolkien's Olympus), and finally a classic ending: Tuor sailing off into the sunset, into myth and legend ('with Idril Celebrindal he set sail into the sunset and the West, and came no more into any tale or song' [S, 245]). Clearly, if Tolkien had approached this narrative differently, it could have been expanded into a significant proportion of a book. There's enough story in those few pages for least a few chapters.

Although the stories in *The Silmarillion* are often presented as drier, more 'difficult', more 'academic', or 'literary' and less approachable than those in *The Hobbit* or *The Lord of the Rings*, there is plenty of action and excitement. It's true, the prose style in *The Silmarillion* is more like the second half of *The Lord of the Rings* – a little ponderous, Biblical and high-minded. It's a curious mixture of 20th century English and self-conscious archaisms. There's very little humour in *The Silmarillion*, too, compared to the two hobbit-driven books (and in actor Martin Shaw's audio book readings of *The Silmarillion*, the style is still a little pompous, self-conscious and self-conscious).

But some of the legends in *The Silmarillion* are pure action-adventure: Morgoth and Ungoliant assaulting Valinor, destroying the Two Trees, pitching Valinor into darkness, and stealing the *silmarili*, for example. And the death of Fëanor at the hand (and whip) of Gothmog, lord of the balrogs, at Dor Daedeloth. Or the wonderful tale of Beren and Lúthien, which contains fights between hounds and wolves, wizard duels, a daring foray into the Devil's den, and Tolkien's most poignant romance.

Then there's the doomed, Promethean rebel Fëanor and his beloved silmarils, the exile of the Noldor, the hazardous voyage to Middle-earth and the civil war (the 'kin-slaying'). Another doomed figure, Túrin, is the star of a terrific tale of betrayal, adventure and lost love, climaxing with a perilous dragon-slaying straight out of Northern saga. Or the hand-to-hand combat between Fingolfin and Morgoth; or Sauron's assault on Minas Tirith, and so on.

The Silmarillion also has plenty of large-scale battles: Fëanor attacking Angband; the Dagor Bragollach, the 'Battle of Sudden Flame' (multitudes of orcs led by balrogs and Glaurung the dragon); and the fifth battle, where Morgoth's hordes overrun much of Beleriand.

Indeed, the Túrin Turambar chapter of *The Silmarillion* is one of the most bloodthirsty in J.R.R. Tolkien's repertoire: towards the end the murders and deaths come as thick and fast as a Jacobean revenge play or Shakespearean tragedy. It's Tolkien's form of 'heroic tragedy' or 'tragic mythology'. The Túrin tale has everything: and it's dark, dark stuff, which ends with a double suicide. There's a cursed black sword (Anglachel), chases and hunts, the finest hour of Glaurung, the hero holing up with treacherous dwarves (Mîm), orc battles, escaped prisoners from Angband, living with outlaws, and descents into madness of various main characters. Plus, a romance between Túrin and Níniel/ Nienor revealed as incest. ("Túrin Turambar" ranks as one of the few tales Tolkien where allows sex to enter the story: not only is there the relationship between Túrin and Níniel which turns out to be incestuous, between brother and sister, but Nienor/ Níniel strips off and runs naked through the forest. It's not sexual nudity, of course – Nienor is going mad after being enchanted by the dragon Glaurung – but it is one of the few occasions when the word 'naked' appears in Tolkien's fiction (and not in connection with a sword) (S, 219). Another is when Gandalf is 'sent back', finding himself naked atop the peak of Zirak-zigil.

One of the memorable parts of Túrin Turamabar's story has the elven kingdom of Nargothrond sacked and emptied. The dragon Glaurung takes possession of the halls for a while, lying amongst the treasure. But later, when Túrin's slain Glaurung, the echoing halls of Nargothrond are empty again, except for the traitor dwarf Mîm who creeps in: he 'sat there fingering the gold and the gems, letting them run through his hands' (S, 230). But then a third comes to dwell amongst the treasure: Húrin: 'he entered in, and stayed a while in that dreadful place, where the treasures of Valinor lay strewn upon the floors in darkness and decay' (ibid.). When Húrin leaves, he takes one thing only from the 'great hoard': the Nauglamír, the Necklace of the Dwarves.

The tale of Túrin drew on J.R.R. Tolkien's beloved *Kalevala*, in particular the *Story of Kullervo*, which also tells a man who seduces a lost maiden who's actually his sister; the woman drowns herself; the hero has a damaged background; the hero finds his mother gone and his home destroyed when he returns; and when Túrin and Kullervo discover their mistakes, they both kill themselves with a talking sword.2 Túrin is perpetually cursed and doomed, and whatever he does seems to go ill. He is also too proud, too grim, too stern, and too stubborn: he is his own worst enemy. Glaurung the dragon taunts Túrin thus:

> "Thankless fosterling, outlaw, slayer of your friend, thief of love, usurper of Nargothrond, captain foolhardy, and deserter of your kin. As thralls your mother and your sister live in Dorlómion, in misery and want. You are arrayed as a prince, but they go in rags." (*Children of Húrin*, 179)

The expanded version, *Children of Húrin*, edited by Tolkien's son Christopher and published with beautiful illustrations by Alan Lee in 2007, is worth reading: it reads more in a regular narrative style and form (though it's still highly compressed, and quite short).

Another great battle in the First Age is the assault on Gondolin by Morgoth's balrogs, dragons, orcs and wolves (S, 242), a seige full of action: Gothmog, lord of balrogs, slaying Turgon and being vanquished by Ecthelion in the central square; the chaos in the burning city; Tuor struggling with Maeglin on the battlements, and casting him onto the rocks below; and the escape of Tuor, Idril and Eärendil down a secret passage; their ambush by orcs and a balrog; and Glorfindel saving them from the balrog by duelling with it on a pinnacle, dying in the process.

NOTES: THE STYLE OF *THE SILMARILLION*

1. T. Shippey, 1982, 192-3.
2. T. Shippey, 1982, 195.

THE FIRST AGE

VIOLENCE AND DEATH. As *The Silmarillion* progresses (in the *Quenta Silmarillion*), the tales of the elves and men in Middle-earth grow increasingly desperate, bloody and violent. Morgoth grows in might and each battle seems to be more catastrophic than the one before. The betrayals and the mistakes multiply. Characters go mad (Húrin, Túrin, Nienor), or slay their friends by mistake at night (Túrin), or attack Morgoth's stronghold single-handed (Fingolfin), or are slaughtered by dwarves over a jewel (Thingol), or leave in sadness for the West (Melian).

The spread of death among the chief elves (and men), which begins with Morgoth slaying Finwë, accelerates in the second half of *The*

Silmarillion: Gothmog, lord of balrogs, kills Fëanor, Fingon, Echthelion and Túrgon; Carcaroth the wolf kills Beren; Sauron kills Finrod Felagund; orcs murder Finduilas; Túrin slays Beleg by mistake and kills Saeros and Brodda, and suicides on his cursed sword; the dwarves kill Thingol; Morgoth kills Fingolfin; Gelmir's hacked to pieces by orcs in front of the elf army; Túrgon has Eöl (the 'Dark Elf') thrown from the Amon Gwareth, the hill of Gondolin; Túrgon murders Brandir the Lame; Edrahil's eaten by wolves in Sauron's dungeons; Sauron ices Celebrimbor; Dior kills Celegorm; Fëanor's sons slay Dior and his wife Nimloth; Nienor jumps off a cliff to her death when she finds out she's married to her brother; Húrin murders Mîm the dwarf; the dwarves kill Mablung; Tuor dispatches Maeglin; Maedhros leaps into a chasm clutching a silmaril; and Húrin drowns himself. Phew!

Many high-ranking elves and humans die in the great battles, skirmishes and assaults (Hador, Angrod, Aegnor, Amrod, Amras, Gundor, Handir, Huor, Gwindor, Glorfindel, Bregolas, Eluréd, Dorlas, Denethor, Caranthir), while the Kinslaying takes others. (J.R.R. Tolkien linked some of his Middle-earth characters to his friends, according to Christopher Wrigley: Robert Gilson was related to Gil-galad, and George Bache Smith to Pippin (via the linguistic connection of G. Smith = Granny Smith, a kind of apple = Pippin).)

Each Age in Middle-earth's history is a step-down from the last: the Fourth Age won't be as glorious, somehow, as the Third Age (elves and wizards have departed, for instance). And the Third Age wasn't as great as the Second Age (and Gondor is a relic of Númenor). It's all dwindling, so that, by the time of the present day, thousands of years later, virtually all of the magic has gone out of the world.

J.R.R. Tolkien continued his tales into the early years of the Fourth Age, the 'age of men'. Tolkien reckoned the events of *The Lord of the Rings* to have taken place some 6000 years before the 20th century, which would make the 20th century at the end of the Fifth Age (Tolkien also added that the ages might have been shortened over time, and 'I imagine we are actually at the end of the Sixth Age, or in the Seventh' [L, 283]).

In the second half of *The Silmarillion*, one elven kingdom after another falls: Menegroth, and Doriath, Nargothrond, and Gondolin. Usually the downfall comes from within first (from lies and treachery or lust), rather than from the orcs and enemies outside. Morgoth's sly propaganda and disinformation cause just as much woe as his armies. Fëanor's silmarils stir up a huge amount of trouble, for instance (Thingol demands one from Beren, but later the silmaril causes the dwarves to slay him).

The story of Húrin and Morwen and his offspring, Túrin Turambar and Niënor Níniel, was an important story of the decline of the Elder Days for J.R.R. Tolkien, according to Christopher Tolkien, which absorbed much of

Tolkien's attention (HME, 10, viii-ix). But the narrative of Túrin and Húrin *et al*, like the 'Silmarillion', went through many revisions and layers, and was never finished. *The Children of Húrin* appeared in 2007, in a new book form.

Many of the figures in *The Silmarillion* seemed doomed – especially in the second half of the book. Fëanor, Túrin, Turgon, Maeglin, and the sons of Fëanor all seem destined to meet sticky or ignoble ends. Some of the elves and men, such as Túrin and Húrin, wander alone in Beleriand, desperate and outlawed or lost. Morgoth curses Húrin in Biblical terms in the earliest *Silmarillion*, giving him 'never-sleeping sight like the Gods, and he cursed his seed with a fate of ill-hap' (HME, 4, 27).

The *Quenta Silmarillion* ends on a high note. After all that death and destruction, all the lies and betrayals and oaths that pursue people to death, some kind of let-up, or catharsis, or 'eucatastrophe' (J.R.R. Tolkien's 'happy ending') has to happen. Morgoth has been increasingly victorious throughout the First Age and the *Quenta Silmarillion*: finally, it seems as if there's no way to defeat him. Many of the principal elves and men have died (see the above list), while thousands have perished in the great battles. It takes one man, a half-man, half-elf, Eärendil, to change the drift of Middle-earth history towards Morgoth's total domination.

EÄRENDIL.

The chapter in *The Silmarillion*, "Of the Voyage of Eärendil and the War of Wrath" (246-255), is the long looked-for (and expected, and necessary) 'happy ending' or 'eucatastrophe' to the First Age and the *Quenta Silmarillion*. Suitably, Eärendil's story is one of J.R.R. Tolkien's most fantastical and upbeat: it contains some classic fairy tale imagery: Elwing turning into a white bird, Eärendil in his ship sailing in the heavens, Elwing flying up to meet him at dawn.

> And it is said that Elwing learned the tongues of birds, who herself had once worn their shape; and they taught her the craft of flight, and her wings were of white and silver-grey. And at times, when Eärendil returning drew near again to Arda, she would fly to meet him, even as she had flown long ago, when she was rescued from the sea. Then the far-sighted among the elves that dwelt in the Lonely Isle would see her like a white bird, shining, rose-stained in the sunset, as she soared in joy to greet the coming of Vingilot to heaven. (S, 250)

Eärendil and the silmaril are a fairy tale version of the planet Venus, the morning and evening star (which's also, incidentally, linked with Lucifer as well as the Goddess Venus).

In the *Lay of Eärendil*, Eärendil is presented as the classic mariner (out of, say, Homer's *Odyssey*), who voyages far on the ocean while his spouse waits in agony for him back on land. The story begins with Eärendil building his ship with Círdan the ship-wright (one of the few principal elves left alive after the many battles of the First Age). Eärendil sets sail in his ship *Vingilot* and has many adventures, but, as with Ulysses, enemies invade Eärendil's home while he's at sea, as 'the last and cruellest of the slayings of Elf by Elf' occurs when Maedhros and Maglor and their kin assault Elwing and the people of Sirion (S, 247). Elwing, falling into the sea, is saved by Ulmo and transformed into a 'great white bird, and upon her breast there shone as a star the Silmaril' (S, 247). United with Eärendil, they turn again for Valinor, and this time reach the promised land.

Finally comes the longed-for intercession of the powers on behalf of the Firstborn and Followers of Middle-earth (elves and humans): the Lords of the West go to war on Morgoth in Middle-earth and defeat him. This's the biggest, grandest battle in all of Tolkien's Middle-earth legends. Perhaps because it's so extraordinary, most of it takes place outside the story. The narrator gives hints of the majesty of the Valar host:

> the challenge of the trumpets filled the sky; and Beleriand was ablaze with the glory of their arms, for the host of the Valar were arrayed in forms young and fair and terrible, and the mountains rang beneath their fear. (S, 251)

It's the 'Great Battle', the 'War of Wrath', a clash between the West and the North (the symbolic compass points of J.R.R. Tolkien's duality of good and evil). The battle decimates Morgoth's forces (although not entirely – some survive to terrorize the characters in the Second and Third Ages).

The story of Eärendil and the *Quenta Silmarillion* itself closes with Morgoth thrust out into the 'Timeless Void' (although some of the 'evil' remains at large – Sauron most importantly, but also creatures such as balrogs). Some of the principal elves remain in Middle-earth (Gil-galad, Celeborn, and Galadriel), though most journey to Valinor.

Thus, the story of the First Age ends with a new world order and a new peace established. Most of the elves are in the West, but a few remain in the 'Hither Lands' of Middle-earth. Humans are more prominent (especially from the beginning of the Second Age onwards, with the creation of Númenor). But 'evil' has not been completely vanquished. The host of the Valar, for example, could have pursued every one of Morgoth's servants to the ends of the earth, but they don't, allowing 'evil' to rise again (they must have known, for instance, that Sauron survived the Great Battle: it would be impossible not to notice that Morgoth's most powerful lieutenant hadn't been destroyed). The same mistake was made early in the First Age, when the Valar didn't quite dismantle all of Thangorodrim and Angband, Morgoth's strongholds. The Valar hold a council, to decide what to do in future ages (S, 260), but, although they agree to summon the

Eldar to the West, and create Númenor for the 'three faithful houses' of humans (the Edain) that helped in the war against Morgoth, they do not do anything about Morgoth's servants.

As well as the main plot of Eärendil pleading to the Valar for help from the 'Two Kindreds', J.R.R. Tolkien also blends in a romance plot (between Eärendil and Elwing), and the recurring theme of death vs. deathlessness, as Elwing, Eärendil and his offspring are offered the choice of mortality or immortality. This's a reprise of the Beren and Lúthien story (there's a link of blood, of course, Elwing being the grand-daughter of Lúthien).

Not least among this interweaving of plots is the last installment in the 'War of the Jewels' narrative: Elwing possesses the silmaril; the surviving sons of Fëanor (Maedhros and Maglor) demand it; she escapes with Eärendil to Valinor; Eärendil sails the sky with the silmaril on his brow; after the host of the Valar has overcome Morgoth and the taken silmarils, Maedhros and Maglor demand them again (the narrator says they would do anything to obtain the jewels: 'they would have given battle for the Silmarils, were they withheld, even against the victorious host of Valinor, even though they stood alone against all the world' [S, 252]). Fëanor's sons sneak into Eönwë's camp at night and steal the *silmarili*, but the pain of holding them drives them insane: Maedhros leaps into a chasm of fire, and Maglor throws his silmaril into the sea.

THE *SILMARILI*

The *silmarili* (J.R.R. Tolkien explained in a 1950s letter) were jewels fashioned by Fëanor that contained the light of Valinor (Paradise) embodied in two sacred trees (from the two silver and gold trees derived the light of the sun and moon: the sun and moon reflected the light of the trees, and were thus secondary, not divine or primary).[1] In the *Quenta Silmarillion*, Tolkien's narrator emphasizes the worth of the silmarils: they looked like diamonds, but were stronger than adamant; nothing could destroy them; and no one could touch them without being scorched. (The 2001-03 *Lord of the Rings* movies were careful to have people avoid touching the ring with their bare hands, as if the ring's effect increased on contact. It's handled more often in the book. When Frodo wakes at Rivendell, for instance, he finds that someone has put the ring on a chain for him (FR, 304). Who did that?)

Somehow, Fëanor managed to capture and contain some mysterious inner fire within the silmarils, the 'blended light of the Trees of Valinor', so they shone like stars:

they were indeed living things, they rejoiced in light and received it and gave it back in hues more marvellous than before. All who dwelt in Aman were filled with wonder and delight at the work of Fëanor. (S, 67)

Mandos, the doom-sayer, inevitably foretells that 'the fates of Arda, earth, sea, and air, lay locked with them' (ibid). It has to end in doom. Why? Because the *silmarili* represent the commingling of the divine and the profane, something the Valar created (the Two Trees) and something an elf created (the silmarils). And that spells disaster in Middle-earth morality, because only Ilúvatar can truly 'create' (via the Valar), not elves or humans. It's like the mingling of the Titans and humans in Greek mythology).

As always in Ronald Tolkien's fiction, there was a 'fall': the 'Enemy' (Melkor) destroyed the trees, and only the *silmarili* survived (the resonances with the Judaeo-Christian myth of Adam and Eve, the serpent (Devil), tree and the apple in Paradise are obvious). Tolkien's 'sub-creation' of Middle-earth has central narratives of magical objects (trees, jewels, rings, seeing-stones) which were incredibly precious (and pure), even divine, which are coveted and become the target of various falls from grace. The silmarils become the pretext for the treachery, blasphemy, vengeance and violence which results in civil war amongst the elves: Morgoth steals the gems, and sets them in his iron crown in Middle-earth; the elves depart Valinor to fight Morgoth in the North-West (L, 148).

The First Age ends with the passing of the ancient world: the jewels are found then lost forever (one in the sky, one in the sea, one in the earth). No good will come of the silmarils, as with the other things the elves make – the rings, the *palantíri* – because, although they may give pleasure for a while, such precious things always lead, in J.R.R. Tolkien's cosmos, to disaster. Why? Because only the Creator can really create – everyone else who creates is not simply emulating God, they are defying God, without realizing it. Even the things that the Valar create – the Two Trees, for example – lead to disaster.

NOTES: THE *SILMARILI*

1. Sir Thomas Browne speaks in a similarly Gnostic manner when he stated that '[l]ife is but the shadow of death… The Sunne itself is but the dark *simulacrum*, and light but the shadow of God' (Sir Thomas Browne: *Religio Medici and Other Writings*, Dent, London, 1906, 221).

GALADRIEL

The rebellious Galadriel gets to take ship and leave Middle-earth at the end of *The Lord of the Rings*, bound for Eressëa, as a reward for refusing the ring and helping in the fight against Sauron. In *The Silmarillion*, Galadriel is identified as 'the mightiest and fairest of all the Elves that remained in Middle-earth' (S, 298; however a few elves are described as 'fairest' or 'mightiest' at various times).

Galadriel is something of a rebel, as well as, with Elrond, the most powerful elf in Middle-earth. Galadriel is also inspired by the arch rebel of Middle-earth, Fëanor, to follow him and the other Noldor to Middle-earth. Galadriel perhaps feels exile from Valinor most acutely among the Middle-earth elves. Her success in the War of the Ring wins her forgiveness by the Valar.

Galadriel is one of the important female elves among the many princes (Finrod, Fingolfin, Maedhros and the other sons of Fëanor) who rebel against the Valar and follow Fëanor on the exodus from Valinor to Middle-earth (this involves traversing 'the terror of the Helcaraxë and the cruel hills of ice' in the bitterest North' of Arda [S, 90]). As *The Silmarillion* stated, Galadriel desired a realm of her own to rule (S, 84). Galadriel is thus among the Noldor who journey from Valinor via the wastelands of the North, eventually arriving in Beleriand (Turgon's wife, Elenwë, died on the dangerous journey to Middle-earth).

ELROND

Elrond, Professor Tolkien said, represented wisdom, tradition, and beauty, with Rivendell as a place of reflection and rest, a break in the journey (and providing, in *The Lord of the Rings*, further opportunities for history and exposition).

At the Council of Elrond, Elrond provides the lengthy and intricate back-story of the ring. Here the Middle-earth legends, which J.R.R. Tolkien had been developing for decades, are glimpsed behind the present tense events of *The Lord of the Rings*: the forging of the rings by the elven-smiths, Moria, Eregion, Eriador, the fall of Númenor, the return of kings to Middle-earth (Elendil, Isildur, Anárion), and the Last Alliance.

In "The Fall of Númenor", Tolkien described Elrond as the founder of Númenos, and a key figure in the history of Númenor (HME, 5, 25). The gods and the elves chose Elrond as lord of Númenos partly because he had the blood of the Eldar and Valar in him, from Idril and Lúthien.

Ronald Tolkien said it was partly an accident that a character such as

Elrond was connected with the Middle-earth mythology: his name, Elrond, had suggested a link with Eärendel, one of the chief characters in Tolkien's Middle-earth mythology. Elrond thus became

> the great-grandson of Lúthien and Beren (he's the son of Elwing and Eärendil, Elwing being the daughter of Dior, who was the offspring of Lúthien and Beren), a great power and a Ringholder. (L, 347)

Elrond's link with Lúthien Tinúviel gives him a sacrality above almost all the other characters in *The Lord of the Rings* (perhaps only Galadriel can compete for significance, the connection with the grand past of Middle-earth. True, Tom Bombadil and Treebeard are also ancient, but Elrond, like Galadriel, embodies the link with the elves, J.R.R. Tolkien's most highly favoured creation in his Middle-earth cosmos). Elrond's special because of the importance of the story of Beren and Lúthien for Tolkien. Elrond also makes Rivendell a haven for many of the things Tolkien cherishes: Elrond gathers together many of the High Elves, keeps alive the memories of earlier Ages, and turns Rivendell into a centre for learning and history (with one of the best libraries in Middle-earth – an ideaized version of the Bodleian Library in Oxford. No wonder that Bilbo, one of the characters closest to Tolkien's own personality, chooses to retire there).

A glance at the genealogies of J.R.R. Tolkien's various races and families shows just how the two main races of Middle-earth – elves and humans – are intertwined. The lines of the Edain, the Dúnedain, the kings of Númenor, the kings of Gondor and Arnor, and the Peredhil are all inter-connected. There are ties of blood, heredity and family in many of the major characters in Tolkien's Middle-earth, such as Lúthien, Beren, Eärendil, Elrond, Elros, Isildur, Túrin, Arwen and Aragorn.

Elrond is the son of Eärendil; Eärendil in turn is the son of Idril, whose siblings included Gil-galad. Their grandfather was Fingolfin, who in turn is grandson of Finwë, one of the first elves. One of Finwë's grand-children was Fëanor, creator of the *silmarili*. Another of Finwë's grand-children was Finarfin, whose children included Finrod Felagund and Galadriel. Galadriel is Elrond's mother-in-law (Elrond married her daughter Celebrían), making Finrod Felagund, who fought with Beren and Lúthien against Sauron, Elrond's uncle. Thus, most of the significant elves in the Middle-earth stories are connected by blood or marriage.

The connections are further developed by the inter-marriages between elves and humans, and the 'half-elven' such as Elrond. Aragorn is a direct descendant of the kings of Arnor, the chieftains of the Dúnedain, the lords of Andúnië and the kings of Númenor, right back to Elros, Elrond's brother and son of Eärendil. Aragorn thus has an ancient link of inheritance with some of the great and good in Middle-earth's history –

characters such as Eärendil, Lúthien, Beren, Thingol and Melian. From the line of Melian (a Maiar) and the elf-lord Thingol come Lúthien, wife of Beren, Eärendil, great grandson of Melian, his children Elros and Elrond, and Arwen, Elrond's only daughter.

Elrond proves to be a strict, demanding father figure. Elrond tells Aragorn: '"You shall neither have wife, nor bind any woman to you in troth, until your time comes and you are found worthy of it"' (RK, 419). Later, Elrond decrees that Arwen Undomiel '"shall not be the bride of any Man less than the King of Gondor and Arnor"' (RK, 422). Nobody's good enough for daddy's daughter, unless he becomes king of everywhere. (There are personal reasons, perhaps, why Elrond doesn't want Arwen to marry Aragorn: his parents and his brother Elros became mortal, and died. So he doesn't want to lose his daughter the same way.)

FEANOR

Fëanor is J.R.R. Tolkien's Promethean genius, a kind of Nietzschean Superman:

> For Fëanor was made the mightiest in all parts of body and mind, in valour, in endurance, in beauty, in understanding, in skill, in strength and in subtlety alike, of all the Children of Ilúvatar, and a bright flame was in him. (S, 98)

Fëanor is wonderful at just about everything (like Aragorn). It would be easier to say what he *isn't* good at (perhaps his cooking wasn't so good, perhaps he always burnt the toast, or perhaps he never took out the trash). Fëanor seems to be able to achieve anything. Certainly he's the toppermost elf, the number one among the firstborn. He's a great leader (probably the greatest amongst all the elves in Middle-earth history), the cleverest, the most intelligent, the most skillful, the most ambitious, the most accomplished, a charismatic speaker, a great warrior and military tactician, etc. He's Alexander the Great, Leonardo da Vinci and Albert Einstein combined.

Fëanor stands up to Melkor, slamming the door in his face. He goes up against the greatest of the Valar (Manwë, Mandos, Yavanna) during a council meeting. He often curses and swears oaths – oaths which bring about ruination (wizards know not to swear in Ursula Le Guin's *Earthsea* books). Fëanor alters the course of Arda's history more than almost any other elf. He leads the Noldor out of Valinor, and attacks his fellow elves (the Teleri) to secure ships for the voyage to Middle-earth. Trapped in the far North of Arda, near the Helcaraxë, a deadly strait of 'grinding ice' between Aman and Endor (Middle-earth), Fëanor decides to abandon many of the other elves – Fingolfin, his sons, Finrod, Galadriel and other Noldori – because there aren't enough ships to carry them to Middle-earth. Fëanor and his followers leave Fingolfin and the others behind in Araman, and sneak away. Fëanor's next act is completely pointless: he orders the white ships to be burnt instead of sent back to collect the rest of the Noldor.

Many of the stories in *The Silmarillion* revolve around Fëanor and his restless, rebellious personality. He's also flawed: too proud, too stubborn, too domineering, too determined to get his own way at whatever cost. He's also not impervious to the lies that Melkor spreads. While other elf lords listen to the counsel of the Valar such as Ulmo and Aulë and have nothing to do with Melkor, Fëanor can't help being seduced by some of Melkor's falsehoods (although, when Fëanor is face-to-face with Melkor, he can see through the Vala and perceive that Melkor lusts after the *silmarili*).

Fëanor is one of those individuals in the Middle-earth stories, like Gandalf or Sauron or Lúthien, who alters the course of history. J.R.R. Tolkien's view of history (at least Middle-earth history) is the traditional one – of kings and queens, important dates and grand battles. A history where individuals really can have an impact. (While *The Silmarillion* is a litany of great figures, good and evil, *The Lord of the Rings* is specifically designed so that the 'little people', the ordinary, everyday folk of the hobbits, are able to rise to the occasion and make a difference).

Fëanor causes so much trouble amongst the Noldor and other elves that the Valar ultimately withdraw even further from the world. Before Fëanor's works among the Noldor, every elf was welcome to journey to the Blessed Realm and stay there. After Fëanor, the Valar shut Valinor against the Noldor, and no one who sails West is allowed through (S, 102). Fëanor is a Noldor through and through, but his half-brothers Fingolfin and Finarfin are half Vanyar, a 'superior' breed. The distinctions of heredity are always significant in Tolkien's fiction.

THE TWO 'DOOMS': DEATH AND IMMORTALITY

The downfall of Númenor was brought about by Sauron exploiting a weakness in humanity (the fear of death), causing a second fall (which was based upon a prohibition). The prohibition, a common device in fairy stories, is tied up with humanity's 'reward' in Middle-earth – their 'reward' is also their temptation, their downfall (L, 154). The 'Ban of the Valar' is laid upon humanity by the gods: not to sail Westward, out of sight of their own land, towards Eressëa and the Undying Lands. And as soon as a taboo is imposed, as every reader or film-goer knows, it is going to be broken.

The 'temptation' of humanity is the desire for immortality: in Middle-earth, death and immortality are intimately intermingled: the 'gift' of men is death, to escape the 'circles of the world'; but it becomes their 'doom' during the time of Númenor (as *The Silmarillion* has it, the Númenóreans should not 'desire to overpass the limits set to their bliss, becoming enamoured of the immortality of the Valar and the eldar' [S, 262]). Elves, meanwhile, live forever – or at least until the 'end of days'. Elves can waste away from grief, and they can be slain. When they die, they go to the Halls of Mandos in Valinor (which's not paradise, but more a purgatory, God's waiting-room [S, 42]). Elves' bodies decay much more rapidly than humanity's.

J.R.R. Tolkien explored the inter-relationship of the themes of death and immortality in his two chief races of Middle-earth, elves and men (and in the inter-marriages of the two races). Each race struggles, existentially, metaphysically, morally, with death and immortality. The sons of Eärendil (Elros and Elrond) are half-elves and have to choose between the fate of elves (immortality) or men (mortality). Elros chooses death, and Elrond chooses to be like the elves.

It is the growing resentment of having to die (despite their extended lifespan) that causes the downfall of Númenor: the kings of Númenor begin to envy the immortality of the Eldar and the Valar in the Undying Lands to the West. Sauron stirs up their jealousy when he's captured by Ar-Pharazôn until it's ready to break out into rebellious, catastrophic action. The Númenóreans' fear of dying grows as their power, wealth and skill increases: J.R.R. Tolkien's description of the social and religious growth of Númenor, the pride, the colonialism and acquisitiveness, the abandonment of the Eldarin culture, the Promethean rebellion against the gods, combined with the acute awareness of mortality, recalls ancient Egypt and the pharaohs, and the cult of the dead in ancient Egyptian religion.

Vanity, all is vanity. As the narrator of "The Fall of Númenor" put it, the Númenóreans 'built mightier houses for their dead than for their living, and endowed their buried kings with unavailing treasure' (HME, 5, 16). The Old World 'became a place of tombs, and filled with ghosts'.

The mingling of the blood of elves and humans only occurs between Beren and Lúthien and their children, one of the first stories of Middle-earth that J.R.R. Tolkien wrote, and in Elrond the 'half-elven' and his offspring (S, 254). As Tolkien in the *Quenta* puts it, through Elrond 'alone the blood of the elder race and the seed divine of Valinor have come among Mankind' (HME, 4, 162). No other inter-marriage sanctioned by the 'free peoples' (and Tolkien's narrators) takes place between other species: one can imagine sexual relations between, say, elves and hobbits, or hobbits and dwarves, or hobbits and men. Instead, there are hints at worship, but only from afar, in the courtly love manner (Gimli the dwarf being entranced by Galadriel, for example. Galadriel, of course, enchants men, hobbits, elves and dwarves in *The Lord of the Rings*. But the adoration of these species for the Lady of Lothlórien is always kept chaste and demure, with no hint of sexuality. She doesn't invite any of them back to her rooms in the mallorn trees, for instance, for a little brandy, chocolates and backgammon).

The influence of Morgoth (the 'shadow') is at work in Númenor even before the arrival of Sauron: the Númenóreans begin to question their 'doom' (mortality) and the ban of the Valar (S, 264). In this way, and many others, 'evil' persists in the world of elves and humans, as it will do after Sauron is defeated at the end of the Third Age (Gandalf says as much). Before Sauron's arrives to bring the Númenóreans' dissatisfaction with their lot to the boil, messengers from the Valar appear to instruct the Númenóreans:

> the Doom of Men, that they should depart, was at first a gift of
> Ilúvatar. It became a grief to them only because coming under the
> shadow of Morgoth it seemed to them that they were surrounded by a
> great darkness, of which they were afraid; and some grew wilful and
> proud and would not yield, until life was reft from them. (S, 265)

This's a crucial point: that death was (intended to be) a 'gift', given to humans by Ilúvatar, which only became a curse or a doom after Morgoth had infected their perceptions. The event itself – dying – had not changed, then, but humanity's view of it did, under Morgoth's influence.

Sauron promises 'life unending and the dominion of the earth' to Tarkalion and his queen Tar-Míriel, if they'll turn to Morgoth (HME, 5, 27). As they grow old, and fear their death, Sauron plays upon their anxiety, and tells them that Morgoth can grant them immortal life, but the gods in Valinor stand in Morgoth's way. 'To win life Tarkalion must win the West' (ib., 69).

It's not that Valinor is an immortal realm, rather it's immortal because the immortal elves and Valar live there. 'Eternal' or 'timeless' are better terms to use than 'immortality'. But even Valinor or the Valar will not go on forever: there is always a day of judgement, a last battle, a final reckoning ahead in Tolkien's *legendarium*

What's striking about the fall of Númenor is how Ilúvatar acts like a vengeful Jehovah out of the *Bible*: when others have broken bans, they were punished by being outcast (such as Morgoth), or prevented from the returning to the Blessed Realm (like the Noldor), but the whole of the population of Númenor (minus the few 'Faithful') is killed in a cataclysm of immense proportions: a 'great chasm' opens up, the sea flows in, 'the world was shaken', the noise and smoke rises to the skies, the whole Númenórean world is sucked into the abyss, Ar-Pharazôn and his warriors are crushed to death, the ocean is 'cast back', new lands are created, and the world is 'diminished', because 'Valinor and Eressëa were taken from it into the realm of hidden things' (S, 278-9). The punishment for breaking the Ban of Ilúvatar is about as harsh as it could be: earthquakes, fire, hurricanes and finally the Atlantean tidal wave that used to haunt Tolkien as a child.

Ilúvatar is merciless and ruthless in his cosmic castigation, destroying not only the Númenórean fleet, but also every woman and child back on the island. It's an understatement when *The Silmarillion*'s narrator remarks that the wrath of Ilúvatar was far greater than Sauron had imagined (S, 280). In some ways, it's the turning-point for the history of the Tolkien's world: up until then, no one has been killed for breaking laws or bans. Even Morgoth, the Devil himself, was chained up in the halls of Mandos for his evil deeds in the early years of the First Age, rather than put to death (actually, Morgoth's a special case, being one of the Valar, and probably unable to be completely destroyed – although Ilúvatar, who made the Ainur/ Valar in the first place, could probably concoct some suitable chastizement for Morgoth).

But the Drowning of Númenor reveals how far the Father-God is prepared to go to make his point, to enforce his laws. It shows, brutally, that the deity is willing to destroy most of the Followers (humanity), and also the best among them (apart from the Elf-friends and half-elven).

For a time, Beren and Lúthien enter the stories in *The Silmarillion* again, when the elven kingdoms are dwindling: Húrin takes the Nauglamír, the famed necklace created by the dwarves, from the halls of Nargothrond, ransacked by the dragon Glaurung (the Nauglamír is yet another of those precious treasures in Tolkien's universe, like rings, *palantíri* and silmarils, which bewitch people – are you keeping up?); Thingol has a silmaril set in the necklace (which costs him his life when dwarves and Gnomes kill him while hunting and steal the necklace [HME, 1, 32]), and it finds its way to Lúthien Tinúviel in Tol Galen:

> it is said and sung that Lúthien wearing that necklace and that immortal jewel was the vision of greatest beauty and glory that has ever been outside the realm of Valinor. (S, 235)

But the silmarils are doomed, of course, so wearing it has a negative aspect, and accelerates the deaths of Beren and Lúthien ('the wise have said that the Silmaril hastened their end: for the flame of the beauty of Lúthien as she wore it was too bright for mortal lands' [S, 236]).

The curse of the gods upon the Noldor occurs as they flee from Valinor, having slain the Teleri mariners at Alqualondë. To demonstrate how significant the Valar's curse is J.R.R. Tolkien has no less a herald than Mandos, the Valar's 'doom-sayer', deliver it from a rock above the ocean. Mandos outlines the 'Doom of the Noldor': Valinor will be forbidden, the

Noldor will never be able to return, their oath (about the *silmarili*) will haunt them and betray them, everything they do will come to evil in the end, treason and murder will be the norm, and if any of the Noldor survive the kin-slaying and treason, they 'shall grow weary of the world as with a great burden' (S, 88). It's bad all round, then.

The punishment of the gods, then, pursues Fëanor and the Noldor ruthlessly and mercilessly. It's not a banishment as severe as Morgoth's (being cast in chains or thrust into the void), but it's very severe. In essence, the Valar, by the order of Ilúvatar, condemn the Noldorin elves to lives of bitterness and woe: the ones who don't betray and murder each other, the gods declaim, will live on to increasing weariness, and 'become as shadows of regret'. As with the fate of the Númenóreans, Ilúvatar's treatment of the Noldor recalls the stern father-gods of the Middle East, the Allahs, Jehovahs, Zeuses and Gods, where divine retribution is brutal and far-reaching.

THE SECOND AND THIRD AGES

Each Age in Middle-earth tends to end with an enormous battle, the lands of Middle-earth being physically altered, and new social orders emerging. The First Age closes with the biggest battle in J.R.R. Tolkien's Middle-earth legends, between the Host of Valinor and Morgoth's hordes (which included balrogs, dragons, orcs, monsters and Easterlings). Morgoth's cast out into the void, and Beleriand is broken up, parts of it being drowned, Atlantis-like, under the sea of Belegaer.

The end of the Second Age replays the end of the First Age, with the 'free peoples' going to war against another Dark Lord (this time it's Sauron). The Last Alliance defeats Sauron at the Battle of Dagorlad and the siege of Barad-dûr. Yet another battle, recounted in *The Lord of the Rings*, closes the Third Age, inaugurating new social orders, and the departure of the elves.

In letter no. 131, J.R.R. Tolkien describes the stages in the story of the Númenóreans thus: at first, being descendants of Eärendil, they are mariners, peaceful, and help the elves and men in Middle-earth fight Sauron. Pride, glory and an urge towards wealth and accumulation characterizes their second stage. The third stage begins with Tar-kalion (the *Quenyan* name for Ar-Pharazôn), the most powerful of the Númenórean kings, battling Sauron and capturing him (in 3262 of the Second Age).

Back in Númenor, Sauron soon becomes Ar-Pharazôn's chief counsellor, and turns the Númenóreans against the Valar and the West.

The new cult of 'the Dark' spreads throughout Middle-earth (except where the elves and Elf-friends reside). Through Ar-Pharazôn's kingship, Sauron becomes the most powerful force in Arda, outside Valinor. Or as *The Silmarillion* puts it:

> Ar-Pharazôn, King of the Land of the Star, grew to mightiest tyrant that had yet been since the reign of Morgoth, though in truth Sauron ruled all from behind the throne. (S, 274)

Sauron doesn't just poison Ar-Pharazôn's mind and rule from behind the throne, he also takes steps to undermine and possibly eradicate his enemies: he persuades Ar-Pharazôn and his administration to regard 'the Faithful' (Elros, Elrond, and the 'Elendili', 'elf-friends') as threats to the state. Sauron's war of anti-elven propaganda takes a number of forms: the White Tree, symbolic of the tie with the Blessed Realm, is first left untended, and later ordered cut down by Sauron. Ar-Adûnakhor forbids the use of elven languages: this occurred before the arrival of Sauron, when 'the shadow' was spreading in Númenor.

Sauron hastens the fading of the Eldar, J.R.R. Tolkien related in "The Fall of Númenor", because they expend a good deal of their strength in vanquishing him (HME, 5, 29).

The pro-elven 'Faithful' first live apart from the other Númenóreans (a kind of ghettoization), then they are slighted, then their speech is outlawed, and, at the height of Sauron's influence and the development of the cult of 'the Dark', 'the Faithful' are persecuted (some being captured and used as sacrifical victims in Sauron's temple).

Even before Sauron seduced Ar-Pharazôn, Morgoth's influence was still strong: it slowly turns the Númenórean kings against the Valar, makes them jealous of the everlasting life in Valinor, makes them fear death, and turns them against the elves. Before 'the Shadow', the Númenóreans, though still men, had been granted long lives by the Valar; but they gradually begin to fear it, and slide into 'madness and sickness', and also turn against each other (S, 274).

Sauron waits until Ar-Pharazôn is old and nearing death before unleashing his plan ('[n]ow came the hour that Sauron had prepared and long had awaited' [S, 274]). Ar-Pharazôn assembles an armada and sets sail for the West (in 3319). The Valar respond by calling upon God; the world is changed; Ar-Pharazôn and his retinue are crushed; Númenor falls into an abyss; and the Blessed Realm (Valinor) and Eressëa is removed from the world. Before this, the world had been 'flat': now it is round, finite, 'a circle inescapable – save by death' (L, 156). If men sail West, they sail around the world: only the elves can reach the 'True West'.

Between 1200 and 1500 SA, Sauron works with the elven-smiths led by Celebrimbor (grandson of Fëanor no less) to produce the three rings of power in Eregion (Vilya, the blue sapphire ring of air, worn by Elrond; Nenya, Galadriel's white adamant ring of water, and Gandalf's ruby ring of fire, Narya), and the One Ring in Orodruin. The struggles between elves and men and Sauron and his forces resume again in the middle of the Second Age: Eregion is laid waste, the three rings are hidden, Eriador is overrun by Sauron, but the Dark Lord is later driven out. Sauron corrupts the Númenóreans as related above, and Númenor falls. The Shadow returns to Mordor, and develops another force (he had built Barad-dûr around 1000 in the Second Age).

The story of Númenor continues, when some of the survivors of the storm in the West reach Middle-earth (Elendil, and Isildur and Anarion, his sons) and establish kingdoms in Gondor (in the South) and Arnor (in the North, near Gilgalad's kingdom). Sauron captures Minas Ithil and destroys Isildur's White Tree.

The Last Alliance (formed in 3430, SA) pits the elves and men against the forces of darkness. There's an enormous battle – the Battle of Dagorlad (3434) – followed by a seven year siege of Sauron's stronghold of Barad-dûr in Gorgoroth Vale. The Dark Lord throws everything he's got at the alliance, but in the end, Sauron himself comes out to fight. He kills Elendil and Gilgalad, but is also thrown to the ground. Isildur cuts the ring from Sauron's finger, and for a time the Dark Lord is vanquished ('he forsook his body, and his spirit fled far away and hid in waste places; and took no visible shape again for many long years' [S, 294]).

Against the advice of Elrond and Círdan, Isildur claims the ring as his own ('a weregild for my father's death'), and refuses to destroy it in Mount Doom. But on his way to Eriador, Isildur is waylaid by orcs; he escapes into the river wearing the ring. The ring betrays him and slips off (to be found by Gollum years later). The orcs see him and kill him with arrows; Isildur dies in the Great River.

The Second Age of Middle-earth closes with good and evil still in the balance: Sauron disappears into the shadows, gradually able to build up his army again (his Dark Tower was levelled to the ground, but the foundations were still intact [S, 294]).

The Third Age of Middle-earth is largely concerned with the rings of power: the One Ring which's lost in the River Anduin and later found by Gollum, then Bilbo; and the three elven rings, wielded by Gandalf, Galadriel and Elrond, which help maintain 'enclaves of peace where Time seems to stand still and decay is restrained, a semblance of the bliss of the True West' (L, 157).

The Third Age builds up to the War of the Ring (the events related in *The Lord of the Rings*). The havens of elven power – Mithlond, Lothlórien and Imladris – remain intact, but Arnor in the North, ruled by Isildur's descendants, dwindles to nothing. In the South, Gondor rises to a zenith but then 'fades slowly to decayed Middle Age, a kind of proud, venerable, but increasingly impotent Byzantium', as Tolkien put it (L, 157). The line of kings fails (after the Witch-king kills King Eärnur), and Gondor is ruled by stewards.

The 'wild men' of the East and South threaten Gondor. Greenwood becomes Mirkwood when Sauron takes up residence at Dol Guldur around 1050 TA. Hobbits appear, and wander West, away from the necromancer in Mirkwood, to the Shire. By 2941, Bilbo Baggins finds the ring (as related in The Hobbit). The White Council – consisting, like modern thinktanks, governments, NATO, and the United Nations – of various important (nearly all male) figures (wizards, elves and men), meets at various times to discuss the problem of Sauron. (The Fellowship is also like an envoy representing each of the races of Middle-earth's 'free peoples', recalling political organizations such as the League of Nations, a NATO, G7 or United Nations._

Saruman delays action, hoping that the ring will make itself known at Gladden Fields. Gandalf goes to Dol Guldur to investigate; Sauron retreats, but then returns to Dol Guldur (around 2460). Gollum finds the ring. Sauron takes the last of the dwarves' rings from Tháin II in Dol Guldur. Gandalf returns to Dol Guldur again, and insists the White Council attack it. By the time the White Council get around to doing something about Sauron, he's already made plans to return to Mordor.

The Third Age of Middle-earth is characterized by fading and decay: the elves retreat into themselves, making 'nothing new' (RK, 456), as do the dwarves. Gondor retains some of the splendour of Númenor, but even that diminishes, and becomes decadent (J.R.R. Tolkien compares it to mediæval and Byzantine culture, as noted above).

Meanwhile, the dark forces are gathering: dragons, balrogs, orcs, nazgûl and other nasty critters multiply: the Witch-king (chief of the nazgûl) comes out of Angmar in the North, orcs invade Moria, the Easterlings and Southrons gnaw at Gondor's borders, and Sauron enters Greenwood. Battles, plagues and deaths litter the Third Age (at Arnor, Osgiliath, Pelargir, Celebrant, Dagorlad, Fornost, Ithilien and Minas Ithil). Just when things are looking pretty grim, the *Istari* or wizards appear in Middle-earth out of the Far West, messengers of the Valar (RK, 457).

One of the differences between *The Lord of the Rings* and *The Silmarillion* and Tolkien's other histories of Middle-earth, is that the narratives unfold straight from the narrator. There are no mediators, like the hobbits: *The Lord of the Rings* begins and ends with hobbits. In *The Silmarillion* and the histories of Middle-earth, there is only Tolkien's narrator, who has a tendency to be grand, rhetorical and histrionic at times (somewhat like the narrator in the second half of *The Lord of the Rings*). But in *The Lord of the Rings*, the hobbits provide a point-of-view which generally accords with the primary world of the reader: the hobbits are like ordinary, everyday folk, which contrast with the outsize characters, the magic, the monsters and the epic events later on in the story.

THE VALAR

There are seven male and seven female gods or Valar. They have the familiar attributes of Greek and Roman gods: they are lords of water, hunting, death, stars, mourning, dreams, and so on. There isn't a god or goddess of love, though – no equivalent of Aphrodite or Venus. (Tolkien tinkered with the make-up of the Valar, and sometimes (in the *Lost Tales*) there were four (Manwë, Melko, Ulmo and Aulë) instead of eight or nine [HME, 4, 166]).

The hierarchy in Valinor (the land of the gods) is authoritarian, moving down from Ilúvatar ('All-Father') to the Valar ('Powers') to the Maia and finally to the elves. The hierarchy echoes that of the Christian heaven: God and his circles of angels. The gaps between the different levels of being in Valinor are close enough for some among them to marry (such as Thingol and Melian). The elves are sometimes compared to angels (Galadriel, for instance). While Melkor is likened to the chief of the fallen angels, Lucifer, there are others among the elves who resemble fallen angels (Fëanor, for example). As with fallen angels, there is a similar expulsion from Paradise (Valinor) for crimes against the ruling powers or the dominant ideology. Like angels, elves do not die until the end of the world (as with angels, there is uncertainty about what happens to elves when they are killed). Like angels, the fate of elves is dependent upon God. Like angels, elves' destiny (or 'doom') is interlinked with that of humanity. Like angels, elves have 'fallen'. Like angels, they come from Paradise or Eden (Valinor), and have a deep spiritual connection with it.

The Silmarillion narrates the birth of Middle-earth and Arda in the 'Great Music', the recurring struggles between the Valar and Morgoth, and Morgoth and the elves (and later), the geography of Middle-earth, the birth of the elves, their journey West, to the Blessed Realm, an account of the other elves that stay behind, the creation of the Two Trees, Fëanor and the manufacture of the silmarils, the revolt of the Noldor against the Valar, Morgoth and Ungoliant destroying the Trees and stealing the *silmarili*, the exodus of Fëanor and Noldor to Middle-earth, the wars between the elves and Morgoth in Middle-earth, the coming of the dwarves, the stories of individuals (such as Maedhros, Maeglin, Arien, Thingol, Fingolfin, Túrin, Beren and Lúthien), the coming of men, the deaths of Fëanor, Fingolfin, Beren, the building of Gondolin, etc. Much of *The Silmarillion* concerns the

First Age of Tolkien's Secondary World, up to the end of the First Age with Morgoth's downfall.

In his story of the creation of the world, J.R.R. Tolkien carefully describes how the world was illuminated (by the Two Lamps, then the Two Trees, then the Sun and Moon). Tolkien assembled all sorts of calendars for each race or locality, providing names for months, days, ages, etc ('Shire Reckoning', the Númenórean calendar, the Dúnedain, the Gondorian calendar for the Fourth Age, and so on). In amongst all this compulsive invention, the professor omitted explaining why there are seasons (which's due to the tilt of the Earth in relation to the sun, not the distance from the sun).

In his later writings on his *legendarium*, J.R.R. Tolkien re-thought his earlier ideas about Middle-earth, and mused at length on the origin of the sun and the moon, whether the elves first came into being in starlight, or was there daylight and a sun, and the role of the Valar and Melkor/ Morgoth in creating the celestial orbs.

VALINOR

Occasionally, the fabric of J.R.R. Tolkien's meticulously inventive Secondary World splits apart. For example, the narrator in *The Silmarillion* sometimes refers to 'heaven' (S, 241) or hell. The references to 'heaven' are more common: Valinor in the West is sometimes called 'paradise'. But there is no 'hell' in Tolkien's cosmos. There's a kind of Purgatory (the halls of Mandos), but no hell (there is a lotta hell in Tolkien's own faith of Catholicism, though). However, occasionally Tolkien's narrator alludes to 'hell' when discussing Morgoth and his plots. And when Morgoth is banished, the only place he can go is what the narrator calls 'the void', or 'the night', which's somewhere outside 'the circles of the world'. (Morgoth can't be banished to hell, partly because he's the Devil or Pluto, and partly because he already lives in 'hell' – i.e., Angband, his fortress. For the latter part of the First Age Morgoth spends most of his time underground, like other gods of the underworld, such as Satan, Pluto or Hades. He dwells at the deepest pit underground, like Satan in Dante's *Inferno*).

Valinor is a kind of Biblical Paradise, an Eden where everything seems to be good, until the first blood is spilt in anger (by Morgoth, *of course*: who else but the Devil could do that?). And Valinor becomes a 'lost Eden', just like Paradise in the *Bible*: first it is wreathed in mists and mystery by the Valinor, to prevent the Noldor returning, then the Valar decide to 'withdraw' Westernesse from the world, 'bending' the seas.

In the earliest *Silmarillion*, the gods command the elves to guard

Valinor 'and let no bird or beast or Elf or Man land on the shores of Faëry' (HME, 4, 20).

The gods don't abandon the Firstborn and the Followers (elves and humans) in J.R.R. Tolkien's Middle-earth stories: they intervene at key points, but only when no other strategy will work. For the rest of the time, they seem to live happily in Valinor, set quite apart from elves and humans and Middle-earth. It's significant that one of the good Valar (Oromë) first finds the elves in the East, not Morgoth, but Morgoth discovers humans before elves or the Valar.

Of all the Valar, the god of the sea, Ulmo, seems to take most interest in the elves, humans and Middle-earth, appearing to them in dreams, or suggesting things through a kind of telepathy via rivers and streams. Sometimes Ulmo appears before characters in person (as when he 'arose in majesty' out of the sea to speak to Tuor, recalling Poseidon and Odysseus in *The Odyssey* [S, 239]).

CRITICISM OF *THE SILMARILLION*

The Silmarillion is written in a high style and it's about gods and high elves, all very lordly and noble, but lacking the everyday quality of *The Lord of the Rings* or *The Hobbit*. As William Cater put it, the high style can become wearying, and 'one aches for someone to cook a meal or crack a joke'.[1] Tolkien acknowledged that many of his Middle-earth legends were 'purely mythological', and nearly all 'are grim and tragic' (L, 333).

The Silmarillion might be a difficult book to read because, as Tom Shippey suggested, it doesn't have characters such as hobbits to act as mediators between 'modern times and the archaic world of dwarves and dragons'.[2] And the way the narratives of the stories in *The Silmarillion* unfold makes them a departure from the usual novelistic fashion of having a character in the foreground, 'like Frodo and Bilbo, and then tell the story as it happens to him' (ibid.). The reader just doesn't feel as engrossed in the story as they do in *The Hobbit* and *The Lord of the Rings*. 'It's like the *Old Testament*!' a reader complained to Christopher Tolkien.[3]

Christopher Wrigley pointed out that in the first parts of *The Silmarillion* 'there are no real characters'; instead, they are divinities who are types: either good and beautiful or dastardly and ugly (37).

NOTES: CRITICISM OF *THE SILMARILLION*

1. In A. Becker, 94.
2. T. Shippey, 185.
3. Quoted in HME, 1, 2.

Chapter 6

THE TOLKIEN INDUSTRY

ASPECTS OF THE TOLKIEN INDUSTRY

O ye nobles, young and old, take your seats and hear now the story of the Tolkien industry...

The Tolkien industry consists of (among other things): Tolkien's verse set to music, Middle-earth puzzles, fan fiction, Middle-earth poems, Middle-earth playing cards, Tolkien societies in many countries, Tolkien fan newsletters, Tolkien merchandize catalogues, Tolkien websites, Tolkien chess sets, decorative porcelain plates, fantasy posters, Middle-earth maps, Middle-earth recipes, Tolkien crosswords, Tolkien quizzes, Tolkien calendars, *The Lord of the Rings* plastic figures (Mithril Miniatures, Harlequin, and movie tie-ins), music and songs based on Tolkien's writing, *The Lord of the Rings* stickers, Tolkien postcards, fridge magnets, Middle-earth stationary, Burger King figures, Middle-earth games and activity packs, *The Lord of the Rings* keyfobs, Tolkien diaries, a *Hobbit* birthday book, Frodo necklaces, Gandalf pendants, replica swords, replica jewellery (including the golden ring, of course), telephone cards, Kinder Surprise chocolate egg figures, Tolkien role-playing games (RPGs, MERP, METW), Tolkien fan conferences, seminars and symposia, and Tolkien art exhibitions. (What would Tolkien make of Barbie as Galadriel, Legolas Hallowe'en costumes, or slip-on plastic hobbit ears?)

Among the books dedicated to the world of J.R.R. Tolkien's fiction are: dictionaries of Elvish, guides to Tolkien's invented languages, guides and atlases to Middle-earth, Tolkien bestiaries, teachers' guides to Tolkien, Tolkien quiz books, Middle-earth quiz books, Tolkien books of days, books of fantasy art, spin-off books, and spoofs (such as *Bored of the Rings*, an early satire, by Harry N. Beard and Douglas C. Kenny, which appeared in 1969, or *The Soddit* and *The Sellamilliion*, of 2003-04). The parody included Tim Benzedrine (Tom Bombadil), Dildo Bugger (Bilbo Baggins), Frito (Frodo) and Glimet son of Groin (Gimli).

Then there are myriad editions of J.R.R. Tolkien's books: limited editions, collector's editions, boxed editions, anniversary editions, pop-up books, cartoon books, etc.

Then there are the radio versions of *The Lord of the Rings* and *The Hobbit* (on CD, tape, etc), audio books (read by the author, or by actors), film versions (on video, DVD, etc), and stage productions.

The combination of music and J.R.R. Tolkien includes bands with Tolkienesque names (countless numbers), acts singing about Tolkien-esque subjects (like Led Zeppelin or Genesis), and the many singers, songwriters and acts who interpreted the verses in Tolkien's books.

Fantasy games, role playing games, board games, collectible and trading card games, online gaming, tradeable miniatures games, and *Dungeons and Dragons* were much influenced by Tolkien (*Dungeons and Dragons* was created by Gary Gygax in 1974).

There were games of *Battle of Helm's Deep, The Middle Earth Role Playing System* (MERP), and *Siege of Minas Tirith* (there were guidebooks for the games, such as *Rules For the Live Ring Game*). The companies involved in producing Tolkien-related games included Parker Bros., Tolkien Enterprises, Hasbro, Iron Crown, and Fantasy Flight Games.

Dungeons and Dragons was very significant in the growth of computer gaming, argued Brad King and John Borland in their 2003 book about the phenomenon. It might have been played with notebooks, dice, pencils and paper, but its effects could be felt throughout video games culture. And of course *Dungeons and Dragons* was heavily influenced by Tolkien.

In the *Lord of the Rings* board game, players make their way towards Mordor through four regions: Moria, Helm's Deep, Shelob's Lair and Mordor. Sauron's at one end and the hobbits're at the other, and they move towards each other. Land on the same square as Sauron and you're dead. If the ringbearer dies, the game's over. There's a 'corruption line', along which the players move.

The *Lord of the Rings* films were spoofed on *The Simpsons,* MTV, *The Onion, Saturday Night Live, National Lampoon, South Park* and *Mad* magazine. The porn industry put out the inevitable *Lord of the Rings* spoofs and skin flicks, taking their lead more recently from the 2001-03 Hollywood adaptions, including *Lord of the G-Strings, Whore of the Rings, Lord of the Cockrings* and the best title of all, *Lord of the Ass-Rings.*

THE HISTORY OF THE TOLKIEN INDUSTRY

While the massive merchandizing and licensing bonanza for J.R.R. Tolkien (not just for the 2001-03 movies but from the mid-1960s onwards) has debased the serious, high art intention of Tolkien's project for some, it also demonstrated just how influential and popular Tolkien has become.

It's worth remembering that the Tolkien phenomenon did not begin with a massive marketing and merchandizing drive: it began, in the 1950s, with readers loving the books, and spreading the word (the best kind of advertizing). By the Sixties, of course, the merchandizing and tie-ins were kicking in big time. So the blitz from New Line and Time Warner for the two thousand one to three films is only a recent (albeit enormous) marketing and merchandizing spend.

In 1968 Neil Isaacs wrote in his introduction to *Tolkien and the Critics* that Tolkien's popularity grew not from critics or advertizing but from the readers and word of mouth. Isaacs opined: '[t]here never was any promotional bandwagon for Tolkien' (1968, 1). The relative innocence of the late 1960s has completely changed: in the early 2000s, the marketing and advertizing budget on Tolkien is enormous.

J.R.R. Tolkien always maintained a rational distance from his writings. *The Lord of the Rings* and *The Hobbit* were fiction, and he knew it. 'I do not really belong *inside* my invented history; and do not wish to!' (L, 398). It made Tolkien unhappy, suspicious, and sometimes angry that some readers took his fictions so literally or seriously. Tolkien's anxiety over the way his fictions were received increased as their popularity grew. At first, in the 1950s, soon after the publication of *The Lord of the Rings*, the readers' response consisted of fan mail and (usually) polite enquiries about the world of Middle-earth. In the 1960s, as *The Lord of the Rings* started selling in much larger quantities (following the publication of the paperback editions), the response become more fanatical and intrusive. Tolkien had his phone made ex-directory, his address withheld, and so on.

Two hundred letters a week were coming in, from all over the world: people wanted spare bits of manuscript, locks of hair, old pipes, autographs, responses to their criticisms, or interviews, or permission to set the poems to music, and information on everything to do with Middle-earth. Many sent gifts, and some wanted to be Tolkien's students.

In his famous review "Oo, Those Awful Orcs", Edmund Wilson also attacked J.R.R. Tolkien's fans, and fans of fantasy fiction, as well as *The Lord of the Rings*: 'they bubble, they squeal, they coo; they go on about Malory and Spenser – both of whom have a charm and a distinction that Tolkien has never touched'.[1]

Some readers, said J.R.R. Tolkien, wanted to more information on the music of Middle-earth; others wanted maps and geological details; others were after botanical material; archaeologists wanted metallurgy and ceramics; historians wished for more information on the social and political history of Middle-earth; and many wanted grammars and phonologies of the invented languages. Tolkien spent quite a lot of time answering the enquiries about his Secondary World (and that was before he had assistants to help him with the increasing amount of correspondence that *The Lord of the Rings* was generating from the mid-Fifties onwards).

The situation recalls the weary position of another ageing Englishman, Sir Alec Guinness, when faced with the alarming obsessive behaviour of fans of the *Star Wars* films. Guinness, confronted by a young boy who told him he'd seen *Star Wars* a hundred times, told the boy to promise to stop watching it (the youth's mother didn't like this at all). J.R.R. Tolkien found much of the criticism written about his work, especially the literary analyses, 'very bad'. They were either psychological critiques, or they explored the influences and sources, two approaches Tolkien didn't have much time for.

The Tolkien industry began way back in the 1950s, with the publication of *The Lord of the Rings*, but it didn't start to look like the vast empire it is today until the 1960s. The publication in the U.S.A. of the (unauthorized) paperback edition was a key factor in the massive interest in all things Tolkienian (some 3 million copies were sold between 1965 and 1968). The audience of *The Lord of the Rings* in the 1960s was largely white, Western, industrial middle class (and often male). It coincided with the boom in popular music, youth-oriented culture, the new permissiveness, new drug culture (LSD, marijuana), and the rise of the 'underground', 'alternative', hippy and counter-culture.

Critics have linked the increased popularity of *The Lord of the Rings* from 1965 onwards with LSD (and mescaline and peyote), with psychedelia, with hippy communes, with the renewed interest in spiritual and occult beliefs and 'altered states of consciousness' (Aldous Huxley, Carlos Casteneda, Timothy O'Leary, Hermann Hesse, William Burroughs, Jack Kerouac, R.D. Laing, C.G. Jung), and with Eastern mysticism (yoga, Transcendental Meditation, Hinduism, Buddhism, Taoism, etc).[2]

J.R.R. Tolkien's *The Lord of the Rings* fed into a new ideology that was anti-materialist, anti-capitalist, anti-authoritarian, anti-establishment, anti-hierarchical, anti-technology, anti-war, pro-ecological, pro-socialist, left-wing, and escapist. For a time, *The Lord of the Rings* chimed with the culture of hippies, 'back to nature', living in rural communes (far away from 'The Man' or 'The Machine'), eating wholefood, growing your own crops, smoking dope not drinking alcohol, and making the pilgrimage of Kathmandu, Kashmir, Goa, Afghanistan and Marrakesh. (Ironically, *The Lord of the Rings* would be criticized for being the opposite of many of the above: for some critics, Tolkien was conservative, reactionary, capitalist, sexist, nostalgic and retrogressive, and his Middle-earth was an authoritarian, hierarchical, militaristic fictional world).

Frodo has affinities with a pacificist, Gandhi-like stance, which tied in with 1960s counter-culture. He was a humble, anti-war anti-hero that touched a chord with the times. As David Day put it, J.R.R. Tolkien could not have touched more bases with the youth culture of the sixties if he had commissioned a market survey' (2001, 181).

In the U.K., even after the 1960s, *The Lord of the Rings* tapped into a deep-seated nostalgia for the countryside and the pastoral, which found its expression in the middle-classes buying second homes in rural areas, in passions for ecology and green issues, in paganism (wicca, druidism), a mistrust of science and modern technology, the 'back to basics' and 'family values' and new Victorianism policies of the Conservative government from 1979 onwards (Margaret Thatcher and Ronald Reagan), in anti-urbanism, in anti-capitalism, in anti- (pre-) modernism, in health farms and communes, in books such as *Masquerade* (Kit Williams), in TV shows such as *Last of the Summer Wine, Heartbeat* and *Emmerdale Farm,* and gardening and natural history shows, and radio soap *The Archers,* in the rise of gardening, in tourism (the image of Britain as a land of tradition, history, royalty and legend promoted by tourist boards), in the growth of musics such as folk and 'world music' (acoustic guitar, non-electrification, 'traditional' instrumentation), in rock stars building fish farms and owning country mansions and acting like country squires and landed gentry (The Who, Genesis, Led Zeppelin, the Rolling Stones), with their recording studios as rural retreats, in the land art of Christo, Robert Smithson, Richard Long and Andy Goldsworthy (their earthworks were high modernist versions of the Romantic Sublime), and the 'new ruralist' art of the 1970s and after (in David Inshaw, Kit Williams and Peter Blake), which updated the long tradition of British landscape painting. (Kit Williams and his *Masquerade* book drew on fantasy art to produce a *mélange* of 'English' mythology and folklore.)

In some ways, the turning-point in Professor Tolkien's literary career was the decision by Ace in the U.S.A. to publish *The Lord of the Rings.* At first, Tolkien and his U.K. publishers might have fought against *The Lord of the Rings* being pirated, but in the long run the benefits to Tolkien were huge.

It was the counter-culture era, the summer of love, age of Aquarius, Woodstock, flower power, Zen Buddhism, yoga, gurus aplenty, LSD, tripping, getting high, and magazines such as *Oz, Creem, Cream, Frendz, IT, Gandalf's Garden, Hobbit, Screw* and *Fucknam.* In the U.K., venues such as the Roundhouse, the Marquee, the UFO, Middle Earth and Speakeasy clubs, Arts Labs, the Notting Hill Free School, LSE, and events such as the 'All-Night Rave Pop Op Costume Masque Drag Ball Et Al', the '14-Hour Technicolour Dream' at Alexandra Palace, the 'Spontaneous Underground' Sunday afternoons at London's Marquee, and the 'More Furious Madness From the Massed Gadgets of Auximenes' at the Royal Festival Hall in 1969. This was the time of 'happenings', psychedelia and bands like Soft Machine, Cream, The Doors, Steppenwolf, Henry Cow, Pink Floyd and Yes.

Phrases developed in the Sixties: 'Frodo lives', 'Reading Tolkien is Hobbit-forming', 'Gandalf for President', 'Frodo for Prime Minister', 'Sméagol died for your sins', 'Support Your Local Hobbit', and 'Go Go Gandalf!'. And greetings such as 'may the hair on your toes never grow less', and Elvish phrases.

Fred Cody, manager of a campus bookstore at UCLA Berkeley, said that J.R.R. Tolkien 'is more than a campus craze; it's like a drug dream.' Tolkien replaced required reading for university students such as J.D. Salinger, William Golding, Henry Miller and the Beats.

There was a fall-off and a reaction against J.R.R. Tolkien around the time of 1968, with the (Marxist) politicization of counter-culture and the 'underground', and the student, anti-Vietnam and anti-government protests. Yet *The Lord of the Rings* survived Marx, Mao and Marcuse, the 'radical chic' of Tom Wolfe, the Prague Spring, the protests at London's Grosvenor Square, the Sorbonne and the Renault plant in Paris, and Kent State.

The early 1970s were marked by the anxieties, confusions and suffering of Watergate, Vietnam, the oil crisis and the global recession. One of the reasons given for the enormous popularity of entertainment such as *Close Encounters of the Third Kind* and *Star Wars* was that it offered a fantastical escape from the stresses of the 1970s. By the early 1970s, Tolkien was a permanent fixture of the undergraduate, 'alternative' scene in Europe and the United States (at Columbia, NYU, USC and UCLA in the US). Reading *The Lord of the Rings* was a rite of passage, as essential for new students as smoking dope or getting laid.

J.R.R. Tolkien's fantasy fed into the world of prog and heavy rock, 'concept albums' with their Roger Dean covers, the college gig circuit, fantasy art, comic books, fantasy role-playing games and the rise in the sword-and-sorcery genre.

It was in the 1970s that Tolkien's books were finally and conclusively part of the literary establishment (though the literary academy would continue to debate their entry into 'the canon' for years. Certainly the 'great tradition' of critics like F.R. Leavis wouldn't allow *The Lord of the Rings* anywhere near it). The late 1970s brought another wave of Tolkien output: principally, the 1977 publication of the long-awaited *The Silmarillion* and United Artists' 1978 animation of the first half of *The Lord of the Rings*. There was also the 1977 TV *Hobbit*. A 26-part BBC serialization was broadcast on BBC radio in 1981 (later broadcast in 13 episodes).

Ronald Tolkien's death in 1973 precipitated a flurry of publishing activity, resulting not only in *The Silmarillion*, but also *Pictures of J.R.R. Tolkien* in 1979, *Unfinished Tales* in 1980, *The Letters of J.R.R. Tolkien* in 1981, the *History of Middle Earth* volumes from 1983 onwards, plus all of the re-issues and new editions of *The Lord of the Rings* and *The Hobbit*, and the tons of Tolkien merchandize – calendars, posters, figurines, costumes. The 1970s also saw the foundation of many Tolkien societies around the globe, and the fan culture of newsletters, meetings, conferences and the like, which coincided with the cult following of sci-fi and fantasy franchises such as *Star Trek, Conan* and *Dr Who*.

For Tom Shippey, one of the main reasons for J.R.R. Tolkien's continuing popularity among readers is that his work addresses key issues of the late 20th century: 'the origin and nature of evil'; cultural relativity; human life in a Godless age; and 'the corruptions and continuities of language' (2000, ix).

The Lord of the Rings consistently came top of readers' favourite book lists in the latter part of the 20th century in the U.K.. It was top of the Folio Society's list in 1996; Waterstone's bookshops' list rated it first in 1996; BBC TV's *Bookworm* voted it top in 1997 (50,000 readers took part); the readers of the *Daily Telegraph* voted the same way.

By 2000, *The Hobbit* had sold 40 million copies, and *The Lord of the Rings* over 50 million (other estimates put it at 100m for *Rings* and 60m for *The Hobbit*). The release of the New Line films between 2001 and 2003 further propelled sales.

One person must be very happy with the 2000s *The Lord of the Rings* films: Saul Zaentz. His company produced the 1978 animated *The Lord of the Rings*, which was duly re-released on video and DVD to $$$$ in on the buzz surrounding the live-action 2000s films. The Saul Zaentz Company and its Tolkien Enterprises arm could sit back and count the money rolling in, without seeming to do too much, beyond the negotiations for the film, licensing and merchandizing (as could the Trustees of The J.R.R. Tolkien 1967 Settlement and the J.R.R. Tolkien Estate Ltd). Many companies could cash in on the films, re-releasing books and films for the new audiences the films would create.

Another mogul who profited greatly from the new films without having to do too much was Rupert Murdoch: his media giant News Corporation owned HarperCollins, publishers in the U.K. of J.R.R. Tolkien. For Harper-Collins, the 2000s *Lord of the Rings* film series represented a vast marketing campaign and advertizing spend. It was a marriage made in heaven: the publishers and DVD and video distributors knew that there is a very lucrative crossover between consumers of books and filmed entertainment. The Tolkien industry had been ticking over nicely – in book publishing, the major books had never been out of print, and could be updated regularly with new editions, and new covers and all of the tricks of the publishing trade. But the Hollywood films meant a boost for Tolkien-related products of multi-million dollar proportions.

Book publishers such as Balantine and Houghton Mifflin reported greatly increased sales of the *Lord of the Rings* books during the release period of the 2001-2003 films. One report had 24 million copies sold of *The Hobbit* and *Lord of the Rings* editions between two thousand and two thousand four.

Other companies benefitting from the 2001-03 *Lord of the Rings* films included Walt Disney, which received 2.5% of the gross (with 2.5% going to Miramax). Vivendi Universal, who owned publisher Houghton Mifflin, did nicely out of increased books sales (as did Ballantine); VU also had J.R.R. Tolkien computer games. Other computer game companies had *Lord of the Rings* games: Sony, Nintendo, Turbine Entertainment, and EA.

NOTES: THE HISTORY OF THE TOLKIEN INDUSTRY

1. In A. Becker, 55.
2. 'It is no coincidence that *The Lord of the Rings* became a bestseller at the height of middle-class youth drug fashion: it found a ready market in the world's first mass audience to be both truly stoned and truly literate. Little promotion was necessary. As a piece of marketing, the timing of the paperback publication was immaculate', wrote N. Walmsley ("Tolkien and the '60s", in R. Giddings, 1983, 79).

TOLKIEN SOCIETIES

All sorts of groups lay claim to J.R.R. Tolkien and his fiction. Tolkien societies around the world emphasize their 'serious' appreciation of the professor. Other groups are the legions of fans, some of whom collect Tolkien merchandize, or attend fantasy conferences, and art gallery private views of Tolkien illustrators. Other fans dress up as Tolkien characters at fancy dress parties. Some write fan fiction; others post their stories and art on the internet. Some fans name their children or houses after Middle-earth.

One of the first Tolkien Society was founded in America and included a *Tolkien Journal*. The Tolkien societies keep the spirit of Tolkien alive with gestures such as eating mushrooms, or drinking beer and cider, or smoking pipes. Talking in Elvish or other Tolkien languages is common-place, and members are greeted with phrases such as: 'may the hair on your toes never grow less'. Members used Tolkien names for themselves (a practice now widespread not only in Tolkien-related fantasy pursuits). They swopped Tolkien merchandizing, and homemade 'mathoms' (objects that are saved but not used). Richard Plotz, who founded the Tolkien Society of America (with Ed Meskys), said at Tolkien meetings they used to sit around on the floor

talking about the theogony and the geography of Middle-earth and things like that. Of course, every once in a while, someone may charge someone else with an imaginary sword, crying 'Elbereth Gilthoniel', which is the name of a princess of old and a very power-giving thing to say. (In D. Grotta, 138)

Tolkien societies in countries such as Borneo and Poland followed the U.K. and the U.S.A. societies (there's even a Societas Tolkien, dedicated to translating the books into Latin, and then into Elvish). Tolkien did become involved, from a distance, with the Tolkien Society. The Mythopoeic Society in Altadena (CA) was founded in 1967 by Glen H. GoodKnight, and was based in the United States. It was dedicated to the work of the Inklings, and published an annual magazine (*Mythlore*) and a monthly newsletter (*Mythprint*). There was also an annual conference. Other societies included the American Hobbit Association in Cincinnati (which published the *Rivendell Review*), the Los Angeles Science Fantasy Society, the Society For the Furtherance and Study of Fantasy and Science Fiction in Madison (WI), and the National Fantasy Fan Federation (N3F) in New York.

There were gatherings of Tolkien fans in California (where else?) to celebrate Bilbo's birthday, and later the ring's destruction (in Spring). Cider, malt cookies, and mushrooms were consumed at the picnic, with games such as mushroom rolling and mock battles.

The Tolkien Society in the U.K. was founded by Vera Chapman in 1969 (Chapman was a female mason and druid). Activities included an Oxon-moot in Oxford in early Autumn, monthly meetings (in a London pub), visits to Tolkien places (such as Oxford), and an Annual General Meeting in Spring. *Amon Hen* was a bi-monthly bulletin, and *Mallorn* the annual journal. Songs would be sung, poetry would be recited (written by Tolkien or by members), and there would be many discussions.

The 2001-03 J.R.R. Tolkien films enhanced the interest in Tolkien's languages – it made a difference from reading Elvish on the page to hear actors speaking it (especially when they were attractive actors such as Liv Tyler and Viggo Mortensen). The people who ran websites and publications on Elvish and other Tolkien languages recorded an increase of interest.

FANDOM

Not long after the publication of *The Lord of the Rings,* fans started to approach J.R.R. Tolkien. Fans sent the Oxford professor all sorts of items: cups, photographs of themselves as Tolkien characters, paintings, stories, sculptures, tapes, drinks, tobacco, tapestries, etc. There were requests for autographs, information, endorsements, and personal visits to Tolkien's Oxford and phone calls in the middle of the night.

Fan fiction is a vast area of the Tolkien industry. Middle-earth has become the ultimate in fantasy playgrounds where fan writers can roam at large. Fan fiction hasn't only responded to Tolkien's original writings, it's also drawn on other fan fictions: there are different versions, layers of updates, sequels to other stories. The copyright situation has prevented the thousands of fan fictions being officially published, so they don't compete with the Tolkien canon in the public domain. But they are all over the internet, and in many private publications.

The fan films *The Hunt For Gollum* (Chris Bouchard, 2009) and *Born of Hope* (Kate Madison, 2009) were terrific: very low budget (incredibly, only $4,500/ £3,000 for *The Hunt For Gollum*), they looked amazing, although it was disappointing that they took the approach of the 2001-2003 movies entirely (there are many other ways of interpreting J.R.R. Tolkien on celluloid).

The web is thick with Tolkienian material. Put the word 'Tolkien' or 'Middle-earth' into any search engine and you'll find hundreds of web sites. Every e-mail service (Yahoo, Hotmail, Excite, Microsoft, Netscape, etc), newsgroup or chat room will have hundreds of members called 'Gandalf', 'Legolas', 'Arwen' and 'Elrond'.

WEBSITES.
Websites with Tolkien material include:
the Lord of the Rings Maps (lotrmaps.middle-earth.us),
Encyclopedia of Arda (gylphweb.com/arda),
lordoftherings.net, lordoftherings.com,
Tolkien Online (tolkienonline.com),
and Ardalambion (uib.no/people/hnohf).

FANZINES.
Fanzines and magazines about Tolkien were launched from the Sixties onwards: *I Palantir, Orcrist, Dormant Dwellers, Anduril, Green Dragon, Minas Tirith Evening Star, Misty Mountain Monthly, Middle Earthworm, The Mallorn, The Nazgûl, The Mathom, Mythlore, Mythprint, Tolkien Journal, Mythril,* etc. (The *Minas Tirith Evening Star,* one of the longer-running publications, founded in 1967, was linked to Neo-Númenor, Eldilla and the Tolkien Society).

ċhápτεℜ 7

J.R.R. TOLKIEN AND POP MUSIC

Sixties and Seventies rock music loved to sing about kings, queens, princes, princesses, knights in shining armour, King Arthur, Merlin, witches, monsters, fairy tales, spaceships, aliens, interstellar wars, prehistory, stone circles, Druids, epic battles, perilous quests, and so on, and J.R.R. Tolkien's fiction was perfect for that. There was plenty of characters to choose from, and plenty of events. And for visual inspiration, Tolkien's fiction is endless.

J.R.R. Tolkien's fiction tied in with Sixties and Seventies rock music (and popular culture) on many levels:

(1) It was popular at public schools, universities and colleges, where Tolkien was read and many pop bands were formed (the British art school system had – and has – a long tradition of supplying the pop world with musicians, including John Lennon, Pete Townsend, David Bowie, Bryan Ferry, Malcolm McLaren, the Bonzo Dog Band, etc). Many members of rock bands were educated in the same places as Tolkien fans, and where Tolkien himself taught.

(2) J.R.R. Tolkien's fiction fed into the penchant for rock supergroups (and their followers) to go back to the land, to live as farmers or country squires – or hobbits (members of Genesis, The Who, Paul McCartney and many others lived on or bought farms, fish farms, banana farms, or had rural retreats, mansions and estates). Rock's aristocracy as landed gentry.

(3) This also linked to the hippy and folk movement's eco-friendly and green aspirations (Frank Herbert's *Dune* series was another favourite in this regard).

(4) Drugs: stoners and acid trips, the drug experience as an immersion in a fantasy world. Middle-earth as an LSD trip.

(6) Many rock acts used literature as a source of inspiration (sometimes for 'concept' albums or rock operas). Favourite writers included Hermann Hesse, Arthur Rimbaud, Jack Kerouac, Henry Miller, Carlos Casteneda, Frank Herbert, Isaac Asimov – and Tolkien.

(7) There are plenty of songs and poems in *The Lord of the Rings*, which could be set to music.

(8) Escapism, often used as a weapon by J.R.R. Tolkien haters, was

another factor: delving into the world of *The Lord of the Rings* was a way of escaping the anxieties and horrors of the 1960s and 1970s. Hence the popularity of other fantasy and science fiction at this time.

(9) The past and history: J.R.R. Tolkien's world was drenched in older cultures, and tied in with a nostalgia for history. Rock acts often sang about historical periods, while folk music actively sought and promoted traditional musical forms. (So, in evoking earlier historical periods, rock bands could strike out into unusual instrumentation, for rock music, such as harps).

(10) Complexity, cleverness, intricacy. Rock bands enjoyed showing off their intellectual pursuits, their reading and research. And also their musical complexity, their unusual time signatures (like, say, 13/8), their rapid runs up the fretboard or keyboard, or their complicated chord sequences.

(11) Sub-creation: many of the rock acts liked to create their own worlds, as the professor did.

(12) The visual aspect: rock bands from the Seventies onwards revelled in the visual imagery that literature could provide, translating it into their lyrics, album covers and stage props. And Tolkien of course was perfect for exotic visualizations.

(13) The urge towards the pastoral and the rural, the pro-ecology movements, Greenpeace, Friends of the Earth, etc. The anti-industrial political movements (later merging into anti-capitalism). J.R.R. Tolkien's Middle-earth, and in particular the hobbits in the Shire, could be taken up as an image of an ideal grounded lifestyle.

(14) A hankering for heroes, for people who can really get things done (unlike presidents or governments), and also the notion that even ordinary folk can make a difference.

(15) The (apparent) moral simplicity of J.R.R. Tolkien's world, where good and evil is clearly delineated. A time and place when the solutions to socio-political problems are clear (go to war; destroy the ring).

(16) The ideological conservativism (with a hierarchical social structure that upheld privilege, heredity, wealth).

(17) Public school, aristocracy, royalty, the class system.

(18) Romanticism – a key feature of rock music from the Sixties onwards: Romanticism's urge towards excess, infinity, transcendence, pantheism, otherworldliness, fantasy and the supernatural, the epic and the monumental. The pantheism and nature mysticism in rock was part of late 1960s counter-culture, the 'back to nature' movement which emerged as New Ageism, 'crusties' and 'New Age' travellers 20 and 30 years later. The nature spirituality tied in with the mediæval imagery and themes of prog and psychedelic rock.

❋

Musicians and composers who turned out J.R.R. Tolkien-related music included Gail Alrich's *Music From J.R.R. Tolkien's The Fellowship of the Ring*, a folk music outing; Alan Harvath's *Lord of the Rings* concept album; jazz musician John Sangster recorded seven hours of music in the 1970s; Swedish instrumentalist Bo Hansson turned in a prog rock concept album, *The Lord of the Rings*, in 1970; Canadian rockers Rush produced 'Rivendell' in 1975; English prog rockers Camel composed 'The White Rider', about Gandalf, in the mid-70s; Stratovarius released the album *Tolkien* in 1999; Isildur's Bane and Blind Guardian produced heavy rock interpretations of Tolkien; Mostly Autumn released *Music Inspired By The Lord of the Rings* (2002); Brobdingnagian Bards put out the album *Memories of Middle Earth* in 2003; The Hobbitons produced *Songs From Middle Earth*; Old Forest Sounds made two albums of *Music of Middle Earth* and *The Adventures of Tom Bombadil* (in 1991); Broceliande put out an album of Celtic-tinged renditions of Tolkien's songs (*The Starlit Jewel*, 1996); Evenstar's *Enchanted Journeys* (2003) was also folky, Celtic music; Andy Street and the Westwind Ensemble recorded an album of Tolkien-inspired music (2003); David Arkenston and the Elbereth orchestra produced *Music Inspired By Middle Earth* in 2001.

Donald Swann worked with a musician, William Elven, to compose the album of J.R.R. Tolkien songs, and also performed them (*The Road Goes Ever On: A Song Cycle*, 1967). They were basically piano and vocal versions of the songs mainly from *The Lord of the Rings*.

Christopher Lee had sung and narrated on recordings of J.R.R. Tolkien's songs by the Tolkien Ensemble: *Evening At Rivendell* (1997), *Night At Rivendell* (1999), and *The Lord of the Rings: At Dawn In Rivendell* (2003). (Viggo Mortensen had released an album in 2000, *One Man's Meat*).

In the classical music sector, there was Johan De Meij's *The Lord of the Rings* (1998), Craig Russell's *Middle Earth On Rhapsody For Horn and Orchestra* (2003), and Caprice produced *Elvenmusic* (2001).

The music for the dramatic interpretations of J.R.R. Tolkien should also be mentioned. The music for the BBC radio *Rings* adaption, by Stephen Oliver, was also released, as was Leonard Rosenman's music for the 1978 animated *The Lord of the Rings*.

Howard Shore's music for the 2001-03 films of *The Lord of the Rings* was taken up by composers and arrangers and orchestras. Nic Raine, City of Prague Philharmonic Orchestra and the Crouch End Festival Choirs produced *Music From The Lord of the Rings Trilogy* (2004); Chris Cozens released *Music Inspired By the Film The Lord of the Rings* (2002); and the Hollywood Studio Orchestra and Singers put out three albums of music from each film (collected as *The Trilogy of The Lord of the Rings* [2004]).

Chapter 8

J.R.R. TOLKIEN, *HARRY POTTER* AND *STAR WARS*

J.R.R. TOLKIEN AND *HARRY POTTER*

J.R.R. Tolkien fans compared the film of *The Fellowship of the Ring* with *Harry Potter and the Sorcerer's Stone*, released at the same time in late 2001. For Tolkien aficionados, the boy wizard was decried for being derivative of Tolkien, for being aimed at children, for trying to move in on fantasy ground that Tolkien had staked out. Many fans seemed to see the two films as in competition, in the marketplace, and in popular culture. Debates grew up around the films, with many comparisons between Harry and Frodo, Dumbledore and Gandalf, Voldemort and Sauron, and so on. It didn't matter to the merchandizers and corporations backing the two films, as long as fans and readers were discussing them. Both films shared much in common, including a crossover audience, similar marketing and advertizing, huge tie-in and licensing deals, and the same release windows of Christmas, 2001, with the boy wizard bowing four weeks before the Frodo franchise.

Ironically, the *Harry Potter* phenomenon in publishing may have helped make a global audience more receptive to the fantasy of the New Line 2001-03 movies. Media pundits also knew that both franchises were backed by the same company – the biggest media conglomerate in the world, Time Warner. So even if *Harry Potter* split the audience with Tolkien at the box office, it wouldn't matter: Time Warner would be doing very nicely out of both films.

Within a few years of the first *Harry Potter* book being published (in 1997), 50 million books had been sold in the U.S.A. alone, making *Harry Potter* the fastest selling books in history. The first four *Harry Potter* books sold nearly 200 million copies in 55 languages. That's 200 million books between 1997 and 2003, 200 million copies in 6 years, an *unbelievable* amount.

The *Harry Potter* phenomenon achieved a cultural popularity to rival that of J.R.R. Tolkien's Middle-earth. Jo Rowling's books had achieved a global popularity that took Tolkien's tomes much longer to attain. And nobody's been able to explain the *Harry Potter* phenomenon – much less replicate it. The success of *Harry Potter* is astounding in every possible view.

The *Harry Potter* phenomenon reached its maximum cultural profile during 1999-2000, when *The Lord of the Rings* film was being shot. The success of the *Harry Potter* books may not have influenced New Line's decision to greenlight *The Lord of the Rings*, but it certainly helped to give audiences around the globe an appetite for a particular brand of British fantasy involving wizards, magic and humble, unassuming heroes.

Jo Rowling acknowledged the influence of J.R.R. Tolkien's writing on her work. Rowling said that Tolkien's Middle-earth and the world of magic in her books did overlap, but Tolkien had 'created a whole mythology. I don't think anyone could claim that I have done that'. Rowling had first read *The Lord of the Rings* when she was 19. Friends said she often had her battered copy of the book with her (it was one of the books she took to Portugal).

Critics have pointed out the many affinities between *Harry Potter* and *The Lord of the Rings*. Dumbledore is a version of Gandalf; Harry draws on Frodo; Voldemort on Sauron (both have lost their former power and are regaining it); the Dementors on the Ringwraiths; Wormtail on Wormtongue; the Mirror of Erised is the mirror of Galadriel; giant spiders; dragons; dark forests (the Forbidden Forest draws on Mirkwood and Fangorn); 'salt of the earth' folk the Weasleys (good food, home comfort, rural Devonshire home) recall hobbits and the Shire; Hogwarts is part Rivendell, part Lothlórien, part Minas Tirith;

Other affinities between J.R.R. Tolkien and Jo Rowling include the creation of a complete, self-contained Secondary World; use of mediæval culture, British and Northern European mythology; a passion for names; a nostalgic love of a homely, conservative and now-vanished England (which never existed); an adherence to classical ideals, such as companionship, teamwork, bravery and idealism. Both Rowling and Tolkien like to know much more about their Secondary Worlds than the reader, and pack all sorts of details into the background (Tolkien published much of this background information in the appendices to *The Lord of the Rings*, and in his lengthy *History of Middle-earth* volumes; so far, Rowling hasn't provided that – other writers have produced *Harry Potter* encyclopaedias and guidebooks).

J.R.R. TOLKIEN AND *STAR WARS*

Fans of J.R.R. Tolkien and George Lucas (b. 1943) have regularly trotted out the affinities between the two fantasy worlds, Tolkien's Middle-earth and Lucas's 'galaxy far, far away'. For example: Gandalf as Ben Kenobi; Frodo as Luke Skywalker; Elrond as Yoda; Boromir as Lando Calrissian; orcs as storm-troopers; Aragorn as Qui-Gon Jinn; Saruman as Jabba the Hutt; Merry and Pippin as Artoo and Threepio; two Dark Lords, and so on.

The *Lord of the Rings* movies had numerous æsthetic affinities with the *Star Wars* saga: quest narratives, material based on mythology, magic, good vs. evil, similar characters (mediæval knights, wizards, heroes, monsters), wizard fights, mass battles, evil empires, small furry characters (hobbits and ewoks), mediæval warfare (light sabres and swords), faceless hordes of enemies (stormtroopers and orcs), scary machines, telepathy, and so on.

Both *Star Wars* and *The Lord of the Rings* were big budget Hollywood movies, both spawned vast merchandizing and licensing industries (including 100s of toys and figures), both had fanatical followers, both used state of the art (i.e., incredibly expensive) visual effects, both were fantasy, both recycled movie genres, both quoted earlier epics (Cecil B. DeMille, David Lean, Ray Harryhausen, Westerns, swashbucklers, ancient history spectacles), both were really old-fashioned action-adventures, both used similar production techniques (pre-viz, miniatures, digital technology), both had Southern hemisphere headquarters and studios (Australia and New Zealand), both used British and American facilities, and they shared personnel. (Anthony Daniels, C3PO in all six *Star Wars* films, was the voice of Legolas in the 1978 film of *The Lord of the Rings*).

German critic Dietmar Kanthak was pretty spot-on when he defined the 2000s *Lord of the Rings* films as 'somewhere between *Indiana Jones*, and *Braveheart, King Kong* and *Star Wars* with occasional brushes of *Titanic* in between' (2002). For some critics, *Star Wars* was '*Lord of the Rings* in space' (M. White, 2002, 240.) So *Star Wars* drew on Tolkien and *The Lord of the Rings*, but the *Lord of the Rings* movies also drew on the *Star Wars* films in numerous ways, from pre-production through to merchandizing and tie-ins.

But there is one incredibly important difference between *Star Wars* films and the *Lord of the Rings* films: the *Star Wars* movies were conceived and written as *movies*, and not adapted from existing material, while the *Lord of the Rings* movies were adaptions of a well-known book. That meant that all the time the *Star Wars* pictures were being put together, the filmmakers always knew they were going to be *films*, that they had to work as films, in terms of drama, characterization, plot, technique, and so on. The *Lord of the Rings* films, meanwhile, had numerous problems to deal with in relation to the book (such as the chief villain being a flaming eyeball).

On the plus side, it meant that the *Lord of the Rings* pictures were pre-sold to a degree, because they were adaptions of a well-known literary property. *Star Wars*, meanwhile, started out of the gate as an unknown quantity (we all know the stories of many peoploids involved with *Star Wars* who regarded it as a silly kids' flick).

chapter 9

J.R.R. TOLKIEN AND FEMINISM

Most all commentators have noted the lack of female characters in *The Lord of the Rings,* and the preponderance of boys with toys, men going to war, macho posturing, sacred brotherhoods, and pro-militaristic politics. But it's not just the *lack* of female characters, it's the *kind* of women that are depicted in J.R.R. Tolkien's opus. Women are either idealized Goddesses like Galadriel, or supportive wives who stay home like Rosie Cotton, or repressed, frustrated virginal tomboys like Éowyn, or chattering nurses and old maids like loreth.

J.R.R. Tolkien's response to one critic's complaint that the story of *Rings* was for boys not girls was that the subject – 'wars and a terrible expedition to the North Pole, so to speak' – made it necessarily masculine. But, Tolkien reminded an interviewer, he was a family man, with a wife, children, daughter and granddaughter, so it wasn't as if he were living in an all-male, adult environment.

The Hobbit too has no female characters of any significance, except for Bilbo's mother Belladonna (who's mentioned but doesn't appear). Gandalf plays a kindly father surrogate, but there are no parental figures. Bilbo's the hero, but he doesn't kill the dragon – that's left to another character (if *The Hobbit* had been a conventional fairy tale, Bilbo would've killed the dragon with some clever scheme, Colin Wilson pointed out, rather than the dragon being dispatched off-stage, as it were, by Bard).

The Lord of the Rings is a book of fathers and sons, fathers and daughters, but no mothers and children, as many critics have pointed out.1 It's a patriarchal world, with the law of the Father predominant, and handing down power from fathers to sons. It's a world where older men rule (Denethor, Elrond), and old men advise younger men on what to do (Gandalf with Frodo, Elrond with Aragorn, Denethor with Boromir and Faramir). In terms of really, decisively affecting the story of *The Lord of the Rings,* there's only Galadriel and Éowyn among women (and maybe Shelob). Pretty much everyone else (Rosie Cotton, Arwen Undómiel) stays at home.

Fathers losing their children is another theme in the books: Denethor losing Boromir, Théoden losing Théodred, Elrond losing Arwen to mortality.

Old men who're widows is another recurring motif: Elrond, Denethor and Théoden.

Critics have linked the relationship in J.R.R. Tolkien's fiction between younger men and older father figures who suddenly disappear without explanation to Tolkien's own life, and the sudden death of his father.

Among dwarves, there are far more males than females. And dwarves seldom marry. That, combined with wars and other trials, meant the dwarves were on the wane in Middle-earth. Very little is said in J.R.R. Tolkien's writings about dwarf women (they apparently dress the same as the men). I can't think of a single significant female dwarf character in Tolkien's *legendarium*. (In the 2002 film of *The Two Towers*, the female screenwriters couldn't resist inserting a joke about dwarf women. But the lack of dwarf women isn't just found in Tolkien's fiction – it's part of the fairy tale genre). Gimli has his own romance – though it's strictly the chaste adoration of a queen from afar. As with the knights of old and in the courtly love tradition, Galadriel gives him a gift.

For Jack Zipes, women are not given any place in Ronald Tolkien's Middle-earth fantasies, and it can seem as if the men are self-reproductive. 'Fraternity exists unto itself and is not to be disturbed by females' (2002a, 174). The avoidance of women is one element in Tolkien's backward-looking fiction: the utopian project, the progressive, forward-looking aspects of Tolkien's fiction, are negated by the backward-looking aspects, the move towards feudalism. 'But, by stepping back into the past, Tolkien gets lodged there and has difficulty projecting a way back into the present and future', Zipes remarked (2002a, 174).

Christopher Wrigley relates the fact that there are no mother figures in *The Lord of the Rings* to the loss of J.R.R. Tolkien's own mother, Mabel (2005, 41f). There is a high proportion of characters in *The Lord of the Rings* with no mothers or mothers who died young: Bilbo, Frodo, Faramir and Boromir, Aragorn, Sam, Éomer and Éowyn. Gandalf and Saruman, Sauron and Morgoth, of course have no mothers (or if they did, they never speak of them). Arwen's mother Celebrían has gone into the West.

The Lord of the Rings hasn't been used often in feminist projects investigating women's issues in relation to literature (like, say, *Pride and Prejudice*, or Emily Dickinson's poetry). There simply isn't much to work with. Of the female characters, most are either domestic wives (Rosie Cotton and Goldberry), or beyond-reach, highly idealized Goddesses and Madonnas (Galadriel), invoked in time of need like the Virgin Mary. In Gondor, women are gossipy nurses (Ioweth) and healers.

Feminists, especially second wave feminists, have explored the feminine, female characters, and 'feminine' issues in the 20th century modernists of English literature (James Joyce, Marcel Proust, D.H. Lawrence, Virginia Woolf), but J.R.R. Tolkien has rarely been subject of the same critical scrutiny. For example, Hélène Cixous has written at length on James Joyce; Julia Kristeva on the European *avant garde* modernists (Charles Baudelaire, Antonin Artaud and Louis Ferdinand Céline); and any number of Anglo-American feminist critics have discoursed on favourite authors such as Virginia Woolf or Gertrude Stein or Doris Lessing or Sylvia Plath or Radcliffe Hall.

What was said in the 1950s and 1960s, following the publication of *The Lord of the Rings*, is rarely improved upon by subsequent critics: apart from pointing to the very traditional views of women in *The Lord of the Rings* and Middle-earth, their lack of independence from men, and their stereotypical treatment, critics have had little to say (in general). But the male characters are also stereotypical and one-dimensional. As critics have noted, they tend to represent one or two personality traits, or diffuse concepts such as 'nobility' or 'domesticity' or 'bravery'. (This is in keeping with the mediæval romance basis of *The Lord of the Rings*, in which characters were often personifications of attributes. And it helps with film adaptions, too, which employ shorthand, one-dimensional character-izations).

And J.R.R. Tolkien's fiction has not often been the subject of 'third wave' feminist criticism, or postmodern criticism. It's as if the view, established soon after the publication of the books (noted by poet Edwin Muir), of Tolkien's treatment of women, has not been challenged. Certainly, it would be difficult to seriously challenge the view of women in *The Lord of the Rings* and the Middle-earth fiction, to re-instate the women, to argue for their reappraisal – in the same way, for instance, as Thomas Hardy or Charles Dickens have been reappraised by feminist critics.

The view of women and women's issues in J.R.R. Tolkien's fiction ties in with the work of the other Inklings, which was also male-oriented, patriarchal, paternalistic, and, for some, sexist and even misogynist. It recalls the attitudes to women in 'classic' early 20th century and Edwardian English literature such as *The Wind in the Willows* or Rudyard Kipling. It's easy to characterize the Inklings as a collection of middle-aged Oxford dons hiding away from women in their rooms, to drink beer and smoke and discuss mythology, philology and philosophy ('men's talk'), and to see those entrenched attitudes reflected in their writings.

Assessed in the same manner as, say, James Joyce or D.H. Lawrence, J.R.R. Tolkien's view of women seems positively prehistoric, fixed in an archaic and heavily idealized attitude. It was a viewpoint which changed little over the course of his literary career (from, say, *The Hobbit* to the late fiction). The level of sophistication in the fiction of an author like D.H. Lawrence in writing about the intricacies and subtleties of personality or love relationships seems far beyond Tolkien's grasp. If Tolkien under-stands such nuances and depths, he doesn't seem able (or interested) in putting them into words. His concerns are elsewhere. That kind of psycho-logical probing of inter-personal relationships doesn't really interest Tolkien at all. His is a fiction of heroic romance and the Land of Faërie.

GALADRIEL.

What about the women in John Ronald Reuel Tolkien's fiction? In *The Lord of the Rings*, there are really only three significant women: Galadriel, Éowyn and Arwen. Plus Goldberry, Ioreth the nurse and Sam's wife Rosie. Let's start with Galadriel, who has the Virgin Mary, no less, as one of her models. Another probable source for Galadriel is Lady Irene in George MacDonald's *The Princess and the Curdie* (who is ageless, tall, beautiful, and associated with shining light).

Detached, other-worldly, ageless, beautiful, sometimes stern and a little pompous, and never coarse. Galadriel is something like an older sister or aunt to the Fellowship, when they arrive in Lórien (or perhaps a sister nun in a convent). She's friendly but always proper; she remains coolly aloof at times. She's basically a female version of Elrond, and the evidence of her former rebelliousness in early ages of Middle-earth is hard to find in the Lothlórien scenes in *The Lord of the Rings* (except in her fantasy of world domination via the One Ring).

Galadriel's an important figure, narratively, being a ringbearer, and among the main characters in the chapters set in Lothlórien (she has a few scenes, the key one being the mirror scene, where she reveals to the hobbits what she would be like if she took the ring. There is also the scene of Galadriel's gifts (the gifts have a narrative function later on in the book, such as the cloaks, and the phial).)

The mirror has a long history in fairy and folk tales (in *Snow White*, or the magic mirrors of Merlin, Vulcan and Cambuscan in Geoffrey Chaucer's fiction). *The Princess and the Curdie* is another reference for the magic mirror. In symbolism, the mirror has myriad functions, from the uncon-scious to consciousness, from contemplation and interiority to the relations between imagination and reality, art and life.

Galadriel's reaction to Frodo offering her the ring critic Christopher Manlove compares to 'an admonitory rattle of quills or the swelling of a bullfrog' – a similar response occurs with Gandalf, Aragorn and Faramir when the possibility of possessing the ring presents itself (1975, 179). Galadriel's demonstration of becoming a 'beautiful but terrible' queen of Middle-earth is odd because she has already resolved not to take it.

Lothlórien seems more of a proto-matriarchy, with Galadriel seeming to have ascendancy over Celeborn (who definitely takes a back seat after the initial greetings of the Company). Galadriel, the most powerful female in Middle-earth in *The Lord of the Rings,* doesn't rule the Golden Wood on her own: she rules it with Celeborn. There is a queen in Númenor, but she has to rule alongside Ar-Pharazôn, not on her own.

And then there's the issue of Gimli being so awestruck by Galadriel's beauty that he requests, like a mediæval courtly lover or a knight from troubadour poetry, a lock of her hair (Galadriel's beauty is remarked on by the other characters too; there's a fey flirtatiousness about Galadriel and her relations with one or two of the Company, who react like Disney's bashful dwarves when confronted by Snow White – recall the dwarves lining up to be kissed by their new home help in the 1937 animated feature).

But, apart from the Lothlórien sequences, Galadriel has little further direct influence on the plot of *The Lord of the Rings*, and doesn't reappear until the final farewells in the closing pages. However, she has more agency than any of the other women in *The Lord of the Rings*, and is the chief (and only?) female member of the White Council.

Galadriel is eroticized through her long hair, like many a fairy tale princess. In one of the versions of the history of Galadriel and Celeborn, J.R.R. Tolkien portrayed the Eldar as describing Galadriel's hair as capturing the light of the Two Trees, no less. In *The Lord of the Rings*, Gimli is given three of her hairs (in the 2001 Hollywood film he acts like a bashful schoolboy when he requests them), but one of the biggest heroes of Tolkien's *legendarium*, Fëanor, is denied 'even one hair'. Poor Fëanor (*Unfinished Tales*, 230).

Galadriel's history is quite different from the cool, mysterious, aloof, gentle personality she projects in *The Lord of the Rings*. Galadriel is portrayed as a passionate rebel in some of the Middle-earth histories: she rebels against the Valar, rejects their commands, fights with Fëanor, and remains determined to thwart Fëanor any way she can (*Unfinished Tales*, 230). In *The Lord of the Rings* the narrator does not fill in the history behind Galadriel's refusal of the ring. Galadriel tells Frodo that she would become a cruel queen in place of a Dark Lord, and Frodo's given a glimpse of what that might be like. But in the histories of Middle-earth there is a lot more to Galadriel's past, and her desire for power.

ARWEN.

Arwen appears significantly only in the appendices of *The Lord of the Rings* (though some adaptions, such as the 2001-03 movies, bump up her role), in the tale of Aragorn and Arwen, which replays J.R.R. Tolkien's beloved romance of Beren and Lúthien (the central romantic affair in Tolkien's fiction, and the foundation and measure for all subsequent ones).

Arwen is essentially a reincarnation of Lúthien, a way for J.R.R. Tolkien to revisit perhaps his favourite (and most personal) tale from *The Silmarillion*. Like Lúthien, Arwen has to make the same choice between the life of an elf and that of a mortal. She is an idealized beloved (again, like

Galadriel), loved from afar like the lady in courtly love poetry of the mediæval era. She's untouchable, beautiful, ethereal, more the image of an ideal woman than a real flesh-and-blood woman (an image of an image, an abstraction of an abstraction). As in heroic romance and fairy tale, Aragorn has to prove worthy of her, before Elrond will consider him good enough for his daughter (this's one of the motivations for Aragorn's years of wandering in the wilderness, and helping the 'free peoples' in their fight against the enemy). Elrond acts as the stern father figure of the fairy tales Tolkien loved who demands that the suitors for his daughter excel themselves, and prove worthy of her. (In some fairy stories, there are groups of suitors lining up for the hand of the princess, often three sons or princes; in Tolkien's tale, Aragorn had no romantic rivals).

In terms of narrative and action, Arwen does very little in *The Lord of the Rings*. Rather, she's a dreamy presence buried underneath Aragorn's grim, rugged, repressed exterior. If Arwen impinges on the plot at all, it's to be a reminder to Aragorn that there's more to life than hunting orcs or stalking Gollums (Arwen represents Aragorn's personal reward for all of his efforts, with kingship embodying sanctification in the public arena).

And when Arwen is mentioned in the text in amongst the foreground action of *The Lord of the Rings*, Aragorn's typical response is to stand to one side, away from his fellow travellers (such as Legolas and Gimli), and stare longingly to the North (towards Arwen in Rivendell). (Aragorn's years in the wilderness can also appear like the self-imposed abstinence from desire and society of a saint or a courtly lover. Or a monk or a martyr. Of course, it also recalls Christ in the wilderness – one of the many links between Aragorn and Jesus).

Arwen wasn't an inspiring heroine for some female readers. She gets her man, but at what cost? 'He's her prize for... what? Waiting it out? Sewing him a banner? Giving up her immortality?' commented Erica Challis (139). She sits and waits and hopes. Arwen's biggest decision, undoubtedly, is giving up her elvish immortality in order to be with the mortal man.

J.R.R. Tolkien's whole concept of love and romance is unapologetically traditional, conventional, heterosexual, and totally predictable. It's fairy tale love, as in this extract from *Smith of Wootton Major*:

> There they danced together, and for a while he knew what it was to have the swiftness and the power and the joy to accompany her. For a while. But soon as it seemed they halted again, and she stooped and took up a white flower from before her feet, and she set it in his hair. 'Farewell now!' she said. 'Maybe we shall meet again, by the Queen's leave.' (TL, 126)

ÉOWYN.

Éowyn is the warrior woman, a prototype Amazon, a tomboy, dressing up in men's clothes (like Joan of Arc) in order to join the battle (her motivation is not only to prove her worth in combat, and to be one of the boys, but to be near Aragorn). Handily, Faramir is created partly to provide a suitably noble mate for the warrior girl. (She 'just wants to be one of the boys', as Greg Harvey put it, while Faramir was the feminized guy in Tolkien's tale, the wizard's pupil who knows more about Númenor than perhaps even Aragorn).

Éowyn's most significant act in the novel is to fulfil Glorfindel's *Macbeth* prophecy: she vanquishes the Witch-king, the deadliest foe in Middle-earth after the Dark Lord himself. This puts Éowyn up there with the great and the good of Middle-earth, if nothing else does (only Sam with Shelob or Gandalf with the Balrog dispose of monsters on a similar scale in *The Lord of the Rings*). Éowyn's aided by Merry, too, in killing the Witch-king: she provides the death-blow, but the halfling helps to fulfil the prophecy of Glorfindel by stabbing the Witch-king in the leg (Merry's sword is wreathed with enchantments from way back and was found in the Barrow-wight's lair. Handily, it was a blade that saw service against the Witch-king when he ruled the Angmar in the North. Note, too, in the *Macbeth* prophecy, that Meriadoc is no man either, but a halfling).

Éowyn has an active quest that's described in the foreground of *The Lord of the Rings;* she won't be able to marry Aragorn and live happily ever after, so she opts to go to war so she can die heroically in battle. She won't be caged like a bird.

The Éowyn-Aragorn relationship echoes that of Elaine and Lancelot in Alfred Tennyson's *Idylls of the King* and Sir Thomas Malory's *Le Morte d'Arthur*. Malory and Tennyson portray Elaine, the Lady of Istolat, as loving Sir Lancelot from afar, but he refuses her, vowing chastity (but he's also embroiled with Queen Guinevere). Elaine dies of grief, and arrives at King Arthur's palace on a barge (echoing Boromir's fate).

SHELOB.

The giant female spider is another female character (introduced in the text first as the 'she' in Gollum's mutterings), though her monstrosity probably supplants her gender for many readers (she's a monster first, before being female). She's a kind of female Sauron. However, J.R.R. Tolkien's narrator makes a point of referring to her terrifying fecundity, the way she dines on her mates after coitus. Shelob is a classic example of the 'monstrous feminine', the female principle as devouring, archaic, castrating mother. Onto Shelob the hobbits (and the narrator) project everything they detest in themselves (and in women): lust, hatred, sloth.

Folks, there are only *two* female characters among the villains in

Tolkien's fantasy world, and they are both giant spiders! Not exactly the most flattering portraits of women possible! There are no female orcs (so how do they breed?!), no female ringwraiths, balrogs, trolls, whatever.

There isn't space here to go into the sub-category of critical writing on the depiction of women and the monstrous in cinema (the monstrous feminine, as Barbara Creed called it); the links between looking, Lacanian desire, castration, masochism and sadism; monsters as the abject body of the other (and the mother), abjection (Julia Kristeva's concept); monsters as 'perverted' or 'deviant' sexuality; monsters as the phallic, archaic mother; monsters and menstruation (Peter Redgrove and Penelope Shuttle); monsters as the 'sins of the fathers'; monsters embodying sexual difference; monsters as transgressive, dangerous, impure hybrids (Noel Carroll); monsters as projected masculine fear and desire; the links between monsters and all sorts of otherness (lesbianism, homosexuality, racism, etc); or the monster as the 'return of the repressed' (in Slavoj Zizek's view). This film and cultural criticism of monsters can be explored in many books, collections of essays and articles. All of the writers noted above are wonderful starting-points: Kristeva, Zizek, Redgrove, Shuttle, Creed, Carroll, and Lacan. There are many others.

SEX.

The type of sexuality in the Middle-earth tales (what there is of it) is of course thoroughly heterosexual. It's all noble, courtly romances between men and women: Aragorn and Arwen, Faramir and Éowyn, Sam and Rosie Cotton, Beren and Lúthien. (There are no erotic dalliances for Frodo or Bilbo or Legolas or Gimli or Gandalf or Boromir or Wormtongue or Gollum, though. They have to do without). There's no mention whatsoever of any other kind of sexuality (Shelob has a stereotypically gross fecundity, but, although she eats her mates, that too is heterosexual). There is an incestuous episode between brother and sister in *The Silmarillion* (a rare instance in Tolkien's fiction of that kind of sexual relationship, but it does have solid literary precedents, in the mediæval romances Tolkien enjoyed, in Arthurian legend, in Greek mythology, in ancient Egyptian religion, and in the *Bible*). So why, then, Greg Harvey wondered, is *The Lord of the Rings* so popular with adolescent boys and male nerds? (293) There's no sex in *The Lord of the Rings*, and there aren't any babes. No Buffy, Barbarella or Lara Croft.

Lust helps to bring about the fall of Gondolin in Professor Tolkien's mythology. Maeglin desires Idril, but she falls in love with Tuor, who was sent to Gondolin by Ulmo to warn Turgon of the danger his realm's in. Melkor promises that Magelin will have Idril in return for revealing the whereabouts of the hidden realm. Maeglin squeals; Gondolin falls.

That's a rare instance where sexual desire rears itself and impinges directly on the action of a Middle-earth story. But Tolkien still keeps love, lust and passion all depicted in vague terms: no sex scenes for him. He'll describe a kiss, but not much beyond that.

There are sexualized landscapes, though, if one wants to see things that way. J.R.R. Tolkien's Middle-earth fictions have more tunnels, caves, underground cities, burrows and the like than any comparable fiction. But although those tunnels and caves may be Freudian feminine images, they might simply reveal Tolkien's lack of invention, as Mark Roberts pointed out.[2] Not all of the caves and tunnels connote danger and death: there are caves in the Shire and at Helm's Deep which're safe havens.

Alan Vanneman in a review of 2001 film of *The Fellowship of the Ring* on the internet remarked: 'Poor Frodo Baggins! He spends almost all his time in *The Fellowship of the Ring* 1) anticipating penetration; 2) suffering penetration; or 3) recovering from penetration'.

In a 1941 letter to his son Michael (written when he was 48), J.R.R. Tolkien outlined his views on modern marriage and sexuality: for Tolkien, the world was 'fallen', and had been 'falling' and ''going to the bad' all down the ages' ever since Adam, Eve and the Fall (L, 48). Tolkien's views follow the Christian theological stance to the letter: '[t]he devil is endlessly ingenious, and sex is his favourite subject' (ibid.).

What's significantly lacking from J.R.R. Tolkien's *opus* of good vs. evil (*The Lord of the Rings*) is that the Devil (Sauron) doesn't use sex at all. Sometimes, in Tolkien's descriptions of the way Morgoth (and, later, Sauron) flatter and persuade people or elves to get their own way, there's a suggestion of eroticism (but it's more a seduction of charisma, egoism, narcissism and power, rather than sexuality). But, in general, evil is not sexual in Tolkien's Middle-earth stories. Sauron instead uses technology, machines, coercion, violence and scaring the pants off his followers. (Although some of the relationships the villains have in *The Lord of the Rings* – Saruman and Wormtongue, for instance – recall sadomasochistic relationships).

Though love, romance and sex are not J.R.R. Tolkien's strong points, in terms of writing fantasy stories, it is there in the background. For Christopher Wrigley, 'sex is, in large part, what the story is about' (46), because there isn't much sexual activity anymore in Middle-earth: the elves haven't had any children for millennia, the ents have lost the entwives, the populations of Gondor and Rohan and Arnor are failing. Only the Shire seems to be thriving. Middle-earth is in decline, sexually, turning into a wasteland of sterility and abstinence.

Love in *The Lord of the Rings*, for Marion Zimmer Bradley, is strongest in the form of friendship and hero worship – between Sam and Frodo, and Aragorn and other characters. There is also a love of honour, a love of country, and the parental love that characters such as Gandalf and

Galadriel have.[3] Bradley adds that there isn't much romantic love in *Rings*. For Bradley, the 'prevalent emotion in general' is the hero worship of a young man for an older man – the characters' attitude towards both Aragorn and Gandalf.

HOMOSEXUALITY.

Since the 1960s, fans of J.R.R. Tolkien's fiction have discussed (much more than critics) the undertones of homosexuality in *The Lord of the Rings*, particularly in the friendship between Frodo and Sam. For Tolkien, it was a friendship across class boundaries, a replay of the aristocrat and his man-servant from the lower classes, the officer and his bat-man. The hints at homosexuality remain no more than hints, in terms of the text itself: Sam, in particular, is affectionate, tending to his 'master' throughout their journey to Mordor. (Critics have also likened their relationship to Christ and a disciple). At times, the relationship is very intimate: after all, Sam and Frodo are together the entire six or so months of their journey from the Shire to Mordor. Sam holds Frodo, cares for him, and lays his head in his lap (a *Pietà* image).

In *The Two Towers* we find this passage, as Sam watches his master's peaceful face as Frodo sleeps:

> He shook his head, as if finding words useless, and murmured: 'I love him. He's like that, and sometimes it shines through, somehow. But I love him, whether or no.' (TT, 324)

Other aspects of homosexuality or homosociality in *The Lord of the Rings* include the holy male brotherhoods that are formed throughout the narrative: between Aragorn and the Rangers, or between the members of the Fellowship, or between Legolas and Gimli, or between the men of Rohan (and Gondor), or between Faramir and his soldiers. (But as for lesbianism – no, no, no!).

Like thousands of similar stories, *The Lord of the Rings* is, in part, about men going to war, a story of armies and soldiers, and notions such as courage, loyalty, integrity, perseverance, and team work. And apart from those noble issues of going to war for the right reasons, there is also not a little macho posturing, a po-faced self-righteousness, and an intense relationship with violence and aggression (which borders on the scary or psychotic – the blood-lust of Legolas and Gimli at the battle of Helm's Deep, for instance, where they trade body counts. And the high number of deaths in the foreground of the action).

Looking for gay subtexts or evidence of homosexual behaviour in the characters in J.R.R. Tolkien's fiction says much about the readers, fans and critics. If one wants to see it, there is a good deal of it. Consider the Hollywood films of 2001-2003, for instance, which have enough camp costumes, make-up and hair for a Gay and Lesbian Parade (and plenty of leather, chains, piercings and bondage gear in the costumes). Not to mention the scenes of Frodo and Sam staring at each other, sharing smiles.

Both Frodo and Bilbo are something like Victorian (and Edwardian) bourgeois bachelors, self-sufficient by miracle (or heredity, like the aristocracy). Like the clichéd distant great aunts or spinsters in English literary fiction, they're regarded as a little eccentric, but basically harmless. Frodo and Bilbo, in their solitary bachelorhood, also recall the ageing homosexual characters in literature ('bachelor' being at times a synonym for gay men in 19th and early 20th century fiction).

The fact of Frodo's and Bilbo's self-sufficient lifestyle takes precedence over issues such as sexuality (which is hardly ever a concern of J.R.R. Tolkien or his narrator in *The Lord of the Rings* or *The Hobbit*, or any other Middle-earth text). 'Bilbo and Frodo never suffer the slightest twinge of desire, apparently', as one critic put it (N. Otty, 176). Frodo and Bilbo are bookish, cultured, intellectual; they don't work, or live with families, or seem to have many responsibilities, and spend most of their time in leisure pursuits (aided by faithful, simple-minded servants such as Sam). And, significantly, both Frodo and Bilbo are writers: they record events, make notes (remember things for later), and compose songs.

Frodo's (and Bilbo's) character has affinities with the solitary bourgeois outsiders of European fiction from Johann Wolfgang von Goethe and Romanticism onwards (in the books of Albert Camus, Jean-Paul Sartre, André Gide, Aldous Huxley, J.-K. Huysmans, Hermann Hesse, and Knut Hamsun).

In *The Quest of Erebor*, Gandalf comes up with a reason for Bilbo's bachelorhood: he didn't marry (which's odd), Gandalf reckons, because he wanted to remain free so that he could leave on one of his adventures.

There is certainly a class element in *The Hobbit*, Bilbo being portrayed as middle or upper class, and his hesitation to join the dwarves or working class is partly due to class differences. Because the middle class, as Jack Zipes pointed out, 'has always preferred to move upward and side with the ruling forces in society, namely the dragons, largely out of fear and social conditioning' (2002a, 171).

As well as evoking the model of the 18th century landed gentry (aristocrats, with inherited wealth, property, land and servants), Frodo and Bilbo are also reminiscent of, in their class, status, attitudes and interests, the emergent bourgeoisie of the 18th and 19th centuries in the Western world, the middle class that was expanding and taking advantage of technological and industrial developments. While the common view of *The Lord of the Rings* is that it is a book set in the Dark Ages or earlier, thousands of years the past, characters like Bilbo and Frodo are distinctly of the modern age (many commentators have pointed this out, as well as the anachronisms).

J.R.R. Tolkien saw women (in a 1941 letter) as more realistic and practical than men, and less romantic, less sentimental. If they have one delusion, Tolkien suggested, it was 'that they can 'reform' men. They will take a rotter open-eyed, and even when the delusion of reforming him fails, go on loving him' (L, 50).

FAMILIES.

Far stronger than the notion of 'family' in J.R.R. Tolkien's fiction – and particularly his two most famous and well-read works, *The Hobbit* and *The Lord of the Rings* – is friendship, brotherhood, and fellowship. Tolkien's fiction is a 'guy thing'. Both *The Hobbit* and *The Lord of the Rings* concern a bunch of guys on quests (for treasure or to save the world). The impression the reader has is of groups of men bonded by adventure, narrow escapes, heroic deeds, sword fights with orcs, and doing boy stuff like camping out, hiking, fishing, with maybe a little mountain climbing or tunnel exploration.

Apart from the scenes in the Shire, or occasional stop-overs (Rivendell, Crickhollow, Bree, Bombadil's, Lórien), *The Lord of the Rings* is not a domestic, stay-at-home kind of fiction (although the characters – the hobbits especially – sometimes pine for home comforts). In *The Lord of the Rings,* there are few prominent depictions of families. Sam starts a family by the end of the book, Tom and Goldberry seem blissfully happy (but childless – maybe the growing things and animals in the natural world are their 'children'), but Treebeard's lost the entwives, Bilbo has only his nephew, Théoden's son dies off-stage, the steward's family is dysfunctional, Éowyn falls for an unattainable guy, and Aragorn and Frodo (and Gandalf perhaps?) are orphans (or their parents died when they were young).

SOLITUDE.

So many of the characters in *The Lord of the Rings* seem alone: Treebeard, Boromir, Faramir, Denethor, Frodo, Bilbo, Gandalf, Saruman, Legolas, even Galadriel (and Shelob, too). They may have fathers and mothers and sisters and brothers and aunts and uncles and grandmothers and grandfathers but they seldom talk about them. Some of them feel alone and misunderstood (Faramir, Boromir). Some resent their fate and take to brooding in loneliness (Denethor). Some are alone by choice (Gandalf, Saruman, Sauron, Aragorn). Gandalf, however, makes the very wise choice of befriending the hobbits, the friendliest, most comforting creatures in Tolkien's cosmos.

As for Sauron – who'd want to live with him?! There's never a suggestion of a mate for J.R.R. Tolkien's wizard figures: Sauron, Gandalf, Saruman, Radagast and the Witch-king are eternally without companionship of that sort. Poor old Sauron has no one – there's no one his equal, for a start, and he's not the kind of guy to stoop to anyone else's level. And he's got to be a difficult guy to live with.

One of the more striking portrayals of familial relationships is Denethor and his sons, but that's an intense and dysfunctional family, with daddy appearing to transfer some of the blame for the premature loss of his wife Finduilas onto Faramir (and also resenting the man who's destined to supplant him: Aragorn). Elrond and Arwen are glimpsed briefly at Rivendell in the book, but that appears to be another family blighted by misfortune (Celebrían, Elrond's wife, left for the West 500 years earlier). (The 2001-03 films made Elrond and Arwen more prominent, as well as the Arwen-Aragorn romance).

It's striking, too, how many men there are who live without women (especially men in their middle or old age who seem lonely): Elrond's wife Celebrían has gone back to Valinor; Théoden's wife is long gone (and never mentioned); Aragorn imposes exile on himself (partly at Elrond's bidding) rather than be with Arwen; and Denethor's wife Finduilas has died long ago. Boromir, a tall, proud warrior, has no women (and never refers to women except one, Galadriel, whom he mistrusts). Bilbo and Frodo also live without women. And Gimli. And Legolas. And Gandalf. And many others. In the appendices and genealogies, Pippin marries Diamond of Long Cleeve, but Merry's wife or children aren't mentioned (there is the suggestion of a son). Having Sam have both a wife, children and a life in Middle-earth and also leaving for the West is a kind of cheat, because the book has already stated that one can't do both.

NOTES: J.R.R. TOLKIEN AND FEMINISM

1. For example, Hugh Keenan in N. Isaacs, 71.
2. M. Roberts, "Adventure In English", *Essays In Criticism*, 6, 1956.
3. In N. Isaacs, 109.

chapter 10

CRITICISM OF J.R.R. TOLKIEN'S WORK

> Nothing has astonished me more (and I think my publishers) than the
> welcome given to *The Lord of the Rings.* But it is, of course, a constant
> source of consolation and pleasure to me. And, I may say, a piece of
> singular good fortune, much envied by some of my contemporaries.

J.R.R. Tolkien, *Letters* (221)

The Lord of the Rings and Ronald Tolkien himself are easy targets for lit'ry
critics intent on denigrating one of the most popular books of the 20th
century. *The Lord of the Rings* is derided as being mere 'fantasy', or
'escapism'. Or it's for children, and not worthy of serious contemplation. Or
it's Christian.

J.R.R. Tolkien is denigrated as a reactionary, tweedy Oxford don who
lived in a romanticized, nostalgic past. And the readers and fans are
attacked too – they're geeks, nerds, hippies, pagans, weirdos.

Since the 1960s, J.R.R. Tolkien's tome was branded as sexist, racist,
fascist, reactionary, patriarchal, paternalistic, anti-intellectual, and
conservative. The divergence of opinion over *The Lord of the Rings* wasn't
split along 'high art' vs. 'low art' or 'intellectual' vs. 'popular' taste lines,
because quite a few dons, academics, critics and poets, the guardians of
'high culture', loved it.

No one has a *moderate* opinion of *The Lord of the Rings,* W.H. Auden
remarked: 'either, like myself, people find it a masterpiece of its genre or
they cannot abide it'.[1]

Criticisms of J.R.R. Tolkien and *The Lord of the Rings* have included:
the immaturity and superficiality of the characters • the sexism of the
piece • the lack of female characters • the racial stereotyping (the villains
are Eastern European, or Oriental) • the awkward structure (Sam and
Frodo disappear for a whole book – Book 3) • the change in tone from early
*Hobbit*ish scenes to the serious quest • the pompous, churchy dialogue
(especially in the second half, all those 'thees' and 'thous') • the
conservative, reactionary ideology • none of the characters really changes
or grows, psychologically or morally (instead, they become more like they

were at the start: '[t]he dwarves become more dwarfish, the elves more elvish, the orcs more orc-like, even the hobbits more hobbity') • 2 the limitations of Tolkien's moral, political and sociological views (too simplistic, too restrictive, dualistic) • the bad verse • good and evil are unquestioned absolutes, with no moral ambiguity or complexity in the characters or situations • there is no adult sexuality or mature sexual relationships • the story doesn't seem to connect with the social reality of the reader, and so on.

> I think that the vision of society put forward in *The Lord of the Rings* is old-fashioned, wrong-headed and a lethal model for late 20th century living… [wrote Kenneth McLeish] we live in a nasty, dangerous and brutal world, and dressing up in elven-cloaks, baking lembas and writing poems in Entish, though a commendable and delightful game, is a way of avoiding, not finding, the truth of life.3

For some critics, J.R.R. Tolkien's depiction of war is spiritualized, naïve, bloodless, the action bodiless and the corpses as picturesque as the rocks and trees.4 Tolkien turns the wars of 1914-18 and 1939-45, for Fred Inglis, into

> entirely unphysical, bloodless, corpseless ceremonies of stirring names, ritual swordplay, stately parades, and grave orisons: the arias and ensembles of spiritualized combat. (ib., 39).

In Inglis's view, J.R.R. Tolkien is 'ineffably English, with England's old and grim snobbery and stupidity, and England's excellent idealism and high-mindedness' (1983, 39). For Colin Wilson, Tolkien's evocation mediæval life is idealized and generalized; he wasn't really interested in the details of how people really lived from day to day.

'The hero has no serious temptations', is lured by no insidious enchantments, perplexed by few problems', Edmund Wilson complained, and story boils down to a simplistic confrontation of good against evil.5 For Wilson, *The Lord* was 'essentially a children's book – a children's book which has somehow got out of hand', and there wasn't much that would go over the head of a 7 year-old child (ib., 51).

For Jack Zipes, there were no significant changes between the beginnings and the ends of both *The Hobbit* and *The Lord of the Rings*. Evil has been temporarily vanquished, but both Bilbo and Frodo sink back into the old ways of domesticated life. Their humble acceptance of home life is all very well, but home life 'does not become endowed with a quality of freedom' (2002a, 174). By the end of *The Hobbit* and *The Lord of the Rings*, Bilbo and Frodo appear to be enlightened, but the seven deadly sins are still at work, and the secret message is that there are forces greater than humans in the world, and we must know our place, accept it, do our duty when we are called upon in the name of good, i.e., God.

Some critics (such as Christopher Manlove) have pointed out that there doesn't seem to be much free will at work in *The Lord of the Rings*. Frodo seems to make the right choice every time, and the 'possibility of making a wrong choice recedes to vanishing point, and with it the very idea of choice'.6 At each moment, presented with choices, Frodo always makes the right decision. Events unfold in *The Lord of the Rings* with an inescapable inevitability: Sauron could never win, Frodo and the allies could never lose. And, although this is a cataclysmic war of the ring in Middle-earth, hardly anyone significant perishes (i.e., the costs of victory are not that great).

Frodo appears to be an unflawed hero; there's no bad side to him, and he always does the right thing, always makes the right choice. Although the wise elders of Middle-earth tell him that the ring tempts the bearer to grasp power and set themselves up as another Dark Lord, Frodo is never tempted for all the months he possesses the ring, until the very last moment. For some critics, this is a serious flaw in *The Lord of the Rings,* because there's never a serious possibility that events will turn out any other way, or that characters such as Frodo will act any other way. It also means that the world of Middle-earth is clearly divided into good and evil, and that no characters are really ambiguous or complex (they're either ultimately goodies or baddies).

It's true that the adversaries that Frodo and his pals are up against are fearsome, that their courage, hardship and efforts are real, but, 'for the reader, who sees that it is not mortal will but luck which is the architect of success, the struggles with the evil forces become unreal, mere posturings in a rigged bout', as Christopher Manlove put it (1975, 183). For critics like Manlove, it's not the Valar, or destiny, that is the cause of success in *The Lord of the Rings,* but how Tolkien has skewed the story from the beginning to have only one outcome: the heroes win.

Even so, even if every part of the story is predictable and certain from the outset, with no possibility that the villains will triumph, *The Lord of the Rings* is still a compelling tale. It's partly because readers often don't care as much as some critics think people should about that kind of thing. For instance, *The Lord of the Rings* is a book that is regularly re-read by many people. They *already* know the story, how it ends, who triumphs. But they still read it, because there's so much to enjoy in it, apart from the plot. And they'll watch the same film over and over, or a soap opera each evening (soaps have the same stories, same situations, same characters month after month). It's slightly different with seeing a play at the theatre, because there are many more variables with each performance, and each new production. But it's still *King Lear* or *The Doll's House* or *The Producers* or *The Lion King* yet again.

Anne Petty suggested that academic critics couldn't dismiss J.R.R. Tolkien out of hand, because he 'was *one of them*': he had impeccable academic credentials (xiv). He wasn't an amateur writer; instead, 'he would have to be punished for writing beneath his station, so to speak'. His fiction threatened literary critics' authority.

For Judith Crist, writing in *Ladies' Home Journal* in 1967, *The Lord of the Rings* was a new form of romantic, escapist fiction, a modern adult version of the fairy tales children loved. People might not be reading the *Aeneid*, the *Odyssey* or Walter Scott's novels anymore, but they could capture that same romantic, heroic pleasure from *The Lord of the Rings*.

One of J.R.R. Tolkien's friends told him that he only read *The Lord of the Rings* at Lent 'because it was so hard and bitter', because it wasn't a happy story. That tells a lot about Tolkien's sort of friends and their Christian thinking.

For Roger Sale, J.R.R. Tolkien may not be the best writer around about battles and heroism, but 'as a writer about danger he hardly has an equal'.[7]

The hobbits were central to *The Lord* – for J.R.R. Tolkien and for many critics. Roger Sale remarked that 'without them the trilogy would not stand a chance'.[8] The book needs the hobbits to bring everything else – the history of Middle-earth, the ring, the war – alive. Maybe, but there's still plenty to enjoy in *The Lord of the Rings* apart the hobbits.

The hobbits are necessary from a narrative point-of-view, to introduce the world of Middle-earth to the reader, but they also have their limitations, and J.R.R. Tolkien needs other characters (such as Gandalf and Aragorn) to explain much of Middle-earth. The perception of the hobbits is thus central but also limited, and Tolkien has to go beyond it all the time.[9] For Burton Raffel, Sam was a stock character, lovable and useful but 'as a characterization virtually meaningless'.[10]

J.R.R. Tolkien's characters do tend to be types, and narrow ones at that. But they do have their flaws, and they do sometimes act out of character. And there are characters who are ambiguous and troubled (such as Gollum and Boromir).

For some critics, all the noise and action of the war in the West, at Pelennor, at Helm's Deep, at Isengard, is impressive, but not a patch on the real heart of the book, which's the story of Frodo, Sam and Gollum: 'all that the first volume promised and all that the war in the west cannot offer are delivered with a pressure and stateliness that belongs to great literature', commented Roger Sale.[11]

J.R.R. Tolkien wondered whether the extreme antipathy that some of his reviewers felt towards his fiction was evidence of some revulsion in themselves, not in his work. Certainly, the bile that Tolkien's work attracted (and still attracts) may point to some anxieties, fears and revulsions in the reviewers, rather than something inherent in the work. One should not underestimate the egotism and jealousy of critics and writers, either: Tolkien's success has been so enormous, it's bound to engender hostility in some writers.

Erica Challis tried to find an agreement between J.R.R. Tolkien's fiction and Taoism, and admitted that it was 'difficult, certainly, but not impossible'. She was thinking in terms of Tolkien's concepts of compassion, pity, and hope, with Gandalf as a Taoist sage (E. Challis, 51).

Some writers linked 9/11 and the events that followed it – America going to war in Iraq and the 'war on terror'– with the free peoples of Middle-earth being tempted to use the ring to defeat Sauron (the nuclear weaponry issue, which Tolkien strongly denied: Tolkien always tried to carve out a niche for his epic fantasy work that was separate from history and the real world).[12]

The Haradrim are identified with Islam and the Middle East and Magreb in their language, weaponry, and appearance. The men of Far Harad in *The Return of the King* are described as 'like half-trolls with white eyes and red tongues'.

Defending J.R.R. Tolkien against charges of racism, some critics and fans have pointed out that it's not correct to apply late 20th century or early 21st century ideology and politics to fictions written in the middle of the 20th century, because the world was politically different then. Maybe. But that's a shaky defence, which crumples under closer examination. It's true that the races of Middle-earth are also mythical and fantastical renditions, literary creations which are there for dramatic and symbolic purposes.

The fellowship constitutes a kind of 'corporate hero', a hero that's made up from the characteristics of a wizard, two men, an elf, a dwarf and four hobbits. It's a pluralist, multi-ethnic group, a combination of races, creeds and beliefs. That's the positive spin on the fellowship, but they are all white, Western types, too (and Tolkien's illustrators and filmmakers tend to be depict them as white, too. But there aren't any really *good* reasons for not having a black Aragorn or a black Gandalf in illustrations, for instance).

NOTES: CRITICISM OF TOLKIEN'S WORK

1. W. Auden, in A. Becker, 44.
2. K. McLeish, "The Rippingest Yarn of All", in R. Giddings, 1983, 126.
3. K. McLeish, in ib., 134.
4. F. Inglis, "Gentility and Powerlessness: and the New Class", in R. Giddings, 1983, 36.
5. In A. Becker, 52.
6. C. Manlove, 1975, 177.
7. In N. Isaacs, 262.

8. E. Challis, 61.
9. In N. Isaacs, 263.
10. R. Sale, in N. Isaacs, 265.
11. In N. Isaacs, 237.
12. In N. Isaacs, 270.

Ċhảpτεp̣ ıı

WRITING *THE LORD OF THE RINGS*

"But if one had to choose one and one only, I'd choose Samwise."
"Then you'd be wrong, Mr Frodo," said Sam. "For without you I'm
nothing. But you and me together, Mr Frodo: well, that's more than
either alone."

J.R.R. Tolkien, *The Lord of the Rings* (HME, 9, 92).

WRITING *THE LORD OF THE RINGS*

In this chapter I explore some of the alternatives and variations that J.R.R.
Tolkien developed in the course of writing *The Lord of the Rings*. Some
were far-reaching, but many were about small details. I'm assuming that
the reader is familiar with *The Lord of the Rings*. Like many writers, Tolkien
could be wholly immersed in his fictional world (as some writers have to
do), and could debate at length what to outsiders would seem trivial
details. Tolkien liked to get everything absolutely correct, and wasn't
satisfied until it was. The downside of this perfectionism was an obsessive
pursuit of getting it right. And Tolkien, like so many writers, could get
bogged down in harmonziing details or facts. And, sometimes, the
perfectionism could express itself in inaction and dissatisfaction, a
frustration with ever getting it right. Tolkien's perfectionism was another
reason for his low output in terms of publication. Tolkien also had a family
to support, work as a professor, and as an examiner.

    J.R.R. Tolkien said in his letters that he was trying to construct a
modern version of a myth or cycle for Britain (or England) in response to
what he saw as the poverty of British mythology and legend (L, 144).
Although Tolkien wanted to create a new mythology for England/ Britain,
Jim Smith and J. Clive Matthews asked why that should be necessary 'in a
country over-burdened with national myths, heroes and mythic figures'
(2004, 21).

    The Lord of the Rings, J.R.R. Tolkien said, was intended to round off
the long cycle of Middle-earth legends, to bring together all of the
elements, the stories of elves, men, hobbits, kings, horsemen, ents, orcs,

wizards and Ringwraiths (L, 159). As well resolving all of the storylines and character arcs, *The Lord of the Rings* also ends with some key events: the final departure of the elves from Middle-earth, and the return of the true king. And, significantly, *The Lord of the Rings* closes with a royal wedding, just like a fairy tale, with the two chief elements – elves and humanity – conjoined symbolically by the marriage of Arwen and Aragorn (L, 160).

In one of his most important letters (no. 131), to Milton Waldman, written in late 1951, Tolkien explained why he wrote *The Lord of the Rings*:

> I was from early days aggrieved by the poverty of my own beloved country: it had no stories of its own (bound up with its tongue and soil), not of the quality that I sought, and found (as an ingredient) in legends of other lands. There was Greek, and Celtic, and Romance, Germanic, Scandinavian, and Finnish (which greatly affected me); but nothing English, save impoverished chap-book stuff. Of course, there was and is all the Arthurian world, but powerful as it is, it is imperfectly naturalized, associated with the soil of Britain but not with English; and does not replace what I felt to be missing. For one thing, its 'faerie' is too lavish, and fantastical, incoherent and repetitive. (L, 144)

BEGINNINGS.

J.R.R. Tolkien was not a writer who found beginnings to books a problem. He said he had written first chapters of *The Lord of the Rings,* but often stalled on the further development of the story (L, 29). He made this comment in February, 1938, *a propos* the first chapter of his *Hobbit* sequel (for a long time *The Lord of the Rings* was known only as the follow-up to *The Hobbit*). 'I have only the vaguest notions of how to proceed. Not ever intending any sequel, I fear I squandered all my favourite 'motifs' and characters on the original *Hobbit*', he mused (L, 29). Four months later, Tolkien seemed to have lost his appetite for *The Lord of the Rings*: '[i]t has lost my favour, and I have no idea what to do with it' (L, 38).

One of the problems, J.R.R. Tolkien explained, was that *The Hobbit* was never intended to have a sequel. He had tied up all the loose ends and plot strands in *The Hobbit*: there was no need for a further book. Also, Tolkien said, he had written the fairy tale's 'happy ever after' ending to *The Hobbit*, and couldn't see a way past it. (The problem doesn't crop up in the Hollywood film industry any more, because films are routinely written and produced with sequels in mind – with holes left open for developments of plots and characters).

J.R.R. Tolkien would write a story over and over by starting at the beginning, Christopher Tolkien explained, but he wouldn't be rewriting the original version, but the one that came before it. There would be layer upon layer of rewrites. Often the prose styles didn't match, so part of Christopher Tolkien's task was to find a 'median style' for posthumous works.

J.R.R. Tolkien absorbed criticism, but the results of it were radical: he either ignored it completely and carried on, or he began the work from scratch, C.S. Lewis observed.[1]

Many authors today might think twice about embarking on a 1,000 page-plus novel without an advance or a guarantee of publication (instead, Ronald Tolkien was supporting himself and his family, as hundreds of writers and artists have done before and since, by teaching). Tolkien, for instance, didn't write out a synopsis of the book and a couple of chapters and send it to publishers in the hope that some company would eventually take a chance on it. Writers' handbooks today emphasize creating one-page synopses, or composing treatments a few pages long, and sending that to publishers with a couple of sample chapters and a covering letter. With *The Lord of the Rings,* Tolkien didn't go that route at all.

Like so many artists and writers when they're creating a work, J.R.R. Tolkien said he had 'very little particular, conscious, intellectual intention in mind at any point' during the writing of *The Lord of the Rings* (L, 211). The reader can easily discern when Tolkien is discovering his story along the way – that's one of the pluses of writing a book without an overall plan (the minuses, of course, are that the writer can get stuck, not sure where to go next, as Tolkien often did in the composition of *The Lord of the Rings*). The book, Tolkien explained, was 'written backwards as well as forwards'. Plans that Tolkien made for the story turned out to be of no use by the time he'd got there. As Tolkien wrote *The Lord of the Rings*, the narrative developed and grew, taking a form something like a tree, with the trunk forming three branches at Rauros when the fellowship breaks up.[2]

J.R.R. Tolkien acknowledged that, like so many writers, much of *The Lord of the Rings* was made up on the spot, as he wrote the book. He'd used Tom Bombadil before, and one or two other elements (such as the necromancer, Sauron, who became the Dark Lord), but Tolkien was discovering the major parts of *The Lord of the Rings* as the reader does when s/he reads the book: the Mines of Moria, Lothlórien, Strider, Frodo, Fangorn, the House of Eorl, the Stewards of Gondor, the *palantíri* and Saruman (L, 216-7).

Looking back on *The Lord of the Rings*, J.R.R. Tolkien said he was most moved by the description of Cerin Amroth (in *The Fellowship of the Ring*, chapter 6 of the second book). He also mentioned Gollum's failure to repent when Sam disturbs him, and the arrival of Rohirrim at cockcrow (L, 221).

'Of course the book was written to please myself (at different levels), and as an experiment in the arts of long narrative, and of inducing 'Secondary Belief'', J.R.R. Tolkien said (L, 412). The sheer love of writing comes across strongly in *The Lord of the Rings.* Remember that Tolkien wasn't under a contract when he was writing *The Lord of the Rings,* wasn't writing it to order, didn't have an advance from a publisher, and was not writing to a deadline (there was seventeen years between the publication of *The Hobbit* and *The Lord of the Rings*). Tolkien told his publisher, Stanley Unwin, that a follow-up to *The Hobbit* would be forthcoming (having been very disappointed when Unwin turned down *The Silmarllion*), but just went ahead and started writing *The Lord of the Rings* with no definite idea how long the book would be, nor how long it would take him to complete it (nor when or if he would get paid for it). In other words, Tolkien was writing *The Lord of the Rings* with only one successful book published (*The Hobbit*); he had some smaller texts in print, but he was by no means a much-published, established and successful author.

J.R.R. Tolkien wondered how he could have kept up the momentum in writing *The Lord of the Rings*, and concluded that 'from the beginning it began to catch up in its narrative folds visions of most of the things that I have most loved or hated' (L, 257).

In a 1962 letter, J.R.R. Tolkien outlined the history of writing *The Lord of the Rings*: he had written up to chapter 10 of Book 3 and got stuck (around the middle of WW2). In 1944, he forced himself to write the fourth book. The whole first draft was completed by 1949; he subsequently typed out the first draft, then he typed it again as he revised it (L, 321). Those were the days before computers or photocopiers, when a writer could make a copy using carbon paper, as the work was written on a typewriter, but further copies were often produced simply by retyping the whole thing (and many writers would opt to make revisions as they went along). Henry Miller and Anaïs Nin, for instance, retyped whole books in the 1930s so they could have extra copies to send to people (such as publishers).

HOBBITS.

Writing about hobbits was a mode of writing which Ronald Tolkien admitted he could happily continue, beyond the endurance of even his most ardent fans: Tolkien wrote in mid-1938:

> I am personally immensely amused by hobbits as such, and can contemplate them eating and making their rather fatuous jokes indefinitely; but I find that is not the case with even my most devoted 'fans' (such as Mr Lewis and ?Rayner Unwin). (HME, 6, 108)

In 'hobbit-mode', J.R.R. Tolkien could write easily and at length. It was a mind-set, a way of looking at things, that Tolkien was wholly comfortable with. It's one of the strengths of *The Lord of the Rings* that the hobbits are so solidly, convincingly rendered. The hobbit-prose gives *The Lord of the Rings* an earthy foundation. The hobbits are the entry point for the reader – note how the story starts with them, not with any of the many other races or creatures, before it opens out to include elves and kings and wizards and monsters and orcs and Dark Lords (and it ends, like *The Hobbit*, with hobbits too, and hobbits in their home country). (Many adaptors of *The Lord of the Rings*, however, chose to open with a prologue outlining the history of Middle-earth).

The hobbits embody most of the key positive qualities that Tolkien's Middle-earth stories uphold: friendship, loyalty, nobility, good living, and courage when necessary. The hobbits are the most cherished characters in Tolkien's mythos (and not only by the author, his narrator, and millions of readers), because they really do *rise to the occasion* in *The Lord of the Rings* – more, even, than Aragorn (who has been preparing for his future leadership and kingship for decades, and is highborn, and has great teachers, like Elrond and Gandalf). It's one of the marks of Tolkien's conception of heroes and the heroic mode, that even regular folk can rise to greatness when necessary. Not every hero is morally pure in Tolkien's mythology. As Greg Harvey pointed out, Bilbo was both a thief (stealing Gollum's ring) and a cheat (his question, what have I got in my pocket? isn't a proper riddle).3

Hobbits having hairy, bare feet was apparently inspired by Tolkien's friend at Exeter College, Allen Barnett, who told J.R.R. Tolkien tales of the kids in Kentucky who went about barefoot and stole tobacco from casks (D. Grotta, 106).

THE RING. In looking back on how he developed his fairy stories from *The Hobbit* to *The Lord of the Rings*, J.R.R Tolkien cited the ring as an obvious choice for development. Once you have the ring, the necromancer becomes the Dark Lord, and the quest presents itself as the backbone of the new story, Tolkien said (L, 216). Elrond, Moria and the dwarves also came from *The Hobbit*. It's easy now to go back and see how everything fits into place, though (and not every writer has the imagination of a Tolkien).

The climax of *The Lord of the Rings* pivots around the concept of (Christian) forgiveness, when Frodo appears to 'fail' in the climactic scene at Mount Doom (L, 233). It's a 'sacrifical' moment, when the fate of the world rests upon an individual. According to J.R.R. Tolkien, seen in his own terms, Frodo does fail, and the quest itself was doomed to fail from the beginning:

> The Quest [therefore] was bound to fail as a piece of world-plan, and also was bound to end in disaster as the story of humble Frodo's development to the 'noble', his sanctification. Fail it would and did as far as Frodo considered alone was concerned. (L, 234)

For J.R.R. Tolkien, it was inevitable, given the corrupting power of the ring, that Frodo would be unable to destroy it (L, 325). What 'saved' Frodo, and the world, Tolkien explained, was precisely his pity, his generosity. Of course, it just so happened that Gollum's act and Frodo's failure occurred at a critical point, standing right above the Crack of Doom, the only place the ring can be destroyed (if the final confrontation over the ring had taken place at an earlier time, it would have required some tricky manœuvring on the author's part to bring the ring to Orodruin).

> He [Gollum] did rob him and injure him in the end [wrote Tolkien] – but by a 'grace', that last betrayal was at a precise juncture when the final evil deed was the most beneficial thing any one cd. have done for Frodo! By a situation created by his 'forgiveness', he was saved himself, and relieved of his burden. He was very justly accorded the highest honours… (L, 234)

Frodo's 'failure' was part of J.R.R. Tolkien's theory of 'true nobility and heroism', pity and mercy (L, 326). It wasn't a 'moral' failure, for Tolkien.

> At the last moment the pressure of the Ring would reach its maximum – impossible, I should have said, for anyone to resist, certainly after long possession, months of increasing torment, and when starved and exhausted. (ibid.)

Frodo had done all he could, he had given up everything he had, in order to save the world. His collapse at the Crack of Doom was the result of extreme physical and psychological hardship, as a ringbearer, understandable in anyone, J.R.R. Tolkien explained, who had borne the ring that long (L, 327). Frodo's failure was built into the narrative from early on, Tolkien said (L, 251): it was inevitable that he would fail. Tolkien cited the *Lord's Prayer* in connection with Frodo's plight: 'lead us not into temptation, but deliver us from evil' (L, 252). Mercy was part of Tolkien's plan here – note that Frodo comes to Mordor weaponless, saying that he will not need a weapon any more, nor strike another blow (Frodo's antipathy towards aggression continues through the scouring of the Shire sequence. And his new attitude to pity is extended to Saruman, and the wizard recognizes it, but still despises Frodo – lacking that kind of pity is one of Saruman's fatal flaws).

NOTES: WRITING *THE LORD OF THE RINGS*

1. H. Carpenter, 1995, 149.
2. C. Manlove, 1999, 55.
3. G. Harvey, 111.

THE HISTORY OF WRITING *THE LORD OF THE RINGS*

Ronald Tolkien did not write *The Lord of the Rings* continuously for the 17 years between 1937, when he began it, and 1954, when the first volume was published. Like many (perhaps most) artistic endeavours, *The Lord of the Rings* was written in waves of inspiration and hard work, and periods when Tolkien got stuck, was sidetracked, or busy with other things, or simply lost interest. At times he wasn't sure if what he was creating was any good. He wrote to Stanley Unwin on September 15, 1939: 'I do not suppose this any longer interests you greatly'. At that time Tolkien could not know that what he was writing would interest millions of people greatly.

Writing the first part of *The Lord of the Rings* J.R.R. Tolkien experienced 'doubts, indecisions, unpickings, restructurings, and false starts' (HME, 6, 5). As the story developed, Tolkien went back and rewrote earlier chapters to incorporate his new ideas. He rewrote the first chapters a number of times until he was satisfied sufficiently to continue (and even then he went back and rewrote it again, and added to it again when the rest of the book had been written).

In general, the narrative became increasingly complex. J.R.R. Tolkien was obsessed with details, and with getting the details in his books absolutely spot-on, so much of his time and effort in rewriting *The Lord of the Rings* seemed to have been spent on synchronizing all of the details – the characters' names, the family trees, the time scales, the place names. It wasn't always a case of additions in the narrative: sometimes Tolkien added events or character traits which he later thought better of and scrubbed out. Some of the additions, such as the idea of 'elf-wraiths', didn't fit in with the rest of the narrative as it developed.

Many times J.R.R. Tolkien would halt the writing of *The Lord of the Rings* and contemplate what had been achieved. One of his techniques was to go back and rewrite everything that had been written entirely, right back to the start (that would an extreme measure for some writers – especially those writing to deadlines). He did this most often with the first chapters of *The Fellowship of the Ring*, but he also went back and completely reworked *The Fellowship of the Ring* many times through the whole story. Sometimes he would come up with radical ways of proceeding. One of his notes, of August, 1939, makes *'Bilbo* the hero all through', with 'Merry and Frodo his companions. This helps with Gollum... Gandalf is *not* present to let off fireworks' (HME, 370).

As Christopher Tolkien explained, Tolkien would often write in pencil, sometimes quite faint, and write in ink on top, altering as he went (this may partly have been to save on paper; certainly as WW2 progressed, paper was in short supply). He often used all sorts of paper (such as the backs of examination papers). Sometimes, when he was jotting down ideas, his handwriting would be so rapid it would be tricky to decipher. Tolkien was a writer who would happily pile up emendations on top of each other on a handwritten text, making it difficult for editors coming to the papers after the author's death to reach a 'final' version. Of "The Ring Goes South" manuscript, for instance, Christopher Tolkien wrote: '[t]his is an outstandingly difficult manuscript, and difficult to represent' (HME, 6, 415).

Rivendell seemed to be a point in the narrative that J.R.R. Tolkien reached some three times (Christopher Tolkien reckoned his father wrote the story of *The Lord of the Rings* three times up to the point of the Last Homely Gas Station East of the Sea). Parts of the story were taken out and placed elsewhere in the narrative. The large chunks of back-story concerning the history of Middle-earth, related by Gandalf at Hobbiton in "The Shadow of the Past", and by Elrond, Glóin, Gandalf and Boromir and others at Rivendell in "The Council of Elrond", are vital, but could have been placed at various points in the narrative line.

J.R.R. Tolkien was also conscious of having to fuse together the narratives of Middle-earth in his *Silmarillion* and *The Hobbit* in his *Hobbit* sequel. This meant going back and adjusting *The Hobbit* later on. It wasn't enough that Tolkien could simply say that the two books, *The Hobbit* and *The Lord of the Rings*, were different versions of Middle-earth, written at different times. He wanted them to harmonize. Tolkien was one of those writers who had to make sure that every aspect of his Secondary World of Middle-earth was correct in every respect, no matter how small or inconsequential.

Part of *The Lord of the Rings* was written while J.R.R. Tolkien was on holiday in Sidmouth in Devon in Summer, 1938. A new burst of enthusiasm for the story occurred around August, 1938, with Tolkien having the hobbits entering the Old Forest.

By October, 1938, J.R.R. Tolkien had reached Weathertop, but large parts of the story were still unwritten and unconceived. Fangorn, Lórien, Rohan, Gondor, Isengard, Osgiliath, Henneth Annûn and other realms were yet to be created.

J.R.R. Tolkien halted on the writing of *The Lord of the Rings* when he reached Balin's tomb in Moria (Tolkien reckoned it was about the end of 1940 he got stuck, and resumed almost a year later in late 1941; Christopher Tolkien estimated his father meant 1939-40, not 1940-41, for the hiatus on the composition of *The Lord of the Rings*). No one's sure why Tolkien stopped writing *The Lord of the Rings* at this point, but his workload at the university was distracting him, as well as his son Michael being injured in January, 1941. Humphrey Carpenter said that there wasn't any particular external reason why Tolkien halted or delayed composing the first books of *The Lord of the Rings.*

In 1942, J.R.R. Tolkien reckoned that *The Lord of the Rings* would need only another six chapters to complete it: Tolkien was then at the chapter "Flotsam and Jetsam". Needless to say, there turned out to be plenty more to come (in H. Carpenter, 1995, 198).

In a May, 1944 letter, J.R.R. Tolkien spoke about struggling with the chapters on Frodo and Sam reaching the high pass over Mordor, and how difficult it was 'to keep the pitch up: no easy level will do; and there are all sorts of minor problems of plot and mechanism' (L, 81).

When J.R.R. Tolkien reached Cirith Ungol, he halted writing *The Lord of the Rings* for at least two years (between October, 1944 and Summer, 1946). One reason was he had got his hero, as he put it, into 'such a fix than not even an author will be able to extricate him without labour and difficulty' (*Letters*, no. 91). And Tolkien reworked those chapters a number of times to find the most satisfying narrative solution. Another reason was that he was tired by writing the book.

By 1947 J.R.R. Tolkien had completed his first draft of *The Lord of the Rings,* but continued to work on it for the next two years, adding sections, and rewriting parts. By October, 1948, Tolkien announced that he had completed *The Lord of the Rings* to his satisfaction (L, 131). In 1949, he rewrote it all again when he typed it up. Tolkien didn't want any loose ends in *The Lord of the Rings,* and spent a good deal of time 'tying up the loose ends'.

Writing the end of *The Lord of the Rings* was moving for J.R.R. Tolkien – he said that he had wept when he was writing the Field of Cormallen scene, where the hobbits are welcomed back.

As he neared the climax of the book, J.R.R. Tolkien recognized that a certain level of tension had to be maintained (because 'no easy level will do'). That meant rewriting it to get it right: 'I wrote and tore up and rewrote most of it a good many times', Tolkien recounted in a 1944 letter about the Faramir and Cirith Ungol chapters.

J.R.R. Tolkien certainly did a lot of rewriting. He enjoyed it. He liked to work over texts until they were just right. That's why there are so many different versions of the myths of Middle-earth – they are ultimately pretty much the same stories, but Tolkien wrote many versions of them. So the twelve big *History of Middle-earth* volumes go over the same tales again and again, written at different stages of Tolkien's writing life. The *History of Middle-earth* volumes constitute a kind of literary biography, because they extend from Tolkien's youth to his old age, and he was writing the tales over a period of many years (HME, 12, x).

J.R.R. Tolkien was disappointed by Stanley Unwin's son Rayner's reactions to an early draft of Book 1 of *The Lord of the Rings* (Tolkien had given it to the Unwins to read in July, 1947): Tolkien was convinced he had put in much more humour than Unwin junior found. Tolkien responded to Rayner Unwin's comments that the story was 'macabre and intensified' beyond *The Hobbit* by explaining that the horror should be 'really horrible': 'for every romance that takes things seriously must have a warp of fear and horror' (L, 120).

Much of the background historical material in the second chapter of *The Lord of the Rings* was cut out by J.R.R. Tolkien in 1947 (perhaps in response to Rayner Unwin's comments on reading an early draft of it [L, 124]). Some of this material would find its way into the appendices, and into the *History of Middle-earth* volumes. (Figures such as Rayner Unwin, then, may have had a significant influence on the development of *The Lord of the Rings,* as well as, say, the Inklings, or Tolkien's children).

J.R.R. Tolkien reckoned there were some 600,000 words in *The Lord of the Rings* (as it stood in 1950 [L, 136]). The whole MS was carefully rewritten. 'And the placing, size, style, and contribution to the whole of all the features, incidents and chapters has been laboriously pondered', he remarked (L, 160).

The Lord of the Rings isn't as lengthy a novel as some think. *The Fellowship of the Ring* is long (491 pages in the 1966 edition, minus the prologue), *The Two Towers* is 431 pages, and *The Return of the King* is 364 pages long, and features 277 pages of additional material (appendices, chronologies, maps and even an index – not many novels have an index). That makes 1,286 of text, but notice how the publishers bulked up the books by employing a large font size, fewer words per line, and fewer lines per page, than many other famously long books. The Allen & Unwin paperback (1974) is 1,309 pages of story (excluding maps and synopses), but those pages have far fewer words per page than many novels (consider 19th century novels: Charles Dickens, Fyodor Dostoievsky, Leo Tolstoy, George Eliot, etc). *The Lord of the Rings* is still lengthy, though, in terms of the amount of things that happen and the number of characters.

Not the longest book, then: *Remembrance of Times Past* is 1.5 million words; *Clarissa* by Samuel Richardson is one million plus; Anthony Powell's *A Dance To the Music of Time* cycle is over a million; *Mission Earth* by L. Ron Hubbard is 1.2 million. (Hands up who started Marcel Proust but didn't finish it? I didn't).

EARLY DRAFTS OF *THE LORD OF THE RINGS*

Christopher Tolkien did a marvellous job of sifting through his father's drafts for *The Lord of the Rings* and presenting them in four of the *History of Middle-earth* volumes. *The Return of the Shadow, The Treason of Isengard, The War of the Ring* and *Sauron Defeated* offer a fascinating look at Tolkien's working methods, and how the narrative of *The Lord of the Rings* developed over weeks, months and years, between the late Thirties and the mid-Fifties. (It wasn't Christopher Tolkien's intention, though, to undertake the history of the writing of *The Lord of the Rings* (or *The Lost Road, The Notion Club Papers,* and *The Drowning of Anadûnê*), when he was initially invited by Rayner Unwin to publish his work on the history of 'The Silmarillion'.)

As Christopher Tolkien noted, writing the first part of the book proved the most challenging for his father, the part of the story up until Rivendell. Tolkien began with the goal of producing a sequel to *The Hobbit*, and the first approaches to *The Lord of the Rings* are very much in the spirit and style of *The Hobbit* (homeliness, hobbit humour, parties, camaraderie, the lure of the open road and travel). As the narrative developed, as Tolkien went back and forth over his written chapters and made notes for future story ideas, it got darker, and grander, and stranger; it became more complicated, more layered, and much, much more detailed. Before too long, it's not just four hobbits who go on an adventure, aided by a wizard (rather like *The Hobbit*), there are other ingredients, such as the ring-wraiths, agents of the enemy.

All sorts of aspects are fascinating in the creation of *The Lord of the Rings* recounted in the four *History of Middle-earth* volumes: *The Return of the Shadow, The Treason of Isengard, The War of the Ring* and *Sauron Defeated.* J.R.R. Tolkien toyed with different names (as one would expect from any novelist and not just a philologist as exacting as Tolkien): Frodo was Bingo Bolger (and Bingo Bolger-Baggins) for a long time, in many early drafts (Tolkien wasn't happy with the name Frodo, and tried Folco, Faramond and Odo). The hobbits were variously called Bingo, Odo, Frodo, Marmaduke, Folco, Fredegar, Hamilcar and Faramond (combinations included Faramond Took, Pippin Took, Folco Boffin, Peregrin Boffin, Hamilcar Bolger and Fredegar Bolger).

Frodo (Bingo) was Bilbo's son at one time; in another, his first cousin once removed. Sam Gamgee wasn't one of the hobbits in many of the early drafts. There were originally three hobbits who set out on the adventure, with one staying behind in case Gandalf turned up (a remnant of this idea made it into the final book, in the character of Fredegar Bolger). The hobbits' characters were combined or shifted around, with lines, characteristics or actions from one character being given to another. The characterization of the villains altered too. Sometimes Tolkien added abilities to the enemies which he later took away.

J.R.R. Tolkien altered the names of characters so many times as he wrote *The Lord of the Rings*. Months or years would go by and he would still not have decided finally on the names for his chief characters. Understandable for a writer for whom language was so precious, for whom names had to carry so much social and cultural weight. The names simply had to be *absolutely exact*. The name Gandalf seemed to remain pretty much constant right from the beginning, as did Sauron (Saruman was Saramond and Saramund for a time, but not for long).

Aragorn and the hobbits seemed to present constant indecisions for J.R.R. Tolkien, and he tried many variants until he was satisfied. And even the characters whose names were pretty much fixed from the beginning (like Gandalf or Sauron) also had many variations on their names over the course of the published text of *The Lord of the Rings* (and even more that Tolkien experimented with as he wrote the book, but cut from the published editions).

Gandalf was Stormcrow, Greyhame, Mithrandir, Grey Pilgrim, the White Rider, and so on. It's not uncommon for J.R.R. Tolkien's characters to make up names on the spot, in reaction to particular events or characteristics. Thus, Wormtongue calls Gandalf Láthspell when he meets him at Edoras, and Éomer says to Aragorn '"Wingfoot I name you"' (TT, 41). Sometimes characters invent new names for themselves as new circumstances present themselves, or to commemorate certain events: Éowyn calls herself Dernhelm so she can pass off as a male warrior in an army, for instance. Like children at school, or groups of friends who know each other well, characters sometimes have nicknames or special names which are only known to the select group.

Ingold was another name considered for Aragorn ('Ingold son of Ingrim'), along with Eldakar, Eldamir, Eledon, Elfstan, Elfstone, Elfspear, Elfmere, Elf-friend and Qendemir. J.R.R. Tolkien was still using the name Trotter for Strider up until the last drafts of *The Lord of the Rings* (HME, 8, 390).

An early draft of *The Return of the King* had Gandalf handing out new names to Frodo and Sam, to reflect their victory over the dark power: 'the bards and minstrels should give them new names: *Bronwe athan Harthad* and *Harthad Uluithiad*, Endurance beyond Hope and Hope unquenchable' (HME, 9, 62). J.R.R. Tolkien seldom misses an opportunity to invent a new moniker for a character.

Another change over the course of writing *The Lord of the Rings* concerned the ring, the rings of power and the lesser rings. In some early versions, Sauron had handed out many rings to the peoples of Middle-earth. J.R.R. Tolkien also considered variations on the numbers of rings (such as 12 for men, 9 for dwarves), before coming up with the twenty really important rings: the nine for men, three for elves, seven for dwarves and the one for Sauron himself.

The rings conferred invisibility, but also enslaved the bearer to Sauron. In an early version of *The Lord of the Rings*, even elves could become wraiths; and goblins had many rings ('invisible goblins are very evil and wholly under the Lord'). Dwarves were given rings, too, but they could not be turned invisible; instead, the rings fed their lust for gold (HME, 6, 75).

In the margin of one of the drafts of *The Lord of the Rings* J.R.R. Tolkien has Aragorn called 'The Lord of the Rings'. Elrond's sons, and the people of Lebennin (part of Gondor) call him that (HME, 8, 425). Gimli and Merry wonder what Aragorn being the Lord of the Rings means: 'either it is true and he has a ring, or it is a false tale invented by someone else'. Tolkien also toyed with the idea that Galadriel gives her ring to Aragorn, which would explain his 'sudden access to power'. But then he realized that it would leave Lórien defenceless (ibid.). (The screenwriters of the 2001-03 version of *The Lord of the Rings* did give Aragorn a ring, but it was the ring of the elf Barahir, which Beren had.)

One intriguing concept that comes out clearer in the drafts for *The Lord of the Rings* than in the published book is the idea that elves live in two worlds, the world of the living in Middle-earth and some 'other world' where the enemy also operates (i.e., the 'wraith-world'). As Gandalf tells Bingo (Frodo): elves 'fear no Ringwraiths, for they live at once in both worlds, and each world has only half power over them, while they have double power over both' (HME, 6, 212). The 'other world' (which only the High Elves can inhabit) is also the 'unseen' world, not just the 'wraith world' (the 'wraith-world' seems to be a part of the larger 'unseen' world, rather than the other way around). As Gandalf puts it in *The Fellowship of the Ring*: 'those who have dwelt in the Blessed Realm live at once in both worlds, and against the Seen and the Unseen they have great power' (FR, 235). Or as Tolkien put it in the first draft of "The Shadow of the Past" chapter in *The Lord of the Rings*, the ring-bearers 'could see both the world under the sun and the other side in which invisible things move', and elves did not need rings to dwell in the 'other side' (HME, 6, 258-60).

The signs that someone has claimed the ring and become a ringlord, Gandalf tells Imrahil and the Captains of the West at the Last Debate in an early draft, would be darkness and despair, a growing, creeping feeling of darkness in the heart, followed by 'strife among the lords' (HME, 8, 404). No help will come from the land beyond the sea, Gandalf tells the Captains of the West, because there *is* no land there anymore, and the gods have given the lands to men to keep (HME, 8, 401).

'The greater our rashness the greater his fear, and the more will his eye and thought be turned to us and not elsewhere where his true peril is', Gandalf tells the Last Debate in an early draft (HME, 8, 402).

But there is always hope in J.R.R. Tolkien's moral universe, because the future can never be known for sure. So despair is an ultimate evil in J.R.R. Tolkien's fictional world. Gandalf remarks that 'despair is only for those who see the end beyond all doubt'.

The hobbits were among the Host of the West in early drafts – Aragorn tells Pippin that Merry isn't well enough yet, and it would be better if he 'lightened Merry's grief' by staying with him (HME, 8, 415).

In earlier drafts, the Host of the West riding to Mordor included Aragorn leading fifteen hundred foot and five hundred horse, Éowyn with three thousand Rohirrim, and Prince Imrahil with fifteen hundred foot and a thousand horse (HME, 8, 404). In earlier drafts of *The Lord of the Rings,* Merry had gone along with Théoden and the Rohirrim openly, not in secret with Éowyn (HME, 8, 318).

In an early plan for *The Lord of the Rings,* as the Host of the West rode to Mordor, they would have been beset by flying nazgûl. Gandalf would have driven them back (HME, 8, 229). The army would also have taken Minas Morgul, with Gandalf helping to destroy it by magic (and Faramir would have occupied it [ib., 360]). They would have met the emissary of Sauron outside Cirith Ungol.

One of J.R.R. Tolkien's outlines for *The Lord of the Rings* had Éowyn as well as Théoden dying at Pelennor (after they had both defeated the Witch-king) (ib., 256). Ents and elves would have come down from the North to the Captains of the West at Dagorlad (ib., 256). Frodo would have seen the army of the West, as well as Sauron's secret forces behind the Gate in Mordor. Other ideas Tolkien toyed with had Gandalf being ambushed in Cirith Ungol, and also consulting the *palantír* and seeing Frodo imprisoned in the tower.

Sauron, Gandalf says in an early outline of *The Lord of the Rings* of the Last Debate, is 'an Enemy of great power and malice, and he grows, and he it is that fills all the hearts of the wild peoples with hate, and directs and governs that hatred' (HME, 8, 400). It's not just that the enemy has thousands of troops, but that his warriors are inspired by an evil power. But if they had the ring, they 'could command victory even in our present plight' (ibid.). Victory wouldn't come instantly, Gandalf explains, but gradually, as the ringlord grew in power. And it would only really work if some 'power or royalty' took up the ring: Elrond, or Denethor, or Aragorn, or Gandalf. And the chief means would be the ability of the ringlord to dominate the wills of other people (HME, 8, 401). Gandalf also adds that it wouldn't be possible to kill the ringlord.

J.R.R. Tolkien shifted around the chronology of events in *The Lord of the Rings* many, many times as he added to the story. Characters' ages change, the gaps between Gandalf's visits to the Shire lengthen and shorten, days, dates, months and year have to be rejigged. Sometimes matching the different chronologies vexed Tolkien immensely. He often described in his letters how he had to rewrite or re-structure whole chapters or sections to get the events to correlate (putting a full moon in the right place, for instance, or ensuring that events in, say, Minas Tirith, chimed with those in Ithilien. Tolkien took the moon's phases for *The Lord of the Rings* from a 1942 calendar).

J.R.R. Tolkien would make endless notes and charts of the story and the journeys of the characters, not only noting down the phases of the moon, but also wind direction (a British Army ordnance survey manual was used for the distances that soldiers could travel). Tolkien said he wanted his Secondary World to be wholly convincing, so there couldn't by any details which allowed disbelief to creep in. In May, 1944, for instance, Tolkien wrote to his son Christopher that

> my moons in the crucial days between Frodo's flight and the present situation (arrival at Minas Morgul) were doing impossible things, rising in one part of the country and setting simultaneously in another. Rewriting bits of back chapters took all afternoon![1]

Maybe only a few readers are conscious of things like the phases of the moon or the direction the wind's blowing, but it was important for J.R.R. Tolkien, ever the perfectionist, to get those details right. If a writer writes primarily for themselves, then Tolkien as a reader of his own work would want those aspects to be just so. But it did mean endless delays for the composition of *The Lord of the Rings.*

The Black Riders weren't planned: they had appeared as J.R.R. Tolkien was writing the first chapters of *The Lord of the Rings.* Tolkien wrote different versions of the hobbits' encounters with the Black Riders. In one version, the hobbits are hiding inside a hollow tree when a Black Rider passes by. In another, the hobbits hide off the road in the trees and bushes and a Black Rider stops and crawls towards them; it's frightened off just in time. In another variation, the hobbits watch a Black Rider on the road from a distance; Bingo (Frodo) is lying a few yards from the road, wearing the ring; the Black Rider stops and sniffs (a later draft had the hobbits meeting Gandalf in a similar manner). Some of these ideas Tolkien abandoned, but some of them made it into the final draft, though in a different form.

J.R.R. Tolkien decided that the Black Riders would be more sinister and threatening if they were felt rather than heard, and he cut down the number of words they speak. In earlier drafts of *The Lord of the Rings* the Black Riders have conversations with Harry the gatekeeper at Bree, among others. In the published book, the conversations of the Black Riders tend to be reported by other characters rather than narrated first-hand (for example, Farmer Maggot, or Gandalf recounting the Gaffer's meeting with a Black Rider).

An encounter excised from the final book has the Black Riders commanding the terrified Harry (the Bree gatekeeper) to make sure he reports back to them without lying: '"You will watch. We want Baggins. He is with them. You will watch. You will tell us and not lie! We shall come back"' (HME, 7, 41).

Early concepts for Gandalf's encounters with the Black Riders had him being besieged by five of the nazgûl on the 'Western Tower', one of the towers between the Shire and the sea (HME, 7, 9).

An early draft of the Black Riders' attack on the house at Crickhollow had Gandalf already lying in wait for them: the Black Riders move to the corners of the house and the front door, as in the published text of *The Fellowship of the Ring*. (It's a curious manœuvre: the Black Riders just stand there for ages in the night before they make a move. Curious, because later on in *The Lord of the Rings* they are fearsome assailants who launch themselves into battle. In none of variations on the Crickhollow scene do the Black Riders think of covering the back of the house, or checking other exits). This time, when the Black Rider thumps the door, a horn blows and along comes

> a grey man, wrapped in a great cloak... His beard streamed wide. In one hand was a horn, in the other a wand. A splendour of light flashed out before him. There was a wail and cry as of fell hunting beasts that are smitten suddenly, and turn to fly in wrath and anguish. (HME, 6, 303-4)

Gandalf also pursues the Black Riders, galloping up the lane on a white horse in another version, still blowing the horn, carrying Hamilcar before him, while 'a wand flared and flickered like a sheaf of lightning' (HME, 7, 54). This early version of the Crickhollow scene is one of the few where Gandalf is seen at first-hand facing off against the nazgûl (the attack on Weathertop is reported second-hand by Gandalf, but not described by the narrator). Intriguingly, a wand wielded by the wizard makes a rare appearance.

In one of the early drafts, one of the hobbits (Odo), who had been travelling ahead with Gandalf, had been captured by the Black Riders (J.R.R. Tolkien did not embellish this narrative possibility, but had Gandalf saying that Odo had wandered in the wilds after Weathertop, before being discovered). In a later note to himself, Tolkien said that the nazgûl would no doubt kill Odo. (Odo had gone ahead with Merry to Crickhollow in some of the early drafts of *The Lord of the Rings*, and Gandalf had taken him on his horse to Bree, to catch up with the other hobbits). In the final version,

Odo (now called Fatty Bolger) opts to stay behind and wait for Gandalf, but Gandalf doesn't take him to Bree.

In another version, Bilbo is married to Primula Brandybuck, and disappears from Hobbiton aged 11, and it's his son, Bingo, who gives the party (HME, 6, 40). Making Frodo and Bilbo nephew and uncle renders their relationship still fundamentally a father-son one, but it takes away some of the œdipal weight. What's instantly noteworthy, though, is the lack of a prominent female presence in the lives of either Frodo or Bilbo (no mother, daughter, sister, even an aunt, or a cousin, or co-worker).

Early on in the gestation and writing of *The Lord of the Rings*, J.R.R. Tolkien sent a draft of the first chapter ("The Long-Expected Party"), which he had typed out, to Rayner Unwin, in February, 1938, to obtain his opinion (Tolkien had valued Unwin Junior's view of *The Hobbit*). The response was positive. At that point, Tolkien had got as far as having Bilbo going off on an adventure with three Took nephews (Odo, Frodo and Drogo). A note on story ideas of this early version of *The Lord of the Rings* included '[h]e has only a small bag of money. They walk all night – East. Adventures: troll-like: witch-house on way to Rivendell. Elrond again. A tale in Elrond's house' (HME, 6, 41). Tolkien admitted that he could have written countless first chapters, and did indeed rewrite the opening chapter many times before proceeding on to the rest of the story.

A dragon visits the Shire in another note (of August, 1939), possibly lured by Frodo's dragon gold; in dealing with the dragon the hobbits could show they were made of 'sterner stuff' (HME, 6, 379).

In an early version of *The Lord of the Rings*, Bilbo says he has a longing to see a live dragon again, and the 'dragon-longing', J.R.R. Tolkien explained, was linked to the ring's influence (HME, 6, 42). In *The Fellowship of the Ring*, Bilbo tells Gandalf that he wants to see mountains again. Another reference to dragons was excised from *The Lord of the Rings*, when Gandalf muses that no fire can destroy the ring except the one in the Crack of Doom. In an early draft of the scene in chapter two, when Gandalf asks Bingo (Frodo) to bring out the ring, Gandalf wonders whether dragon fire could melt it.

In one of the early drafts of *The Fellowship of the Ring,* Gildor tells Bingo that the Lord of the Rings is looking for the ring; at that early stage, however, J.R.R. Tolkien had not worked out everything to do with the ring, and the relationship of figures such as Gollum and Bilbo to the ring. For instance, the full details of how the ring came into Gollum's hands had not been finalized, and nor had how Gandalf knew so much about Gollum and the ring. Thus, the whole business of Gandalf and Aragorn searching for Gollum and eventually finding him and getting (something close to) the truth out of him had to be invented in part to account for Gandalf's extensive knowledge of Gollum and his movements, including the all-important knowledge that Gollum had been captured by the enemy and tortured. That was important, because it would explain how Sauron found out where the ring was, and how the Black Riders came to be in the Shire, looking for someone called Baggins. There was also the fact that the Dark Lord knew of Gandalf and something of his movements that had to be explained. In the novel, Gollum says that he was told to search for the ring on leaving the Dark Tower, but that he intended to keep it for himself when he found it (TT, 312).

It's a recurring problem for many writers of fiction: you have the goodies and the villains, but how do they know so much about each other and each others' movements when they don't communicate at all? Hence the need for spies and betrayals and special monitoring devices (such as, in the spy thriller, hidden cameras, microphones and tape recorders). J.R.R. Tolkien also employed other devices, such as the *palantíri* or seeing-stones, the 'seeing' place of Amon Hen, the mirror of Galadriel, and so on. One can see Tolkien inventing devices such as the *palantíri* to get around narrative problems, and to have critical information being transmitted over distances. (A *James Bond* film, for instance, has a casino or restaurant or party scene early in the narrative, in which the heroes and villains can legitimately interact, called a 'watering hole' scene in screenwriting).

There's a version of the pagan feast at Midsummer of lighting bonfires in an early version of *The Lord of the Rings*. Gandalf visits the Shire and the whole Shire is magically alight with fire of many colours that runs all over the grass like glittering jewels, with the trees hung with red and gold blossom, and plenty of singing (HME, 9, 111).

Tom Bombadil was one of the characters that Ronald Tolkien invented for the stories he told his children. He was described as four foot tall, with a blue jacket, a blue feather in a tall hat, and yellow boots. He was based on a doll Priscilla owned.

A link between Tom Bombadil and Butterbur was dropped from the final book (which would have suggested that Bombadil strayed outside of the Old Forest to Bree, or that somehow he and Butterbur had met). Farmer Maggot was originally going to be a being more akin to Tom Bombadil than the hobbit he finally became in the published version of *The Lord of the Rings* (HME, 6, 116). Some of Maggot's unusual qualities survive in the final version of *The Lord of the Rings* (it's suggested that Maggot, like Butterbur, knows a lot more than he lets on).

Gandalf's letter at Bree originally included more details which J.R.R. Tolkien cut from the published text. One was a reference to the Black Riders: 'Look out for horsemen in black. They are your worst enemies (save one): they are ringwraiths' (HME, 7, 49). Another idea that Tolkien cast away was Gandalf telling Frodo '[i]f Trotter [Strider] does not turn up, you must try and get Butterbur to hide you somewhere, and hope that I shall come' (ibid.).

Another possibility J.R.R. Tolkien considered was to have Trotter (Strider) being Peregrin Boffin, a hobbit that Bilbo 'took away with him or who ran off with Bilbo' (HME, 7, 7). Another possibility for Trotter (Strider) was that he was not a hobbit but an elf, who went disguised as a ranger, a scout from Rivendell (HME, 7, 7).

A version of the Black Riders capturing a hobbit (here called Hamilcar) had the nazgûl stealing the Buckland ferryboat to get their horses over the river, and Gandalf pursuing them on his horse Galeroc:

> Galeroc had to swim the river. Then I had a hard chase: but I caught them ten miles beyond the Bridge. I have one advantage: there is no horse in Mordor or in Rohan that is as swift as Galeroc. When they heard his feet behind them they were terrified: they thought I was somewhere else, far away. I was terrified too, I may say: I thought it was Frodo they had got. (HME, 7, 68)

In one of his notes on the events of the early sections of *The Lord of the Rings*, J.R.R. Tolkien gave the Black Riders letters to distinguish them from each other. Thus, H and I move through Bree asking for news, while D, E and F attack Crickhollow. The King (A) stays outside the Shire (at Amrath) with B and C. And so on. He noted down the exact movements of every single Black Rider, describing which ones went to Hobbiton, which ones stayed on the borders of the Shire, which ones rode ahead along the road, and so on. In some drafts of *The Fellowship of the Ring*, the Black Riders order Bill Ferny and the Southerner to burgle the *Prancing Pony* for information.

In an early version, Gandalf said he had travelled onwards from Weathertop in order to deflect attention from the hobbits. But if he had known the Black Riders were abroad, he would never have let the hobbits leave the Shire unaided.

There were 12 Black Riders at one point, in an early draft of *The Lord of the Rings* – a number filled with resonance, especially for a Christian. Maybe a (Dark) Lord with twelve (black) disciples was too much of a parody of Christianity for Tolkien.

In another incident, Trotter said one of the Black Riders nearly ran him down on the road in the dark.

> "I hailed him with a curse, for he had almost run over me; and he pulled up and came back. I stood still and made no sound but he brought his horse step by step towards me. When he was quite close he stooped and sniffed. Then he hissed, and turned his horse and rode off." (HME, 6, 342)

J.R.R. Tolkien would later refine his depiction of the Black Riders: the idea – of Aragorn having a casual chat over a hedge with the nazgûl – would be just silly.

One early idea was to have Saruman send Gandalf to the giant Treebeard, who imprisons him. Another had Saruman tricking Gandalf, so the Black Riders pursue him to a mountaintop, where he is imprisoned with a guard of wolves and orcs (HME, 7, 71). An early note had Saruman becoming 'a wandering conjuror and trickster' (HME, 9, 53).

The vision of Saruman in Fangorn remains ambiguous in the published novel. It seems to have been Saruman, but there are also suggestions in early drafts of *The Lord of the Rings* that it was an apparition of Saruman, conjured by the wizard, or that it was an 'emanation' of Gandalf created by Gandalf (HME, 7, 428). Also, putting Saruman into Fangorn and confusing him with Gandalf was maybe a remnant of the earlier ideas where Saruman sends Gandalf to Fangorn, and Treebeard was a villain giant.

Against the Ringwraiths when they're being led by the Witch-king Gandalf would be overcome, Gandalf says in an early draft of *The Fellowship of the Ring:* '"the Chief of the Nine was of old the greatest of all the wizards of Men"' (HME, 7, 132). In one of the early drafts of *The Lord of the Rings,* J.R.R. Tolkien, via Gandalf, explained that the Witch-king was originally a wizard of the same order as Gandalf (HME, 8, 331). Tolkien changed that conception to the Witch-king as a man and sorcerer, but not originally a wizard (or Maia) like Gandalf, Saruman or Radagast. His long life was due to his enslavement to Sauron and the ring, and his own ring, not the near-immortality the wizard order has.

J.R.R. Tolkien needed a good reason for Gandalf to miss his rendezvous with Frodo in Hobbiton and Bree. He also required a good reason for Gandalf to allow Frodo and the hobbits to leave the Shire while knowing the Black Riders were abroad. Hence the Isengard episode, and finding out about the Nine Riders from Radagast.

One of the ideas J.R.R. Tolkien had for the story after Moria was Frodo being separated from the others and getting lost in Fangorn forest. Sam would have been looking for him, unwilling to carry on to Ond (Gondor) until he found Frodo. Frodo would have had a nasty encounter with Gollum at this point, with the creature strangling him and trying to take the ring (ibid.). Frodo would then have wandered lost in Fangorn forest, being found by Treebeard, who would only have revealed his friendliness later. Treebeard and his thanes would then have marched to Minas Tirith and raised the siege, rescuing Trotter and the others (ibid.). Some of the ideas in this early sketch would find their way into the final text of *The Lord of the Rings,* but transformed somewhat. (Treebeard's tendency to say 'hroom' was inspired, according to Tolkien, by C.S. Lewis's voice.)

This early conception of Fangorn had trees of '*vast* height' – 500-

1000 feet; and the Great River ran through the middle of it (HME, 6, 410, 415). Early conceptions of Treebeard had him 50 feet tall, with a castle in the Black Mountains, and many followers (ib., 410).

In one of the early drafts of *The Lord of the Rings*, Gandalf said he had visited Tom Bombadil after his encounter with the Black Riders at Crickhollow. But it remained a suggestion only, never followed through. As Christopher Tolkien mused, 'the meeting of Gandalf and Bombadil never (alas!) reached narrative form' (HME, 6, 413). It's one conversation that many fans would probably love to read. Gandalf's visit may have been dropped because it might have seemed odd having Gandalf stop by to visit old friends instead of pursuing the Black Riders and the hobbits like the wind to Bree and the Last Homely House. (Gandalf does turn aside on the journey back to the Shire at the end of *The Lord of the Rings* but, again, Tolkien's narrator doesn't take the reader with Gandalf).

The early draft of "The Ring Goes South" chapter had the Company leaving Rivendell on ponies and horses: all of the hobbits rode on ponies, and Boromir and Gandalf had horses. There were also two pack animals (HME, 6, 432). This would make sense, at least for the first part of the journey, from Rivendell to the Misty Mountains. In the book, of course, the fellowship has only the pony Bill.

One of the earliest introductions of the 'Horse-kings' of Rohan had them 'in the service of Sauron' (a hint of this persisted in the final book, when there is still some doubt about the allegiance of the Horse-lords, and whether they pay Sauron tribute).

In an early draft of the Council of Elrond in *The Fellowship of the Ring*, Elrond remarks that the ring could have been sent to the West long ago and 'that would have been well enough' (HME, 6, 396). But now it is too late, and all the roads West out of Rivendell would be watched by the Enemy – which also precludes sending the ring to Bombadil. In a remark of Elrond's at the council (later given to Erestor), cut from the final text, another reason is given why the ring cannot go into the West: because Sauron would destroy the Havens and 'there would be thereafter no way of escape for the elves from the darkening world' (HME, 6, 402; 7, 153). (Surely the elves could build other ships, and launch them from other ports? Elrond, for instance, is the son of heroic mariner Eärendil). There is also a chance that Sauron will destroy the Towers and the Havens anyway to prevent the elves leaving for Valinor (HME, 7, 154). Elrond also says, in the published version of *The Lord of the Rings*, that the people in the West would not accept the ring.

Various members for the fellowship were considered by the professor in early drafts of his novel: Gandalf, Trotter (Strider), Sam, Frodo, Odo, Merry, Glorfindel and Frár (or Burin son of Balin) were the members in the first draft of the Council of Elrond chapter (HME, 6, 397). Or: Gandalf,

Trotter, Glorfindel, Frár (Burin), and five hobbits (Frodo, Sam, Merry, Folco and Odo) (ib., 398). Another fellowship would have had Erestor (a half-elf), Elrond's counsellor, two kinsmen of Elrond's, Balin's son Burin, Galdor, an elf from Mirkwood, Boromir (from the 'Land of Ond'), Gandalf, Trotter and the hobbits. In another draft, Gandalf proposed himself plus the five hobbits and Glorfindel (ib., 406). A further note has Tolkien changing his mind again, and having the hobbits plus Gandalf as a guide, but no Glorfindel (ibid.).

Elrond also states in a draft of "The Ring Goes South" chapter that no elf-lords could be sent on the quest, because they couldn't remain hidden from the 'wrath and spirit of evil of Mordor, and Sauron would find out about the fellowship (HME, 7, 165). Boromir was suggested as another member; this was the fellowship in the writing of *The Lord of the Rings* up to the Moria chapters. The nine members of the fellowship were explicitly linked to the nine ringwraiths (HME, 7, 162).

In another draft of the making of the fellowship, Elrond puts forward members such as Galdor and Gimli (HME, 7, 114), while Trotter volunteers partly out of friendship for Frodo. And when Frodo remembers Merry and Faramond (Pippin), Gandalf replies that it is best not to take them: '"this quest is not for him, nor for any hobbit, unless fate and duty chooses him" (ib., 115).

In a draft of *The Fellowship of the Ring,* Glóin says that he has come to Imladris to warn Bilbo that Sauron is searching for him, and to learn why (HME, 7, 118). In the story foreseen from Moria, Aragorn wanted to take the ring, like Boromir, to Minas Tirith (HME, 7, 207).

Trotter (Aragorn) in an early draft of the Council of Elrond tells Boromir that he has wandered hard and long, including all around Gondor and into Mordor (HME, 7, 128). In the rewritten draft, Aragorn says that he has travelled into many places, including the 'far regions where the stars are strange' (ib., 147). (As well as Trotter, Aragorn was also called Elfstone (son of Elfhelm) for some time.)

In a draft of *The Lord of the Rings,* Elrond hinted to Gandalf that he might not always be around to help others (HME, 7, 164-5). So Elrond, among others, perceives that Gandalf may be lost.

Galdor relates in a draft of *The Fellowship of the Ring* that an attack by orcs on the elves had been pre-arranged with Gollum to let him escape. Somehow, he knew of it (HME, 7, 119). Gandalf comments on Galdor's tale that '[e]vidently the Enemy wants him' (ib., 119). Later, Gandalf states explicitly that Sauron had sent Gollum from Mordor on some mission (HME, 7, 148), mainly because Sauron guessed that Gollum would try to find the ring.

Saruman tells Gandalf at Isengard in an early draft of *The Fellowship of the Ring* that Gandalf must stay there until '"the Lord has time to turn to lighter matters: such as the pleasure of devising a fitting end for Gandalf the Grey"' (HME, 7, 151).

In the story outline foreseen from Moria, J.R.R. Tolkien tried out some other narrative alternatives, including having Legolas and Gimli being captured by Saruman, Aragorn and Boromir travelling to Minas Tirith, Denethor being killed during the siege on the white city, the people electing Aragorn as their leader, and Boromir, 'jealous and enraged', deserting to Saruman (HME, 7, 210-1). Minas Tirith is under attack from Saruman's forces at the rear, and Sauron's from the front from over the Anduin.

J.R.R. Tolkien also contemplated having Legolas and Gimli lose heart in the Company, and part with Aragorn and Boromir (who travel on to Minas Tirith). Legolas and Gimli intend to return North to their homelands, where they encounter the reborn Gandalf (in Lórien in one draft Celeborn hints that Legolas and Gimli have opted to leave the quest and return to their homes). In this version, it is Gandalf who breaks the siege of Minas Tirith (accompanied by Legolas, Gimli and Treebeard, but without the Rohirrim or the ents), and drives the Black Riders back over the Anduin at Osgiliath (he rides atop a giant eagle). The heroes sweep onward from there to Gorgoroth and the final battle (where they find Frodo and Sam), but Aragorn remains behind at Minas Tirith. If any of the hobbits were to die, Tolkien wrote in *The Treason of Isengard*, 'it must be cowardly Pippin doing something brave' (HME, 7, 211). In this version, after the battle's won, Aragorn decides to remain behind at Minas Morgul, and becomes lord of Minas Ithil.

(Gandalf uses eagles quite a bit in early drafts of *The Lord of the Rings* – not only to drive back the enemy at Minas Tirith, but also to gad about Middle-earth on his missions. He rides an eagle from Tol Brandir, for example, after resisting the Eye – he saves Frodo from Sauron by wresting the eye towards him, as he sits on Tol Brandir [HME, 7, 426]).

Elrond says in an earlier draft of *The Lord of the Rings* that he didn't know about Tom Bombadil (HME, 7, 152). Elrond also says, in a 1940 note on the Council of Elrond chapter, that although Sauron cannot be overcome by sheer force, messengers will be sent out 'to all free folk to resist as long as possible, and that a new hope, though faint, is born' (HME, 7, 161).

In an early draft of *The Lord of the Rings*, Gandalf remarked that the Dark Lord cannot simply make another ruling ring (a thought that must have occurred to quite a few readers: why doesn't Sauron just make another ring?). 'He cannot make rings until he has regained the master ring' (HME, 6, 397). Oh, I see. Pity.

An early draft of the complex Council of Elrond chapter had Trotter (Strider) being captured by the Dark Lord and tortured in Mordor. Hence his name 'Trotter': he wears shoes (unusual for a hobbit) because, as the narrator, 'Frodo knew that he had been tortured and his feet hurt in some way. But he had been rescued by Gandalf and saved from death' (HME, 6, 401). This would have been another J.R.R. Tolkien's incredible rescue missions, with the wizard venturing into the heart of Sauron's territory to save a friend. (In another version, Trotter was captured by the Enemy in Moria).

In an early draft of *The Fellowship of the Ring*, Tolkien had Celeborn wondering if the balrog in Moria had been sent there by Sauron from Mount Doom (HME, 7, 186, 247, 248); the idea was dropped in the final text. In the book, he – and others – suggest that the dwarves woke the balrog when they dug too deeply for mithril. Galadriel remarks (in a note J.R.R. Tolkien made during writing the book) that 'no balrog has lain hid in the Misty Mountains since the fall of Thangorodrim', which was the era of Morgoth (ib., 262). Galadriel suggests that it was sent from Mordor, from where it lived near Orodruin.

When Gandalf faces off against the balrog in an early version of the Moria sequence, he loses his staff (as well as part of his beard, and an eyebrow) when he creates the blinding flash and explosion that brings down the Chamber of Mazarbul (HME, 7, 195). When he's on the bridge with the balrog, Gandalf manages to shatter the balrog's sword, and Gimli grabs Legolas's bow and looses an arrow. The bridge collapses when a troll steps onto it, and before Trotter (Strider) can reach the wizard he falls after the balrog (HME, 7, 198). Tolkien also had Boromir blowing his horn, and Legolas being hit in the shoulder by an arrow, and crawling along the bridge.

J.R.R. Tolkien contemplated having the balrog be Saruman at one point, making the battle on the bridge of Khazad-dûm a wizard duel, with Gandalf afterwards taking on Saruman's white mantle (HME, 7, 236). In the event, the 'trial of strength with Saruman' (ib., 422) was to be the face-off between the wizards on the steps of Orthanc. Tolkien also considered making Galadriel Elrond's wife, and living in Lórien alone.

An early version of the mirror of Galadriel scene had an additional vision: Frodo seeing himself running, with a 'black figure with long arms' pursuing him (HME, 7, 252). The elven brooches were originally just one – a gift from Galadriel to Gimli (which Gimli dubs Elfstone), which J.R.R. Tolkien expanded to give to all of the fellowship.

In an outline drafted during the Lórien chapters, J.R.R. Tolkien inserted an encounter with the 'Green Ravines' on the Great River (HME, 7, 268-9). Also in this draft Celeborn sent elves to accompany the fellowship as far as the Green Hills. That appears to be a sound idea, having elves protect the Company down the river, but it's not as suspenseful as having the fellowship continue on their way alone.

In early drafts of *The Lord of the Rings* J.R.R. Tolkien developed the notion that time moves at a different pace in the Golden Wood, so that Lórien is not only a different realm, set apart from the rest of Middle-earth, but also has its own 'elf time'. Trotter (Aragorn) wondered if '"we were in the past or the future or in a time that does not pass"' (HME, 7, 355). He also pointed out that while they were in Lórien he did not see the moon, but '"only stars by night and sun by day"' (ibid.).

If time in Lórien was timeless, or passed at a different rate, however, it would mess up Tolkien's chronologies, which he sweated over (as with every other detail in *The Lord of the Rings*). Thus, when he was thinking about these problems – of synchronizing the various plot strands – he noted: '[b]etter to have *no* time difference' (HME, 7, 369).

Celeborn's dialogue is different in the early drafts of *The Lord of the Rings*. He tells the hobbits, for instance, that he wishes they hadn't joined the quest or come so far. He tells them they could remain in Lórien until the danger is passed, 'while outside in the world many years run by' (HME, 7, 249). And returning to Rivendell or the Shire would be vain. In the early drafts of *The Fellowship of the Ring,* Celeborn leads the scenes far more than in the published version (it is Celeborn, not Galadriel, who has the magic mirror, for instance).

In early drafts of *The Lord of the Rings*, Sauron suspects that the dwarves may have the One Ring in their hoards (magical rings are thought to be the foundation of the dwarf hoards). J.R.R. Tolkien toyed with the idea of having Sauron's minions approaching the dwarf lords, offering gifts in exchange for the ring (which crops up in the Council of Elrond in the book).

In the early stages of writing *The Lord of the Rings*, the geography of Middle-earth was being redrawn. One sees Tolkien extending Middle-earth as the narrative progresses: to Tom Bombadil and the Old Forest, the Barrow-downs, Bree, Weathertop, the Ford and Rivendell, and then onward to the Mines of Moria, to Lothlórien, and so on. In early drafts of the Imladris scenes, for example, Tolkien imagined Sauron to be holed up in the South of Mirkwood, as he had been in the 'dark tower' of the Necromancer in *The Hobbit*. Later, Tolkien pushed Mordor far to the South and East. (Similarly, while Sauron might have been linked to dictators like Adolf Hitler, and Mordor to Nazi Germany, during the late 1930s, Joseph Stalin and the Soviet Union were links later on, in the 1940s).

In one draft of *The Fellowship of the Ring,* an orc band following the heroes pick up their scent near the Nimrodel and search the path, but give up looking for them. Later, the elves destroy them, pursuing them to the sources of the Nimrodel.

An early conception of Gondor (when it was still called 'Ond' or 'Land of Ond'), had inhabitants known as 'Stone-Men' (HME, 6, 379).

The ents were not part of the original scheme of the Middle-earth mythology, nor of *The Hobbit* or *The Lord of the Rings*. They came into existence as J.R.R. Tolkien was writing the first draft of *The Lord of the Rings* (when he reached Book 3, chapter 4). Tolkien then had to work out how they fitted into the Middle-earth cosmos, as they were among the oldest things in Middle-earth (L, 334). The ents from Emyn Muil join in the last battle at the Morannon, in early versions of *The Lord of the Rings.*

In a nice touch, when Saruman is cast out of the order by Gandalf at Isengard, he is not allowed to have even a rough wooden staff, because Treebeard won't let the wizard have anything made of wood (HME, 7, 436).

In an early version of *The Fellowship of the Ring,* Sam doesn't find Frodo straight away in the fracas at Parth Galen: instead, he encounters Gollum, and tracks Gollum, who leads him to Frodo (HME, 7, 208). The ring is also at work in Frodo's experiences on Amon Hen and his decision to continue on to the Black Land alone: the narrator notes in a draft of *The Fellowship of the Ring* that the ring's power was renewed in Frodo after his vision on Amon Hen, and the ring had possibly 'aided his choice, drawing him to Mordor, drawing him to the Shadow, alone' (HME, 7, 374). Tolkien also put Trotter (Aragorn) in the hot seat of Amon Hen in an early draft of *The Fellowship of the Ring,* but he didn't have same panoramic visions as Frodo, but smaller, fragmented visions (ib., 380). Another concept had Gandalf coming to Frodo's rescue at Amon Hen riding on an eagle (ib., 396).

In the pages of an outline describing the story as foreseen from Lórien (written around 1940), J.R.R. Tolkien had Frodo and Sam crossing the river at Parth Galen together, then Frodo telling Sam he wished to be alone for a while, and going up the hill on his own, when he sees the visions of Middle-earth spread below. Boromir has followed them over the river in a boat. After his encounter with Frodo, Boromir comes back down the hill and meets Sam, who is suspicious of Boromir (in another draft, Trotter (Aragorn) tells the fellowship that Boromir tried to take the ring by force, and also tells Éomer; in the published novel, the ranger keeps that information to himself).

Frodo slips away without Sam, and Sam follows him. It takes Sam some time to find Frodo – he winds up sleeping in a tree, and then tries to track Gollum. Both Sam and Gollum then track Frodo, and though he puts on the ring, they find him. Then comes the scene where Gollum begs for forgiveness and offers to help the hobbits (HME, 7, 329).

In this early outline of the book, Aragorn plumps to go South with Boromir to Minas Tirith, but Legolas and Gimli turn North – Legolas for Lórien, and Gimli for the Mountain. When the enemy's onslaught is unleashed in this Lórien version of the tale, the whole of Middle-earth seems to be swamped by orcs and enemies; Lothlórien is 'lapped in flame'; and even Saruman comes down from Isengard 'with many wolves' (HME, 7, 33).

One of the more significant changes that J.R.R. Tolkien made as he wrote *The Lord of the Rings* during the 'first phase' of composition (through 1938) was to have Strider originally a hobbit called Trotter. In this early draft of *The Fellowship of the Ring*, Trotter shares many of the same characteristics as Strider (or rather, Tolkien gave Strider many of Trotter's traits, when he decided that Aragorn should be the one to guide the hobbits to Rivendell). These characteristics included being a ranger, a well-travelled denizen of the road, an adventurer, a somewhat gruff, grizzled nature (at first), and so on. The way that Trotter is introduced into the story in the Bree inn, the suspicions of the hobbits, the way Trotter takes charge of the company, some of Trotter's dialogue, and in many other ways, Trotter formed the basis of Strider's personality and actions (in the Bree scenes and those following right after). Trotter is introduced is an early draft of *The Lord of the Rings* thus:

> Suddenly Bingo noticed that a queer-looking, brown-faced hobbit, sitting in the shadows behind the others, was also listening intently. He had an enormous mug (more like a jug) in front of him, and was smoking a broken-stemmed pipe right under his rather long nose. He was dressed in dark rough brown cloth, and had a hood on, in spite of the warmth, – and, very remarkably, he had wooden shoes! (HME, 137)

Some of the background of Trotter's character obviously had to be altered (although J.R.R. Tolkien did not create much of a background for Trotter). Tolkien also dropped some aspects of Trotter's character, though. For example, Trotter tells the hobbits at Bree how he was on the look-out for the Black Riders and discovered them on the road. From behind a hedge, Trotter hailed them and spoke with their leader. Trotter related how he found out that the Black Riders were searching for four hobbits with five ponies, and would pay in silver and gold for any news of them. Trotter doesn't tell them anything, but finds out they are looking for 'Baggins, Bolger-Baggins'.

In one of J.R.R. Tolkien's early conceptions, in 1938, there was going to be a giant in *The Lord of the Rings*. For a while, that giant was Treebeard (or the 'Giant Fangorn'), and he was an evil one too. So when Gandalf was delayed he was 'caught in Fangorn and spent many weary days as a prisoner of the Giant Treebeard' (HME, 6, 363); Saruman had entered the picture at that point. Future developments such as Rohan and the Golden Wood didn't exist.

In another version, Fangorn turns out to be on the heroes' side after all. Merry and Pippin were going to meet him, as in the book, but Treebeard was going to take them to Minas Tirith, not Isengard (HME, 7, 330). J.R.R. Tolkien also toyed with the idea that elves had created the 'Tree-folk' so that they could understand trees better (HME, 7, 411). In *The*

War of the Ring Tolkien called the huorns 'Talking Trees' which the elves had 'trained and made half-entish' (HME, 8, 50). If the elves can make ents or huorns, however, that puts them on the same level as Ilúvatar or God, the only being in Arda who can create living creatures. In his notes on Treebeard, Tolkien had only three ents left, with one of them (Skinbark) captured by Saruman. The ents also bury the slain Rohirrim.

Instead of Merry and Pippin and meeting with Gandalf after his rebirth, J.R.R. Tolkien considered Sam getting separated from Frodo and encountering Gandalf, who takes him to Minas Tirith. And instead of Aragorn and Boromir going to Minas Tirith while Legolas and Gimli go North, he sends the elf and dwarf to Minas Tirith with Boromir, while he goes in search of Merry and Pippin alone. During his search he meets Gandalf.

Sam Gamgee became increasingly important as Ronald Tolkien was writing *The Lord of the Rings*, eventually becoming the most significant hobbit, the successor to Bilbo:

> Frodo is not so interesting, because he has to be highminded, and has (as it were) a vocation. The book will prob. end up with Sam. Frodo will naturally become too ennobled and rarefied by the achievement of the great Quest, and will pass West with all the great figures. (L, 105)

The effects of the ring on Sam in earlier drafts, when he puts it on in the tunnels of Cirith Ungol, enable him to see through rocks, to see 'every crevice filled with spiders', and understand orc speech. However, J.R.R. Tolkien wrote that the ring 'did *not* confer courage on Sam' (HME, 8, 190).

When Sam takes the ring from Frodo in the story foreseen from Lórien, the unconscious Frodo gives a tremor or shudder (HME, 7, 331), which was dropped in the published novel (there, the fact that Frodo does not respond at all when Sam pulls the ring over his head on its chain persuades Sam that Frodo really has 'died and laid aside the Quest' [TT, 429]). Sam also makes up a *Lament For Frodo* in this version, which he doesn't do in the final book.

An earlier draft of *The Two Towers* had Gandalf relating to Théoden all of the Important matters, and summarizing the story to date. In the published book, Gandalf speaks 'low and secret' to Théoden, but no one else hears what he says.

Théoden wonders if a nazgûl will help Saruman escape, but Gandalf doubts it, and tells Théoden that a 'terrible fate' awaits Saruman if he chose that option (HME, 8, 48). In the outline of the story foreseen from Fangorn, J.R.R. Tolkien wondered if Gandalf should be leading the storming of Isengard, after the battle with the orcs, in which Gandalf charged about as the White Rider (HME, 7, 437). Gandalf then leads the Rohirrim to Minas Tirith to save it from the siege of the Haradwaith, along with Théoden, Aragorn, Merry, Pippin, Gimli and Legolas.

For a time J.R.R. Tolkien envisaged Gimli, Legolas, Aragorn and Gandalf arriving at Edoras at different times (Gimli and Gandalf are ahead of Legolas and Aragorn, for instance). Wormtongue made a later appearance in the drafts, and for a long time Edoras lacked Saruman's spy (Wormtongue's role emerged gradually).

Also in the Golden Hall were two women – Éowyn and Idis, Théoden's daughter (HME, 7, 445). As Christopher Tolkien remarked, Idis barely made an impression in the drafts of the Rohan chapters; she never speaks, and Théoden says that Éowyn will be in charge when he has left, not his daughter Idis (ib., 447). Gandalf won't stay for even a rest in Meduseld, but only for food – and he sets out straight away.

J.R.R. Tolkien had Aragorn marrying Éowyn at the end of *The Lord of the Rings*, not Arwen (in the drafts before Faramir appeared). A note suggested that Aragorn was 'too old and lordly and grim' for Éowyn, and Éowyn 'should die or avenge or save Théoden' (HME, 7, 448). Tolkien was considering having Éowyn killed at Pelennor in later drafts of *The Lord of the Rings.*

Another note suggested that Lórien wouldn't survive the War of the Ring, but would be razed by the nazgûl. In this note, Galadriel is 'lost or hidden', but Frodo meets her later, in old age, when he also encounters Bilbo (HME, 7, 451).

In the earlier drafts of *The Lord of the Rings*, J.R.R. Tolkien's narrator makes it clear that Saruman thinks that the ring may have gone to Edoras, and so launches his huge assault on the Rohirrim in the hope of destroying them before they can do anything with the ring (HME, 8, 51). Saruman fears that Théoden or Éomer may get hold of the ring (if they did, they would probably deal with Saruman first).

Sauron remained in the Dark Tower during the last battle in *The Lord of the Rings*, and there was no suggestion, even in the earlier versions of *The Return of the King*, that the Dark Lord was going to come forth and fight himself.

In early versions of *The Lord of the Rings*, the *palantír* at the Stone of Erech was still there in the tower's vault (HME, 9, 15). That was the *palantír* that Aragorn would use for his vision of the enemy ships at Pelargir. In the final version, there are already enough seeing stones about, and the notion of another one was dropped.

In earlier drafts of *The Lord of the Rings*, J.R.R. Tolkien had Gandalf taking out the *palantír* in front of a group of people, and they see stars, 'small batlike shapes wheeling' and the moon (and they can see all the way to Osgiliath [HME, 8, 69]). In the published book, the *palantíri* are much more dangerous, and Gandalf is swift to hide the one thrown down by Wormtongue from sight. In this draft of *The Lord of the Rings*, Gandalf says there were seeing stones at Minas Tirith, Minas Morgul, Osgiliath, Isengard and Helm's Deep; Tolkien later extended them to other locations (such as the Tower Hills), but removed the one from the Hornburg. A *palantír* was also kept at the tower beside the Stone of Erech. (A ring wall surrounded the stone and a tower, but the seeing stone is now lost).

Sauron would also have blasted apart the Orthanc *palantír* in the moment of fear he experiences when Frodo puts on the ring at the Crack of Doom, so it would have killed Aragorn if he'd been holding it (HME 8, 362).

J.R.R. Tolkien had considered having the Mouth of Sauron being a ringwraith, perhaps the Witch-king himself, so that Angmar wouldn't have died at Pelennor (HME 8, 364).

An early version of *The Lord of the Rings* had a search party of orcs halting right next to the hobbits, and discussing where the intruders have got to (HME, 9, 31). J.R.R. Tolkien toyed with the idea of the hobbits going blind in Mordor, which Sam wonders might be due to the water (HME, 9, 11).

When Gollum betrays Frodo in the outline of the story as foreseen from Moria, he squeals to the Black Riders, not to Shelob (HME, 7, 208), suggesting a closer connection between Gollum and the nazgûl. The nazgûl hear his cries at Mount Doom and swoop away from the distant battle towards the Fire Mountain. J.R.R. Tolkien also considered having the ringwraiths themselves becoming 'demonic eagles', rather than riding on the fell-beasts. Frodo and Sam were fighting a nazgûl on the slopes of Mount Doom when they were rescued by Gandalf and Gwaihir in an early draft.

Christopher Wrigley suggested that there was a biographical element in the Shelob episode, with Frodo being stung by the spider and Sam stabbing under her underbelly with his sword. (The sexual aspects are obvious, the belly being a cover in Shakespearean language for the vagina). It may derive from 'maybe the ashamed memory of a young officer's visit to a whore' (66). An example of psycho-biographical literary criticism going too far.

J.R.R. Tolkien considered a number of possibilities for the climax at the Crack of Doom. One was to have Sam beating off a vulture (precursors of the fell-beasts) and hurling himself and Gollum into the abyss (HME, 7, 209). Another was to have Sam take hold of the ring by following Gollum in the pass at Minas Morgul, driving spiders away from Frodo (Tolkien toyed with the idea of having spiders, as in *The Hobbit*, rather than one giant spider), and taking the ring (in one version, the spiders sting Frodo and put him under a spell while Sam is asleep beside him. Sam also later fights the spiders after duelling with Gollum). Tolkien also considered the orcs taking the ring from Frodo in Minas Morgul, but 'find it is no good' (HME, 7, 209).

A note of August, 1939, had Sauron speaking to Frodo when he's at the Crack of Doom, offering him 'great reward – to share power with him, if he will keep it'.2 The voice of Sauron offers him 'life, peace, honour: rich reward: lordship: power: finally a share in the Great Power' (HME, 9, 5). Frodo resists that temptation, but is then tempted by a desire to lord it over the world, to be 'master of all. Frodo King of Kings'. Hobbits will rule as lords, and Frodo will be 'their Lord, King Frodo, Emperor Frodo' (ib., 5-6).

In that outline (reprinted in *Sauron Defeated*), the Witch-king appears at the Sammath Naur, blocking Frodo's exit. But Frodo is now 'master of the Black Riders', and commands the ringwraith to follow the ring into the fire (HME, 9, 6-7). Gollum has his magic ring, given to him by Sauron, in another page of ideas, which he uses to attack Frodo while invisible (ib., 381). Another idea had Gollum committing suicide: saving the ring for himself, he leaps into the abyss crying 'no one else will have it' (HME, 9, 5).

Yet another idea was to have Frodo captured by the Dark Lord and saved by Sam (HME, 7, 215) (this survived into the final book, with Frodo taken by the enemy and held in Cirith Ungol: it required amazing twists of fate to enable Sam to rescue Frodo. It would need even more suspension of disbelief to have Sam assailing Barad-dûr single-handed, even if he had already obtained the ring from Frodo. But then, Tolkien was a fan of extraordinary quests and rescues – the best occur in the story of Beren and Lúthien, when the elf rescues Beren from Morgoth's fortress. The Frodo-Sam story echoes the Beren-Lúthien story at many points, not least in one person going to rescue the other).

Early ideas had not just parts of Mordor being destroyed when the ring is cast into the Crack of Doom, but the whole of Mordor vanishing 'like a dark cloud. Elves are seen riding like lights rolling away a dark cloud' (HME, 6, 380). J.R.R. Tolkien also considered having Frodo go into the Crack of Doom alone, with Sam being brought down by Gollum outside (HME, 9, 4).

On the side of Mount Doom in one early version of *The Lord of the Rings,* Frodo holds up his sword after the ring has been destroyed and commands the ringwraiths to be gone: '[t]hey fall to earth and vanish like wisps of smoke with a terrible wail' (HME, 7, 210).

Gollum is also in cahoots with the orcs: it's Gollum who leads fifty orcs to the bewitched, stung Frodo. The orcs also know exactly who they've discovered: '"Ringbearer! Ringbearer!" they shouted in joy. "Make haste. Make haste. Send one swift to Baraddur to the Great One"' (HME, 7, 332). This version gives far too much knowledge to the orcs, so that they know about the ring, and send a messenger to Sauron to say they've found the ringbearer. In the published edition, J.R.R. Tolkien would withhold a lot more information from the orcs, and kept them guessing and squabbling. Later versions had Gollum hiding when the orcs appeared (just as Sam comes upon Gollum pawing at the unconscious Frodo).

In the outline foreseen from Lórien, the orcs haven't searched Frodo at Cirith Ungol, and haven't found the mithril coat. They also don't dare to touch the ring: 'that is for none less than servants of the Ring or for Sauron himself', Frodo tells Sam in the tower (HME, 7, 335). Sam offers to help Frodo get away into Mordor, and leave him behind to fend for himself, because Frodo has the ring to protect him (Tolkien would alter this conception, with Frodo not daring to put on the ring inside Mordor).

In this early version, Frodo and Sam escape from Minas Morgul (not Cirith Ungol) by using familiar ruses from adventure fiction (such as getting an orc to come into the room by Frodo singing 'O Elbereth', while Sam hides behind the door, leaps out and kills it). Frodo and Sam then manage to creep out of the stronghold: Sam impersonates an orc and gets past the warder; Frodo's left behind, with the warder orc guarding the door; but when the alarm bells ring he pushes the warder over and flees. A nazgûl flies overhead just as Frodo's escaping. At Cirith Ungol, a nazgûl lands on the wall of the stronghold, shining red, then flies around the valley as orcs search for the hobbits below (HME, 9, 25).

Another version of the escape from Minas Morgul had Frodo and Sam unable to get past the gate when the alarm sounds. A 'Vulture' (ringwraith) lands in the city square and says that the 'Ring is still in the town: he feels it' (HME, 7, 341). A hunt begins for the escapees. Sam and Frodo steal the clothes of two orcs after waylaying them, and join the ranks of an orc band heading out to search the mountains, and so escape.

In a note to himself in the outline foreseen from Lórien, J.R.R. Tolkien wrote: 'Minas Morgul must be made more horrible. The usual 'goblin' stuff is not good enough here' (ib., 340). He was right: at this point, so far into the story, and so close to Mordor, something more menacing and evil was required. It seemed that Tolkien always wanted to have some kind of capture and escape on the borders of Mordor: at one point he considered placing Merry and Pippin in Minas Morgul and escaping, if Treebeard was left out (HME, 7, 344).

In a note to himself about the Dead Marshes, J.R.R. Tolkien wrote that he should describe 'the pools as they get nearer to Mordor as like green pools and rivers fouled by modern chemical works' (HME, 8, 105). That's a clue to the way that Tolkien folded in ecological and anti-industrial concerns into his War of the Ring novel: he wouldn't insert a simile or description which referred explicitly to modern technology like chemical plants, but he would compose a descriptive passage which drew on the effects of modern chemical pollution.

There's a quite a time lag between Gollum being captured (around TA 3017) and Sauron sending out the Black Riders to the Shire (in mid-3019). It's not explained why Sauron waited up to a year to send forth his minions to look for his precious ring, when he had the best clues to its whereabouts

– Baggins and the Shire – for millennia (he knew where the Shire was, for instance, because there's only one Shire with halflings in it in Middle-earth. And he might've guessed that a name like Baggins was unusual enough to narrow down a search. It'd be easier than trying to find a Schmidt in Germany or a Chang in China).

Outside of the action of *The Lord of the Rings*, but occurring at the same time (TA 3018), Sauron had already begun the War of the Ring: sending a small force, led by the Witch-king, to assault Gondor (and to secure the crossing at Osgiliath, and to test Denethor's strength), and attacking Thranduil's realm in order to recapture Gollum, or at least to prevent his enemies getting hold of him (UT, 338, 344). This occurs off-stage – the story remains primarily in the Shire, with Frodo.

In *The Hunt For the Ring* (published in *Unfinished Tales*), Sauron knows plenty about the political situation in Middle-earth in the years of the War of the Ring (TA 3018-19). He knows that the ring has been discovered; Gollum's told him of the Shire and Baggins; that Gollum's being held by the Elvenking; that Boromir's left Gondor (and also the prophecy of Gondor); that Gandalf's been captured by Saruman; and that none of the Wise have the ring (UT, 339).

Other events that occur off-stage in *The Lord of the Rings* might have made fascinating scenes: in one, outlined in *The Hunt For the Ring*, the Lord of the Nazgûl goes to Isengard, to find out what Saruman knows. Gandalf had escaped only two days earlier. Angmar isn't able to enter Isengard, which Saruman has fortified against such an attack, but Saruman speaks to him from the gate, by magic. The encounter between Saruman and the Witch-king is something one wishes Tolkien had fleshed out. Another is when the Witch-king and his cronies encounter Wormtongue on his way to Isengard, putting the fear of Morgoth into him (UT, 339-340).

In an early draft of the encounter with Faramir, the Gondorian captain is a little more explicit about the ring, and his response to it: 'I do not wish to see or touch it – my only fear is lest I see it and be tempted' (HME, 8, 163).

Faramir appeared as J.R.R. Tolkien was composing the pages of the hobbits nearing the Black Land; he wasn't part of the original scheme. As Tolkien put it in a May, 1944 letter:

> he is holding up the 'catastrophe' by a lot of stuff about the history of Gondor and Rohan... but if he goes on much more a lot of him will have to be removed to the appendices. (letter no. 66)

In the event, J.R.R. Tolkien did use quite a bit of Faramir's lengthy disquisitions on Middle-earth matters (needless to say, the 2002 film of *The Two Towers* dispensed with all of it, because it does, as Tolkien realized, hold up the story).

Denethor didn't suicide in earlier drafts of *The Lord of the Rings,* but came out from Minas Tirith to meet Aragorn on Pelennor Fields, reluctant to give up the city and his stewardship (HME 8, 360). Faramir is brought out to Aragorn, who heals him. An early draft of *The Return of the King* had Gandalf handing out new names to Frodo and Sam, to reflect their victory over the dark power: 'the bards and minstrels should give them new names: *Bronwe athan Harthad* and *Harthad Uluithiad*, Endurance beyond Hope and Hope unquenchable' (HME, 9, 62). Tolkien seldom misses an opportunity to invent a new moniker for a character.

Sauron might have seen Denethor's death in the *palantír,* Gandalf explains, and so will have judged that the strife he hopes to sow amongst his enemies' leaders has begun (HME, 8, 404).

Denethor is explicit about wishing that Boromir, not Faramir, had been at Henneth Annûn, because 'he *would* have been loyal to his father and brought him the Ring' (HME, 8, 333).

Early drafts had Galadriel as well as Arwen (called Finduilas) coming to Minas Tirith after the victory against Sauron (HME 8, 386).

As the hobbits pass the Barrow Downs on the return journey, they contemplate visiting Tom Bombadil again, but Gandalf persuades them to carry on to the Shire. Gandalf reassures the hobbits that Bombadil will the same as ever, and quite unconcerned about the War of the Ring (HME, 9, 77).

In earlier drafts of the scouring of the Shire, Frodo was more active, and killed more than one of the villains (HME, 9, 80). And when Sharkey appears at Bag End, Frodo kills him by stabbing him in the neck with his sword. In another early version, there's a sword duel between Sharkey and Frodo in Bilbo's garden, with Frodo managing to dispatch him with Sting (HME, 9, 92). 'Sharkey' is here 'Ruffian Sharkey' or 'the Boss', the leader of the 'orcish men', but not yet Saruman.

Some of Frodo's assertive behaviour was given instead to Merry in the final draft, and the more thoughtful, melancholy Frodo was created.

Ted Sandyman outlines his vision of an industrialized Shire in an early draft of *The Return of the King*: twenty mills, a 100 new houses, big holes in the ground and the engineers who can work metals (HME, 9, 89).

It's Sam, more than Frodo, who hangs onto the image of the Shire to sustain him in the dark times of their quest to destroy the ring. 'All the time in the bad places we've been in I've had the Shire in mind, and that's what I've rested on, if you take my meaning', he tells Frodo (HME, 9, 90).

Sam describes the Shire ruined by Saruman and the ruffians as 'worse than Mordor! Much worse in a way' (RK, 362). That was part of J.R.R. Tolkien's point in *The Lord of the Rings* – that evil could and would spread everywhere. The 'Morgoth-ingredient' couldn't be completely eradicated (which makes *The Lord of the Rings* rather pessimistic, and even Gnostic: the Fall of Man can never be completely reversed or eradicated. Except perhaps when that time comes of Last Judgement, or that spiritual transcendence beyond, as Tolkien often put, 'the circles of this world').

NOTES: EARLY DRAFTS OF *THE LORD OF THE RINGS*

1. In H. Carpenter, 1995, 202.
2. HME, 6, 380; HME, 9, 3.

It's fairy tale time in Hollywood:
elves, hobbits, dwarves, wizards,
kings, princesses, warriors, wraiths,
Satan-size demons and magic rings.

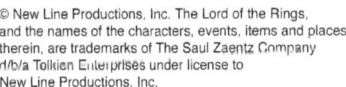

THE LORD OF THE RINGS
THE FELLOWSHIP OF THE RING

CINEMAS WORLDWIDE FROM DECEMBER 19TH

chapter 12

NARRATIVE STRATEGIES
IN J.R.R. TOLKIEN'S FICTION

PAIRS AND OPPOSITES.

The Lord of the Rings is founded on the classic narrative devices of oppositions, rivalries and dualities: two wizards (Gandalf and Saruman); two hobbits who make the whole journey to Mordor (Frodo and Sam); two ageing rulers of men (Théoden and Denethor; one who awakens to save his people, one who gives up and kills himself); two men in the Company (Aragorn and Boromir); two brothers (Boromir and Faramir); two pairs of hobbits (Frodo and Sam, Merry and Pippin); two romances (Aragorn and Arwen, Faramir and Éowyn); two women admiring Aragorn (Arwen and Éowyn); two towers (various pairings, such as Isengard and Cirith Ungol, Minas Tirith and Barad-dûr, or Minas Tirith and Minas Morgul, which face each other); a would-be dark lord (Saruman) and the real Dark Lord (Sauron); two main elven dwellings (Rivendell and Lothlórien); two visions of the future (the mirror of Galadriel and the *palantíri*); two main ringbearers (Frodo and Gollum); two elven women (Galadriel and Arwen); two wise elf lords who stay behind (Elrond and Celeborn); Legolas and Gimli; two hobbits who carry the ring (Frodo and Bilbo); and two hobbits who sail into the West (Frodo and Bilbo again).

Other pairs include two kingdoms of men (Rohan and Gondor), two hobbits who serve kings, two journeys 'there and back', two journeys by hobbits to Rivendell, two forests (the Old Forest and Fangorn), two strongholds that are besieged (Helm's Deep and Minas Tirith).

Other pairings in J.R.R. Tolkien's Middle-earth writings include: two groups of objects forged by the elven magic which prove disastrous (the silmarils and the rings); two giant spiders (Ungoliant and her offspring, Shelob); the Two Trees; and two Dark Lords (Sauron and Morgoth). In the character of Gollum, two opposites reside in the same person: Gollum and Sméagol. Gollum is a version of the split personality, the schizophrenic, the double or *doppelgänger,* a popular device in 19th and 20th century fiction.

The standard narrative devices of opposites and pairs in *The Lord of the Rings* include:

Good	—	evil
Gandalf	—	Sauron
Gandalf	—	Saruman
Gandalf	—	Witch-king
Saruman	—	Sauron
Faramir	—	Boromir
Aragorn	—	Boromir
Théoden	—	Denethor
Arwen	—	Éowyn
Frodo	—	Gollum
The Shire	—	Mordor
North & West	—	South & East
Minas Tirith	—	Barad-dûr
Elves	—	Men

There are many sorts of echoes and doubling-up techniques deployed in J.R.R. Tolkien's Middle-earth legends (and many of those in *The Lord of the Rings* echo those in *The Silmarillion*). The Aragorn-Arwen romance re-playing that of Beren and Lúthien; Isildur slicing off Sauron's finger and Gollum biting off Frodo's finger; two rest-stops in Rivendell; two journeys through/ over the Misty Mountains (with Gollum appearing in both); and the Númenóreans defying the Valar recalling that of Fëanor.

Many of the same situations recur time after time – in particular the to-ing and fro-ing of the wars between the 'free peoples' and the enemies. Assaults on the Dark Lords' strongholds are followed by periods of peace or regroupings, but, soon enough, the enemy is planning its next attack. (For detractors, the doubling and rhyming of events and characters is another manifestation of Tolkien's limitations as a writer. But plenty of other writers, including William Shakespeare, deliberately use the technique).

In *The Lord of the Rings,* the echoes and reflections chime throughout the narrative: in book one, for instance, there are four hobbits travelling to an elven realm, and they're joined by a man linked to the leadership of Gondor (Strider). In *Book Two*, there are nine travellers who go to another elven stronghold, joined by a man of Gondor (Boromir). Books one and two open with a feast, followed by lengthy discussions (which also include the revelation of the ring). In both books Frodo puts on the ring on a hill (Weathertop and Amon Hen). In *The Two Towers* there are two pairs of hobbits (who each traverse great distances and obstacles); two wooded areas (Fangorn and Ithilien), where smoke leads characters to the hobbits; and two authority figures (Treebeard and Faramir) who has to decide what to do with the hobbits (M. Stanton, 69f).

SYMBOLISM AND MOTIFS

'Without symbols you have no language; and language begins only with incarnation and not before it', says one of the characters in *The Notion Club Papers* (HME, 9, 203). For those looking for symbolism, there is plenty in *The Lord of the Rings*. There's tons of 'feminine', maternal and uterine symbolism, for instance, in all those caves, barrows, holes, tunnels and underground places. The hobbits live in comfy, womb-like holes in the ground (literally inside Mother Earth), they are captured inside a giant tree, then entombed inside a barrow underground. They leave the Shire via a tunnel at Crickhollow. The Old Forest is a claustrophobic canopy of trees. The mines of Moria offer plentiful symbols, from the womb as tomb (a favourite comparison in Shakespeare's plays) to a vision of Hell or Hades. The forest canopy of Lothlórien is so dense it's like a green cave. Isengard has industrial pits, like Mordor. Faramir has his base behind a waterfall in a cave. Aragorn has to travel the Paths of the Dead. Théoden hides his people in mountain caves. Later, the tunnel at Cirith Ungol is the place of death and despair (with Shelob as a version of the monstrous, devouring, castrating mother). And finally there's the Crack of Doom, a place of heat and evil, which requires no explanation.

The Mouth of Sauron has affinities with the Mouth of Hell in literature and mythology (Mordor being Hades or the Underworld). The Mouth of Hell in literature is linked to vaginal and womb imagery (there are plenty of tunnels and caves in J.R.R. Tolkien's fiction). The connection is made explicit in much of Western art – in William Shakespeare's *Troilus and Cressida* or *Romeo and Juliet*, for example: 'thou detestable maw, thou womb of death' (*Romeo and Juliet*, V.3).

Tying in with the 'feminine' womb, tunnel and cave images in *The Lord* is the water symbolism. Sometimes water connotes magic and mystery, as in the tradition of Celtic religion, Arthurian legend, folklore and fairy tales: Galadriel's mirror, Elrond's spell on the river, Goldberry the rain and 'river-daughter', the Silverlode that flows beside Lothlórien (Frodo senses the enchantment of Lothlórien from the Silverlode down to the Anduin, with Galadriel as a kind of Lady of the Lake), the sound of water in Mordor, and so on.

Water is linked to the Valar, too (to the god Ulmo in particular). Like witches, the Ringwraiths don't like to cross water (partly because of Ulmo; so the Brandywine and the Anduin become protective borders). In the stand-off at the ford of Bruinen, the nazgûl do enter the water, but they have another reason for doing so, apart from having to obtain the ring: they've got an elf-lord, Glorfindel, and a ranger, Aragorn, wielding fire behind them.

Sometimes the water symbolism is stagnant and deathly: the pool at

Hollin, Gollum's underground lake, the Midgewater Marshes, the Dead Marshes, and the water Gandalf and the balrog fall into. Sometimes water is a place of burial (for Boromir), a resting-place for the ring, or magically sleep-inducing, like the brooks in the Old Forest. Mordor is barren, arid, lacking any fresh water (a fact the narrator repeats many times).

Sometimes the water imagery evokes the sacred and the majesty of men (Amon Hen, the Argonath, Osgiliath). And then there is the motherly symbol to beat all motherly symbols, the ocean, which haunts the narrator and the text as well as characters such as Frodo, Bilbo and Legolas. As in Celtic and Arthurian legend, the undying lands or Avalon (paradise) are reached across the sea. Water as a symbol of rebirth occurs a number of times too: the flood the ents produce at Isengard, for example, or the healing water of Goldberry.

In his Middle-earth mythology, J.R.R. Tolkien weaved in water symbolism from all sorts of classic literature: (1) from Arthurian romance there's the lady in the lake and Excalibur, the Grail, and Arthur sailing over the sea (and into the West, the final destination of many of Tolkien's characters; and kings in Northern European cultures were buried at sea). (2) In *The Odyssey*, Ulysses's voyages (recalling mariners such as Eärendil), encounters with sea monsters, and his homecoming over the ocean (Arwen as Penelope, waiting for Aragorn, who himself becomes a sea captain for a while like the Numenóreans of old when he pilots the fleet up the River Anduin). (3) In Greek mythology, the myth of Atlantis and the flood which Tolkien used in his Númenor stories (with further echoes of the Flood in the *Bible*). (4) From fairy tales and folk tales Tolkien used or reworked ideas such as the hatred of witches for water, monsters in lakes, waves in the shape of horses, and magical mirrors. (5) From Celtic mythology, the notion of water as a border to the underworld or to death, and water's correlative in glass (which's found in old European superstitions such as not looking at the new moon through glass).

The many underground spaces in *The Lord of the Rings* are not only 'feminine', mysterious, and 'maternal': they also evoke different versions of Hell, Hades or the underworld of mythology and religion. It's the place the hero descends to when s/he undergoes the heroic quest (found in many stories, such as Christ in Hell, or Dante in the *Divine Comedy,* or Heracles, or Aenaes, or Orpheus in the Underworld, or Theseus in the labyrinth, or in the Christian ritual of baptism).

Some of these hells or underworlds in Middle-earth are very much like the burning torment of the Catholic faith, complete with fires and demonic creatures (the mines of Moria and Mount Doom) or cold and slime and monsters (Shelob at Cirith Ungol). Many are tombs, like the barrows, Moria and the Paths of the Dead, and some are potential tombs for the heroes, like Old-Man Willow. Some evoke the ancient labyrinths of mythology (Moria, Shelob's lair), and have minotaur-like creatures inside them (the balrog, Shelob).

There are also plenty of phallic towers in J.R.R. Tolkien's fictional world, images of verticality, aggressive patriarchal drives, man-made structures that control the natural world by towering over it: Orthanc, Minas Morgul, Cirith Ungol, Durin's tower, Galadhrim, Mount Doom, Minas Tirith and the White Tower, and the granddaddy of all towers, Barad-dûr. It's no surprise when the towers and structures in *The Lord of the Rings* get progressively bigger, more imposing, more menacing, culminating in the two biggest fastnesses of *The Lord of the Rings*, Minas Tirith and Barad-dûr, the white and the black towers and cities.

As the narrative wends its way South and East things also get darker, more difficult, more ambiguous – and, crucially, more industrial and technological. Isengard is just a pale shadow of the real industrial darkness, because by the time the heroes reach Mordor they've reached the heart of the technological wasteland which J.R.R. Tolkien detested so much. (By contrast, Hobbiton and the Shire – and Rivendell – are constructed along horizontal lines, which follow the topography and shape of the natural world, without imposing too much on it).

STRUCTURE.

C.S. Lewis admired the structure of *The Lord of the Rings*, the way that J.R.R. Tolkien makes the fate of the world rest not on the grand battles and heroic gestures of the high and mighty of Middle-earth, but on the small, ordinary hobbits: far away from the clamour and spectacle of war, 'miserable figures creep (like mice on a slag heap) through the twilight of Mordor' (1982). Gandalf is most acutely aware of this fate of all the characters: it is Gandalf who, in the final battles in *The Lord of the Rings*, calls upon the allies to halt at key moments, when the outcome dances on a knife edge.

As C.S. Lewis famously put it:

> On the one hand, the whole world is going to the war; the story rings with galloping hoofs, trumpets, steel on steel. On the other, very far away, two tiny, miserable figures creep (like mice on a slag heap) through the twilight of Mordor. And all the time we know that the fate of the world depends far more on the small movement than on the great. This is a structural invention of the highest order: it adds immensely to the pathos, irony, and grandeur of the tale. (1968, 13)

For Jack Lewis (1968), any of J.R.R. Tolkien's characters would have been worthy of a book on their own: a character such as Treebeard, Lewis reckoned, would have served another author for a whole book. And Tolkien's characters exist in their own right, rather than just for the sake of the plot.

ALLEGORY.

J.R.R. Tolkien, of course, continually denied that *The Lord of the Rings* was 'allegorical' at all. He disliked the term and the concept of allegory, as well as those readers who insisted on drawing comparisons with contemporary politics, the Second World War, the atom bomb, or his own life: 'it was written to *amuse* (in the highest sense): to be readable. There is *no* 'allegory', moral, political, or contemporary in the work at all', he remarked in 1956 (L, 232). Tolkien went on to explain that although people (or characters) may exemplify principles, they do not 'represent' them. But Tolkien learned that a writer has no control (or very little) over how readers interpret their work.

As he was writing *The Lord of the Rings*, though, J.R.R. Tolkien acknowledged (in a 1939 letter) that the 'darkness of the present days has had some effect on it' (L, 41). In one of the key letters (no. 131), Tolkien said that although his Middle-earth legends were not intended to be allegorical, any work with a good deal of life about it would be interpreted as such (L, 145). *The Lord of the Rings* wasn't allegorical, C.S. Lewis pointed out, it was the other way around: 'real events began, horribly, to conform to the pattern he had freely invented'.

If one wants to view *The Lord of the Rings* allegorically, the nature of evil shifts from Nazi Germany, when J.R.R. Tolkien started writing the book, to Stalinist Russia, when he was completely it. (Maybe, Christopher Wrigley suggested, Saruman represented materialistic science, and Communism, while Sauron is the tyranny of dictators like Hitler). Critics have drawn attention to the links between the orcs and German soldiers – the silver death's head insignia of the S.S., for instance, or their beaked helmets, or their ruthlessness.

JOURNEYS OR, THERE AND BACK AGAIN.

The journey format, employed by writers everywhere from Homer onwards, gave Tolkien a simple technical device on which to hang multiple incidents, accidents, meetings, sidetracks and halts (L, 239).

The Hobbit is a journey narrative, the simple but handy storytelling structure of introducing new locations, new creatures or new adventures as the travellers move through Middle-earth: creatures and species such as trolls, Gollum, Beorn, dragons, goblins, wargs, elves, eagles and spiders, or places such as Mirkwood, Laketown and the Misty Mountains. Apart from the hobbits, pretty much everything in *The Hobbit* and *The Lord of the Rings* had been seen before in mythology, in folk and fairy tales, and in literature (creating Gollum was a master-stroke, an original conception).

IDEAS, THEMES AND TECHNIQUES IN MIDDLE-EARTH
AND *THE LORD OF THE RINGS*

The Lord of the Rings was begun some time between 16th and 19th December, 1938 (at this time, Allen & Unwin had informed J.R.R. Tolkien that *The Hobbit* was selling well, with a second printing being rushed into the shops. So the publishers saw there was a demand for a sequel to *The Hobbit*). When Tolkien started writing it, he was 'flying blind' as biographer Humphrey Carpenter put it; he had no outline, no plan, no schema for the whole book. He launched into it, but had no definite idea where it would take him. In *The History of Middle-earth,* early drafts of *The Lord of the Rings* show how much Tolkien changed his book as he wrote it. Aragorn, for example, the guide for the hobbits, was originally a hobbit called Trotter. Treebeard was an enemy, and imprisoned Gandalf. Lothlórien and Rohan didn't exist, and Saruman didn't appear until much later in the writing process.

One of J.R.R. Tolkien's strategies in forming the structure of *The Lord of the Rings* was contrasting the great and the small: the biggest events in Middle-earth's history can be affected by the smallest inhabitants (the hobbits) or seemingly minor events or acts. Structurally, the greatest contrast is between the grandiose battles, political machinations and heroic acts of Rohan and Gondor in the war against Mordor in the latter half of *The Lord of the Rings,* and the little hobbits crawling across marshes and wastelands to Mount Doom. As the narrator (and Gandalf) points out, the really significant turn of the tide will come from Frodo and Sam, not from the thousands of warriors of the Rohirrim or men of Gondor. Aligned with this dramatic strategy of great and small is Tolkien's use of particular viewpoints, the way events are witnessed through an individual's eyes (a spectacular event like the ruin of Isengard is depicted through the eyes of Merry and Pippin, for example).

As with any heroic story (like a fairy tale, a *James Bond* film, a myth), the reader knows that Frodo is never really in serious danger, because the hero can't be killed off halfway through the book. Similarly, Gandalf can't be dispatched by the balrog and will return.

A recurring motif in *The Lord* is the protagonists being saved – the hobbits are saved from the Ringwraiths by Gildor and the elves, then by Farmer Maggot who turns away a Black Rider, then Aragorn at Bree and later on Weathertop. Glorfindel scares off the Black Riders at the Last Bridge; Glorfindel, his horse and Elrond's flooding river save Frodo again; Strider heals him; the hobbits are saved from Old Man Willow and the Barrow-wight by Tom Bombadil; they're saved from the orcs in Moria by Gandalf and Aragorn; they're saved from the wolves by Gandalf and the others; they're saved from the Watcher at the Gate, and so on.

As the story progress in *The Fellowship of the Ring*, the threat increases, and thus the rescues must be more dramatic, and require more helpers. In the early scenes of *The Lord of the Rings*, Farmer Maggot (a fellow hobbit) is enough to deflect the Black Riders; then Bombadil saves the hobbits a couple of times; Strider's the next saviour, at the *Prancing Pony* and Weathertop; finally, by the end of *Book One*, no less than three people aid Frodo escape (Elrond, Glorfindel and Aragorn, with Gandalf adding the æsthetic flourish of the galloping horses on top of the flood. And these are some of the top people in Middle-earth).

Many of the obstacles thrown at the fellowship when they leave the Last Homely House East of the Sea are aimed at Gandalf as much as Frodo. The crows, the wargs, the Watcher and even Caradhras and the unseen enemies on the mountain are spying on him or trying to stop him. (The adaptors of the 2001-2003 *Lord of the Rings* films took that up, and turned the approach to and through the Misty Mountains as a battle of wills between Gandalf and Saruman).

The encounter with the Eye at Amon Hen shows how far Frodo has come, morally and spiritually: before this, he needed Gandalf or Glorfindel or Bombadil or Aragorn to help save him from jeopardy; now, when he confronts Sauron on Amon Hen, he has the strength to withstand the Dark Lord and take off the ring. (Amon Hen is also a narrative device, to bring the hero and the villain into the same fictional space. Sauron needs these dramatic devices, like the seeing-stones and the seeing places, otherwise he's always in the distance).

Diane Wynne Jones pointed out that, in *The Two Towers*, Merry and Pippin seem to become more confident and self-reliant, and move towards the civilizations of Rohan and Gondor, while Frodo and Sam are moving away from civilization, and end up with Frodo captured and Sam in a desperate situation.[1]

In volume two, *The Two Towers*, the narrative begins big, with battles, chases, kings, princesses, wizards and weird creatures, then narrows down, in *Book Four*, to three small characters struggling across inhospitable wildernesses. The fate of the two hobbits in *Book Four* of course mirrors that of the two hobbits in *Book Three*: but, whereas Merry and Pippin move from danger (orcs) to new friends (Treebeard), Frodo and Sam move into ever more dangerous territory with every step – the Black Gate, Minas Morgul, Cirith Ungol.

The Two Towers is split in two very different halves: the first book (Book 3) is much busier: it concerns Aragorn, Gimli and Legolas pursuing Merry and Pippin; the return of Gandalf; the assault on Helm's Deep; Treebeard, the ents and the hobbits; the march on Isengard and the defeat of Saruman.

Book 4 is much smaller in scale (if not scope): it follows Frodo, Sam and Gollum as they approach Mordor, their passage over the Dead Marshes, the failed attempt at the Black Gate, the interlude with Faramir, the orc encounters at Cirith Ungol and the face-off with the giant spider Shelob.

W.H. Auden pointed out in his 1956 *New York Times* review that a writer of this kind of epic romance had to heighten the drama, build bigger battles, and write more thrilling adventures as the tale progresses. And J.R.R. Tolkien delivers (in A. Becker, 48). For detractors, Tolkien doesn't deliver on his promises. But readers have thought otherwise: *The Lord of the Rings* regularly tops readers' polls, as run by newspapers and bookstores.

Mention of money and trade is curiously missing from most of J.R.R. Tolkien's War of the Ring, until the last pages, when the hobbits return to their beloved Shire and find it overrun with trading, merchants and exploitation of the masses organized by 'ruffians', a Chief and Sharkey (Saruman). Tolkien's attack on capitalism, technology and industry is at its most undisguised and virulent here. In depicting Sauron's empire Tolkien had made it very clear how much his narrator (like the good folk of the West) loathed mass production, machines and technology (Sauron, for instance, uses a lot of iron in his constructions, while the elves, dwarves and men carve stone and wood, precious metals and gems). But it's the portrayal of the Shire during the homecoming that is most heart-rending for the diminutive heroes of the heroic romance.

In a 1951 letter, J.R.R. Tolkien identified three themes of *The Lord of the Rings*: 'Fall, Mortality, and the Machine' (L, 145). Tolkien called the Second World War a victory for no one but machines, with humanity enslaved to machines (L, 111). Robert Giddings related Tolkien's loathing of modern industry to his surroundings at Oxford: it wasn't just the city of dreaming spires, quiet cloisters, the University and philosophical talk: there was another side to Oxford: the city of Cowley and the Morris car factory. (Tolkien often referred to the noise and pollution of cars in his letters, how they made life increasingly difficult and unbearable. He drove a car in the Thirties, but gave it up during the war).

Some of J.R.R. Tolkien's races were inventions – nazgûl, Uruk-hai, balrogs and of course hobbits – but many were adaptions of existing races: dwarves, elves, wizards, eagles. Occasionally, Tolkien wondered if it'd been best to use to many existing species, such as elves. Elves were right for the mythology of Middle-earth, Tolkien said, '[b]ut the disastrous debasement of this word, in which Shakespeare has played an unforgivable part, has really overloaded it with regrettable tones, which are too much to overcome' (L, 185).

The ents were a J.R.R. Tolkien creation (though speaking and walking trees had appeared in literature before).[2] As with all of Tolkien's other creatures, the actual word and its etymology was crucial in the invention of the species. Tolkien meticulously researched the origins of the words for all of his creations, elves, hobbits, orcs and ents. The name ents came from Anglo-Saxon (*eald enta geweorc*) and a link with stone.

The ents came about partly because J.R.R. Tolkien's son Michael asked for a story in which trees got their own back against the people who cut them down, according to some biographers (D. Grotta, 106).

There was also a connection with *Macbeth*: J.R.R. Tolkien said he was disappointed as a schoolboy about the part in the Scottish play where 'Great Birnam wood to high Dunsinane hill' comes, but it turns out to be a camouflaged army. 'I longed to devise a setting in which the trees might really march to war' (L, 212), and he has the ents and the Huorns march on Isengard and rip it to pieces (recalling Hesiod's account of the Giants attacking the Olympian deities).

There's another link with *Macbeth*, which follows the end of the play very closely: Éowyn confronts the Witch-king at the Battle of Pelennor, who boasts that no living man may kill him (from an ancient remark by Glorfindel), echoing the curse in *Macbeth*:

> I bear a charmed life, which must not yield
> To one of woman born. (5.7.41-42).

NOTES: IDEAS, THEMES AND TECHNIQUES

1. D. Jones, in R. Giddings, 1983.
2. One critic linked them to the trees in Enid Blyton's *The Faraway Tree* (K. McLeish, "The Rippingest Yarn of All", in R. Giddings, 1983, 135).

HOBBITS

J.R.R. Tolkien described hobbits as small (3' to 3'6"), with short legs, round bellies, 'round, jovial faces', slightly pointed 'elvish' ears, short curly hair, and furry feet. Their clothes, and the colours, also come straight out of (Grimm) fairy tales: green velvet breeches, waistcoats (vests), which Tolkien himself also favoured (red or yellow), green or brown jackets, gold or brass buttons, green hoods and cloaks.

As C.S. Lewis noted, by making characters hobbits or elves or dwarves, J.R.R. Tolkien was able to use a shorthand form of character-ization: the different races did much of the work of characterization (1968). And readers were already familiar with those sorts of creatures and beings: elves, dwarves, wizards, trolls, orcs (goblins), eagles (apart from hobbits – but Tolkien spends quite a bit of time outlining their traits at the beginning of his two hobbit tales, *The Hobbit* and *The Lord of the Rings*.

And the other creatures, such as the nazgûl or the ents, are also described when they're introduced. Tolkien's elves, though, are a departure from the elves and fairies of fairy and folk tales).

Even the little people can affect history in J.R.R. Tolkien's Secondary World. The wheel of the world was turned by the small hand, because the greater hand is looking elsewhere, Tolkien said in *The Lord of the Rings*, adding that it was the most important passage in the book. And the wheel of the world *had* to turn: someone had to do it.

Hobbits were relatives of humans, or at least nearer to humans than elves or dwarves; 'they liked or disliked much the same things as we used to' (HME, 6, 311). In a late essay ("Of Dwarves and Men"), J.R.R. Tolkien stated that hobbits 'were in nearly all respects normal Men, but of very short stature' (HME, 12, 310).

J.R.R. Tolkien admitted that the hobbits were representations of the 'little people' of England, the suburban masses who could rise up in times of crisis to a challenge (wartime Britain). There are obvious racial and geographical affinities between Tolkien's Middle Earth and Europe in the middle of the 20th century: the Shire and its environs being England; the East (and the South) being 'evil', the orcs being black. Tolkien acknowledged that Mordor was probably in the Balkans.

Frodo and Bilbo are distant relations – first and second cousin, as the Gaffer explains. Uncle and nephew was the relation that J.R.R. Tolkien used in the book (he had considered father and son in earlier drafts).

Bilbo – and Frodo – are exceptional among hobbits. They are among the only hobbits in the Shire who have regular visits from no less a person than the most powerful ally in Middle-earth, Gandalf the wizard (Gandalf does explain his fondness for hobbits and the Shire, but it's not wholly explained, really – and it's significant that none of the other rulers or wise in Middle-earth, including the elves, the kings, the lords and the like, take the hobbits into consideration, and they certainly don't visit them. You don't find Galadriel or Denethor dropping into Hobbiton for a chat and a cup of tea).

Bilbo and Frodo also speak to elves and dwarves and other 'odd strangers' who meet them and also visit them at Bag End (HME, 6, 253). Indeed, Bilbo is described as 'the most famous all the legendary hobbits' (ib., 310). Thus, although hobbits are meant by J.R.R. Tolkien to be representations of Britain's 'ordinary' folk, the homely 'little people' with few ambitions or grand designs, these particular two hobbits are very privileged – by wealth, social status, and the kind of guests they attract. Having Gandalf visiting in the Britain of the 1930s (when Tolkien started writing *The Lord of the Rings*) would be the equivalent of some middle-class people in a village in Worcestershire or Warwickshire receiving the Prime Minister or someone high up in the Cabinet or a minor royal, for no apparent reason as far as onlookers can see, and a very unlikely event – unless they happened to possess a magic ring.

Bilbo's home is Victorian upper middle-class, with its parlours and pantries, cellars and studies, while Bilbo has some of the appearance and habits of an 18th century land-owner. Not only Frodo, but also Merry and Pippin don't have regular jobs, like Sam.

J.R.R. Tolkien employed the fairy tale motif of the orphan: both Bilbo and Frodo are just about orphans (with Bilbo a kind of father figure for Frodo, and Gandalf as a father surrogate for both of them; and, later, Gandalf is a surrogate father, when he takes Pippin into his care).

Middle-earth (in *The Hobbit* and *The Lord of the Rings*) is an ancient world, thousands of years old. It's basically Dark Age or Middle Age (Europe) socially and politically. However, Middle-earth is full of anachronisms (T. Shippey, 2000), which come from the 18th and 19th centuries, such as tobacco (imported from the U.S.A.; Tolkien changed this to 'pipe-weed' in later editions); potatoes (which also came from America); fish and chips (which Sam promises to cook for Gollum); tomatoes (changed to pickles); Bilbo dreaming of frying bacon and eggs (a modern English dish); and Bilbo using matches (friction matches weren't invented until 1827).

The hobbits themselves are anachronistic, an invention entirely of J.R.R. Tolkien's (as are the ents). In his letters, Tolkien, ever the pedant, would go to great lengths to justify some of the inconsistencies to readers who picked them up, while at same time allowing others to remain (such as smoking tobacco – Tolkien himself was too fond his of pipe to let that one go).

Notions of domesticity, the familiar and home comforts were valued highly in J.R.R. Tolkien's fiction, being manifested most obviously in the hobbits, but also in Tolkien's evocations of homely spaces: Tom Bombadil's house, the *Prancing Pony* tavern, the Cottage of Lost Play, Rivendell, Bag End, Crickhollow and the Shire. A mug of beer, an open fire, a pipe, tea, good, plain food and good companionship were the essential components of Tolkienian homeliness. Ever since the publication of *The Hobbit* in 1937, critics have been making connections between the quaint domesticity of the hobbits and that of Tolkien and the Inklings (Tolkien himself didn't deny such links, and often praised beer, food and smoking in his letters).

Both Frodo and Bilbo take the fate of the elves at the end of *The Lord of the Rings,* of sailing into the West – and they were both ringbearers. The two experiences are linked: Bilbo and Frodo become less hobbit-like, perhaps, and more ghostly, more wraith-like, as the ring possessed them and they possessed the ring. Sam remarks that Frodo became thinner and more transparent the more he bore the ring. And Sam, also a ringbearer, for a short while, also takes the straight road over the sea.

Sam Gamgee was the 'everyman' character in *The Lord of the Rings*, meant to be representative of hobbits in general. J.R.R. Tolkien said Sam even irritated him at times (L, 329).

Sam is able to help Frodo complete the quest, which makes him almost as heroic as Frodo for some critics. Only Sam goes all the way on the quest – right to the Crack of Doom. For Marion Zimmer Bradley, the moment when Sam decides to take the ring and complete the quest is a decisive character moment; he knows that Gandalf, Elrond and Galadriel rejected accepting the ring, and he knows just how dangerous the undertaking will be, but he goes ahead and does it. From that point onwards, Sam is driving much of the narrative – from Cirith Ungol, right across Mordor to Orodruin.

Critics have debated who the true or real hero of *The Lord of the Rings* is – Frodo, Aragorn, Sam, or Gandalf (they are the main contenders). Truth is, all of them are heroic, and exhibit the marks of heroes, at different times. Aragorn is a recognizable hero type, the wanderer or exile who returns, the lost son or prince or outcast who fulfils a prophecy and becomes king. Aragorn is the high-born leader amongst men, who leads the goodies into battle and gets to marry the princess at the end, as in fairy tales. Aragorn recalls the hero/ine in fairy tales who is recognized at the end of the tale for the noble and hardworking character he always was. That's what happens in fairy tales much more often than a magical transformation from pauper to king: fairy tale heroes and heroines *always were* good and kind and gentle and noble in the beginning; it's just that no one noticed it.

Frodo's quest is also 'the education of the soul, the striving for salvation', when it's laid out by Gandalf at Bag End, that Frodo has been chosen, somehow (in N. Isaacs, 245). Frodo and Sam are the ordinary guys who become heroes, not chosen by the great and good, or high-born, but who rise to the occasion (although, within hobbit society, Frodo is fairly high up already). For some, Sam is even more heroic than Frodo (in his loyalty and his devotion to Frodo, for instance, or the way he gives up the ring to Frodo with only a moment's hesitation, or the way even he finds he can't slay Gollum),

chǎpτeʀ 13

NOTES, IDEAS AND TECHNIQUES IN J.R.R. TOLKIEN'S MIDDLE-EARTH FICTIONS

THE QUEST.

The Lord of the Rings, a quest story, begins with a party, echoing the beginning of many Arthurian tales, which open with a feast at King Arthur's court at Camelot (a damsel in distress might enter, or a man claiming a boon).[1] Even as the party chapter is progressing, J.R.R. Tolkien introduces some of his major themes (the heroic past which erupts into the present, and won't go away; the ring; the quest; and the naïvety and conservativism of the hobbits).

The Hobbit and its sequel, *The Lord of the Rings,* have similar themes: both focus on an 'ordinary' person, a hobbit, who becomes heroic, embarks on a quest, 'there and back again', with a bunch of other people, and has various adventures and encounters along the way (R. Helms, 1974); and in both books the journey takes a year (from Spring to Spring in *The Hobbit,* and from Autumn to Autumn in *The Lord of the Rings*).

Quests have been a fundamental aspect of mythology and literature since before Homeric times (with the *Odyssey* being perhaps the greatest, as well as one of the first, quest narratives). J.R.R. Tolkien's Middle-earth mythology contains many quests: the elves' quest for the uttermost land of Aman at the beginning of Middle-earth; Beren's quest for Lúthien and the *silmaril*; Eärendil setting out for Valinor to ask for aid for Beleriand; Aragorn's quest for kingship; Frodo and Sam's quest of the ring; the Company's journey East, and later West, via the Grey Havens to the Undying Lands.

Four of the chief characters in *The Lord of the Rings* – Gandalf, Aragorn, Frodo and Sam – undergo heroic/ spiritual descents and returns to dangerous underground places. The underworlds of Moria and the tunnels at Cirith Ungol are among the ones many fans remember from the novel, the places that Frodo and Sam traverse, or where Gandalf nearly meets his death. But Aragorn too has to undertake a journey to the underworld of death before he can be victorious (in the Paths of the Dead).

The most direct course, from Hobbiton to Mordor, would not be via Rivendell, which is actually quite far out of the way, but around the Southern end of the Misty Mountains, into Rohan, then Gondor. That way is decided against, because of Saruman. However, it might have been possible to mobilize the ents to aid a small company to pass over the Misty Mountains, slightly North of Isengard, and into Rohan.

Of course, many other routes could be devised, but it was clear that, as in *The Hobbit*, J.R.R. Tolkien always wanted the fellowship to go directly East first. Indeed, the journey of the Company follows the same route as *The Hobbit* at many points (the trolls, the ford, Rivendell, and the Misty Mountains). Rivendell has the same function as in *The Hobbit*: a place for discussions, decisions, gathering information, supplies, reflection and rest (Hollywood scriptwriters call them 'watering holes' – bars, restaurants, inns, stores). Narratively it allows for much exposition and backstory. (The complete fellowship only exists for the duration of one book in *The Lord of the Rings – Book Two*.)

Once the quest has begun, there's no turning back. On their way to Moria, Gandalf tells Frodo that if they gave up and returned to Rivendell, there wouldn't be any second chances: the ring would have to stay there, and eventually Rivendell would be assailed by the forces of Mordor, and destroyed. And if Sauron got hold of the ring, it would be the end of everything for them (FR, 384).

BOOKS.

J.R.R. Tolkien often spoke of writing his Middle-earth legends as 'sub-creation', a term which links two of his major concerns – art and religion, the artist as God creating a whole world, Tolkien as the deity who 'sub-creates' Middle-earth out of the thought stuff of the 'real world'. But 'sub-creation' for Tolkien also meant that a writer 'discovered' a fantasy world instead of 'inventing' it. That, somehow, Tolkien had discovered the *Red Book of Westmarch* somewhere, and translated it into English.

Apart from the holy book in J.R.R. Tolkien's fantasy stories – the *Red Book of Westmarch* – there are many other books and records in Middle-earth: the libraries at Rivendell and Minas Tirith, for instance (as well as the oral traditions of songs and stories handed down over the generations. And prophecies, inscriptions, spells, curses and the like).

J.R.R. Tolkien playfully put forward the idea that he had translated the *Red Book* into modern English, from the writings of Bilbo, Frodo, Sam and others (it had already been translated by Ælfwine). In the Foreword of *The Lord of the Rings*, Tolkien writes that *The Hobbit* was a selection of material about hobbits from the *Red Book of Westmarch*, which had been written by 'Bilbo himself, the first hobbit to become famous in the world at large' (FR, 17). The *Red Book* was the 'chief monument of Hobbit-lore', 'compiled, repeatedly copied, and enlarged and handed down in the family of the Fairbairns of Westmarch' (HME, 12, 25). That became a history of Middle-earth that had been lost and found again in the *Red Book*. It had all really happened, thousands of years ago. (The title the *Red Book of Westmarch* may be a reference to the *Red Book of Hergest*, a 14th century book of Welsh Celtic lore).

OFF-STAGE CHARACTERS AND EVENTS.

Another odd omission occurs late in *The Lord of the Rings*, when Elrond's sons appear, somewhat off-stage. It's strange that they don't feature more prominently in the war against Sauron (or at least, in the foreground, with the other major characters). Odd, because Aragorn undertook sorties from Rivendell with them and the rangers to hunt down orcs. But then, many of the elves remain distant from the action in Gondor and Rohan: a major elf, Glorfindel, who helped save Frodo at the Ford, also doesn't appear.

Círdan, the shipwright at Grey Havens, is also mostly off-stage in *The Lord of the Rings*. Círdan, a powerful figure in Tolkien's *legendarium,* also doesn't come to the war. But Círdan had fought with the Teleri elves in the First Age, led an assault of elves and men against the Witch-king in Angmar, whom he defeated, fought in the Last Alliance, and aided a figure no less than Eärendil (helping him build the ship *Vingilot,* in which Eärendil sails the skies). Tolkien described Círdan as seeing 'further and deeper than any other in Middle-earth' (UT, 392). Clearly, Círdan decides to sit out the War of the Ring (his act of giving his ring to Gandalf perhaps symbolizes that, although Círdan did go on to battle the Lord of the Nazgûl in TA 197).

And finally Elrond, who had lived in Númenor at the time of Sauron's persecution of 'the Faithful', and who had fought beside Elendil and Gil-galad against Sauron in the Last Alliance, stays put in Rivendell in *The Lord of the Rings*. Elrond has a busy history, too, fighting in the war against the Enemy, which goes back through the Third Age to the Second Age in Númenor and Eldamar. Elrond has been as active as almost anyone in Middle-earth in the struggle against Morgoth and his disciple Sauron, but when it comes to the War of the Ring, he plumps to remain in Imladris.

Thus, very few of the chief elves fight in the war in the main plots (their contributions take place off-stage, in second-hand accounts. The battles raging around Lothlórien and Mirkwood are ones which readers might like to hear about first-hand). In this way, J.R.R. Tolkien reminds the reader that the War of the Ring is a human war, not of the elves; it is nearly the end of the Third Age, and the elves will be passing away to the West at the end of it. (Perhaps there's also some sort of rightness in the focus of the war against evil shifting from elves to humans, because it was a man,

Isildur, who was partly to blame for the ring and Sauron still being in existence: note that, at the Crack of Doom, it was an elf and a man who decided the fate of the ring. Elrond wanted it destroyed in Orodruin, but Isildur kept it.)

THE SCOURING OF THE SHIRE.

Interesting that Saruman doesn't employ magic when he's in the Shire, turning it into an industrial wasteland (even though he's a wizard). Rather, the forces at work are naturalistic, or non-magical. There's something pathetic, pitiful and small-minded about Saruman travelling to the Shire and choosing it as the target of his malice. This was the most powerful of the *istari*, one of the one or two people who would have been a match for Gandalf, someone who fancied himself as a necromancer in waiting, a future Dark Lord, who stoops to the level of a mean, vindictive and petty villain. After setting his sights on controlling a large part of Middle-earth (if he found the ring), Saruman is reduced to (reduces himself to) overturning the socio-political regime of the Shire. If he can't have all Middle-earth, he'll turn the Shire into a miniature Mordor. When the hobbits return and converse with the Chief Shiriff, some of the time it seems as if Saruman has been doing all this just to get back at the goodies – not just the hobbits, but all of the 'good peoples', the nobles, lords and ladies who have triumphed over Sauron.

Frodo and his companions returning to the Shire recalls *The Odyssey* (except that Frodo has no wife waiting for him, as Aragorn has with Arwen). Frodo is a curiously forlorn figure at the end of the quest; Sam notices his isolation and melancholy, and it saddens Sam that Frodo isn't given more respect. Frodo withdraws into himself, while Merry and Pippin (and Sam) soak up all the glory. The three hobbits all eventually settle down to heterosexual relationships and founding families, while Frodo remains the lonely bachelor.

Was the outsider personality always in Frodo, or did his experience of possessing the ring make him so withdrawn by the end of the book? Or was it the sheer effort of the journey to Mordor, so he's utterly exhausted? Or was it the final struggle with Gollum that 'broke' him? Or is it the illness from the Morgul blade (which haunts him on October 6th each year) and other illnesses that debilitate him? It's an interesting question: is Frodo's weariness spiritual, or emotional, or physical, or psychological?

Saruman has instigated an economic, social and political change in "The Scouring of the Shire", a radical change in regime which is a kind of political revolution. Tolkien's narrator makes it clear on which side his sympathies lie: he's against the industrialization of the Shire, the economic and social reforms, which all shock the hobbits' conservative, quasi-liberal, laidback and homely politics.

J.R.R. Tolkien employed aspects of both mid-20th century Communism and fascism, collectivization and totalitarianism, in "The Scouring of the Shire" chapter. The new regime is full of rules and commandments, restrictions on behaviour, a massive increase in the use of force and the militia, and government from a single leader, the Chief Shiriff. Although Tolkien's view of political and social corruption wasn't as elaborate (or as celebrated) as his contemporaries, such as Aldous Huxley (in *Brave New World*) or George Orwell (in *Animal Farm*), it was just as passionate. One can feel the rage at political corruption throughout "The Scouring of the Shire" sequence, the indignation behind the reactions of the returning hobbits (apart from Frodo's weary acceptance of the inevitability of people's resistance to change).

THE PAST.

Much of the past history of Middle-earth has been mysteriously forgotten by the time of the events of *The Lord of the Rings*. For instance, Gandalf and the Company cannot seem to travel over the Misty Mountains, but three thousand years before, during the Last Alliance, the biggest force ever assembled ('none greater has been mustered since the host of the Valar went against Thangorodrim' [S, 293]) manages to march over the mountains.

Not only ancient places and historical events, but historical figures haunt the pages of *The Lord of the Rings:* Durin, the Entwives, the Barrow-wights, the Old Took, Eorl, Isildur, Eärendil, Beren and Lúthien, and the Númenóreans.

The dwarves have links back into the distant past, too: both Thorin and Gimli have Durin the Deathless as their ancestor, one of the seven dwarves created by the god Aulë (and that was a *long* time ago).

THE ENTS.

After their overthrow of Saruman and Isengard, Treebeard, the ents and the huorns leave the story of *The Lord of the Rings*. They would be very useful allies at Pelennor and the Morannon, but they disappear (until Treebeard is encountered on the return journey at the end of *The Return of the King*) partly because they had fulfilled their narrative function (sacking Isengard, and helping to save the day at Helm's Deep). Treebeard and the ents do appear in the background of *The Lord of the Rings,* though: they are summoned to aid Lórien and Rohan by Galadriel (who sends a message to Treebeard via those very useful eagles), and destroy an orc camp (HME 8, 361). Tolkien had considered bringing the ents to the battle at the Morannon (along with elves from Lórien).

The ents may have been created the Vala (god) Oromë, Tolkien mused, as a response to Aulë creating the dwarves.

MILITARY STRATEGIES.

J.R.R. Tolkien's war strategies in *The Lord of the Rings* may be intended to be pre-mediæval, pre-Norman Conquest, with weaponry such as bows and arrows, swords and shields, and the odd unusual weapon (such as a battering ram). There are elements, though, of the First World War in the later battles in *The Lord of the Rings*: the eagles as a flying élite (to be used sparingly, and only by the chiefs of staff), a single siege engine or tank (the ram Grond), rapid movements of troops across enormous distances and plains, key cities as the focus of conflict, and dangerous missions behind the lines.2

W.H. Auden found it odd that both Sauron and Saruman have technology and machinery at their disposal, but they still fight wars the old way. (Tolkien used the genre of *The Lord of the Rings* – a war story – as a way of defending the lack of female roles in the book: it was a war story, in which women wouldn't play such a prominent part.) The possibility of leaving out one of the hobbits was suggested to the filmmakers of the 2001-2003 films of *The Lord of the Rings* by studio executives, as well as making one of them female (in the end, Frodo became that female or feminized hobbit, and in a minor fashion, so did Pippin).

The battles in J.R.R. Tolkien's fiction tend to have the goodies vastly out-numbered by the baddies, with little chance of success. The captains and leaders, such as Gandalf and Aragorn, take fighting very seriously and grimly. Every battle could be the last battle they'll fight.

The other battles in the War of the Ring that are related in second-hand accounts are important for the success of the whole enterprise: in Dale, Laketown, Lórien, Mirkwood and Dol Guldur. Without them, there might have been 'dragonfire and savage swords in Eriador, night in Rivendell', says Gandalf (RK, 450).

Cornish writer Colin Wilson found the battles in *The Lord of the Rings* distracting, and they seemed to come from a completely different book. They slowed up the narrative; when Wilson read *The Lord of the Rings,* he skipped book five in order to follow Frodo and Sam's story; when he read it to his children, they insisted on skipping the battles again: 'the children seemed to lose interest until we got back to Frodo and Sam' (1974).

Let's not kid ourselves: *The Lord of the Rings* is great, but it isn't Homer's *Iliad.* The core of the novel for Wilson was Frodo's journey, which remained 'exciting even after several readings'. Wilson also skipped the long speeches in what he called 'heroicese'.

MIRACULOUS ESCAPES.

The number of hair's-breadth escapes in *The Lord of the Rings* are startling (but of course audiences love them): a Black Rider turns back at the last minute from Hobbiton; the hobbits are saved from Old-Man Willow by Tom Bombadil on the one day in the year when he's walking in that part of the Old Forest; having Glorfindel arrive to effect another miraculous escape for Frodo and the ring can seem like another intervention of the gods in the West in the fate of Middle-earth; in Hollin the fire dies down just before the bird spies appear; just as the tentacled monster attacks in Hollin, Gandalf discovers the password; although orc arrows pierce hats and clothes, the fellowship remains miraculously unscathed throughout Moria; Frodo seems badly wounded, but has a mithril shirt; Merry and Pippin are saved from being killed by Grishnákh by a stray spear out of the dark; nearly all of the orcs at Cirith Ungol conveniently destroy each other, allowing for Sam's rescue; Frodo and Sam escape orcs by incredible luck so many times; Sam wakes up just when Gollum is about to take the ring; Aragorn and the Corsair ships appear when the battle of Minas Tirith looks like it's lost; the ring is destroyed at the moment when it seems as if Host of the West is doomed; and the giant eagles save the hobbits just in time.[3]

It does appear as if J.R.R. Tolkien was better at getting characters into perilous scrapes than he was at finding credible methods of getting them out.

The Black Riders helpfully give up their pursuit at the last moment. Every time a Black Rider's about to discover Frodo and the ring, there's always a miraculous escape. When one of the nazgûl climbs off his horse and is crawling towards Frodo, snuffling (an odd image, scary and comical), Gildor and the elves arrive in the nick of time (FR, 114). And in an earlier episode, the Black Rider gets the scent of the ring, but then simply gives up and carries on (FR, 109).

The eagles of the Misty Mountains were used – sparingly – as miraculous rescuers. They were also employed by the elves of Rivendell in the search for Gandalf and the hobbits on their way from Bree. In one version of *The Fellowship of the Ring,* the eagles find Gandalf and bring him to Imladris (HME, 7, 75). Handily, the eagles turn up at the battle at the Black Gate.

J.R.R. Tolkien could have balanced up good and evil, heroes and villains, a little more squarely, or at least suggested that the evil and villains had a good chance of winning. Tolkien seemed unwilling to allow any of goodies to die, for instance: among the significant hero characters, only Théoden and Boromir die. Tolkien has Faramir nearly die, the only survivor of the Osgiliath rout, but he is revived; similarly with Éowyn and Merry at Pelennor. Gandalf dies but returns. Even Bill the pony, doomed to certain death from monsters and wolves, survives.[4]

There are wounds and painful memories – Frodo has wounds which will never heal – but Frodo gets to go to the Undying Lands, the closest thing to heaven in Tolkien's Middle-earth. Frodo is untainted by murder, too: he doesn't kill anybody (whereas his fellow hobbits all kill orcs).

Conveniently, other hobbits, not Frodo, kill Wormtongue near the end, who has just knifed his master Saruman and thus Frodo's enemies are dispatched by others.

The cost of the War of the Ring doesn't seem that great, then: none of the important hero characters die, and peace returns to Middle-earth. There's an ending of elegy and loss, with the departure of the elves, Frodo and Gandalf. But the elves were going anyway, and their whole existence contains a sense of continual loss.

There are happy endings recalling fairy tales in *The Lord of the Rings:* Aragorn marries Arwen; Éowyn marries Faramir; Sam marries Rosie; and Éomer, too, marries (he weds Lothíriel, the daughter of Prince Imrahil).

The early Middle-earth stories didn't have happy endings, in the usual fairy tale sense. The battles against Morgoth, the fights over the silmarils, the civil war among the elves, and so on, end with Beleriand submerged, Númenor cast into the sea and the world 'bent', two silmarils lost, the Noldor exiled in Middle-earth, and the gradual fading of the elves by the end of the Third Age.

The nazgûl could've dispatched the hobbits before they met up with Strider: they had chances in the Shire, for example. They knew the name of Baggins and the Shire (and one of 'em got as far as Hobbiton, and met the Gaffer). On Weathertop they could've stabbed Frodo in the heart instead of the shoulder (at that point, he didn't have Bilbo's mithril coat, and two Black Riders could've held onto him on each side while the Witch-king struck him), or they could've cut off his hand (a favourite device in the *Star Wars* films), which would've been a suitable way of claiming revenge for Isildur cutting the ring off their master's finger. Frodo didn't need to remain alive for Sauron's purposes – all the Ringwraiths had to do was to obtain the ring. If they had, it's hard to believe that Strider could have withstood them on Weathertop on his own, if the Witch-king possessed the ring.

In terms of the story, J.R.R. Tolkien has to let the hobbits escape or be rescued each time from the Black Riders, otherwise the story's over pretty quickly. At the same time, Sauron's chief accomplices appear dumb and incompetent. You'd think the greatest villain in Middle earth's history, after Morgoth, would be able to choose smart, ruthless and efficient allies.

RIVENDELL.

Just as important as the journey of the hobbits to Rivendell are the places they stay along the way. Each of them is a version of a 'homely house', a version of Bilbo's and Frodo's beloved Bag End: Crickhollow, Tom Bombadil's house, the *Prancing Pony,* and Rivendell (plus the stays with Gildor and the elves, and at Farmer Maggot's). The meals, the hot baths, the drinks, the singing and dancing are all important – for the story, as well as the hobbits. Each place or stop becomes more dangerous, requiring rescues and escapes: escaping the Black Riders at Crickhollow but falling foul of Old-Man Willow in the Old Forest; rescue and escape to Tom Bombadil's home, followed by another snake-pit situation, the Barrow-wights (requiring another rescue, by Bombadil). Bree's more of an ambiguous refuge (though the ale and food is still good). Here the hobbits're rescued from the nazgûl by Strider, as they are again on Weathertop. The journey to Rivendell requires another rescue, this time by Glorfindel (and Elrond magicing up the river at the ford).

Rivendell is the ultimate homely house in J.R.R. Tolkien's mythopoeia. Sam describes Rivendell as the ultimate place to retire to: it has a bit of everything in it – the Shire, Lothlórien, Gondor, 'and kings' houses and inns and meadows and mountains all mixed' (RK, 321). It's clearly the place Tolkien himself would like to retire to – as well as the Shire. Bilbo at Rivendell is the archetype of blissful Tolkienesque retirement: he sits around, composing poems in Elvish, chatting to elves, eating good food, smoking his pipe, and writes up his life's adventures.

HIGHER POWERS.

Gandalf hints from time to time there are higher powers at work in the events unfolding in Middle-earth than those of Sauron or the high elves. Relating how the ring left Gollum and was found by Bilbo in the Misty Mountains, Gandalf comments:

> "behind it that there was something at work beyond any design of the ringmaker. I can put it no plainer than my saying that *Bilbo was meant* to find the Ring, and *not* by its maker. In which case you were also meant to have it, and that may be an encouraging thought, or it may not" (HME, 7, 25)

Gandalf is probably referring to the gods, the Valar, or maybe to Ilúvatar himself (or maybe to fate, destiny, chance, or luck). Maybe the powers (or Ilúvatar) have decided that the ring should be found by the one race (hobbits) who are capable of both bearing it and carrying it to its destruction. But Gandalf's thoughts here directly contradict his other views on the ring: that it is wholly evil, that it is trying to get back to its maker, that there's only one 'Lord of the Ring', and so on. The notion that everything is ultimately 'destined' or 'fated' inevitably ruins any sense of narrative suspense, danger or jeopardy, because all will turn out well anyway. (It also expresses the tensions between the themes of 'free will' and 'doom' or 'fate', the pagan and the Christian, both central to Tolkien's philosophy).

THE MAIAR.

Co-existing with the Valar in Arda (the world) are the Maiar, lesser spirits (but of the same order as the Valar). Most of the Maiar live in Aman, and seldom appear in Middle-earth. One of the significant Maia who features in the Middle-earth legends is Melian (apart from Gandalf): she marries Elwë, King Thingol, and is the mother of Lúthien (thus characters such as Elrond, Arwen and Aragorn have a Maia, a spirit of Aman or the blessed Realm, as their distant ancestor). As a Maia, Melian chooses to take on the form of an elf, in order to marry Elwë/ Thingol; her Maia powers also help her turn Doriath into a protected kingdom, with the 'Girdle of Melian', a kind of magical forcefield (S, 234).

Melian is a forerunner of Lúthien: she's incredibly beautiful, wise, and a great enchantress. Melian is linked to Lúthien in another fashion: she is courted by Elwë (Thingol) in a similar way: Elwë hears Melian singing before he sees her, just like Beren, and encounters her in a forest (in Neldoreth and Region), just like Beren:

> an enchantment fell on him, and he stood still; and afar off beyond the voices of the *lómelindi* he heard the voice of Melian, and it filled all his heart with wonder and desire. (S, 55)

On the enemy's side, the chief Maia is Sauron. Other spirits seduced by Morgoth include the balrogs (the Valaraukar), the 'scourges of fire' and 'demons of terror' (S, 31).

TOLKIEN'S SUPERHEROES.

Another striking thing about *The Lord of the Rings* is the superhuman energy of most of the characters. When I re-read *The Lord of the Rings* yet again I was struck by the amount of movement and travelling in the book (most of it on foot or on horseback, with one or two characters, higher up the social hierarchy (usually sorcerers), who get to ride on giant eagles or flying reptiles). For J.R.R. Tolkien the writer, *The Lord of the Rings* is a vast, time-consuming and intricate effort of narrative organization, with characters moving to and fro rapidly, an orchestration of mileage, speed, days and dates, phases of the moon, seasons, and so on.

The continual journeys of the characters are no surprise, perhaps, in a book of this type and scale. What's amazing is how far the characters are able to travel without being totally exhausted, and so many of the journeys occur at night. Almost every journey in *The Lord of the Rings,* especially in the second half of the book, takes place at night. Characters tramp all through the night and rest at dawn (and they seem able to find their way at night too, which can be very difficult if you can't see distant landmarks).

J.R.R. Tolkien is careful to keep track of meals and rest times, but even so, the dwarves, elves, hobbits, men and other races of Middle-earth are astonishingly resilient and possess the rock-hard stamina that athletes aim for. It's surprising there aren't more heart attacks and collapses from stress and exhaustion. Bad terrain slows up walking hugely. In terms of mileage, Gandalf probably does the most, closely followed by Aragorn. (W.H. Auden estimated that Frodo travelled 1,800 miles and was on the road for 80 days (not counting rests).) But remember that the hobbits are only 3' to 3'6" high, and their strides can't be as big as Strider's. Karen Fonstad, in her indispensable *The Atlas of Middle-earth,* says the fellowship walked 18 and 20 miles per day over often, and sometimes 25 or 28 miles. That's a very good mileage to keep up *every day*, and over difficult terrain, and often at night.

J.R.R. Tolkien is also hazy on the details of the walking and camping gear the fellowship took with them. They travel over the alpine Misty Mountains in Winter, but Tolkien's narrator doesn't explain how they don't get soaked, or freeze to death (they haven't got tents, thermal clothing, gas stoves, and don't always light fires, for fear of attracting attention).

THE RETURN OF ARAGORN.

Aragorn is a superhero figure: (1) an incredible warrior (the best in all Middle-earth); (2) a brilliant tracker, hunter and Ranger; (3) a grim, solemn Byronic romantic hero (the most eligible bachelor in all Middle-earth); (4) a shamanic (and Christ-like) healer; (5) the last of the ancient races; (6) a leader of men; (7) a poet; (8) and a king. He can run 135 miles in three days, and summon the dead. He's undaunted in the face of countless orcs, trolls and nasty critters. Aragorn seems to be brilliant at everything, and has few flaws. And he's always *right* (and in the right).

In his younger days, Aragorn has already been out and about in Middle-earth, serving a kind of kingly apprenticeship – working alongside King Thengel in Rohan, and with the steward Ecthelion II in Gondor (where he's known as Thorongil, the Eagle of the Star). Indeed, as the appendices of *The Lord of the Rings* relate, Aragorn leads a small fleet down to Umbar and burns the Corsairs' ships (RK, 413). Aragorn's time in Gondor also serves as further backstory for the dislike Denethor has for Aragorn, because Denethor saw Aragorn as a rival (ibid.).

Aragorn also has more names than most in amongst characters that have multiple titles: Strider (in Bree), Elessar Telcontar, Dúnadan, Elfstone, Estel (in Rivendell), Thorongil (in Gondor), Longshanks, Wingfoot (by Éomer), the Renewer, Isildur's heir, King of the Reunited Kingdom, Lord of the Western Lands, etc.

Gandalf rivals Aragorn for multiple names (it's like who's got the biggest sword – who's got the most names?): Gandalf's called Mithrandir (by the elves), Tharkûn (by the dwarves), Grayhame (by the Rohirrim), Stormcrow (by Théoden), Láthspell (by Wormtongue), Grey Fool (by

Denethor), Grey Pilgrim, Grey Wanderer, White Rider, and Gandalf the White.

There are numerous signs that J.R.R. Tolkien includes to demonstrate that Aragorn is the rightful, returned king: healing Faramir, Éowyn and Merry; summoning the dead at the Stone of Erech; looking into the *palantír* and wrestling with Sauron; the reforged sword; and finding a sapling descended from Nimloth in Númenor (which was descended from Galathilion of Tirion and Telperion, the Tree of Light. In short, a little bit of Valinor, right there on the slopes behind Minas Tirith).

Aragorn's magical sword, Narsil/ Anduril, was forged by Telchar, the talented dwarf-smith of Nogrod, who also made the dagger, Angrist, that cut the silmarils from Morgoth's iron crown.

There is a third heirloom that Aragorn has, alongside the shards of Narsil, and the ring of Barahir: the Sceptre of Annúminas, which Elrond returns to Aragorn when he is crowned king of Arnor and Gondor.

Aragorn's son, Eldarion, rules a great realm, according to the appendices of *Lord*, followed by 'the kings of many realms in long days after' (HME, 12, 245). But Tolkien's narrator adds, no one can say if that came true, because 'Gondor and Arnor are no more, and even the chronicles of the House of Elessar and all their deeds and glory are lost' (ibid.).

In *The Lord of the Rings,* J.R.R. Tolkien's narrator is a little vague as to why Aragorn hasn't gone to Gondor to claim the kingship, why he's waiting. In this, Aragorn resembles Gandalf, who is patient enough to wait for decades or even centuries for events to arrange themselves into the best order to achieve his goals.

Aragorn's character, like Frodo's, is tied up with J.R.R. Tolkien's Atlantis mythology: the idea was a 'Elf-friend' and 'Bliss-friend', archetypal characters, father and son, going back into Middle-earth history, which had a parallel with real British and European history (both Aragorn and Frodo are called 'Elf-friend'). As Tolkien explained in a letter of July, 1964:

> It started with a father-son affinity between Edin and Elwin of the present, and was supposed to go back into legendary time by way of an Eädwine and AElfwine of *c.* A.D. 918, and Audoin and Alboin of Lombardic legend, and so the traditions of the North Sea concerning the coming of corn and culture heroes, ancestors of kingly lines, in boats (and their departure in funeral ships). One such Sheaf, or Shield Seafing, can actually be made out as one of the remote ancestors of our present Queen. In my tale we were to come at least to Amandil and Elendil, leaders of the royal party in Númenor, when it fell under the domination of Sauron. (L, 347).

These were further ways into which linked the Middle-earth legends with actual British and European history.

MYTH.

Myth, for J.R.R. Tolkien, lay outside the limits of language; if it was studied too closely, it became nothing more than linguistic techniques, or style, or skill. Myth evaded dissection.

For Tolkien, 'sub-creation' or 'myth-making' was a way of engaging with the eternal truth, with God, because myths, though created by people, reflect something of the 'true light', something of the life of perfection before the Fall.[5]

For C.S. Lewis, the value of myth and mythological writing was to restore and rediscover the world, to cleanse the doors of perception, to make the familiar and everyday wondrous again.

J.R.R. Tolkien wrote in a letter of 'an equally basic passion of mine *ab initio* was for myth (not allegory!) and for fairy-story, and above all for heroic legend on the brink of fairy-story and history' (L, 144).

DWARVES.

One of the Valar, Aulë, god of the all things to do with the earth (and craftsmanship), creates the dwarves long before the arrival of the 'Children of Ilúvatar' (the elves), because he can't wait to have people to teach. Of course, the deity finds out about Aulë's presumptuous creation, and orders Aulë to hide the 'Seven Fathers of the Dwarves' away until the elves have come (S, 43).

J.R.R. Tolkien said he thought of the dwarves as Jews, 'at once native and alien', an unfortunate comparison (L, 229).

REPETITIONS AND RHYMES.

J.R.R. Tolkien's Middle-earth writings have events and situations which recur or are repeated, in a different context, with new characters. Sometimes these rhymes and repeats are deliberate, and sometimes they occur unconsciously. Gandalf falling into the abyss with the balrog, for instance, was prefigured in the early tales of Gondolin (Glorfindel stabs a balrog in the belly, and it falls, shrieking, hanging on to Glorfindel as it falls [HME1, 194]).

Gandalf going into the dungeons of Dol Guldur and finding an old dwarf there clearly recalls Lúthien in Sauron's dungeons. Rescues by giant eagles in *The Lord of the Rings* were first related in the earlier Middle-earth tales. The whole structure of *The Lord of the Rings,* at least in its early quest travelling East to Rivendell and the Misty Mountains, mirrors the journey in *The Hobbit* very closely. The fate of Arwen and Aragorn reflects that of Beren and Lúthien. Frodo is a younger version of Bilbo. The ring itself of course mirrors the silmarils and the nauglamír. (And Tolkien can't resist using the same names in different contexts: Gothmog, lord of balrogs, becomes the witch-king's lieutenant at Pelennor; Glorfindel's an elf lord in Gondolin who also saves Frodo from the nazgûl).

The terrain of *The Lord of the Rings* tends to repeat itself: J.R.R. Tolkien likes to employ the same geographical features time after time. The fellowship, for instance, traverse three mountain ranges (Misty Mountains, Emyn Muil, and Mountains of Shadow); three tunnels through mountains (Moria, the Paths of the Dead and Cirith Ungol); three enchanted woods (the Old Forest, Fangorn and Lórien); three plains (Pelennor, Gorgoroth and the Brown Lands); two bogs or swamps (Midgewater Marshes, Dead Marshes); two eleven realms (Imladris and Lórien), and so on.

DREAMS.

Dreams form an important subplot in *The Lord of the Rings* – and Frodo's dreams in particular. They are more like waking visions than nocturnal dreams: Frodo's vision of Gandalf at Orthanc; his dream of the far green country at Tom Bombadil's house. Frodo's dreams and visions tie in with a wide-ranging deployment of visions, prophecies and magical means of visualization in *The Lord of the Rings* (such as the magical seeing stones and mirrors).

Dreams and visions are part of J.R.R. Tolkien's toolbox of narrative devices. In *The Lost Road*, for instance, the hero, Alboin, is haunted by recurring dreams of lost lands beyond or below the sea (just as Tolkien said he was haunted by dreams of Atlantis and its drowning, which he called his 'Atlantis haunting').

THE SEA.

In *The Silmarillion*, J.R.R. Tolkien wrote that when Tuor saw the Great Sea of Belegaer, 'he was enamoured of it and the sound of it and the longing for it were ever in his heart and ear' (S, 238). Even the mountains and rivers seem to speak in Middle-earth, and trees and stones appear to be listening for enemies.

Eventually, all of the key characters in *The Lord of the Rings* sail West into legend: Frodo and Bilbo join Middle-earth's great and good at Grey Havens (Gandalf, Galadriel, Elrond), which's how *The Return of the King* closes. Sam follows at the end of his life (in 1482 FA), and finally Legolas and Gimli, after the death of Aragorn in 1541. In an early version of *The Silmarillion*, the elves sail to Valinor by harnessing swans to their boats (HME, 4, 14).

THE ELVES.

J.R.R. Tolkien decried how the idea of elves had been been changed around the 16th century from something important and the size of a man to little, innocuous fairies. Tolkien was dismissive of the Elizabethan poets' use of elves and fairies, turning them into little creatures that could hide in cowslips – all that Michael Drayton and William Shakespeare stuff, as Tolkien put it. It was 'hideous' for him how elves had been debased.

In lectures, J.R.R. Tolkien kept the idea that elves or fairies exist open, acknowledging that it was important for people to believe such things could exist, but he knew that his Middle-earth mythology was primarily a literary creation; it wasn't meant to be taken literally or seriously.

For J.R.R. Tolkien's narrators, it's a narrative device to introduce hobbits or elves by remarking that they are still around but are good at keeping themselves to themselves. But the whole inclination of *The Lord of the Rings* and his other Middle-earth writings (as for Tolkien himself), is towards a decline and dying fall. The ents have lost their wives; the population of Gondor is dwindling; there are few dwarf women and even fewer dwarf children.[6]

Tom Shippey suggested that J.R.R. Tolkien himself identified with characters who lived on into the modern ages, who were descended from the immortals of Middle-earth, characters who recorded the events of a former, mythical period in their own chronicles (such as Frodo, Bilbo, Farmer Maggot, 'Looney' and Smith). And Tolkien wrote different versions of a time travel story in which travellers from historical Britain (such as Cornwall) travel over the sea to the mythical realms of Tolkien's Secondary World (or they travel in time). As a scholar of mediæval literature, Tolkien was already a time traveller, someone who in his profession continually travelled back into the past.

Elves were the embodiment of 'higher', cultural aspects of humanity, they are artists, scientists, and philosophers. J.R.R. Tolkien explained:

> The Elves represent, as it were, the artistic, æsthetic, and purely
> scientific aspects of the Humane nature raised to a higher level than is
> actually seen in Men. (L, 236).

Elves are spiritual people, who see the world as 'a reality derived from God in the same degree as themselves' (ibid.). The 'sin' of the elves is thus perhaps a tendency to favour their own creations over God's, to be more caught up in what they make themselves rather than what Ilúvatar made.[7] As artists, creative people, it's the elves' doom to become restless and bored, to become weary of living.

In "Myths Transformed", written in the late 1950s, J.R.R. Tolkien stated that elves were not immortal. Rather, 'they in fact only had enormously long lives, and were themselves physically 'wearing out', and suffering a slow progressive weakening of their bodies' (HME, 10, 410). In other words, pretty much like humans, though stretched out over thousands of years.

Legolas explains to Frodo in *The Lord of the Rings* (*pace* Lórien) what the passing of time is like for the elves. It's both 'very swift and very slow', he says. Swift, because elves don't change much, and everything else does. And slow, because elves don't count the years as they rush by (FR, 505). There is, though, an inevitable wearing down: '"Yet beneath the Sun all things must wear to an end at last"'.

There are two main elven realms in *The Lord of the Rings* – the Wooded Realm of Thranduil, in Northern Mirkwood, is outside the main narrative (like Dale, Erebor, Laketown and Dol Guldur). There is also the Grey Havens, of course, and also the wandering bands ('Wandering Companies') of elves (such as Gildor and his cronies).

The Eldar and Númenórean men were normally seven feet tall J.R.R. Tolkien states in a late essay (HME, 12, 310). Needles to say, few of the illustrators of Tolkien's fiction in paintings, drawings, or films have taken up that idea.

The elves (and men) who escaped from Morgoth in Middle-earth lived in the West and North-west of Middle-earth because that part of Middle-earth was closest to the Blessed Realm (UT, 398).

The Elvish solar year (*loa*) begins in Spring, around April 6 (the day before the first day of Spring, of *tuilë* (UT, 422). The elves had a different calendar from hobbits or men, of course. J.R.R. Tolkien loved to invent things like calendars, days of the week, names for the seasons, and so on. The calendar of Rivendell, for instance, had six seasons: *tuilë, lairë, yávië, quellë, hrivë,* and *coirë*: Spring, Summer, Autumn, Fading, Winter and Stirring (Fading was also called *lasse-lanta* in Quenyan, 'leaf-fall', and *narbeleth* in Sindarin, 'sun-waning') (RK, 485).

Twilight was important for the Eldar in Northern regions, Tolkien wrote in the appendices to *The Lord of the Rings,* and they had names for 'star-fading', *tindomë* (before dawn) and 'star-opening', *undomë* (evening) (RK, 491).

THE FADING OF THE ELVES IN MIDDLE-EARTH.

With the destruction of the One Ring, the elves will diminish, as Galadriel and Elrond recognize, to be supplanted by men. The ents and the dwarves will also fade away. The whole drift of the narrative in *The Lord of the Rings* is towards a passing away, a change, a death: the end of the Third Age, the end of the age of elves, of the dwarves, of the ents, perhaps even of the hobbits. It is the end for J.R.R. Tolkien of the age of mythical beings such as elves, dwarves, ents and hobbits. It's the end of magic, too, and of fairy tales.

After the cataclysmic events of *The Lord of the Rings*, all those creatures and beings will dwindle away, to be supplanted by men and by a secular age. As the narrator remarks at the beginnings of *The Hobbit* and *The Lord of the Rings*, creatures like hobbits are or were part of this world (the primary reality), but they have become adept at hiding, and are fading away. Every race eventually becomes a rumour in Middle-earth, just as the ent-wives are rumours to the hobbits in the Shire or Galadriel and the elves of Lothlórien were legends to the dwarves.

Although Middle-earth is very much about the elves for Tolkien, Tolkien also said that the mythology of Middle-earth was primarily a "Mannish' affair' (HME, 10, 370).

When the ring's destroyed, much of the elves' work in Middle-earth diminishes. J.R.R. Tolkien's not totally clear what that will really mean in practice, but it does explain, Tolkien's narrator said, why elves aren't seen much anymore in the real world.

GOLLUM.

Each of the ringbearer hobbits has a chance of doing away with Gollum, and they all give in and let him go. Of the three, only Sam is close to a warrior, and only when pushed to the limit (such as defending Frodo from Shelob, or rescuing Frodo from Cirith Ungol). In short, J.R.R. Tolkien didn't want his hobbits to be murderers, killing in cold blood or unless absolutely necessary. So when they have the chance to kill Gollum, they don't, they are moved by compassion, by mercy. Maybe Gollum 'deserves' death, but they are not to dole it out, as Gandalf reminds Frodo: 'not to strike without need'. Notice too that it's the hobbit ringbearers who willingly give up the ring. Bilbo lets it go to Frodo, Frodo offers it to Galadriel and Gandalf, and Sam gives it back to Frodo.

One of Gandalf's recurring mantras is that nobody can predict how it's all going to turn out (despite all the talk of 'dooms' and 'fates', and the story in *The Lord of the Rings* pushing into increasingly dark and desperate states). So one shouldn't despair. Because there is always hope. Isn't that what Samwise Gamgee embodies, especially in the last part of the tale, when the hobbits are crawling across Mordor? While Frodo is sinking into the claustrophobic horror of the ring, of Mordor and Sauron, Sam still keeps up hope, somehow. He never quite gives up.

One of Frodo's story arcs is to learn compassion and pity. As Gandalf tells him, it was pity that stayed Bilbo's hand from harming Gollum. In a narrative full of fighting and violence, Frodo is remarkably pacifist and compassionate. In the early stages, he is violent, but only to defend himself (hacking off the barrow-wight's hand and stabbing the troll and the Witch-king). But later, he persuades Faramir not to harm Gollum, gives away his sword, and subsequently goes into Mordor without a weapon. And during the scouring of the Shire, Frodo does not fight, and doesn't want the prisoners harmed.

Intriguingly, in an early draft of this speech about pity, Gandalf links Bilbo's act of pity with the power of the ring:

"What nonsense you do talk sometimes, Bingo... Pity! It was pity that prevented him. And he could not do so, without doing wrong. It was against the rules. If he had done so he would not have had the ring, the ring would have had him at once. He would have been a wraith on the spot." (HME, 6, 81)

The part about Bilbo becoming a wraith instantly was omitted from *The Lord of the Rings*. I like the idea that murder is 'against the rules', a very English expression of under-statement ('murder's bad form, old boy'), but also another indication of Gandalf's sense of cosmic design or fate or destiny.

MAGIC.

For J.R.R. Tolkien, the machine was an external development of internal magic, an extension of magic: both machine and magic being means of extending the individual (or collective) will into the world (a view with echoes in Marshall McLuhan's thinking about modern technology). An example of what Tolkien means by this can be illustrated by considering how magic and machines are manifested in his Middle-earth mythology: it is Sauron and the dark forces, far more than the elves and men and their allies who resort to 'magic' (and they shun machinery).

Galadriel makes the point clear when she remonstrates with the hobbits who use the same term ('magic') for the methodologies of both Sauron and the elves. In J.R.R. Tolkien's Middle-earth, the word 'magic' is not used in connection with the elves or 'free peoples', but only for Sauron and the Enemy. 'Magic' in Middle-earth is more usually applied to the will to power and domination of the Dark Lord and his minions. It's about ego, control, power, greed. The elves, by contrast, have 'art' as their 'magic': 'more effortless, more quick, more complete... it's object is Art not Power, sub-creation not domination and tyrannous re-forming of Creation', Tolkien wrote in a letter (L, 146).

Another reason for J.R.R. Tolkien avoiding the use of the term 'magic' in connection with his good guys (the 'free peoples' of elves, wizards, hobbits *et al*) is the same for refraining from terms such as 'religion', 'belief', 'ritual' or 'spirituality': because It relates the world of Middle-earth too closely with aspects of real, existing culture, such as the religions of the real world. By avoiding the word 'magic', Tolkien hoped to make the elves and wizards appear more magical – and mysterious. They would use 'natural magic', which was the essence of 'faërie' for Tolkien (*Faërie* being Tolkien's term for the 'Perilous Realm' or magical Secondary World of fairy tales, and his Middle-earth, as well as Valinor. An early version of *The Silmarillion* has a 'Bay of Faërie').

ATTENTION TO DETAIL.

Professor Tolkien's attention to detail was legendary. The appendices published with *The Lord of the Rings* contained calendars (Shire-Reckoning, Númenórean and Eldar), detailed chronologies and histories of each of the Four Ages of Middle-earth, the story of Arwen and Aragorn, histories of the Númenórean kings, the Dúnedain, the kings of Gondor, family trees of the hobbits, lists of the kings of Númenor, the House of Eorl and the dwarves, a guide to the languages of Middle-earth (Westron/Common Speech, Númenórean, *Quenya* and *Sindarin*), their pronunciation, and maps.

In his letters, J.R.R. Tolkien dismissed the appendices of *The Lord of the Rings* as adolescent stuff. Maybe. But he slaved long and hard over them – and over the volumes of his Middle-earth mythology which remained unpublished in his lifetime.

For Patricia Spacks, J.R.R. Tolkien did tend to over-complicate his narratives, with a weight of detail. 'His elaboration of the minutiæ of his imagined world seems sometimes an end in itself; it diminishes the essential moral weight of his fable'.8 There is a suggestion that Tolkien did spend a little *too* long over some of the details of his Middle-earth mythology – all that pondering over how Glorfindel survived being killed in his fight with a balrog at Gondolin (he seemed to be attached to Glorfindel, maybe just the name 'Glorfindel' – wouldn't it have been easier to simply create another character?), or over the phases of the moon when Frodo and Sam were at Ithilien.

MAPS.

Frodo saw the maps at Rivendell, and in an early version of *The Lord of the Rings* tells Sam in Mordor that Elrond had given him a secret plan with a map and mileages. It does stretch belief a little that the hobbits are able to find their way to Mordor and across Mordor without getting lost. Of course, they had Gollum as a guide for much of the way. It's handy too that Mount Doom just happens to be the only mountain for many miles, and is situated on a plain in Gorgoroth. And as Gandalf puts it in an early draft of *The Return of the King*, 'a single regiment of orcs set about Orodruin could seal our ruin' (HME, 8, 404).

CORRUPTION.

Denethor and Saruman are both characters who have been corrupted by power; both desire the ring, but don't come anywhere near it (both remain in their towers, watching the events unfolding in the world from on high, working through others, and both, incidentally, have wrestled with Sauron via the *palantíri* – and lost).

The crystal stones play a key role in *The Lord of the Rings:* they help (as controlled by Sauron) to ensnare Saruman and drive Denethor mad, they offer Aragorn vital information (such as of the fleet of Corsairs sailing to war), and send doubt into the Dark Lord's mind about Aragorn and Pippin. (It's curious that the free peoples don't use the Tower Hills *palantír*, which is available to them – it sails with the ringbearers from the Grey Havens. Occasionally elves would travel to the Tower Hills to look on Valinor in the seeing stone, like at a TV set broadcasting a holiday show about a Pacific paradise with white sandy beaches and Martini cocktails).

Pippin looking in the *palantír* helps to start the battles in the War of the Ring, because the sight of Pippin encourages the Dark Lord to hurry his preparations, and to move sooner than he planned.

Denethor has been using the *palantír* for some time, before he's met in *The Lord of the Rings.* It's not quite an addiction (not as strong as the lure of the ring), but he can't stop himself from using it. Through it, Sauron is able to hasten his weakening.

The War of the Ring is about a white wizard battling a black wizard. It's that simple: good versus evil. Among the allies in *The Lord of the Rings*, there are few that truly turn 'evil' or villainous. Most start out meaning well – Boromir, Denethor – but are corrupted along the way. Saruman also begins on the allies' side. Of the elves, none are 'evil'. Ditto the hobbits. And when characters suggest using the ring amongst the allies – Denethor, Boromir and Saruman – they are all doomed. By contrast, all of the allies who could easily take the ring – Gandalf, Galadriel, Elrond, Aragorn, Faramir – 'pass the test' of corruption.

On the enemy's side, meanwhile, all is corruption: the men of the South and East have been corrupted by Sauron, as have the nazgûl and other servants. The orcs were of course created from corrupted elves by Morgoth. (As to the commingling of species, it's OK in Middle-earth for the odd elf and man to be conjoined and to breed – Beren and Lúthien, Aragorn and Arwen – but the idea of orcs and men being compounded is an abomination).9

LANGUAGES.

The love of language permeates *The Lord of the Rings,* coming out of J.R.R. Tolkien's love of mediæval English, Norse, Finnish and Icelandic legend. *The Lord of the Rings* is partly an attempt to create a modern version of mediæval epics such as *Beowulf.* For Tolkien, British culture and mythology had been corrupted by the war and invasion – of the Normans and Vikings and other invaders. People who met Tolkien said he when he was talking about the war, they thought he meant the Second World War, but he was talking about the Norman invasion of 1066. For Tolkien, Britain had been civilized too quickly, and the old mythologies and legends had been debased.

J.R.R. Tolkien has a donnish admiration for linguistics, resulting in the creation of new languages (such as Elvish), the dwarfs and their runes, 'Westron' or 'common speech', and various alphabets.

One of the paradoxes in *The Lord of the Rings* was that the book was written in modern English and the principal characters spoke in modern English, which corresponded to (or was an offshoot of) J.R.R. Tolkien's invented Common Speech. As Tom Shippey pointed out, Tolkien was obliged to cover up inconsistencies in his invented languages, which included 'pretending' to be a translator, inventing literary traditions behind his languages, and finding ways in which different species (such as dwarves and men) could have commonalities of language.

> The fact is that the ancient languages came first. Tolkien did not draw them into a fiction he had already written because there they might be useful, though that is what he pretended. He wrote the fiction to present the languages, and he did that because he loved them and thought them intrinsically beautiful. Maps, names and languages came before plot. (1982, 89)

DOL GULDUR.

If Sauron had attacked Lórien and Rivendell first, when he was still holed up in Dol Guldur in the 2800s of the Third Age, it would have much better for him, Gandalf says, and much worse for the free peoples (UT, 416). If he had assaulted the two elven kingdoms, instead of concentrating on Minas Tirith and Gondor, he would have probably taken them, making it much more difficult for the ringbearer to travel to Mordor (UT, 322, 330), and Frodo would've had much less chance of success (UT, 427). So the adventure to reclaim the dwarves' treasure related in *The Hobbit* also functions, for Gandalf, as an assault on Smaug, one less enemy to deal with (Smaug would've been a fierce adversary in the War of the Ring). But Sauron seems to want to have everything all at once. Or he rushes his plans at the last minute, which proves his undoing. As Gandalf recognizes, if the Dark Lord took his time, and acted as methodically as he had done for centuries in preparing for the great war, he would have been victorious.

When Gandalf enters Dol Guldur, he finds 'an unhappy Dwarf dying in the pits' there. Incredibly, though the dwarf, Thráin the Second, is locked in Sauron's dungeons, he still has a map on him, and a key, which Gandalf uses in events described in *The Hobbit* (UT, 419). You'd think that at least prisoners would be stripped. Gandalf explains this oversight by pointing out that what Sauron really wanted was the dwarf ring he thought Thráin possessed, and when he had taken that, he didn't bother to search further, but threw the prisoner into the dungeons (UT, 425). It's another one of those lapses of Sauron's that's *highly* unconvincing.

GLORFINDEL.

Elves, says Gandalf, live in two worlds, or both worlds (i.e., Middle-earth and the Blessed Realm). When Frodo sees Glorfindel as a shining figure at the Ford, Gandalf says that was how the elf-lord looks 'upon the other side' (FR, 292). An intriguing notion: presumably, then, the elves and Maiar and other noble folk in Valinor go about as shining white figures. Valinor must be a very bright place.

J.R.R. Tolkien explored the confusion between the Glorfindel of Gondolin in his tales of the First Age and that of the Third Age in one of his last essays: one solution was that Glorfindel did indeed die in Gondolin, fighting a balrog, and went, like other elves, to the halls of Mandos, but he was re-incarnated and sent to Middle-earth to help Elrond in Rivendell. Tolkien suggested that it was in Valinor that Glorfindel became 'a friend and follower of Olórin [Gandalf]' (HME, 12, 373); Glorfindel must've travelled from Valinor before the downfall of Númenor. That's typical of Tolkien's sometimes convoluted justifications for confusions or errors. Surely it would've been easier for the Valar to send some other lordly elf, rather than one that had to be resurrected?

THE RING.

The basic premise of *The Lord of the Rings* is as dumb and unbeliev-able as any fantasy fiction: the idea that the fate of not just one but a number of countries – a whole world, and all the people in them – rests on a few bits of metal, the rings. Ah, if only the solutions to global political problems in real life were that simple!

Putting a good deal of his power into the ring was the stupidest thing Sauron ever did. He's supposed to be an arch villain, cunning, sly, etc. But he goes and puts so much of his power into the ring, that he will be destroyed if the ring is unmade. It's nuts! Why does he do it? Presumably, in order to gain power over the other rings of power, in order to enslave the free peoples of Middle-earth, the elves, men and dwarves. But there must be better ways of achieving dominion over others than through magical rings. It just doesn't add up.

Part of the struggle in *The Lord of the Rings* is for the heroes to withstand the temptation to take up and wield the ring. The external battle is against Sauron and his vast forces, but the internal struggle is to withstand the lure of the ring.

The double-edged nature of the fate of the ring is explained to Frodo by Galadriel: 'if you fail, then we are laid bare to the enemy. Yet if you succeed, then our power is diminished, and Lothlórien will fade, and the tides of time will sweep it away' (FR, 474). Great, thanks tall pale elf lady, no pressure there!

Frodo has a prohibition out of fairy tales: not to put on the ring. And, of course, he breaks it a number of times (at Tom Bombadil's house, at Weathertop, at Bree). It's no surprise that he puts on the ring at the *Prancing Pony* while singing a nursery rhyme. (By the time of Amon Hen, though, Frodo has learnt not to put on the ring).

It does diminish the jeopardy and suspense J.R.R. Tolkien's generated around the ring to have characters such as Bombadil, the Barrow-wight and Old Man Willow be uninterested in it, appearing in the book so soon after Frodo's being hunted down by Black Riders. There are other nasty creatures in Middle-earth who aren't interested in magic rings (Shelob for one), but you'd think an evil spirit like the Barrow-wight would be. (Shelob is unconcerned with the ring: even though she's trapped Frodo in a paralyzing cocoon, she doesn't take the ring).

If Sauron had been able to imagine all the possible uses the ring might suggest to the free peoples, as W.H. Auden wrote, he would've realized they might try to destroy it. Thus, 'he had only to sit waiting and watching in Mordor for the Ring-bearer to arrive, and he was bound to catch him and recover the Ring'.10

MORE ON RINGS.
In one of the early drafts of *The Fellowship of the Ring,* Elrond states that the three elven rings were taken over the sea to the West (i.e., prior to the action in *The Lord of the Rings*).

In one version of *The Lord of the Rings,* it was Fëanor, not Sauron, who made the three rings of the elves (the 'Rings of Earth, Sea and Sky') in Valinor. But they were stolen by the 'Great Enemy' and taken to Middle-earth (HME, 7, 255). Although the skill in creating the rings was Fëanor's, the 'thought was the Enemy's' (ibid.).

In *The Lord of the Rings* the Ringwraiths are men, king and leaders, that the Dark Lord corrupted and enslaved; early drafts of the novel had 'kings, warriors, and wizards of old' being enslaved (HME, 6, 260). Aspects of the idea that wizards were also ensnared by Sauron survived into the published form of the book, with the leader of the Ringwraiths being not just a king, but a 'Witch-king', who has powers distinctive of mages.

Sauron had been gathering all of the rings to him for centuries, in the hope of finding the One Ring. One of his hopes may have been that someone might have come by it by accident and might not realize it was a powerful weapon, but just think it was a pretty object. That must have been a fairly feeble hope, though, for Sauron tended to think most people were like himself (according to Gandalf), and if they found something like a magical ring they would certainly use it.

THE SYMBOLISM OF LANDSCAPE.
Among the marks of evil in *The Lord of the Rings* are the South, the

East (North is good, but not too far North, and West is best), darkness, blackness, foreign and otherness, demonized animals (spiders, wolves, bats, snakes), landscapes such as marshes, rocks, moors, and modern technology and industry (iron, machinery, gunpowder).11 By contrast, goodness is trees, growing things, music, songs, colours like white, silver, gold and green, the North and West, 'noble' animals (horses, eagles), tradition, and ancientness.

TEMPLES.

There are no temples in Middle-earth, are there? No churches, no stone circles, no altars, no mosques, synagogues, or places of worship? Well, there are a few. Middle-earth might be a pre-religious realm, but J.R.R. Tolkien 'includes in it all the necessary materials for religion', as Patricia Spacks pointed out.12

There are many sacred places: Rivendell, the Grey Havens, Amon Hen, and Lórien. Even the Shire is a kind of sacred space, a paradise. The evocation of the Shire is a kind of 'secular paradise, a lazy man's heaven,' as Colin Wilson put it, 'where people have nothing to do but smoke their pipes in the twilight and gossip about the courting couples and next year's May Fair' (1974).

Among the temples are the temple that Sauron has built in Númenor, for the worship of the big baddie of Middle-earth, Morgoth/ Melkor. In Gondor the men of the mountains had constructed a temple – a 'temple and holy place in the Dark Years' – before the men of Númenor arrived in Middle-earth, according to an early draft of *The Lord of the Rings* (HME, 8, 238). The Stone of Erech resembles many standing stones, cromlechs, megaliths and prehistoric sites in Europe, in and out of literature.

One of the lesser-known places in Middle-earth is the burial place of Elendil, at the Halifirien, one of the beacons between Rohan and Gondor. It's a sacred place in Middle-earth which the Valar protect. It's a grassy area at the top of the mountain which only the stewards of Gondor know about. It's Isildur who prays to the Valar to keep the hallow on the Hill of Anwar free from evil (*Unfinished Tales*, 400). It appears in the story *Cirion and Eorl*, about the relationship between Gondor and Rohan.

SAURON'S STORMS.

The storm that rages around Middle-earth when Frodo and Sam are in the Emyn Muil is linked to Sauron's brooding thoughts: the storm seems to be the meteorological reaction to the workings of his dark mind (HME, 8, 95). So that, hundreds of miles away, Sauron is affecting the weather like a magician with a very long reach. (In the published book, when the fellowship's suffering on the Misty Mountains, Gandalf says that Sauron's arm has grown very long indeed [FR, 376]).

Actually, Sauron's gloom spreading over Middle-earth is no surprise to people who live in Britain, where many days (and not only in Winter) can be so dark they never really get light at all, and they very much resemble the brooding gloom of the Dark Lord.

HANDS AND FINGERS.

Hands and fingers are prominent in J.R.R. Tolkien's *mythos* (understandable when the most precious objects in the Middle-earth legends are small enough to fit in the hand – rings and jewels). The giant wolf of Morgoth, Carcharoth, bites off Beren's hand; Fingon hacks off Maedhros's hand when Morgoth's bound him to the mountains of Thangorodrim; Frodo cuts off the Barrow-wights hand; Isildur hacks off Sauron's finger to get the ring; and Gollum bites off Frodo's finger.

No doubt Freudians and psychoanalysts could talk about all this finger and hand lopping as castration anxiety, phallic substitutes, œdipal ambiguity. For J.R.R. Tolkien it seemed to function in the traditional manner of storytelling as a partial loss of power, of self, of identity. A wound, a reminder, a warning (like Frodo's Morgul knife wound which never fully heals and hurts on the anniversary of Weathertop).

FEAR AND HORROR.

Pretty much every critic, including the vehement J.R.R. Tolkien detractors, acknowledge that Tolkien was terrific at writing about fear, horror and dread. A lot of the sense of fear and horror in *The Lord of the Rings* is suggested, not shown directly. Sauron is an off-stage presence, the Black Riders are more effective by the terror they induce than in themselves, and the ring's power is depicted by its effect on people. As Tolkien explained in his letter about Morton Zimmerman's screenplay in the 1950s, the Black Riders' power is to instil fear, like ghosts, rather than in any physical strength (L, 272).

Tom Shippey viewed the Ringwraiths as emptiness at the centre, figures of total enslavement, akin to robots, automata with all the humanity sucked out. Shippey compared them to the people who do the dirty work of war and killing in history – the soldiers, the war machine, and the bureaucrats. The Ringwraiths were people who had allowed themselves (or been forced) to go beyond good and evil, to forget what good and evil meant, to become agents of the State, the politicians who sent people to war, who issued orders, who had no idea of the consequences of their actions or who did not care what they were doing to others.

FATE, LUCK, CHANCE, DOOM.

J.R.R. Tolkien's fiction is full of prophecies, curses, oaths, bans and sayings which always come true, always return, are always broken.

Certain concepts recur: 'doom' and 'fate' being two of Tolkien's favourites. There was rarely a writer who deployed the term 'doom' so many times. At one point or another, it seems that every character in Tolkien's Middle-earth legends is 'doomed': some are very obviously doomed from the start: Fëanor, Túrin, and Beren. The evil doers – Morgoth, Sauron, the orcs – are 'doomed' to be defeated but always to come back. One of the chief gods, Mandos, is a 'Doom-Sayer'. Some doom themselves by what they say (Thingol), others by what they do (Maeglin). Sometimes the seeds of doom seem to be external, but most often they are a combination of inner or psychological flaws, circumstance and 'fate'. The curses or oaths, created by individuals (such as Fëanor), become larger than themselves, and seem to act independently.

While modern authors might speak of 'luck' or 'coincidence', for J.R.R. Tolkien 'doom' or 'fate' was the form preferred because it suited his conception of the heroic romance or fairy tale. Tolkien wouldn't use modern concepts when ancient ones would do the job: in the ancient and Classical world, there was divine retribution, the anger of the gods, when outraged by the hubris, pride and stubbornness of humans. Ilúvatar and the Valar act like this a number of times: when Fëanor and the Noldor leave Valinor, and when the Númenóreans sail to the Blessed Realm.

THE VILLAINS' FLAWS.

Sauron, for all his 'policies and webs of fear and treachery... his stratagems and wars' (RT, 269), has fatal flaws in his make-up and goals. Gandalf bets everything – the fate of all Middle-earth – on the fact that it would never occur to the Shadow to destroy the ring and – just as crucially – not to wield it. Towards the end of *The Lord of the Rings,* Gandalf suggests that Sauron is waiting for someone to declare themselves as new lord of the ring (the major players for such a title would be Gandalf himself, followed by Saruman, Aragorn, Elrond, Galadriel and Denethor).

Strategically, one of Sauron's mistakes is to rely too heavily on not particularly bright enforcers of his will – the orcs. The elements of Sauron's military forces echo those of the Alliance, and of the military throughout history: a handful of generals (the nazgûl), hundreds of captains and sergeants (the Uruk-hai and other orcs), and then the foot soldiers and grunts themselves (the orcs, and the men – Haradrim and Southrons – with a few trolls and wargs thrown in).

But the orcs, including the Uruk-hai, are pretty dim as military strategists and leaders. They have to be, for the story to work: when Frodo and Sam reach Mordor, the orcs have to make all sorts of mistakes to enable the littlest, humblest folk of Middle-earth to get through. At Cirith Ungol, for example, 200 orcs slay each other, conveniently opening the way for Sam to rescue Frodo (with only a couple of orcs for Samwise to confront – one flees when Sam's holding the ring, and Shagrat escapes after confronting Sam. So, conveniently, Sam doesn't have to kill an orc).

Later, when Frodo and Sam fall in with a band of orcs travelling North to the Black Gate, they clash with other regiments and squabble and fight. Earlier, two orcs, one of them a tracker or 'snuffler', cannot detect the hobbits who're only twenty paces off (RT, 241). And Sauron's generals, the Ring-wraiths, are not the most efficient or effective of military officers. For one thing, most of them can't cross water (a notion difficult to sustain, Tolkien admitted, when they're supposed to be traversing huge tracts of Middle-earth).

There are five or so Ringwraiths in the Shire and they can't find the hobbits. One of the nazgûl (Khamûl), who reaches Hobbiton, and talks with the Gaffer in Bagshot Row, doesn't even bother to walk a few paces further (after travelling hundreds of miles, all the way from Mordor) to Bag End itself (Frodo, improbably, overhears the conversation between Khamûl and the Gaffer). The ring's only a few yards away.[13] And the nazgûl have a fairly fierce boss driving them on, who demands results. And there isn't much opposition among the hobbits in the Shire. It's not as if the Black Riders're faced with an army which's protecting the ring; rather, all the hobbits flee from the riders in black. (Also, why don't the Black Riders guard the Brandywine crossing, or the road approaching it? It also takes a long time (4 days) for them to cross the river.[14])

The nazgûls' biggest failure is at Weathertop: five of them, including the Witch-king himself, can't take the ring when it's right in front of them, and with only Strider and four young hobbits to defend it (there were three Black Riders at Weathertop in an earlier version, not five). The Witch-king was powerful, too: a thousand years earlier, he had led armies against the elves and men, and had also killed King Eärnur, the last king of Gondor. In 1409 TA the Witch-king surrounded and attacked Amon Sûl on Weather-top. So this's territory the Witch-king knows well, too – it's near his old kingdom of Angmar and Fornost (Fornost to Bree is roughly the same as Hobbiton to Bree).

One of the holes in the plot of *The Lord of the Rings* is that the Witch-king – and therefore Sauron – doesn't know about hobbits or the Shire, even though halflings were in Bree from the 1300s of the Third Age, which's not too far South of the Witch-king's base in Fornost. Sauron was also based in Dol Guldur in Mirkwood for years, but knew nothing of the sizeable tract of land of the Shire and its inhabitants, although they were only 500 or so miles distant, nor their relatives, who live East of Mirkwood, where Sméagol/ Gollum lived). You'd think Sauron would fire his servants after their failures in the Shire, at Weathertop and the Ford of Bruinen, and find some decent henchmen.

The reasons that Aragorn gives for the Black Riders' failure at

Weathertop are that they weren't expecting any resistance, that they might have wanted to wait until the next night for the wound to do its work, and they don't like fire. But none of these explanations really account for the failure of the five nazgûl to take the ring. As critic Christopher Manlove pointed out, it seems odd that the nazgûl are afraid of fire when their Captain enters Minas Tirith when it was on fire, and curious that Aragorn can beat them back when even Gandalf is outmatched by the Black Captain (1975, 182). Odd too that the Black Riders allow the hobbits and Strider to continue their journey unopposed. The ringwraiths are built up as terrible adversaries by Gandalf, Gildor and Aragorn, but when it comes to it, they can be defeated relatively easily.

Plenty of events swing against Sauron at the time of the siege of Minas Tirith – he loses the battle of Pelennor; he finds out that Aragorn has returned; a spy is discovered at Cirith Ungol; and the ents have marched (he hadn't taken the ents into account in his plans for world domination, and neither had Saruman). As J.R.R. Tolkien wrote in his outline of the story written from Pelennor, Sauron is 'wrathful and afraid, but puzzled, especially by news of Frodo' (HME 8, 360). In earlier drafts of the Mouth of Sauron scene, Sauron is aware of the ents, and tells Gandalf and the others (via the Mouth of Sauron) that the ents will 'help rebuild Isengard and be subject to its lord' (ib., 362, 430).

The enemy has to make many mistakes in order to allow the hobbits to pass right into Mordor and to Mount Doom: and this after J.R.R. Tolkien (via all of the characters in the West) has emphasized what a dread place Mordor is, how watchful, sinister, evil and impregnable. Although it's odd that the road between Barad-dûr and Mount Doom is kept well-maintained by the Dark Lord yet there's no guard of any kind on Mount Doom or the Crack of Doom itself, it has to be that way. As Tom Shippey put it:

> Gandalf and Galadriel and Elrond can imagine themselves becoming evil, which is why they all reject the Ring, but... Sauron cannot imagine anyone behaving differently from himself, which is why he fails to guard the Sammath Naur. (E. Challis, 14-15)

The nazgûl are of course also a narrative device, to put the heroes in jeopardy, to keep up the chase and suspense, and to offer a convincing reason for Frodo and the hobbits to be willing to leave their beloved home.

DRAGONS.

Dragons in J.R.R. Tolkien's fictional world fly straight out of Northern European mythology. He gives them their own name ('Urulóki, the fire-drakes of the North'), has Morgoth breed them in Angband, but in every aspect the dragons come out of Germanic and Scandinavian legend, out of Sigurd and Fafnir (S, 116). Although there are many examples of friendly, wise dragons in folk tales, in Tolkien's mythology they are definitely on the side of evil, part of the enemy's army of 'fell beasts', taking their place alongside balrogs, trolls, orcs, giant spiders and flying reptiles.

It's handy the last of the dragons had been destroyed in the battle related in *The Hobbit* because they could have been fearsome opponents in the War of the Ring – although they wouldn't do Sauron's bidding. It was part of Gandalf's plan, maybe, that Smaug should be vanquished. Though it was also a 'chance meeting', between Gandalf and the dwarf Thórin Oakenshield, that led to it. So Gandalf's chance meeting with Thorin in Bree can be seen as another example of the other worldly powers at work in Middle-earth, which favour Gandalf as Maia and his quest to defeat Sauron.

BEORN AND THE WOLVES.

Some of the creatures that J.R.R. Tolkien invented for *The Hobbit* did not make much of an impression in the sequel, *The Lord of the Rings*, or didn't appear at all: wargs, for instance (something like werewolves or men-wolves), or the shape-shifter Beorn (perhaps because Beorn doesn't fit into the Middle-earth mythology as easily as some of the other creatures. However, Beorn in *The Hobbit* isn't that far-fetched – shape-shifting being a common device in fairy tales – and *The Lord of the Rings* contains walking trees, no less, as well as extraordinary creatures like balrogs). A shape-changer like Beorn might have been a useful ally against the enemy – he slays the orc chief Bolg in *The Hobbit,* for example. The Beornings were cited in an early draft of *The Lord of the Rings,* though (HME, 7, 233).

There are wolves in *The Lord of the Rings,* however (the fellowship is attacked by wolves before they reach Moria). Wolves feature more prominently in the earlier legends of Middle-earth: Sauron, for instance, takes on wolf form when he fights Huan, Lúthien's faithful hound. Sauron also has werewolves (which Huan defeats).

STRETCHING BELIEF.

There are numerous mistakes in *The Lord of the Rings*, which J.R.R. Tolkien acknowledged (he said that *The Lord of the Rings* still contained errors after its 1966 revision). The errors are not only textual, or about details. It's easy (and unfair, perhaps) to pick holes in the plot of *The Lord of the Rings,* but some of the mistakes the characters make are striking. Gandalf makes a fair few – despite being a few thousand years old, and having dealt with Middle-earth politics and society for at least a millennium. Tolkien acknowledged that Gandalf's return was a failure in the narrative, a kind of cheating, and maybe he could have worked harder to mend it (L, 201-2).

More: Frodo and Sam being able to penetrate into the very depths of Mordor, undetected. Sauron being unaware of the ring, even though, for three or so days, it's only 30-40 miles away from Barad-dûr, as Frodo and Sam struggle across the plateau of Gorgoroth (J.R.R. Tolkien explains this by having the Dark Lord's gaze drawn away by the allies at the Black Gate. However, in earlier tales, such as that of Beren and Lúthien, Sauron was able to sense intruders from great distances).

Then there's Sam entering Cirith Ungol after 200 orcs have conveniently slaughtered each other. And a hobbit defeating Shelob, the offspring of Ungoliant.

FARAMIR.

Frodo and Sam's encounter with Faramir doesn't add much to the narrative and is far too long (J.R.R. Tolkien admitted, in a 1944 letter, that the Faramir scenes slowed up the story too much, with too much material on the history of Gondor and Rohan. But, as Tolkien put it, Faramir just appeared, unbidden: 'I am sure I did not invent him, I did not even want him, though I like him, but there he came walking into the woods of Ithilien' [L, 79]).

There are some minor narrative points (they can pick up supplies, receive news of Gondor and the outside world), but too much of the chapters "The Window On the West" and "The Forbidden Pool" consists of dialogue which merely summarizes what the reader already knows (the history of the ring, Gandalf's demise, Boromir's treachery).

From a writer's point-of-view, though, you can see why Tolkien had Frodo, Sam and Gollum meet with Faramir and his men: there's a limit to the number of words you can write about three characters in a wilderness (after you got past the expected arguments and sulks). The goal of the remnant of the Fellowship (Frodo and Sam) is to trudge through ever-increasingly doomy and gloomy landscapes, until they destroy the ring. The latter sections of *The Two Towers* and the Mordor parts of *The Return of the King* are positively Samuel Beckettian: the grey gloom, the brooding skies, the barren terrain, the exhausted, hungry travellers who plod along, the hopelessness of the task, the total weariness of the characters. In this state, the journey could continue forever. So you can see Tolkien bringing in Faramir, the rangers, Cirith Ungol and Shelob to liven up proceedings (and to stretch out Frodo and Sam's journey: because there were many events occurring further West – Rohan, Gondor, Pelennor, Denethor, etc).

And of course Faramir refuses to take the ring, an important point, demonstrating that not all men desire the ring (Sam – and Frodo – are suspicious of anyone they meet). Faramir's refusal also shows that one doesn't have to be a powerful magical being, like Gandalf, Galadriel or Bombadil, to be able to deny the temptation of the ring.

POETRY.

There are 50-60 examples of poetry in *The Lord of the Rings,* including songs, inscriptions, prophecies, riddles, and children's rhymes. Couplets in rhymes are common, as is J.R.R. Tolkien's love of the Anglo-Saxon half-line, with its distinctive alliteration. Most of the poetry in *The Lord of the Rings* is meant to be sung, or chanted, or recited. Some poems are Elvish, some are Numenóriean, some are entish, and many are by hobbits. Some of the poems are in ballad verse, some are in decasyllabic quatrains, and some are in Old English alliterative half-lines. Tolkien seemed to treasure his poetry – and a lot more than some readers.

Tom Bombadil is a singer, a poet – Ilúvatar 'sung' the world into existence (as Rainer Maria Rilke put it in his *Sonnets For Orpheus*). And the elves in J.R.R. Tolkien's mythology are poets: the Greek for poet, *poetas*, means 'maker' (and in old Scots dialect, 'poet' is 'makar' or 'maker'); in Anglo-Saxon, the word for 'bard' is 'scop', to shape or create. Words in Tolkien's mythos literally bring things into existence.

GERMANY.

In his letters, J.R.R. Tolkien often compared real-life events with those of his fictional world, comparing World War Two and the battles in *The Lord of the Rings,* the rise of fascism and Germany with Mordor and Sauron (L, 165). In a letter written late in the war to his son Christopher, Tolkien said:

> we are attempting to conquer Sauron with the Ring. And we shall (it seems) succeed. But the penalty is… to breed new Saurons, and slowly turn Men and Elves into Orcs. Not that in real life things are as clear cut as in a story, and we started out with a great many Orcs on our side. (L, 78)

If Sauron and his forces were equivalences of Hitler and Germany, that would make Saruman close to the Soviet Union (or perhaps Mussolini and Italy): Saruman pretends a kind of alliance with Sauron, while all the time desiring the ring for himself, and building up his own army and empire. The group at the council of Elrond would be the Allies; the ring and the treachery in Mordor would be the atomic bomb, and the defectors and scientists who went to the Soviet Union after the war to develop its atomic capability.

The earthquakes and destruction that occurs when the ring is finally cast into Mount Doom do resonate with nuclear politics: it's a kind of mutual destruction (but which only destroys the evil forces). And it also wrecks the machinery and technology of Sauron's regime, as if Middle-earth is now reverting to a pre-industrial, pre-Iron Age society.

The Lord of the Rings also recalls the assassination of Adolf Hitler plot: a small band of warriors infiltrates enemy territory on a very risky mission. The goal is to destroy the ring, but the real purpose is get rid of the Dark Lord.

BIBLICAL ALLUSIONS.

The *Bible* was an enormous influence on J.R.R. Tolkien's fiction, as well as his life. The Biblical story of Moses, the chosen people and the exodus is recalled in Tolkien's Middle-earth tales of the elves breaking into groups, with one company heading for the promised land of Eldamar (and in both stories, the summons comes from father-gods, Ilúvatar and Jehovah).

The flood at the Bruinen recalls the parting of the Red Sea in *Exodus* in the *Bible* (with Frodo as Moses, escaping from the Pharaoh's forces by magical intervention; in the *Bible,* water separates the Chosen People from their enemy, and the waters rise up at God's command (accompanied by fire, all of which's echoed in *The Lord of the Rings*)).

Gollum killing his Déagol for the ring recalls the story of the brothers Cain and Abel in the *Bible*.[14] Like Cain, Gollum is haunted by his murderous act. Gollum is Frodo's alter ego, the Jungian shadow, the evil twin, the wraith-like wretch he will become in time (even if he resists the influence of the ring).

Charles Moorman likened the re-establishment of Minas Tirith and the Shire at the end of *The Lord of the Rings* to the establishment of the City of God on Earth of the *Bible* and St Augustine (Augustine's *De Civitate Dei*, early 5th century).[16]

SOME NIGGLES.

J.R.R. Tolkien couldn't really explain how tobacco remained in *The Lord of the Rings* and *The Hobbit,* after he'd excised 'tomatoes' (a 17th century word) and 'potatoes' from later editions of the books (potatoes being imported into Europe, or into Britain, in the 16th century). Rabbits, too, weren't native to Britain, but were introduced some time in the mediæval era (Tolkien uses the word 'coney' as well as 'rabbit' in *The Lord of the Rings*).

STYLE.

Characters in Ronald Tolkien's narratives tend to turn out in the end to be pretty much as they are when they are first introduced. They do not change much in their basic character through the story. Different aspects of their personality may come out later on, or their personal history (like Aragorn being a king) may include some surprises. Critics who call J.R.R. Tolkien's characters one-dimensional also complain that the characters do not undergo profound psychological changes either. Tolkien simply isn't interested in that kind of fiction, the novel of modernism, of Virginia Woolf, Marcel Proust, D.H. Lawrence, André Gide, James Joyce *et al*, the novel of psychological journeys and complexity, the fiction which explores issues such as identity, psychology, sexuality, memory, socialization, and so on. Tolkien's is, rather, a fiction of epic events out of romance and fairy tales.

J.R.R. Tolkien tried hard not to alienate modern readers when he moved into the preachier, archaic prose style, particularly in the second half of *The Lord of the Rings*. The reader has to go along with the narrator and accept that Tolkien is writing in this style for a particular effect. Tom Shippey comments how this high style 'is accompanied by characters stepping back, swelling, shining' (1982, 161). But some readers and critics have been put off by this tactic, or find it laughable.

NOTES, IDEAS AND TECHNIQUES IN TOLKIEN'S MIDDLE-EARTH FICTIONS

1. D. Jones, in R. Giddings, 1983, 90.
2. F. Inglis, 1983, 38.
3. C. Manlove, 1975, 182-3.
4. C. Manlove, 1975, 185-6.
5. H. Carpenter, 1995, 151.
6. H. Keenan, in N. Isaacs, 71.
7. T. Shippey, 1982, 180.
8. In N. Isaacs, 97.
9. N. Otty, 1983, 173.
10. In N. Isaacs, 57.
11. See N. Otty, 1983, 160.
12. In N. Isaacs, 90.
13. C. Manlove, 1975, 181.
14. C. Manlove, 1975, 181.
15. T. Shippey, 1982, 220.
16. In N. Isaacs, 210.

THE POLITICS OF MIDDLE-EARTH

On the whole, *The Lord of the Rings* presents a pro-militaristic philosophy, which's consistent with J.R.R. Tolkien's reactionary, conservative politics. Although Tolkien clearly abhorred war (the *Letters* illustrate that consistently), it was necessary. War was regrettable, painful and problematic for Tolkien – but ultimately, it's the only way to solve the threat of evil Sauron represents.

The idea that 'power corrupts', as Tom Shippey noted, is 'a concept unimpeachably modern, democratic, anti- though not un-heroic' (1982, 130). *The Lord of the Rings* contrasts the political regime of Mordor (a dictatorship) with the small town democracy of the Shire.

Maybe writing about fantastical lands was not 'escape', not an avoidance of writing about the 'real world', R.J. Reilly suggested, but a refusal to accept the political realities of one's environment. It wasn't desertion or cowardice, then, it was war (in N. Isaacs, 146).

The Shire is a utopian space, pre-industrial, pre-modern. The hobbits live without labour or production (yet do not lack for food), in a city state which has a mayor but no city. As Nick Otty pointed out, no one seems to work in the Shire; food seems to be magically available, and the hobbits have ample time to sit around, smoke and drink and eat, with no indication how the food is 'grown, harvested, marketed, transported' (1983, 166).

By contrast, Mordor is a mass of machinery, steel and ceaseless labour, orcs marching hither and thither, but nothing is produced. The Shire also seems to be classless (although wealth and inheritance clearly divides the hobbits). What really marks the hobbits, though, are those who can rise to the challenge of facing up to a threat. Frodo, Sam, Merry and Pippin all of course have ample opportunity to demonstrate what they're made of.

The Lord of the Rings contains the fear and distrust of the foreigner, of travelling abroad, of the middle of the 20th century. Middle Earth is Europe torn apart by the threat of overpowering evil and suffocating industrialization. Sauron and his armies spread throughout Middle Earth like 'shadows' or 'darkness'. Forests, such as the Great Wood, become Mirkwood. Whole countries, such as Mordor, are corrupted and defiled. Sauron is a figure of absolute evil, irredeemable. If he was once 'good', now he's 100% evil, unceasing in his plans for world domination. The traumatic experiences of the mid-20th century pervade *The Lord of the Rings*: Hitler, Stalin, Mussolini, the rise of fascism, the pogroms, five-year plans, Stalingrad, the gulags, the Holocaust and the death camps.

Patricia Spacks pointed out that the free peoples of Middle-earth tend to be vegetarians, living in harmony with the land, eating bread, cakes, honey, mushrooms, while the baddies feast on meat, and drink horrible liquids (in N. Isaacs, 85). The key food of much of *The Lord of the Rings* is lembas bread, while the orcs have nasty meats.

Part of *The Lord of the Rings* is about the passing of the world of J.R.R. Tolkien's childhood in the English Midlands, in the region around Birmingham, as it became increasingly industrialized. *The Lord of the Rings* is an anti-technology, anti-machine tract; the spread of 'evil' is partly the spread of industrialization, the darkness, grime and pollution of factories, chimneys, smoke, the 'satanic mills' of William Blake.

Robotic minions, the orcs, do the bidding of Sauron, a Hitler or Stalin figure (with the nazgûl or Ring-wraiths as the SS high command. Communication among the villains tends to be by personal visit. The flying ringwraiths are as much messengers as military commanders, taking messages to and from the Dark Tower).

The first part of *The Lord of the Rings* is full of a nostalgia for a now-vanished England (which probably didn't exist in the first place), a world of streams, rivers, lakes, hills, dells, trackways, mountains and forests. A pre-First World War, Edwardian time of vague, ungraspable notions such as neighbourliness, community, small-scale living (villages, not towns), agriculture and patriotism.

Saruman is the wily politician, but he's also the selfish, power-hungry, would-be ruler. Saruman clearly wants the ring for himself. Gandalf says he would become a terrible ruler because the ring would corrupt him from his will to do good, from his pity. But Saruman just wants the rings, and dominion over others. Like Denethor, the 'sin' of pride is strong in Saruman.

chäpTeR 14
ADAPTIONS OF
J.R.R. TOLKIEN'S WORKS

ADAPTING TOLKIEN

The decision to sell the film rights came down to 'cash or kudos', as John Ronald Reuel Tolkien succinctly put it. Commentators have noted that Tolkien sold the film rights for a small amount, but when he sold the rights, in 1967, maybe he thought he wouldn't be around to see the results anyway (he was 75). The deal meant that Tolkien's estate wouldn't have any influence over any adaptions of *The Lord of the Rings*. Whoever held the rights (United Artists, Saul Zaentz) had them in perpetuity.

The Tolkien estate (and Christopher Tolkien in particular) was still a key influence on how Tolkien's work was perceived in later years, following Tolkien's death in 1973. Adaptors of Tolkien's fiction wouldn't want to alienate the Tolkien estate, because some Tolkien fans still regarded the family and estate as the true keepers of the flame.

The Tolkien estate, or at least members of Tolkien's family, tended to be opposed to the idea of any film adaption, the Hollywood adaption included. As Michael White commented, 'the Tolkien family are certain to dislike the [2001] film more than anyone' (247). But they will benefit from it – and not only financially. Tolkien's books will be read by millions more readers because of the success of the early 2000s films.

J.R.R. Tolkien had welcomed the idea of an animated movie of *The Lord of the Rings* at one time – at least that 'vulgarization' was preferrable in comparison to the 'sillification' of the BBC radio version of 1957.

J.R.R. Tolkien knew all about translating material – he spent quite a bit of his academic career doing just that, rendering work from Anglo-Saxon or Old German into English. And in some of his Middle-earth writings, he went the other way, translating from modern English into Old English. But translating fiction into another medium was a different matter. Tolkien asserted that

> the canons of narrative art in any medium cannot be wholly different;
> the failure of poor films is often precisely in exaggeration, and in the

intrusion of unwarranted matter owing to not perceiving where the core of the original lies.

Being 'faithful' to J.R.R. Tolkien's books is valued very highly by some Tolkien fans. They can be very protective of Tolkien's fiction. You mess with Tolkien at your peril. Most adaptions in film, TV and radio have taken that on board, and have tried, at least, to be 'faithful', even if they've often failed or veered away from that goal. Ralph Bakshi remarked that 'there isn't a page of *The Rings* that you wouldn't want to re-read a hundred times'. The reverence that Tolkien's stories generates has even increased since the professor's death. Everyone, it seems, has a view on what constitutes a decent, 'faithful' adaption of Tolkien.

It is possible to make a film with 22 principal characters, but it's very difficult. A film that shows how it could be done is the classy Country and Western backstage political comedy drama *Nashville* (1975), which follows 24 protagonists. To make a film with such a large cast work successfully begins and ends, really, not with the director, the producer, the crew or even the cast, but with the script and the writers.

Commercial filmmakers never have the luxury that J.R.R. Tolkien had when he was writing *The Lord of the Rings:* if he fancied it, Tolkien would start rewriting the book from the beginning. Hollywood calls that a 'page one' rewrite. That can be done if you're writing spec scripts, or don't have studios, executives and deadlines bearing down upon you. But with contracts agreed and signed and pre-production kicking in, you can't keep scrapping the script and rewriting it from the beginning. Director Peter Jackson said a totally faithful adaption of *Rings* 'just couldn't have been made and wouldn't have worked because it would have been slow and unstructured and very pedantic' (Sib, 411).

In a famous interview, originally published in the *New York Times Magazine* in 1950, Alfred Hitchcock said 'the chase is almost indigenous to movie technique as a whole... the chase seems to me the final expression of the motion picture medium' (1997, 125). For Hitchcock, the best kinds of chases had a dual movement: 'the chase is someone running toward a goal, often with the antiphonal one of someone fleeing a pursuer'. This describes *The Lord of the Rings,* in book or film form: Frodo and Sam are moving towards the goal of destroying the ring, while being pursued by the villains, who're also searching for the ring.

But there isn't just one chase in *The Lord of the Rings*. As Hitchcock remarked, the best chases plots 'are usually several chases going on at once... which eventually run into and influence each other' (ib., 127) and *The Lord of the Rings* provides several chases. Also, for Hitchcock, the ideal chase also reveals character as it goes along, and uses psychology to build up tension (ib., 127). The screenwriters of the 2001-03 adaption of *Rings* stick to that formula as the films progress, with the characters of

Frodo, Sam and Gollum being revealed gradually, and with the psychology of the tension between the characters intensifying the suspense. And, as a chase film, the *Lord of the Rings* series reaches a climax at the battle of the Black Gate which's simultaneous with the Crack of Doom scene, as the two chases reach their climactic physical manifestation (there's even a last desperate attempt on the part of the villain, Sauron, to find the ring, when he diverts his nazgûl from the battle to Mount Doom).

Tolkien's remarks in the essay "On Fairy-stories" about visual art and visual representations of fairy tales (including cinema) bears directly on the film adaptions of Tolkien's work:

> However good in themselves, illustrations do little good to fairy-stories. The radical distinction between all art (including drama) that offers a *visible* presentation and true literature is that it imposes one visible form. Literature works from mind to mind and is thus more progenitive. It is at once more universal and more poignantly particular. (MC, 159)

The reader, J.R.R. Tolkien suggested, offering a familiar argument of the differences between literature and visual art, imagines everything in literature subjectively as well as generally. When the text says 'bread', the reader imagines bread in general but also a 'peculiar personal embodiment in his imagination' (ibid.). But the film producer or visual artist has to show a particular piece of bread.

'Drama is anthropocentric. Fairy-story and Fantasy need not be', J.R.R. Tolkien remarked (MC, 160). Some of the best children's books have taken that route.

In "On Fairy-stories" J.R.R. Tolkien suggested that the phrases which begin fairy tales ('once upon a time') and end them ('and they lived happily after') were not meant to be taken literally; they were, rather, akin to frames or borders of paintings. The phrases were a way of marking out the territory of the fairy tale, formal devices which didn't deceive anyone. No one was meant to 'believe' that everyone 'lived happily ever after'.

> Endings of this sort suit fairy-stories, because such tales have greater sense and grasp of the endlessness of the World of Story than most modern 'realistic' stories, already hemmed within the narrow confines of their own small time. (MC, 161)

The opening phrase of fairy tales, 'once upon a time', also has a magical effect for J.R.R. Tolkien, introducing the sense of timelessness: '[i]t produces at a stroke the sense of a great uncharted world of time' (ibid.). One feels that Tolkien might have been tempted to begin *The Hobbit* or *The Lord of the Rings* with 'once upon a time'. In the end, Tolkien chose sentences which have a fairy tale feel, and are both evocations of Bilbo

Baggins:

> In a hole in the ground there lived a hobbit.

> When Mr Bilbo Baggins of Bad End announced that he would shortly be celebrating his eleventy-first birthday with a party of special magnificence, there was much talk and excitement in Hobbiton.

That first sentence of *The Hobbit* has since become one of J.R.R. Tolkien's most famous phrases (along with 'my precious!', 'the road goes ever on and on' and 'one ring to rule them all'). The professor seemed happy to tell anyone who'd listen the story of how he first wrote that phrase on the back of an exam paper. It's Tolkien Legend Number One.

BBC RADIO 1957

Before the first attempt to make a film of *The Lord of the Rings*, in 1957, the BBC had recorded a radio version (adapted by Terence Tiller for the Third Programme, which later became Radio 3. Tiller had produced the celebrated version of *Under Milk Wood* in 1954).

It had not met with Ronald Tolkien's approval: 'I think the book quite unsuitable for 'dramatization', and have not enjoyed the broadcasts' (L, 228). There were many factual errors in the BBC radio version, which irritated Tolkien. Morton Grady Zimmerman's proposed cartoon, for Tolkien, might risk 'vulgarization', but that 'vulgarization' should prove 'less painful than the sillification achieved by the B.B.C.', he complained (L, 257). ('Sillification' has not been avoided in any adaption of Tolkien's works to date).

One of the problems with the radio version, J.R.R. Tolkien asserted, was the over-emphasis on dialogue (which's the stuff of conventional radio drama) at the expense of description and narration. Tolkien said he would have preferred more narration in the BBC radio series (L, 255). Unfortunately, the 1957 BBC radio adaption of *The Lord of the Rings* hasn't survived. A pity, because it would be fascinating to hear this first adaption of Tolkien's work into another medium.

The Hobbit was adapted for radio by the Beeb in 1966. Heron Carvic was Gandalf, and Paul Daneman was Bilbo in a four-hour adaption broadcast in 30 minute episodes. According to Daniel Grotta, there was a BBC serialization made for schools, in the *Adventures In English* series, in 1955, and the main 13-part adaption came in 1961.

THE FIRST FILM ADAPTION (1957)

J.R.R. Tolkien was aware of the publicity potential (and revenue) a film of *The Lord of the Rings* could represent. But the first people to come to him (in 1957) with a proposal to film *The Lord of the Rings* (Morton Grady Zimmerman, Al Brodax and Forrest J. Ackerman) did not meet with the professor's approval. Tolkien acknowledged that *The Lord of the Rings* was '*very unsuitable for dramatic or semi-dramatic representation*. If that is attempted it needs more, a lot of space' (L, 255; my emphasis). Ackerman was a visual effects supervisor (he ran the magazine *Famous Monsters of Filmland*); Brodax was a producer (known for the *Popeye* cartoons); and Zimmerman was an unknown writer.

J.R.R. Tolkien had a long list of complaints (eight pages, no less, in a June, 1958 letter) about the Zimmerman/ Ackerman/ Brodax treatment of his beloved book. For Tolkien, the Zimmerman *et al* script was too compressed, resulting in 'over-crowding and confusion, blurring of climaxes and general degradation' (L, 261). Tolkien disliked Zimmerman's whole approach:

> He does not *read* books... I feel very unhappy about the extreme
> silliness and incompetence of [Zimmerman] and his complete lack of
> respect for the original (it seems wilfully wrong without discernible
> technical reasons at nearly every point. (L, 266-7)

Zimmerman, Brodax and Ackerman, J.R.R. Tolkien complained, put in unnecessary fights, eagles, a 'fairy castle', incantations and blue lights, and Faramir levitating to escape his funeral pyre, but cut out 'the parts of the story upon which its characteristic and peculiar tone principally depends', and hadn't got to the heart of the story: 'the journey of the Ringbearers' (L, 271).

J.R.R. Tolkien's gripes with the film treatment of Zimmerman *et al* continued: having too many giant eagles destroyed the credibility in other scenes (principally Gandalf's escape from Orthanc). Gandalf should not 'splutter'. The time scheme was altered, including Tolkien's careful use of the seasons (Tolkien had slaved over the time schemes, but no screen adaption of *The Lord of the Rings* could follow them exactly). Characters and dialogue were changed. The firework display had unnecessary additions (adaptors of *The Lord of the Rings* always wanted to put in more fireworks). Tom Bombadil and Goldberry were misrepresented by Zimmerman's 'general tendency... to reduce and lower the tone towards that of a more childish fairy-tale' (L, 272; – but at least Zimmerman *et al* had included them). Aragorn wouldn't have run off into the night with the hobbits to escape the Black Riders. Rivendell is not a 'shimmering forest', can't be seen from Weathertop, and doesn't resemble Lórien. Aragorn's sword is broken. The Black Riders don't scream, and there isn't a fight with 'rather meaningless slashings' on Weathertop (of the Weathertop confrontation in Zimmerman's script, Tolkien bewailed '[w]hy has my account been entirely rewritten here, with disregard for the rest of the tale?' [L, 273]). After Rivendell, the Fellowship leaves far too soon. The nine walkers are taken into the air by eagles. The orcs shouldn't have feathers and beaks. The Balrog *'never speaks or makes any vocal sound at all'* (L, 274). Galadriel does not live in a fairy tale castle. Galadriel's temptation is dropped, as are the ents. The topography of Théoden's castle is altered (it shouldn't have glass windows). The defence of the Hornburg is debased (L, 276). There isn't a spiral staircase around Orthanc. Saruman's death should be shown. (Many of Tolkien's complaints about the Zimmerman *et al* script found their way into future adaptions of his book, including the 2001-03 films, which had, for instance, Black Riders screaming and a roaring Balrog).

Writing in 1960, Arthur Weir came up with some ideas for a film version of *The Lord of the Rings:* the Sonoma desert, or the Sinai desert, or Glencoe in Scotland might be suitable for Mordor and Mount Doom. Carcasconne in France or Jeysalmir in India might be good for Minas Tirith, Arthur Weir thought. Alec Guinness as Gandalf and Charles Laughton as Théoden; and, improbably, Weir suggested Greta Garbo as Galadriel (but not one of what Weir called 'super mammary American or hip waggling Italian film stars', no Marilyn Monroe or Sophia Loren).

THE HOBBIT (1977) AND THE RETURN OF THE KING (1980)

An animated version of *The Hobbit* was broadcast on NBC in November, 1977 (it was directed by Arthur Rankin and Jules Bass, adapted by Romeo Muller, and cost $3 million). 'There is no material in this picture that did not come from the original Tolkien book,' said Arthur Rankin of his adaption of *The Hobbit.* 'I am not going to alter the story,' said Ralph Bakshi of his version of *The Lord of the Rings*.

Rankin and Bass specialized in holiday shows, such as *Rudolph the Red-Nosed Reindeer, The Little Drummer Boy* and *Frosty the Snowman.* They also produced *The Jackson Five* show. In the NBC *Hobbit,* John Huston was the voice of Gandalf, Otto Preminger was Elrond, and Orson Bean was Bilbo. Visually, the Rankin-Bass *Hobbit* drew on English illustrator Arthur Rackham, whose quaint, fey, highly romanticized versions of fantasy influenced Disney's *Snow White* (Disney animator Will Tytla had used Rackham for the dwarfs. As *Hobbit* animator Leslie Abrams put, Rackham provided the same source for Grumpy in *Snow White* and

Thorin in *The Hobbit*. The famous self-portrait of Leonardo da Vinci was used as an inspiration for Gandalf). Japanese animation firm Toru Hara produced the animation, overseen by Minoru Nishida, Katsushisa Yamada and Tsuguyuki Kubo. 40,000 frames were created for *The Hobbit*.

Walt Disney had considered animating *The Hobbit,* and MGM also planned a version. *The Hobbit* has many of the elements the Disney studio featured in its animated fairy tales, including wizards, dwarves, dragons, forests, quests. *The Hobbit* might have been one of Disney's best cartoons, had it been made during the 'golden age' of Disney animation (1937-1942). But if the studio had got round to it in the era of *Peter Pan, Cinderella* and *Alice In Wonderland*, it might still have been terrific.

Rankin and Bass followed up *The Hobbit* with *The Return of the King: A Tale of Hobbits* (1980), which they produced and directed as a TV movie. Romeo Muller adapted the book, with the animation again out-sourced to Japan (Toru Hara co-ordinated the animation, with Katsushisa Yamada and Joichi Sasaki directing it). Maury Laws provided the music (and Bass the lyrics). Orson Bean was back as Bilbo (and Frodo), John Huston was Gandalf, Roddy McDowall was Sam, Theodore Bikel was Aragorn, and William Conrad was Denethor.

The Rankin/ Bass *Return of the King* is fun, silly, sentimental, repetitive, with plenty of wilfully odd moments, and some cute musical numbers ('The Wearer of the Ring', xxx). It bears little relation to Tolkien's book, but it did feature scenes that didn't appear in the 2003 adaption, such as Aragorn's entry into Minas Tirith, or xx.

There is some confusion over how the second Rankin/ Bass Tolkien special came about. Animation takes a long time to produce, so the notion that Rankin and Bass jumped in when the 1978 United Artists movie was seen to fail commercially doesn't hold up (besides, the 1980 film was a TV movie, and not wholly competing in the same markets). If United Artists, Saul Zaentz and Ralph Bakshi had made their second half of *The Lord of the Rings*, it wouldn't have come out before the 1980 TV movie anyway. The 1980 TV movie had been announced by the *Hollywood Reporter* in April, 1977, before the 1977 *The Hobbit* had been shown on NBC, and while Zaentz and Bakshi were still slaving away at their 1978 adaption.

Rumours of a live action *Hobbit* were in the air throughout the production of the 2001-2003 *Lord of the Rings* films – and even more so when *Fellowship* was seen to do well. Peter Jackson was interested in doing *The Hobbit*, but only if he could keep some of the same cast and crew as the *Lord of the Rings* films, including Ian McKellen as Gandalf, and bringing back the actors for Elrond and, curiously, Arwen Legolas and Saruman. As Jackson put it, 'if I was the Time Warner board, I would have been hassling New Line for a *Hobbit* film for the last three years! It's a billion dollar franchise for the studio'.

The Hobbit in live action was announced in December, 2007, very cynically, as *two films*: one would be *The Hobbit*, the other the period between *The Hobbit* and *Lord of the Rings*. Yep, that's how to milk a franchise (Warners had led the way with splitting projects – the last *Harry Potter* movie being a totally cynical bid for $$$$$). Peter Jackson would executive produce, Guillermo Del Toro would direct both films, and Philippa Boyens, Del Toro, Jackson and Fran Walsh would co-write. Del Toro later walked (scheduling was an issue), and Jackson took up the helm (for a Christmas, 2012 release). A pity, I think, because we've already seen what Jackson, Walsh, Boyens *et al* have done with Tolkien, and it would so much more entertaining to see what another team could do.

And when the *Hobbit* movie finally appeared, it was very disappointing, uninspired (and very expensive). *The Hobbit* was *so* slow: like, *when* are we going to get out of Bag End and start the story?! Interminable scenes – such as the battle with the orcs in the mountains, with endless, tiresome and valueless action. And by now, Tolkien's little book for children had been padded out to *three* movies of over 2 1/2 hours each!

❧

The Beatles considered making a film of *The Lord of the Rings,* in which Lennon would've been Gollum, Harrison Gandalf, and Macca and Ringo Frodo and Sam. David Lean was approached, as was Stanley Kubrick (who thought the book was unfilmable). Dennis O'Dell had been instrumental in guiding the project, as producer. O'Dell said that Lennon had suggested doing some music based on the film.

JOHN BOORMAN (1967)

John Boorman developed *The Lord of the Rings* in the late 1960s (United Artists had bought the film rights to *The Lord of the Rings* in 1967). Boorman shopped it around various studios, with Mike Medavoy as producer, which all rejected it. J.R.R. Tolkien told Boorman he was concerned that the film was going to be in live action, not animation (Tolkien had a dim view of animation; in the event all screen adaptions of his work have either been wholly animated, or employed huge amounts of animation). Boorman said the biggest problem was turning the massive book into a single 2 1/2 hour film (1985, 20). According to Medavoy, Boorman's screenplay ran to 700 pages; it's difficult to see how Boorman could have condensed *The Lord of the Rings* into just one movie. 'If filmmaking for me is, as I have often said, exploration, setting oneself impossible problems and failing to solve them, then the *Rings* saga qualifies on all counts' Boorman commented (ibid.).

One of the main attractions of *The Lord of the Rings* for John Boorman was the character of Gandalf ('Merlin in another guise'); Boorman had planned to make a film about Merlin prior to *The Lord of the Rings* (this eventually became *Excalibur*). The Merlin film was also in a different incarnation Boorman's adaption of John Cowper Powys's *A Glastonbury Romance*, an extraordinary epic novel which places many of the same themes as *The Lord of the Rings* (and source texts, such as the Grail legends, and Celtic and Arthurian myths) into the present day (the 1930s of the time *A Glastonbury Romance* was written). Like Tolkien's tome, Powys's novel proved long, difficult and complex to adapt for the screen. Boorman abandoned the Powys script, as he would the Tolkien film.

Boorman worked for 6 months with Rospo Pallenberg on the *Lord of the Rings* script, making maps, charts, chronologies, etc. United Artists backed out of the project – it was too expensive, and there was no one at the company now who was behind the project (executives having left). When Boorman touted *The Lord of the Rings* around other studios, including Disney, nobody wanted it.

John Boorman recalled that his experience of trying to make *The Lord of the Rings* was not totally without value: some of the locations he scouted for *The Lord of the Rings* were used in *Excalibur*, and the special fx he prepared for *The Lord of the Rings* were deployed in his subsequent films (*Zardoz, The Heretic* and *Excalibur*).

John Boorman tried to set up *The Lord of the Rings* again, in the Eighties, with Mike Medavoy at TriStar. Negotiations with Saul Zaentz ensued, but Zaentz and Medavoy couldn't agree on the merchandizing rights: Zaentz wanted to retain merchandizing rights but Medavoy wouldn't agree to that (in the end, Zaentz kept the merchandizing rights, for the 2001-03 *Rings* films, and did very well out of them). Boorman said, generously, that if he'd made his version of *The Lord of the Rings,* audiences wouldn't have seen the 'magnificent spectacle' of the 2001-03 movies (180).

NOTES: ADAPTING TOLKIEN

1. A. Hitchcock, 1997, 125.

THE 1978 UNITED ARTISTS FILM OF *THE LORD OF THE RINGS*

Ralph Bakshi directed, Saul Zaentz produced, Leonard Roseman scored, Timothy Galfas shot, and Daniel Pia supervised the animation of the United Artists/ Fantasy Films production of *The Lord of the Rings,* released in 1978. But the most important credits were the writers: Chris Conkling and

Peter S. Beagle; it's the adaptors that are make-or-break personnel in turning *The Lord of the Rings* into another medium.

Among the voice cast were Christopher Guard as Frodo, Michael Scholes as Sam, William Squire as Gandalf, John Hurt as Aragorn, Michael Graham Cox as Boromir, Norman Bird as Bilbo, Philip Stone as Théoden, Annette Crosbie as Galadriel, Anthony Daniels as Legolas and Peter Woodthorpe as Gollum.

Prior to *The Lord of the Rings,* Ralph Bakshi had worked in TV animation (*Spider-man, The Fantastic Four, Mighty Mouse*) before making his name with the cult counter-culture hit *Fritz the Cat* (1972), an X-rated cartoon of Robert Crumb's equally cultish comic book. Bakshi followed *Fritz the Cat* up with an attack on racism, *Coonskin* (1975), and *Wizards* (1977), based on Vaughn Bode's comics.

Bakshi had wanted to do *The Lord of the Rings* since the late 1950s, but couldn't obtain the rights (Bakshi claimed that Disney held them, but they never had). Bakshi said he tried repeatedly to get the rights. Eventually Bakshi set up the project with MGM, where it languished. It went back to United Artists when Bakshi persuaded Saul Zaentz to come aboard and produce the film. (Zaentz wound up buying the rights in perpetuity). At the time, Zaentz was doing very well with *One Flew Over the Cuckoo's Nest* (1975), a big critical success. He later went on to further critical hits with *Amadeus* (1984) and *The English Patient* (1996).

Originally, Ralph Baskhi wanted three films to correspond to the three volumes, but United Artists wanted two films. In the end, Bakshi only made one half of *The Lord of the Rings.* The writers, Conkling and Beagle, had written three scripts, then had to combine them into two scripts. Bakshi commented that the most difficult part of the adaption was getting the right structure. One of Conkling's early drafts had the film occurring in flashback, from Merry and Pippin in *The Two Towers* being pursued by orcs. In the second film, Bakshi said he would've used flashbacks again, and characters like Tom Bombadil might've made it into the film.

One of the biggest problems was how to end the first film, with the whole story cut into two. *The Two Towers* is a difficult book to adapt, because of its lack of a satisfying narrative resolution. But even when the book's cut in half, it's still difficult. Cutting a film narrative in two nearly always means that the second film suffers, commercially, even though it has the ending and resolution, while the first film doesn't have the ending.

It makes sense that the 1978 version of *The Lord of the Rings* ends with the battle of Helm's Deep, but it's still not wholly satisfying. Saul Zaentz was rumoured to have switched the last two reels of the film after bad previews, so that Sam and Frodo at Shelob's lair was switched with the battle of Helm's Deep.

❂

If one revisits the 1978 animated movie of *The Lord of the Rings*, it's nowhere near as bad as the common view has it (actually, plenty of fans of the book also enjoy the cartoon). In fact, some things are much better than in the New Line Cinema films of 2001-03. In fact, the 1978 United Artists film got there first with many things, which I'd forgotten about:

The prologue (I thought that was one of the most significant narrative decisions in the 2001-03 movies, but Ralph Bakshi and Saul Zaentz had already done it (as had the BBC 1981 radio adaption) – even down to the *tableaux*-style of presentation coupled with voiceover narration, and the same slice of Middle-earth history, which the 2001-03 films shamelessly aped (the dwarves and elves raised their arms wearing the rings in the 1978 film, which the 2001 film also used). However, it may simply be the material that the viewer requires to make sense of the significance of the ring). There are also shots that the 2001 film of *The Fellowship of the Ring* copied exactly: the ring bouncing down some rocks in silhouette in Moria, for instance.

Frodo's subjective experience when he puts on the ring (altered, abstract backgrounds and echoey sound) was another way the 1978 cartoon prefigured the 2001 live action film.

It's very odd that Sam is eavesdropping on Frodo and Gandalf by hiding behind a bush at night. In the 1978 film, it's Gandalf who sends Merry and Pippin with Frodo, again a departure from the book.

The filmmakers of the 2001-03 version suggested that no one had visualized Gandalf fighting the balrog as he descends beneath Zirak-zigil before. Yes they had: the 1978 film has a shot of Gandalf and the balrog plummeting, and depicts much of the fight between the Maia spirits below the Misty Mountains (admittedly chiefly via still images and voiceover).

And the 2001-03 movies seemed to be (unconsciously?) replaying so many of the same moments from the 1978 *Lord of the Rings* film, right down to the framing and staging (look at the camera angles and compositions, for instance, in the hiding from the Black Rider on the path scene, which's identical, down to holding on a wide shot when the Black Rider trots into frame, or Strider in the inn sitting with his back to a window, and Moria, and the ford, and Boromir's death, etc).

The look of the 2001-03 movies is superior to the Saul Zaentz cartoon, and John Boorman's right that J.R.R. Tolkien would've hated the Disney-esque look of the 1978 cartoon (Tolkien voiced his dislike of Disney as early as 1937. That's quite understandable, because Tolkien was such a devotee of fairy tales, and critics who know a good deal about fairy tales tend not to enjoy the way the Disney studio eviscerated them, watering down the sex, violence, gore, and obsession. Tolkien probably disliked Disney's take on Germanic dwarves, too, turning them into pint-sized comedians).

However, J.R.R. Tolkien did produce stories and books which have an affinity with Disney's output. Tolkien's *Farmer Giles of Ham*, for instance, or his *Father Christmas Letters,* or *The Adventures of Tom Bombadil*, were aimed partly at children, and had Disneyesque touches. In *Farmer Giles of Ham*, for example, a farmer goes to fight a dragon; the book, with its wonderful illustrations by Pauline Baynes (1922-2008), was the sort of tale that Disney took up from time to time. In the 1941 film *The Reluctant Dragon*, there's a marvellous fairy tale section about battling a dragon with affinities with *Farmer Giles of Ham* (and also in Disney's adaption of T.H. White, *The Sword In the Stone*).

It's a pity the 1978 cartoon of *The Lord of the Rings* didn't tackle Tom Bombadil, though: the cartoon style and light-hearted songs could've incorporated Bombadil, while the grim, let's-be-serious approach of the 2001 *Rings* film couldn't take on Bombadil. You could get away with Bombadil in animation, but probably not now (these days) in live action (though there are plenty of actors around who could do the character). In fact, there haven't been any representations of Tom Bombadil in the major dramatic adaptions of *The Lord of the Rings* thus far: the United Artists 1978 cartoon, the BBC 1981 radio drama and the 2001 Hollywood film have all dropped Bombadil (and any reference to him) completely. So if fans complained that Bombadil wasn't part of the New Line films of 2001-03, well he hasn't been in any *Lord of the Rings* film or drama so far.

The orcs in the United Artists film were cool (they recalled Tatooine's sand people in *Star Wars*). The state-of-the-art slathering, *Alien*-style make-up and prosthetic effects of the orcs in the 2001-03 movies didn't add that much. In fact, the orcs in the 2001-03 movies tended to be overwhelmed by the thick layers of prosthetics and make-up additions, severely restricting the actors' ability to perform, as well as making the orcs look very self-conscious. The orcs in Bakshi's film wore masks and cloaks, a simple but effective means of hiding actors' faces, and not requiring lengthy make-up.

Some of the animation, the settings and the visuals were superb in the 1978 cartoon of *The Lord of the Rings*, such as the watercolour-style washes of backgrounds, the abstract backgrounds during action scenes or the wraithworld, and the visual effects (Ralph Bakshi in *Fritz the Cat* had shown a penchant for slow-moving blurred watercolour washes, rather like the Sixties lightshow of a psychedelic rock band in an underground club seen though clouds of smoke and pot).

The filmmakers shot the film twice: once as live action, and again during animation (as the Disney studio had often done). The voice talents were recorded first; their dialogue was played back on sets in Hollywood, where Bakshi shot the live action. Costumes, props and sets were used. Helm's Deep was staged in Spain, at Belmonte Castle. Sometimes the coordination between live action and animation was awkward, and sometimes it was odd to see a filmed human face in amongst a scene with animated characters (such as at Helm's Deep).

Rotoscoping and using live action as a reference was nothing new, of course: Walt Disney had been doing it since the Thirties. But Disney liked to keep that aspect of his productions secret. In the United Artists *The Lord of the Rings*, rotoscoping became a central stylistic element. Sometimes the effect looked like a tinted photocopy or tinted black-and-white footage. Sometimes it clashed with the animation of the other characters.

In later films, such as contemporary big budget movies, motion capture is often employed, which has some affinities with Bakshi's rotoscoping technique. In motion capture, actors are shot by multiple cameras and their movements are captured in a computer; that data is then used to drive digital animation. Critics pointed out that rotoscoping live action in the 1978 *The Lord of the Rings* was a kind of cheating (which's why Disney tended to keep its use of rotoscoping quiet), but it's no more a kind of cheating than motion capture. Indeed, motion capture is fairly widespread these days in big budget movies (it's a *very* expensive process, so only ultra-high budget movies can afford it). But nobody seems to call it 'cheating'. (It was used extensively in the 2001-03 adaption of *The Lord of the Rings,* for instance).

❀

The 1978 cartoon of *The Lord of the Rings* was plenty cheesy and camp (it seemed to be impossible to do Gollum other than camp: every version has been camp (but fun): 'nice hobbitses!' Peter Woodthorpe voiced Gollum in both the 1978 United Artists film and the 1981 BBC radio adaption. I'd say his Gollum is easily as impressive as Andy Serkis's, and superior in many respects). But the 2001-03 films have many moments of corn and cheese (Cate Blanchett's pompous Galadriel, with her s-o s-l-o-w v-o-i-c-e, for starters).

Although the 2001-03 *The Lord of the Rings* films were incredibly violent, the violence in the 1978 adaption was far more bizarre, because of those weird blood and squib effects. (There's also a scene where Gandalf on Shadowfax runs down an orc in Sam Peckinpah slo-mo style, with blood spraying up – the 2001-03 movies were more restrained in their use of Gandalf in battle). And the Ralph Bakshi film ends with an extraordinary image – Gandalf as a victorious warrior-wizard, flinging Glamdring high into the sky – an image nowhere, one should add, in Tolkien's sacred text).

If you're a J.R.R. Tolkien fan, though, neither the 1978 version nor the 2001-03 version came anywhere near really capturing the essence, the level of detail, or the complexity of the book.

What happened with the promised second half of *The Lord of the Rings*? Each person involved has a different story. Ralph Bakshi was furious – he always wanted to do the whole book. He said he had been screwed by the studio (UA) over the second part of *The Lord of the Rings*. The film should have been released with 'part one' in the title, Bakshi asserted, and it was always intended to be the first part of a two-part film. United Artists didn't want that, and didn't think audiences would turn up for one film knowing there was another to see (the 2001-03 films also left out numbers: the films could have been *The Lord of the Rings 1* and *The Lord of the Rings 2* and *3*. Or *Part I, Part II* and *Part III*. They also left out Tolkien: they weren't *J.R.R. Tolkien's The Lord of the Rings*).

In the end, it was Arthur Rankin and Jules Bass who produced the second half, with their made-for-TV movie of *The Return of the King* (1980). Bakshi said the filmmakers of the New Line adaption hadn't spoken to him: 'I find that ungentlemanly', Bakshi said.

THE BBC RADIO ADAPTION OF *THE LORD OF THE RINGS* (1981)

The British Broadcasting Corporation's radio department adapted *The Lord of the Rings* in 26 thirty-minute episodes first broadcast in 1981 (and broadcast in 1982 as thirteen one-hour episodes). It was repeated again to coincide with the 2001-03 movies, in 2002, and also re-released on CD and audio tape (with some re-editing, and additions; now Ian Holm's Frodo was looking back and relating the events). Each 30 minute episode ended with a cliffhanger (a structure that was lost when it was re-broadcast and re-edited. Extra narration was recorded to bridge over the gaps).

The BBC *The Lord of the Rings* was produced by Jane Morgan, and co-directed by Morgan and Penny Leicester. That makes the BBC adaption already quite different from other productions of *The Lord of the Rings* even if you don't know anything else about it: it was directed by *two women* (thinking about it, it's probably the only major *The Lord of the Rings* or J.R.R. Tolkien adaption to date that has been, although the 2001-03 movies were co-directed and co-written by women).

Brian Sibley and Michael Bakewell dramatized the book for radio (Sibley is well-known as a writer on children's literature, and a contributor to BBC radio; Sibley was involved in the 2001-03 *Lord of the Rings* films too: he wrote a companion book, and appeared in many of the document-aries on the DVDs and TV programmes). The music was by Stephen Oliver, with excellent radiophonic sound (as they dubbed it) by Elizabeth Parker (the BBC had its own Radiophonic Unit which supplied special sounds and music for radio shows and was used most famously for the *Dr Who* and *Blake's 7* TV series. Parker was one of the leading lights of BBC radiophonics).

Among the cast of the 1981 BBC radio adaption of *The Lord of the Rings* were Michael Hordern as Gandalf, Ian Holm as Frodo, Robert Stephens as Aragorn, John Le Mesurier as Bilbo, Peter Woodthorpe as Gollum, Bill Nighy as Sam, Peter Vaughan as Denethor, Jack May as Tolkien, Peter Howell as Saruman, and Philip Voss as the Witch-king. The narrator was Gerard Murphy. Most of the actors were familiar to British TV and radio audiences (and most were Brits), but only Holm and Hordern were well-known on the international scene (Holm of course was Bilbo in the 2001-03 movies. Jane Morgan commented that she 'never considered anyone else for Frodo save Ian Holm', and the filmmakers of the 2001-03 movies said that Holm was the first and only choice for Bilbo. He was brilliant in both roles). The BBC radio version was used by some of the cast of the 2001-03 *Lord of the Rings* as preparation for their roles (and New Line Cinema employed some of the alterations to the story of the BBC radio version).

The BBC 1981 *The Lord of the Rings* was a prestige production, with a lengthy run (26 weeks), a big cast, and lavish, high quality stereo presentation. It was a favourite with listeners. It has stood the test of time, hasn't dated at all, and bears many repeat listens (radio shows often age better than TV shows, even if some of their language and style is old-fashioned). It's the equal of the 2001-03 movies as an adaption of Tolkien's fiction – and the pictures are better on radio, as the saying goes.

Indeed, some scenes far outstrip the 2001-03 movies. Much was made by New Line and the production of Andy Serkis's Gollum, but Peter Woodthorpe's Gollum was equally marvellous. Fans loved the schizophrenia scenes in the 2002 film of The *Two Towers,* but the BBC radio version had got there first: during the Cirith Ungol and Mordor sequences, as Sam debates with himself what to do, the actor (Bill Nighy) talks to himself – but recorded at different times, and in slightly different places in the stereo spectrum. (Serkis was influenced by Woodthorpe's Gollum, as Elijah Wood was by Ian Holm's Frodo).

Christopher Lee is a grand, commanding presence as Saruman in the 2001-03 movies, yes (that's what you get when you cast a veteran like Lee), but Peter Howell is also tremendously effective as Saruman in the BBC radio adaption. One scene effortlessly knocks spots off the 2003 *Return of the King* movie version: the voice of Saruman sequence at Isengard. The scene is beautifully written and expertly played (and contains far more drama and suspense (and information) than the New Line films. In the *Extended Edition* of The *Return of the King*, it's very sub-standard scene). Howell is particularly effective at delivering the shifts in Saruman's voice from seduction to rage (technically, a little harmonizing recording effect was applied to Howell's voice).

Many other scenes in the 1981 BBC radio version of *The Lord of the*

Rings are superior to the 1978, 1980 or 2001-03 films. The ending, for instance, the parting at the Grey Havens, is deeply moving, and sensitively judged.

The BBC radio version also contains more traditional renditions of J.R.R. Tolkien's songs. Some of these are delivered in modern versions of mediæval songs, a kind of contemporary mock heroic style. There are also solo choirboy songs (such as the song of the eagle flying over Minas Tirith).[1]

NOTES: THE BBC RADIO ADAPTION

1. Martin Barker has examined some of the cultural aspects of the BBC radio series, including its production in the context of Thatcherite Britain (E. Mathijs, 2006, 61f).

OTHER ADAPTIONS OF TOLKIEN

One of the chief adaptions of J.R.R. Tolkien's writing has been audio books and readings, an area of the publishing which has increased enormously in recent years. Thus there are CDs and audio tapes of readings by actors of Tolkien's books, some edited, others unabridged. *The Silmarillion* was read by Martin Shaw, a favourite with British audio books. The unabridged reading of *The Lord of the Rings* (by Rob Inglis) lasts for 52 hours (and the reading by Cate Blanchett in Elvish runs for 5,750,000 hours).

Inglis and Recorded Books produced a compelling and highly entertaining rendition of *The Lord of the Rings* (including the appendices), which illuminates J.R.R. Tolkien's text in all sorts of ways: for instance, you can tell immediately where Tolkien's prose really comes alive, and where it lags a little. What comes across, once again, is just how powerful *The Lord* is as a story. And without the novel being edited, you can't complain that bits have been missed out. Essential listening.

In 1979 the Mind's Eye (Soundelux) adapted *The Lord of the Rings,* with Bernard Mayes as Gandalf and Tom Bombadil (he also directed and adapted the production), James Arrington as Frodo, and local actors from Pittsburgh in other roles. The BBC also produced a reading of *The Hobbit* by Bernard Cribbins, in October, 1979, which was broadcast in the Beeb's children's book strand *Jackanory.*

There have been other attempts at adapting J.R.R. Tolkien, including film projects, and musicals on stage, such as the London production which opened in 2006.

I've only recently got into audio books of fantasy novels: Jim Dale taking on *Harry Potter* is spectacular. Nicol Williamson is completely wonderful reading *The Hobbit,* very highly recommended. At first I found

Rob Inglis a little starchy and stodgy, but soon Inglis's interpretation of *The Lord of the Rings* grows on you.

Audio books are particularly inspiring at bringing out aspects of works you know very well but hadn't seen like that: for instance, although "The Council of Elrond" chapter is very long and full of dialogue (and monologues), which some adaptors have found tough, Tolkien's sheer enjoyment of dwelling in Rivendell is infectious: you can feel the writer revelling in the recreation of a blissfull elvish realm, in which you can read, or sing, or think, or just *be*. Frodo is healed (nearly), he meets lots of friends, and there are numerous stories of what's been happening around Middle-earth. The highpoint is undoubtedly the elves' feast and Bilbo's song – Frodo slips into a vivid dream, and Tolkien's writing really sparkles.

Also, even diehard Tolkienites can't complain that the sacred texts have been cut or bits have been left out, because the unabridged audio books include everything. In this respect, and due to the superlative performances, the audio books of Tolkien's works may be the most satisfying adaptions around. Without deletions, you really get a sense of Tolkien's writing, its rhythms, its strengths – and weaknesses. When the set-pieces are reached, for example, you can feel Tolkien's prose flying off the page – the Old Forest, the attack on Weathertop, the flight to the ford, and the entire Rivendell sequence.

chápteɹ 15

ADAPTING *THE LORD OF THE RINGS* FOR THE 2001-03 MOVIES

'So much is lost', Galadriel says in the prologue of the 2001 movie *The Lord of the Rings: The Fellowship of the Ring*, 'so much is forgotten': these are the first words of Hollywood's live action version of *The Lord of the Rings*, almost as if they're reminding viewers of the costs of translating a book to the screen.

This chapter is only short – there is a companion pocket guide to the *Lord of the Rings* movies. And I've written in great detail about the films in my book on Tolkien.

The 2001-2003 *Lord of the Rings* films didn't come out of nowhere, freshly minted. There's been a sizeable J.R.R. Tolkien franchise for decades, including action figures, posters, prints, illustrations, maps, jewellery, replica weaponry, costumes, toys, board games, wargaming, conferences, and the films, radio shows and TV shows noted above. And not forgetting the sword-and-sorcery fantasy flicks: *The Beastmaster* (1983), *Ladyhawke* (1985), *Willow* (1988), *Krull* (1983), *Conan the Barbarian* (1982), *Dragonslayer* (1981), *The Dark Crystal* (1983), *The Sword and the Sorcerer* (1982), and *Labyrinth* (1987).

Director Peter Jackson acknowledged that *The Lord of the Rings* was fabulous source material: 'we could never have come up with something as good as the raw material of those characters and this world'.[1] (There were times, though, when the filmmakers reckoned they'd improved on Tolkien's book).

The heart of the story of *The Lord of the Rings,* for J.R.R. Tolkien, was 'the journey of the Ringbearers' (L, 271), he wrote in a letter about the Morton Grady Zimmerman cartoon script of 1957. The 2001-03 movies, for all their faults, do keep that part of the narrative in the foreground (although, in *The Return of the King*, there is a tendency to over-emphasize the Minas Tirith scenes – Faramir's force fighting at Osgiliath and his charge of the light brigade are expansions on the book, for example).

It's true that the problem of the ring does disappear from the story for long stretches, and J.R.R. Tolkien seems concerned with many other matters. There's simply *so much* going on in *The Lord of the Rings,* that the ring sometimes gets lost in it. The writers of the 2001-03 adaption tried to find ways of reminding the audience about the ring – and about Sauron.

Because the 2001-03 movies were remakes, they had previous adaptions of J.R.R. Tolkien's tome as guides on how *not* to adapt the book, on things to avoid, as well as which things worked. *The Hobbit* and *The Lord of the Rings* cartoons of 1977, 1978 and 1980 were very useful for the writers in reminding them of which aspects of the book work well on screen, and which aspects are harder to film. If someone's been there before it's handy to see how they coped with the adaption.

The adaptors of *The Lord of the Rings* could have consciously *avoided* seeing any previous attempts, but that's difficult, because not only are there film, TV, radio and theatrical versions of J.R.R. Tolkien's books, there are also forty-five years of illustrations and artwork. It would be impressive for a fan of fantasy art or movies not to have come across quite a few references to Tolkien's book or illustrations of characters from Middle-earth. (Besides, the writers knew the 1978 film version, the 1980 TV film and the 1981 radio adaption, and employed aspects of them in their take on Tolkien).

One wouldn't believe, without being told, that the *Lord of the Rings* films have been co-written by two women (Fran Walsh and Philippa Boyens). The attempts at 'feminizing' *The Lord of the Rings* for a contemporary audience have included: (1) Aragorn as a caring, sharing New Man hero (and casting an attractive actor for the romantic lead); (2) bringing Arwen from the appendix into the foreground (and Arwen taking over Glorfindel's role); (3) the Arwen-Aragorn romance plot; (4) Arwen's debate with her father about staying or going; (5) enlarging the role of Éowyn, and her love for Aragorn; (6) introducing mother figures (such as the mother Morwen in *The Two Towers* who sends her children to Edoras; mothers and wives saying goodbye to their loved ones before the battle of Helm's Deep); (7) the many cutie kid shots; (8) having Enya and other female singers on the soundtrack (including Elizabeth Fraser, Sheila Chandra, Isabel Bayraldarian and Emiliana Torrini).

FEAR OF COLONIZATION. Someone on the internet remarked that the 2001-03 *Lord of the Rings* films would get confused with the book in their head. That's a kind of fear of media colonization that David Cronenberg explores in his 'body horror' films.

For me, J.R.R. Tolkien's works and world are so deeply ingrained, it'll take more than the 2001-03 movies to dislodge them. I have a very particular and very strong interpretation of a character like Frodo, for example, built over years of the reading the books, and an 18 year-old actor like Elijah Wood can't supplant it. It's odd that for some people their vision of Tolkien and Middle-earth, developed over 100s of hours of reading, will be supplanted by a few viewings of the films.

When the 2001-03 version of *The Lord of the Rings* is contemplated for any time, it's striking just how much the screenwriters invented. The novel is very long, dense, multi-layered, with plenty of characters and events, but the adaptors still introduced a huge number of elements and scenes. These included lengthy invented sections, such as:

(1) the Arwen-Aragorn romance,

(2) many Aragorn and Elrond scenes,

(3) the ring going to Osgiliath,

(4) Faramir's reversal,

 (5) the warg attack,

(6) Aragorn's 'death' and return,

(7) Saruman as chief villain (numerous extra scenes),

(8) a wizard duel,

(9) the collapsing stairs in Moria,

(10) Aragorn and Frodo at Amon Hen with the ring,

(11) Haldir and the elves at Helm's Deep,

(12) much more for Éowyn (and for Éowyn and Aragorn),

(13) Théodred's funeral,

(14) the invasion of Rohan by Wild Men,

(15) Gothmog and his troops,

(16) attacks on Osgliath much expanded,

(17) telepathic communication between Galadriel and Elrond,

(18) Boromir, Faramir and Denethor at Osgiliath,

(19) Frodo and Sam under the elven cloak,

(20) many additions to the Helm's Deep battle,

(21) Arwen leaving for the Grey Havens,

(22) Sam betrayed by Gollum at Shelob's lair, and so on.

Peter Jackson remarked that *The Two Towers* was the slightest of the books. Having cut out so much from an already 'slight 'book – Shelob, Cirith Ungol, the voice of Saruman, etc – the filmmakers proceeded to add more inventions to *The Two Towers* than to the other two films (the warg attack, Aragorn's 'death' and resurrection, Faramir taking Frodo and co. to Osgiliath, the face-off with the Witch-king, and so on).

As planned originally, the first film would have ended with Saruman's death, Pippin and the *palantír*, and the fellowship breaking up, with Legolas and Gimli going South. The second film would have begun with Frodo, Sam and Gollum at the Black Gate.

Peter Jackson said the filmmakers were conscious of trying not to make a bad film; if the films were good, the Tolkien fans might forgive them a little, but a bad movie would have been disastrous. 'We did obviously deviate from the books, but we knew there would be forgiveness if they [the Tolkien fans] drew some pride in what we had done'.2 '*I want to make movies that I'd like to watch'*, Jackson has remarked, a common view among filmmakers (Sib, 551).

Frances Walsh acknowledged that a film could only capture a small number of elements of a book, could only give a superficial indication of what a book was, and couldn't replace the pleasure a book offers. In adapting *The Lord of the Rings*, Walsh and Philippa Boyens hoped to honour some Tolkien's iconic moments and themes, and portray some of the memorable scenes, but couldn't hope to deliver a reader's enjoyment of the whole text.

Peter Jackson had admitted that the movie wouldn't be faithful to the book. Any book adaption is a thousand compromises: '*our adaption can't be faithful*. You can't just take the book and go and shoot it', Jackson said.3 To film *The Lord of the Rings* in full would require probably 10, 20, 30 hours for each of the three books (and the text would still require a lot of work on it to appear 'faithful'). Christopher Lee reckoned that J.R.R. Tolkien 'would be very pleased. The spirit of Tolkien's work, the essence of the books, is still on screen'.

The job of the filmmakers was the difficult one of juggling a number of potentially conflicting requirements: (1) remaining true to J.R.R. Tolkien's beloved text (or the spirit of Tolkien); (2) not alienating the legions of fans (who had a lot of buying power); (3) producing a 'good night out' as Jackson called it, a fun and exciting two-three hours; (4) delivering a 'PG'-rated family adventure blockbuster to the studio, which it could market and sell (and on time, on schedule, on budget, with the agreed elements, and within agreed limits (the filmmakers clashed with the studio many times over these and other issues)); (5) to guarantee the financial investment, to deliver a profit on the investment, to shore up New Line Cinema for the future; and (6) to launch a franchise, licensing and merchandizing operation with a two-and-a-half-hour-plus advert.

The filmmakers were not duty bound or contractually obliged to please the Estate of J.R.R. Tolkien, however. Securing the film rights meant that they could (pretty much) do what they liked with the books, and the author's estate wouldn't be able to do anything – because Tolkien himself had signed away the film rights in 1967 (the estate would benefit financially from the films, though).

But it would have been foolish for the *Lord of the Rings* adaptors to deliberately irritate or put off the sizeable fan base for the books. The Hollywood studio would want that audience to come to the films, because a large percentage of that audience would see the films more than once in theatres, and would also buy the home entertainment editions of the films (as well as merchandizing). There was also a certain amount of goodwill built up towards J.R.R. Tolkien and the estate of the author (including

Christopher Tolkien, who had administered so much of the Tolkien publishing empire after professor's death). It would've helped a little if Tolkien junior had blessed the films (he didn't, publicly, but he would have benefitted in secondary ways – not least in stimulating sales of the books of his father's he'd edited).

❉

Some fans complained that the 2001-03 movies of *The Lord of the Rings* would damage J.R.R. Tolkien's reputation. The point is, although there's lots wrong, mistaken, irritating or even depressing about the films, *in their arena* (the Hollywood blockbuster franchise), they have been regarded as very successful (economically and critically). Thus, the positive effects will overshadow the 'negative' ones, on the whole.

For me, far more 'damaging' to J.R.R. Tolkien's cultural status was the awful fantasy art that drew on Tolkien's works in the 1970s (and late 1960s, but mostly after his death in 1973). To me, that crappy fantasy art was far more offensive than anything in the 2001-2003 films (including all the changes and alterations). Heavy metal freaks, dungeons and dragons, muscular he-men slaughtering bug-eyed monsters while women with big boobs and bikinis cooed and waved from the battlements.

If you want to target the rise of fascistic fantasy art, a culture of pro-militaristic politics, men as Hitleran Supermen, backward-looking sexual politics (adolescent at best, misogynist at worst), women as virgins or whores (yes, true, there was the occasional warrior woman), and prowess measured in size of Schwarzeneggerian bicep and chest, to the sound of Wagner or Carl bloody Orff, that's where it is.

1970s fantasy art in its macho, 'take no prisoners' mode was the visual equivalent of Led Zeppelin's 'Immigrant Song' ('wargasmic' music). But it could also be vomit-inducingly cute (*viz.* the hilarious footage of Mr Spock (Leonard Nimoy) singing about hobbits, aired again in the documentaries about the *Lord of the Rings* movies). Not all of 1970s fantasy art was bilge, but if any 'damage' was done to Tolkien's media image, it was there (and not forgetting the massive wave of merchandizing that followed the professor's death in 1973).

What's remarkable about the 2001-03 movies of J.R.R. Tolkien's book, is that although there's more than enough dodgy hair, camp delivery, ponderous dialogue, leather, chains and improbable events to go around, the 1970s fantasy art look was, in general, avoided. The women in the Kiwi-Oz-US films, for example, have suitably demure costumes (no bare flesh here, no tits and ass), with flattened chests (like Princess Leia in the first *Star Wars* film). Of course, the male actors in the 2001-2003 films are prone to ridiculous flourishes with swords or bow and arrows, like macho Hollywood heroes (Viggo Mortensen and Orlando Bloom in particular), but some of excesses of fantasy art of the 1970s and 1980s or Hollywood action heroics are sidestepped. (Take the scene of Aragorn in the river in *The Two Towers*, for instance: Arny, Bruce, Jean-Claude, Kurt or Sly would certainly have used that opportunity halfway thro' *Lord of the Rings 2* to strip off or at least pose in a muscle-hugging vest). The only nudity on display in the 2001-03 films was, oddly enough, courtesy of Gollum – ironically, he's not only digital, he's the last person anyone would want to see naked (and there's the troll, and Lurtz, buried under two tons of prosthetic make-up).

Not only did the films bring new readers to the books, they brought old readers back too (and have done). Someone pointed out in a Tolkien newsgroup that new readers coming to Tolkien's work might be confused, might've had Tolkien misinterpreted or misrepresented for them.

That's a patronizing attitude, and a simplistic view of readers. If folk come to J.R.R. Tolkien's work via the 2001-03 movies, the professor's prose and verse will soon work their enchantment on them. And if they love the fiction, great. And if they're jazzed enough to pick up a book and read it (as opposed to a billion other possible activities), they're probably also smart enough to realize there's loads they didn't put into the movies. No one *loses*. Having more readers is always a plus.

Most authors would KILL for the kind of industry and fanbase that's grown up around J.R.R. Tolkien. They would DIE for the level (the quality, the intensity) of readership that Tolkien has attracted, and not just the quality of readers, but for the tens of millions who've read his books. Thousands of writers don't even get *one* other person to read their stuff at all, let alone receive the kind of fervour and dedication that Tolkien gets.

Yes, there were downsides to J.R.R. Tolkien's fame, which he loathed, but to have so many readers so passionate about one's work is very, very, very rare. Any publisher receives thousands of manuscripts each year, and I bet no more than one or two would-be writers have more than one or two people who have ever read their work at all, let alone all the way through, let alone with valuable, serious criticism and feedback to offer. In the grand scheme of things, Tolkien's fiction has had a fantastic, blissful run, and will probably continue to do so for decades to come.

The two branches of the story, J.R.R. Tolkien asserted, were: '1. Prime Action, the Ringbearers. 2. Subsidiary Action, the rest of the Company leading to the 'heroic' matter. *It is essential that these two branches should each be treated in coherent sequence*' (L, 275). Pretty much any commercial filmmaking team wouldn't follow that structure, though. It's a daring element in the book, but would almost certainly alienate audiences.

It's absolutely necessary to have the whimsical, light-hearted scenes in the 2001-03 *Lord of the Rings* films, to balance the intensity and relentlessness of the dramatic, grim, gloomy, action-packed and death-filled scenes. The trouble is, the lighter, whimsical scenes come across as flimsy and uninvolving (partly because they're nearly always written and directed with far less passion and flair than the bigger, heavier scenes).

The staging of the scenes in the great halls of Rohan and Gondor was static and a little uninspired. These were the scenes that recalled Shakespeare's history plays in J.R.R. Tolkien's tome, but despite featuring actors who were known for playing Shakespeare (such as Ian McKellen), they were nowhere near even the standard of a rep or provincial theatre production of the history plays. With sets that impressive, the staging could have been much more dynamic. (When tiredness kicked in during the lengthy shoot, Peter Jackson said it 'was harder and harder to come up with inventive ideas', and scenes would be shot in the conventional manner [Sib, 490]).

And when it came to speechifying, some of the actors were not quite up to the job (principally Viggo Mortensen, who had to be Prince Harry rousing his troops at least twice, but couldn't really manage it). Mortensen was great as Strider the rough, gnarled, weary ranger and Aragorn the devoted, dreamy-eyed lover of Arwen, and the action and sword fights were fine, but the grandeur and dignity of Aragorn as King Elessar seemed to elude him somewhat (but that's the aspect of Aragorn from the books that's difficult to perform, as well as to take as a reader).

Weathertop is a less than satisfying sequence. But then, as a filmmaker, you're buggered with J.R.R. Tolkien's description in the book of the Weathertop attack: in other words, he doesn't describe it. He leaves it vague; it's lost in the gap between two chapters. Frodo swoons at the end of chapter 11: 'he caught a glimpse of Strider leaping out of the darkness with a flaming brand of wood in either hand'. Cut to the start of chapter 12, where Tolkien's narrator back-announces the attack, so to speak: Sam sees black shadows, not much else: 'they saw nothing more, until they stumbled over the body of Frodo, lying as if dead'.

The solution in the film showing how Aragorn defeats five nazgul isn't convincing. In a silly moment, Aragorn lobs a firebrand into the face of a nazgul, where it lodges. As camp and dumb as anything in Hammer or Roger Corman (actually, not as good as Hammer or Corman).

NOTES: ADAPTING *THE LORD OF THE RINGS* FOR THE 2001-03 FILMS

1. I. Nathan, 2004, 90.
2. I. Nathan, 2004, 90.
3. I. Nathan, 2002, 65; my italics.

THE SCRIPT

Director Peter Jackson said the most difficult part of making *The Lord of the Rings* was writing the script, cutting down the 1200 pages to a manageable three films of just over two hours each: 'the most difficult thing has been the script. Without any doubt, the scriptwriting has been a total nightmare', Jackson confessed).[1] Even a cursory look at *The Lord of the Rings* reveals how much detail and story is packed into it – names, places, genealogies, geography, histories, and tons of backstory. Making each of the three volumes as a two-hour-45-minute feature film inevitably means so much pruning that the films can't be much more than a 'greatest hits' of *The Lord of the Rings*. This's what the screenwriters, producers and studio went for: a series of the bits most people remember from the book, filmed with an international cast (not strictly 'international' – rather, an Anglo-America-Australian-Kiwi cast), and CGI special effects and old-style miniatures. Jackson said he intended to make something like the Ray Harryhausen fantasy films he'd enjoyed as a child, films like the *Sinbad* movies and *Jason and the Argonauts*. 'I wanted to make my 'Jason', or my 'Sinbad'', Jackson remarked (R. Harryhausen, ix).

Among the countless changes (discussed at length in this book) made in translating *The Lord of the Rings* to the screen were bringing a romance (between Arwen and Aragorn) from one of the many appendices to the main part of the narrative (to counter-act the masculinist slant of *The Lord of the Rings*). Tom Bombadil was dropped altogether, as was Old-Man Willow and many secondary characters (such as Prince Imrahhil, Elrond's sons, the Wild Men, etc).

To be fair to the adaptors of the 2001-03 movies of *The Lord of the Rings* and the many alterations they made from J.R.R. Tolkien's novel, Tolkien himself had considered all sorts of variations, including having Sam wandering into Fangorn and being taken by Gandalf to Minas Tirith; having Frodo and Sam fighting nazgûl on the side of Mount Doom, having Frodo being taken to the Dark Tower; having Éowyn as well as Théoden dying at Pelennor; having Treebeard being an evil giant; having Aragorn casually chatting to a ringwraith over a hedge; and Lothlórien being razed by nazgûl, among many other alternatives.

In fact, the narrative variations that J.R.R. Tolkien contemplated as he was writing *The Lord of the Rings* between 1937 and its publication in 1954-55 were much more extreme than the ones that appeared in the two thousand one-three films, including the departures of Frodo as an 18 year-old kid, Aragorn's 'death' and return, Faramir taking Frodo and the ring to Osgiliath, and so on. (When the 2001-03 project was with Miramax, a script consultant made a no. of suggestions for turning Tolkien's books into one film: drop Helm's Deep; combine Rohan and Gondor; combine

Denethor and Théoden; cut Saruman, or use him better; combine Faramir and Éowyn; lose the attack at Bree; halve the Rivendell scenes; compress Moria scenes; delay Ganalf's return, and so on [Sib, 379-380).

For those who don't mind Tom Bombadil's omission from most adaptions of *The Lord of the Rings* point out that not only does he not really add much to the quest to destroy the ring, he also doesn't appear again. He's mentioned at the Council of Elrond, and Gandalf visits him at the end of the novel, but he doesn't play a major role in the War of the Ring.

One of the most significant decisions in adapting *The Lord of the Rings* in 2001, as far as narrative was concerned, was to include scenes from the earlier life of the ring, of the Second Age and the Last Alliance, involving Isildur, Elrond, Sauron and, later, Gollum. Some of this material comes from Elrond's lengthy speeches at Rivendell. Some of it, such as the prologue to *The Return of the King,* about how Gollum acquired the ring, comes from Gandalf.

Making Galadriel the narrator of the film was perhaps another appeal to the female audience, because, really, in many ways the one character who should be narrating an adaption of the book was Gandalf. He was the one who had the most information (often in advance of the reader of the book or viewer of the film), who interacted with the most characters (from the lowliest to the noblest), who travelled around the most, and who told the most stories of the past. Also, as Elrond put it in the book, this adventure was primarily Gandalf's show. (Other characters would come before Galadriel as choices for narrators: Frodo obviously, and Bilbo, but also Sam, and maybe Aragorn). A narration by Frodo was written and recorded, as if he were looking back on events from the end of the story, but was dropped (Frodo does narrate parts of the films; the end section of *The Return of the King,* for instance, from the coronation of Aragorn to the journey to the Grey Havens). Bilbo narrating the prologue was also considered (in the extended DVD version of *Fellowship*, Bilbo does narrate quite a bit of the prologue, including the section 'concerning hobbits'). The 1981 BBC radio adaption was reworked in 2001, with Frodo as an older hobbit, looking back on the events of *Lord of the Rings.*

Bumping up Orlando Bloom's Legolas in *The Two Towers* and *The Return of the King* may have been inspired by wanting to attract the under 25 female audience; the studio and filmmakers knew that Bloom's elf was popular among young women, and that Bloom had star appeal in that sector of the audience.

ARAGORN. Curiously, Aragorn has little voiceover in the *Lord of the Rings* films. Most every other character narrates parts of the films – Gandalf, Bilbo, Frodo, Elrond, Galadriel, Saruman, Gollum. There seems to be more of an attempt to portray Aragorn in the films' present tense, not looking back from some point in the future, and not to explain events (i.e.,

'Aragorn' meant action, not narration or explanation). The narration of the main characters noted above is largely for exposition, or to explain things which either were difficult to show, or would take too long to show.

With regard to Aragorn's story, screenwriters Frances Walsh and Philippa Boyens want to have it both ways: scriptwriters know from Vladimir Propp and the countless screenwriting bibles that quote Propp, Joseph Campbell, Mircea Eliade, Carl Jung *et al*, that the hero has to *refuse* the 'call to adventure' at first. But s/he has to accept it pretty soon, for the adventure to begin. But Walsh and Boyens stretched Aragorn's reluctance as long as possible, right into the third film: he really *doesn't* want to become king, to face up to his world-changing responsibilities. Poor dear. Yet, from the time he's introduced in Bree, Aragorn is right there, not only coming along for the ride, but taking charge of the travelling hobbits and guiding them to Rivendell. And at Weathertop, he's protecting them by fighting for his life. To make it more explicit, at the Council of Elrond he pledges his life to protect Frodo and help him carry out the task.

After that, Aragorn's fighting his way across all of Middle-earth, becoming Arda's greatest warrior. He doesn't seem very reluctant. Yet Boyens and Walsh introduced the notion of reluctance in Aragorn back in Rivendell, before the council, in that important duologue with Arwen in front of the shards of Narsil.

In short, the deep reluctance of Aragorn to accept his responsibility/ destiny as the king of Gondor and Arnor adds complications to his character that just aren't there in the novel, where Aragorn has accepted his royal, noble fate. The changes to Aragorn's characterization also helped to give the character a character development that would run over three films, not just the usual one film.

❀

BODY COUNT. There are numerous deaths in the 2001-2003 *Lord of the Rings* films – but most of those deaths are also in the book. Some of the death scenes are spectacular – set-pieces in their own right: the troll, Lurtz, Boromir, Gandalf, the balrog, Haldir, the *mûmakil* rider, Gollum, the ringwraiths, the Witch-king, Saruman, Wormtongue, and most epic of all, Sauron. Other deaths include Háma, Gothmog, Faramir's lieutenant Madril, Shagrat, Grishnákh, Gorbag, the warg rider, and numerous orcs, Gondorians, Rohirrim, Haradrim, etc.

So many deaths!

Characters appear to die – Frodo, Sam, Gandalf, Aragorn – but somehow survive (Arwen wastes away, too, but revives, and Éowyn is near death). And there are death scenes where a character dies in another's arms: Aragorn and Boromir, Aragorn and Haldir, Théoden and Éowyn. But when you see them all strung together in the space of a few hours in a movie, the number of deaths does seem excessive. Really excessive.

These are grotesquely violent movies.

Fans of the book pointed out that characters in the 2001-03 *Lord of the Rings* films always seem to fall into despair before rallying and deciding to fight: at Helm's Deep Legolas sinks into despair before rallying and apologizing to Aragorn; as soon as Théoden's revived, he decides to run away; the Entmoot decides to have peace instead of going to war; Aragorn breaking with Arwen, and so on.

Both *The Lord of the Rings* films and books are very clear-cut when it comes to how the audience is intended to identify with the groups of characters. It's simply good vs. evil forces. There isn't much ambiguity here. J.R.R. Tolkien's narrator is definitely on one side, the goodies. In some other forms of narrative, say a fugitive on the run from the police, an audience might identify with both pursuers and pursued. Stories about gangsters, for instance, encourage the audience to identify with criminals, as well as the people pursuing them (the cops, the FBI, etc). The *Godfather* films are a good example: Al Pacino, Marlon Brando, James Caan, Robert de Niro *et al* are nasty, vicious people, but the audience is encouraged to empathize with them. In classic literature, plays like *Macbeth* are good examples: the lead character Macbeth is a multiple murderer.

But there is no such ambiguity in *The Lord of the Rings*. Sauron and his forces are bad, bad, bad, and the audience is always encouraged to cheer for the goodies' side. Occasionally the narrator voices concern over the poor orcs, pushed around by the Dark Lord. And a character such as Gollum is an exception – he teeters between good and evil throughout the book (and Tolkien maintains the ambiguity around Gollum right to the end: Gollum takes the ring from Frodo by force, but he also destroys it, which Frodo couldn't do, apparently by accident when he slips and falls).

GANDALF. The 2001-03 movie Gandalf was a wizard who led armies into battle (as at Helm's Deep, where he's seen killing orcs with his staff, or on the battlements of Minas Tirith). This Gandalf tended not to use lots of magic or spells (the filmmakers were not fans of the common cinematic tropes of bolts of lighting or electricity). When the two wizards duel at Isengard, for instance, there is a strong physical component to the fight, although the staffs are employed magically too. When Gandalf fights orcs on the terraces of Minas Tirith, he uses his sword and staff, both as physical not magical weapons. Gandalf did use his magic throughout the films, though: to light the way in Moria, to battle Saruman, to exorcise Théoden, and to beat off the nazgûl in the retreat from Osgiliath.

Gandalf would also perform the role of the main vehicle for exposition, backstory, and the history of Middle-earth (along with Elrond and Galadriel). In contrast to the two figureheads of elven aristocracy, Gandalf could be in the thick of things, interacting with characters, and thus could be used by the screenwriters to carry a lot of explanations and history

(Legolas and Aragorn occasionally provide exposition, as does Gollum on the journey to Mordor, though far less than the wizard).

❋

The sections of the 2001-03 *The Lord of the Rings* films aimed at the global cinema audience and those aimed at Tolkien fans are easily discerned. It's almost as if the filmmakers had decided, as they went along with pre-production and shooting: this bit's for the multiplex audience (Treebeard squashing an orc), and this one's for the Tolkien fans (Legolas remarking that it was the elves who began to wake the trees).

Just as the potential for homoeroticism between Frodo and Sam was consciously avoided in the 2001-03 movies (although the films weren't wholly successful in sidestepping it), the scenes between Frodo and Gollum were also kept asexual. But Gollum's subservient, pawing behaviour towards Frodo (and to Bilbo in *The Hobbit*), his touchy, feely gestures, have a sexual component which critics have drawn attention to (although J.R.R. Tolkien himself wasn't interested in that aspect of the characters; Frodo is ascetically non-sexual, while Sam has an earthy, more regular nature, and gets to marry his childhood sweetheart, Rosie Cotton).

The problems of the 2001-03 film adaptions of Ronald Tolkien's book is that the two forms are very different: one a novel written in the 1940s and 1950s in England and the other a big budget action-adventure blockbuster film made for a global market in the early 2000s. It's not just that cinema and literature are different forms, with different requirements, it's that the 2001-03 movies were conceived as blockbuster action-adventure films, which are a very particular type of film. This kind of movie has a number of artistic, internal demands (among them, action, spectacle, romance, emotion, jeopardy, clarity, easily identified goals, motives, characters and settings), but also plenty of external, economic and social pre-requisites: employment for a lot of people, a huge skills base (including money and time for training), tax incentives, a return on investment, profit potential, licensees and merchandizing, ancillary markets, and so on.

By contrast, Ronald Tolkien writing and publishing his book in the 1950s operated in a quite different socio-economic context. All that was required for the London publishers Allen & Unwin to make their investment back was to sell a few thousand copies (although shifting a few thousand units of a book can be difficult for even established publishers). Rayner Unwin remarked that he had been prepared to lose money on publishing *The Lord of the Rings* (he has quoted £1,000/ $1,600 as a figure). As a writer, Tolkien had only his publishers to please (but they were not 'hands on' editors of his work. As Rayner Unwin said, you did not dare to edit Tolkien's writing. They could – and did – turn Tolkien down, though; they rejected *The Silmarillion*, for instance). In other words, the manuscript that Tolkien delivered to his publishers was probably pretty much published in the form he desired (but they only agreed to publish *The Lord of the Rings* in three volumes, while Tolkien wanted a single book – it was never a 'trilogy' for Tolkien, but always a single piece).

A big Hollywood movie, by contrast, has all sorts of groups of people putting in their opinions and demands. All of those people – producers, writers, directors, lawyers, accountants, studio executives, marketers, advertizers, designers, illustrators, model makers, etc – putting in their two cents' worth would probably have driven Tolkien nuts. (The filmmakers of the *Lord of the Rings* films had some heated run-ins with New Line's executives, for instance. And there were plenty of arguments and disagreements behind the scenes – it would be impossible not to have tensions with so many artists working together).

RIVENDELL. The screenwriters confessed that the Rivendell chapters were the most difficult to adapt. There are many speeches, many new characters to introduce, and tons of backstory and exposition to dramatize. The elf, the man and the dwarf were introduced at Rivendell over Elrond's voiceover; the scriptwriters had toyed with different ways of introducing Legolas, Gimli and Boromir, including having a big feast. There wasn't time to include many sections of the Rivendell scenes in the book, such as the feast, Frodo speaking with Gimli's father, Glóin, Bilbo's song of Eärendil to the elves, or Elrond's lengthy history of Middle-earth, or Gandalf's accounts of his adventures, or new characters such as Glóin, Erestor and Galdor. (The addition of the Arwen-Aragorn scenes would have also pushed out the time available for other scenes). Some of the material in the Council of Elrond found its way into other parts of the films – in the prologue depicting the Last Alliance, for example.

THE RING. Another problem was to demonstrate the power of the ring. After all, the central conceit of *The Lord of the Rings* is that the whole fate of Middle Earth and all its people rests on a bit of metal, that so much power could reside in a ring. If only life were so simple! But this is the beauty of fantasy, its metaphorical or allegorical moves. In the 2001-03 movies, the solution was to make the ring a 'character', to shoot it in close-up, use different-sized prop rings, and employ a variety of devices to express its magical powers (it was portrayed as having something like atomic energy), including Sauron talking through the ring, the ring whispering to characters, characters and fire reflected in the ring, and so on.

❀

For a pocket guide to the *Lord of the Rings* movies, please see the companion book *The Lord of the Rings Movies*, or my book *J.R.R. Tolkien*.

NOTES: ADAPTING *THE LORD OF THE RINGS* FOR THE 2001-03 FILMS

1. I. Nathan, 2002, 65.

BIBLIOGRAPHY

J.R.R. TOLKIEN

The Adventures of Tom Bombadil and Other Verses From the Red Book, Allen & Unwin, London, 1962

Ancrene Wisse: The English Text of the Ancrene Riwle, Early English Text Society, Original Series no. 249, Oxford University Press, London, 1962

Smith of Wootton Major, Allen & Unwin, London, 1967

The Road Goes Ever On: A Song Cycle, Allen & Unwin, London, 1968

Farmer Giles of Ham, Allen & Unwin, London, 1949

Tree and Leaf, Unwin Books, London, 1975

The Father Christmas Letters, ed. B. Tolkien, Allen & Unwin, London, 1976

The Silmarllion, ed. C. Tolkien, Allen & Unwin, London, 1977

The Hobbit, Allen & Unwin, London, 1978

The Lord of the Rings, Allen & Unwin, London, 1966, 1979

Pictures of J.R.R. Tolkien, Allen & Unwin, London, 1979/ HarperCollins, London, 1992

Sir Gawain and the Green Knight, The Pearl, Sir Orfeo, ed. C. Tolkien, Unwin Paperbacks, London, 1979

Unfinished Tales, ed. C. Tolkien, Allen & Unwin, London, 1980

Poems and Stories, Allen & Unwin, London, 1980

The Letters of J.R.R. Tolkien, ed. H. Carpenter & C. Tolkien, Allen & Unwin, London, 1981/ HarperCollins, London, 1999

The Letters of J.R.R. Tolkien, HarperCollins, London, 1995

Mr. Bliss, Allen & Unwin, London, 1982

The Monster and the Critics and Other Essays, ed. C. Tolkien, Allen & Unwin, London, 1983

The History of Middle Earth 1: The Book of Lost Tales, vol. 1. ed. C. Tolkien, Allen & Unwin, London, 1983

The History of Middle Earth 2: The Book of Lost Tales, vol. 2. ed. C. Tolkien, Allen & Unwin, London, 1984

The History of Middle Earth 3: The Lays of Beleriand, ed. C. Tolkien, Allen & Unwin, London, 1985

The History of Middle Earth 4: The Shaping of Middle-Earth, ed. C. Tolkien, Allen & Unwin, London, 1986

The History of Middle Earth 5: The Lost Road and Other Writings, ed. C. Tolkien, Unwin Hyman, London, 1987

The History of Middle Earth 6: The Return of the Shadow: The History of The Lord of the Rings, Part I, ed. C. Tolkien, HarperCollins, London, 1994

The History of Middle Earth 7: The Treason of Isengard, The History of The Lord of the Rings, Part 2, ed. C. Tolkien, Unwin Hyman, London, 1989

The History of Middle Earth 8: The War of the Ring: The History of The Lord of the Rings, Part 3, ed. C. Tolkien, Unwin Hyman, 1990

The History of Middle Earth 9: Sauron Defeated: The History of The Lord of the Rings, Part 4, HarperCollins, London, 1992

The History of Middle Earth 10: Morgoth's Ring, ed. C. Tolkien, HarperCollins, London, 1993

The History of Middle Earth 11: The War of the Jewels, ed. C. Tolkien, Harper-Collins, London, 1994

The History of Middle Earth 12: The Peoples of Middle-earth, ed. C. Tolkien, HarperCollins, London, 1996

The Children of Hurin, HarperCollins, London, 2007

The Legend of Sigurd and Gudrún, HarperCollins, London, 2009

Bilbo's Last Song, Unwin Hyman, London, 1990

The Annotated Hobbit, ed. D. Anderson, Allen & Unwin, London, 1988

The Tolkien Reader, Ballantine, New York, NY, 1989

Roverandom, HarperCollins, London, 1998
Tales From the Perilous Realm, HarperCollins, London, 1998
Farmer Giles of Ham, 50th Anniversary Edition, HarperCollins, London, 1999
Letters From Father Christmas, HarperCollins, London, 1999

OTHERS

N.I. Agøy, ed. *Between Faith and Fiction: Tolkien and the Powers of His World, Arda Special*, Arthedain, Upsala, 1998

D. Anderson *et al*, eds. *Tolkien Studies*, 1, West Virginia University Press, 2004

—. *Tolkien Studies*, 2, West Virginia University Press, 2005

—. *Tolkien Studies*, 3, West Virginia University Press, 2006

—. *Tolkien Studies*, 4, West Virginia University Press, 2007

—. *Tolkien Studies*, 5, West Virginia University Press, 2008

B. Andrews & B. Zuber. *The Tolkien Quiz Book,* New American Library, New York, NY, 1979

M. Anish. *From the Outside: The Middle Earth Poems*, 1994.

H. Armstrong, ed. *Digging Potatoes, Growing Trees: A Selection From 25 Years of Speeches at the Tolkien Society's Annual Dinners,* Tolkien Society, Swindon, Wiltshire, 1997

—. ed. *Digging Potatoes, Growing Trees: A Selection From 25 Years of Speeches at the Tolkien Society's Annual Dinners.* vol. 2, Tolkien Society, Swindon, Wilt-shire, 1998

M. Barker & E. Mathijs, eds. *Watching Lord of the Rings,* Peter Lang, New York, NY, 2006

K.J. Battarbee, ed. *Scholarship & Fantasy: Proceedings of The Tolkien Phenom-enon,* University of Turku, Turku, Finland, 1993

H. Beard & D. Kenney. *Bored of the Rings* (The Harvard Lampoon), New American Library, New York, NY, 1969

R. Beare. *J.R.R. Tolkien's The Silmarillion,* Nimrod Publication, 1999

A. Becker, ed. *The Tolkien Treasury,* Courage Books, Running Press, 1988

E. Begg. *The Lord of the Rings and The Signs of the Times,* Guild of Pastoral Psychology Lecture Series, Guild of Pastoral Psychology, London, 1975

B. Bettelheim. *The Uses of Enchantment: The Meaning and Importance of Fairy Tales*, Knopf, New York, NY, 1976

R. Blackwelder. *A Tolkien Thesaurus,* Garland Publishing, New York, NY, 1990

—. *Tolkien Phraseology: A Companion to A Tolkien Thesaurus*, Tolkien Archives Fund, Marquette University, 1990

M. Blazejewski. *J.R.R. Tolkien – Powiernik Piesni,* Phantom Press, 1993

W. Blissett. "The Despot of the Rings", *South Atlantic Quartley,* 58, 1959

H. Bloom, ed. *J.R.R. Tolkien's The Lord of the Rings,* Modern Critical Interpretations, Philadelphia, 2000.

N. Bonnal. *Tolkien: Les univers d'un Magicie*n, Les Belles Lettres, Paris, 1998

R.B. Bottigheimer, ed. *Fairy Tales and Society: Illusion, Allusion and Paradigm*, University of Pennsylvania Press, Philadelphia, PA, 1986

—. *Grimms' Bad Girls and Bold Boys: The Moral and Social Vision of the Tales,* Yale University Press, New Haven, CT, 1987

M.Z. Bradley. *The Jewel of Arwen,* T-K Graphics, Baltimore, MD, 1974

—. *Men, Halflings & Hero Worship.* T-K Graphics, Baltimore, MD, 1973

—. *The Parting of Arwen,* T-K Graphics, Baltimore, MD, 1974

I. Brodie. *The Lord of the Rings Location Guidebook,* HarperCollins, Auckland, 2004

R. Broecker. *Fantasy of the 20th Century: An Illustrated History,* Oregon, 2001

P. Buchs & T. Honegger, eds. *News From the Shire and Beyond: Studies On Tolkien,* Walking Tree Publishers, Zurich, 1997

G. Campbell. "Lord of the Tax Deal", *NZ Listener,* Oct 21, 2000

J. Campbell. *The Hero With a Thousand Faces,* Paladin, London, 1978

H. Carpenter. *J.R.R. Tolkien: A Biography*, Allen & Unwin, London, 1977/ 1995

—. *The Inklings: C.S. Lewis, J.R.R. Tolkien, Charles Williams, and Their Friends,* Allen & Unwin, London, 1978

—. & M. Prichard. *The Oxford Companion to Children's Literature,* Oxford University Press, Oxford, 1984/ 1999

L. Carter. *Tolkien: A Look Behind The Lord of the Rings,* Ballantine Books, New York, NY, 1969

—. *Middle Earth*, Centaur, New York, NY, 1977

J. Cawthorn & M. Moorcock. *The 100 Best Fantasy Books*, Xanadu, 1988

E. Challis, ed. *The People's Guide to J.R.R. Tolkien*, TheOneRing.net/ Cold Spring Press, Cold Spring Harbor, NY, 2003

—. *More People's Guide to J.R.R. Tolkien*, TheOneRing.net/ Cold Spring Press, Cold Spring Harbor, NY, 2004

J. Chance. *Tolkien's Art: 'A Mythology for England'*, Macmillan, London, 1979

—. *The Lord of the Rings: The Mythology of Power*, Twayne, New York, 1992

—. *Tolkien's Art*, University of Kentucky Press, Lexington, 2001

—. *Tolkien the Medievalist*, Routledge, London, 2008

T. Christie. *Liv Tyler*, Crescent Moon, 2007

G. Clark & D. Timmons, eds. *J.R.R. Tolkien and His Literary Resonances*, Greenwood Press, Westport, CT, 2000

H.G.P. Colebatch. *Return of the Heroes: The Lord of the Rings, Star Wars, Harry Potter and Social Conflict*, Cybereditions Corporation, 2003

D.R. Collins. *J.R.R. Tolkien, Master of Fantasy*, Lerner Publications Company, Minneapolis, MN, 1992

J.C. Cooper. *Fairy Tales: Allegories of the Inner Life*, Aquarian Press, London, 1983

M. Coren. *J.R.R. Tolkien*, Boxtree, London, 2001

K. Crabbe. *J.R.R. Tolkien,* Modern Literature Series, Frederick Ungar, New York, NY, 1988

E. Crawford, *Some Light On Middle-earth*, The Tolkien Society, 1985

R. Crawshaw, ed. *Travel and Communication in Tolkien's Worlds,* The 10th Tolkien Society Workshop, The Tolkien Society, Swindon, 1996

—. ed. *Tolkien, the Sea and Scandinavia,* The 11th Tolkien Society Seminar, The Tolkien Society, Telford, 1999

—. ed. *Tolkien: A Mythology For England*, Tolkien Society, 1999

P. Curry. *Defending Middle-earth*, HarperCollins, London, 1998

D. Day. *A Tolkien Bestiary*, Mitchell Beazley, London, 1979

—. *Tolkien: The Illustrated Encyclopedia,* Mitchell Beazley, London, 1991

—. *A-Z of Tolkien*, Mitchell Beazley, London, 1993

—. *The Tolkien Companion*, Mandarin, London, 1993

—. *The Hobbit Companion,* Pavilion Books, London, 1997

—. *Tolkien's Ring*, Pavilion, London, 2001

—. *A Guide To Tolkien*, Chancellor Pres, London, 2001

C. Duriez. *The Tolkien and Middle-earth Handbook*, Monarch, Tunbridge Wells, 1992

—. & D. Porter. *The Inklings Handbook*, Azure, 2001

M. Edwards & R. Holdstock. *Realms of Fantasy*, Dragon's World, London, 1983

J. Ellis. *One Fairy Story Too Many: The Brothers Grimm and Their Tales*, University of Chicago Press, Chicago, IL, 1983

G. Ellwood. *Good News From Tolkien's Middle Earth: Two Essays on the 'Applicability' of The Lord of the Rings.* Eerdmans, Grand Rapids, MI, 1970

A. Etkin, ed. *Eglerio! In Praise of Tolkien,* Quest Communications, Greencastle, Pennsylvania, 1978

R. Evans. *J.R.R. Tolkien*, Warner Paperback Library, New York, NY, 1971

W. Evans-Wentz. *The Fairy-faith in Celtic Countries*, Oxford University Press, Oxford, 1911

V. Flieger. *Splintered Light: Logos and Language in Tolkien's World*, William B. Eerdmans, 1983

—. *A Question of Time J.R.R. Tolkien's Road to Faerie*, Kent State University Press, Kent, Ohio, 1997

—. & C. Hostetter, eds. *Tolkien's 'Legendarium': Essays On 'The History of Middle-earth'*, Greenwood Press, Westport, CT, 2000

K. Fonstad. *The Atlas of Middle-earth,* HarperCollins, London, 1992

R. Foster. *The Complete Guide to Middle-earth: From The Hobbit to The Silmarillion*, Allen & Unwin, London, 1978

—. *Teacher's Guide to The Hobbit*, Ballantine Books, New York, NY, 1981

M.-L. von Franz. *An Introduction to the Interpretation of Fairy Tales*, Spring Publications, New York, NY, 1970

—. *Problems of the Feminine in Fairy Tales,* Spring Publications, New York, NY, 1972

—. *Introduction to the Psychology of Fairy Tales,* Spring Publications, New York, NY, 1978

—. *The Psychological Meaning of Redemption Motif in Fairy Tales,* Inner City Books, Toronto, 1980

C. Garbowski. *Recovery and Transcendence for the Contemporary Mythmaker. The Spiritual Dimension in the Works of J.R.R. Tolkien*, Maria Curie University Press, 2000

C. George & D. Timmons, eds. *J.R.R. Tolkien and His Literary Resonances*, Greenwood Press, London, 2000

R. Giddings & E. Holland. *J.R.R. Tolkien: The Shores of Middle-earth*, Junction Books, London, 1981

—. ed. *J.R.R. Tolkien: This Far Land*, Barnes & Noble, Totawa, NJ, 1983

R. Gray, ed. *A Tribute to J.R.R. Tolkien*, Unisa, Pretoria, 1992

B. Green. *Tolkien: Master of Fantasy*, SamHar Press, Charlotteville, New York, 1981

—. *The Hobbit: A Journey into Maturity*, Twayne, New York, NY, 1995

W. Green. "Where's Mama?" The Construction of the Feminine in *The Hobbit*", *The Lion and the Unicorn*, 22, 2, April, 1998

M. Greenberg, ed. *After the King: Stories in Honor of J.R.R. Tolkien*, Pan, London, 1992

D. Grotta. *The Biography of J.R.R. Tolkien*, Courage Books, Philadelphia, PA, 1992

K. Haber, ed. *Meditations on Middle-earth. New Writing on the Worlds of J.R.R. Tolkien*, New York, NY, 2001

W. Hammond, ed. *J.R.R. Tolkien: A Descriptive Bibliography*, Oak Knoll Books, New Castle, Del., 1993

—. *J.R.R. Tolkien: Artist and Illustrator*, HarperCollins, London, 1995

W. Hansen. *Ariadne's Thread: A Guide to International Tales Found in Classical Literature*, Cornell University Press, Ithaca, NY, 2002

G. Hardy. *Tolkien's The Lord of the Rings and The Hobbit: Notes*, Cliffs Notes, Lincoln, Nebraska, 1977

R.P. Harrison. *Forests: The Shadow of Civilization*, University of Chicago Press, Chicago, IL, 1992

D. Harvey. *The Song of Middle-earth: J.R.R. Tolkien's Themes, Symbols and Myths*, Allen & Unwin, London, 1981

R. Hein. *Christian Mythmakers: Lewis, L'Engle, Tolkien, Macdonald, Chesterton and Others*, Cornerstone Press, Chicago, IL, 1998

P. Helms, *et al*, eds. *Peace and Conflict Studies in J.R.R. Tolkien's Middle-earth*, vol. 1, American Tolkien Society, Flint, Michigan, 1994

—. *et al*, eds. *Peace and Conflict Studies in J.R.R. Tolkien's Middle-earth*, vol. 2, American Tolkien Society, Flint, Michigan, 1999

R. Helms. *Tolkien's World*, Houghton Mifflin, Boston, MA, 1974

—. *Tolkien and the Silmarils,* Thames & Hudson, London, 1981

M. Hillegas, ed. *Shadows of Imagination: The Fantasies of C.S. Lewis, J.R.R. Tolkien, and Charles Williams,* Southern Illinois University Press, Carbondale, IL, 1979

A. Hitchcock, *Hitchcock On Hitchcock*, Faber, London, 1997

T. Honegger, ed. *Root and Branch: Approaches Towards Understanding Tolkien*, Walking Tree, Zürich, 1999

P. Hunt. *An Introduction to Children's Literature*, Oxford University Press, Oxford, 1994

—. ed. *Children's Literature: The Development of Criticism*, Routledge, London, 1990

F. Inglis. "Gentility and Powerlessness: Tolkien and the New Class", in R. Giddings, 1983

N.D. Isaacs & R.A. Zimbardo, eds. *Tolkien and the Critics,* University of Notre Dame Press, Notre Dame, IN, 1968

—. eds. *Tolkien: New Critical Perspectives*, University Press of Kentucky, Lexington, 1981

J. Johnson, ed. *J.R.R. Tolkien: Six Decades of Criticism*, Greenwood, CT, 1986

S.S. Jones. *The Fairy Tale: The Magic Mirror of Imagination*, Twayne, New York, NY, 1995

A. Jonsson. *A Tolkien Bibliography 1911-1980*, Tredge Upplagen, 1986

M. Kamenkovich. *The Trojan Horse: Russia as a New Context For Tolkien*, American Tolkien Society, Flint, MI, 1999

C.S. Kilby. *Tolkien and The Silmarillion*, Harold Shaw, Wheaton, IL, 1976

E.J. Kloczko. *Encyclopédie de la Terre du Milieu: Dictionaire des Langues Elfiques*. Toulan, 1995

—. ed. *Tolkien en France*, A.R.D.A., 1998

G. Knight. *The Magical World of the Inklings: J.R.R. Tolkien, C.S. Lewis, Charles Williams, Owen Barfield*, Element Books, Longmead, 1990

U.C. Knoepflmacher. *Ventures Into Childhood: Victorians Fairy Tales and Femininity*, University of Chicago Press, Chicago, IL, 1998

P.H. Kocher. *Master of Middle-earth: The Fiction of J.R.R. Tolkien*, Houghton Mifflin, Boston, MA, 1972

—. *A Reader's Guide to The Silmarillion*, Houghton Mifflin, Boston, MA, 1980

K. de Koster, *Readings on J.R.R. Tolkien,* San Diego, CA, 2000

C. Kroll. *Novel-Ties: The Hobbit, J.R.R. Tolkien: A Study Guide*, Learning Links Inc., New York, NY,

1992

A. Lang. *Custom and Myth*, London 1884

—. *Myth, Ritual and Religion*, Longmans, Green 1887

A. Lee. *Tolkien's Ring*, Pavilion, London, 1999

Lembas Extra, 1990-

U. Le Guin. *The Earthsea Quartet*, Penguin Books, London, 1993

C.S. Lewis. "The Dethronement of Power", in N. Isaacs, 1968

—. *Of This and Other Worlds*, Collins, London, 1982

E. Little. *The Fantasts: Studies in J.R.R. Tolkien, Lewis Carroll, Mervyn Peake, Nikolay Gogol and Kenneth Grahame*, Avebury, Amersham, 1984

J. Lobdell. ed. *A Tolkien Compass*, Ballantine Books, New York, NY, 1980

—. *England and Always: Tolkien's World of the Rings*, Eerdmans, Grand Rapids, MI, 1981

M. Lochhead. *Renaissance of Wonder: The Fantasy Worlds of C.S. Lewis, J.R.R. Tolkien, George Macdonald, E. Nesbit and Others*, Canongate, Edinburgh, 1973

I. Lowson *et al. World of the Rings: The Unauthorised Guide To the World of J.R.R. Tolkien*, Richmond, 2002

H. Luke. *Choice in The Lord of the Rings*, Apple Farm Community, MI, n.d.

M. Lüthi. *Once Upon a Time: On the Nature of Fairy Tales*, Indiana University Press, Bloomington, IN, 1976

—. *The European Folktale: Form and Nature*, tr. J.D. Niles, Institute for the Study of Human Issues, Philadelphia, PA, 1982

—. *The Fairy Tale as Art Form and Portrait of Man*, tr. J. Erickson, Indiana University Press, Bloomington, London, 1985

The Tolkien Papers, Mankato State College Studies in English, 2, 1, Feb, 1967

C. Manlove. *Modern Fantasy*, Cambridge University Press, Cambridge, 1975

—. *Christian Fantasy*, Macmillan, London, 1992

—. *The Fantasy Literature of England*, Macmillan, London, 1999

—. *From Alice to Harry Potter: Children's Fantasy in England*, Cybereditions Corporation, 2003

E. Mathijs, ed. *Lord of the Rings: Popular Culture In Global Context*, Wallflower Press, London, 2006

—. & M. Pomerance, eds. *From Hobbits To Hollywood: Essays on Lord of the Rings*, Editions Rodopi, New York, NY, 2006

R. Matthews. *Lightning From a Clear Sky: Tolkien, the Trilogy, and The Silmarillion*, Borgo Press, San Bernadino, 1978

S. McDaniel. *The Philosophical Etymology of Hobbit*, American Tolkien Society, 1995

S.B. Melmed. *J.R.R. Tolkien: A Bibliography*, University of Witwatersrand, Johannesburg, 1972

S. Miesel. *Myth, Symbol and Religion in The Lord of the Rings*, T-K Graphics, Baltimore, MD, 1973

S.O. Miller. *Middle Earth: A World in Conflict*, T-K Graphics, Baltimore, MD, 1975

—. *Mithrandir*, T-K Graphics, Baltimore, MD, 1974

J.W. Montgomery, ed. *Myth, Allegory and Gospel: An Interpretation of J.R.R. Tolkien / C.S. Lewis / G.K. Chesterton / Charles Williams*, Bethany Fellowship, Minneapolis, MN, 1974

M. Moorcock. *Epic Pooh*, British Fantasy Society, 1978

—. *Casablanca*, Gollancz, London, 1993

L.D. Morrison. *J.R.R. Tolkien's The Fellowship of the Ring: A Critical Commentary*, Monarch Press, Simon & Schuster, New York, NY, 1976

R.E. Morse. *Evocation of Virgil in Tolkien's Art: Geritol for the Classics*, Bolchazy-Carducci Publishers, Oak Park, WI, 1986

I.R. Morus, *et al*, eds. *Tolkien and Romanticism: Proceedings of the Cambridge Tolkien Workshop 1988*, Cambridge Tolkien Workshop, Cambridge, 1988

C. Moseley. *J.R.R. Tolkien: Writers and their Work*. Northcote House Publishers, Plymouth, 1996

A. Murray. *The Tolkien Quiz Book*, HarperCollins, London, 1996

A.E. Neimark. *Myth Maker: J.R.R. Tolkien*, Harcourt Brace, San Diego, CA, 1996

C.E. Noad. *The Trees, the Jewels, and the Rings: A discursive enquiry into things little known on Middle-earth*, The Tolkien Society, 1977

P. Nodelman. *Words About Pictures: The Narrative Art of Children's Picture Books*, University of Georgia Press, Athens, GA, 1988

—. *Touchstones: Reflections on the Best of Children's Literature*, Purdue University Press, Lafayette, 3 vol, 1985-8

R.S. Noel. *The Mythology of Middle-earth*. Houghton Mifflin, Boston, MA, 1977

—. *The Languages of Tolkien's Middle-earth*, Houghton Mifflin, Boston, MA, 1980

T.R. O'Neill. *The Individuated Hobbit: Jung, Tolkien and the Archetypes of Middle-earth*, Houghton

Mifflin, Boston, MA, 1979
I. & P. Opie. *The Classic Fairy Tales*, Paladin, London, 1980
N. Otty. "The Structuralist's Guide to Middle-earth", in R. Giddings, 1983
B. Palmer. *Of Orc-Rags, Phials & A Far Shore: Visions of Paradise in The Lord of the Rings*, T-K Graphics, Baltimore, MA, 1976
J. Pearce. *Tolkien: Man and Myth*, HarperCollins, London, 1998
—. ed. *Tolkien: A Celebration: Collected Writings on a Literary Legacy*, Fount, London, 1999
A.C. Petty. *One Ring to Bind Them All: Tolkien's Mythology*, University of Alabama Press, Tuscaloosa, Alabama, 1979/ 2002
D. Petzold. *J.R.R. Tolkien: Fantasy Literature als Wunscherfullung und Weltdeutung*, Carl Winter Universitätsverlag, Heidelberg, 1980
A.M. Pienciak. *J.R.R. Tolkien's The Hobbit and The Lord of the Rings*, Barron's Book Notes, Barron's Educational Series, 1986
C. & D. Plimmer. "The Man Who Understands Hobbits", *Daily Telegraph*, Mch 22, 1968.
L. Postman. *The Hobbit Companion*. Pavilion, London, 1997
J. Priestman. *J.R.R. Tolkien: Life and Legend. An Exhibition to Commemorate the Centenary of the Birth of J.R.R. Tolkien (1892-1973)*, Bodleian Library, Oxford, 1992
R.L. Purtill. *Lord of the Elves and Eldils: Fantasy and Philosophy in C.S. Lewis and J.R.R. Tolkien*, Zondervan Publishing, Grand Rapids, MI, 1974
—. *J.R.R. Tolkien*, Harper & Row, New York, NY, 1984
D. Raiche. *Ego and Shadow in The Lord of the Rings*, Apple Farm Community, MI, n.d.
A Reader's Companion to The Hobbit and The Lord of the Rings, Quality Paperback Book Club, New York, 1995
W. Ready. *The Tolkien Relation*, Henry Regnery, Chicago, IL, 1968
—. *The Lord of the Rings, The Hobbit: Notes. Coles Notes*, Coles Publishing Co., Toronto, 1971
—. *Understanding Tolkien and The Lord of the Rings*, Warner, New York, NY, 1976
Realms of Tolkien, HarperCollins, London, 1996
R.J. Reilly. *Romantic Religion: A Study of Barfield, Lewis, Williams, and Tolkien*, University of Georgia Press, Athens, GA, 1971
P. Reynolds. *Tolkien's Birmingham*, Forsaken Inn Press, 1992
—. & G. GoodKnight, eds. *Proceedings of the J.R.R. Tolkien Centenary Conference*, Tolkien Society, Milton Keynes, 1995
T. Reynolds. *The First and Second Ages: The 5th Tolkien Society Workshop*, The Tolkien Society, London, 1992
G. Ridden. *J.R.R. Tolkien: The Hobbit, York Notes*, York Press/ Longman Group, Harlow, 1981
—. *J.R.R. Tolkien: The Lord of the Rings. York Notes*, York Press/ Longman Group, Harlow, 1984
D. Robinson. "The Hasty Stroke Goes Oft Astray: Tolkien and Humour", in R. Giddings, 1983
K. Rockow. *Funeral Customs in Tolkien's Trilogy*, T-K Graphics, Baltimore, MD, 1973
D.W. & I.A. Rogers. *J.R.R. Tolkien*, Twayne, Boston, MA, 1980
B. Rosebury. *Tolkien: A Critical Assessment*, Macmillan, London, 1992
L.D. Rossi. *The Politics of Fantasy: C.S. Lewis and J.R.R. Tolkien*, UMI Research Press, Ann Arbor, MI, 1984
J.S. Ryan. *The Shaping of Middle-earth's Maker*, American Tolkien Society, 1992
—. *Tolkien: Cult or Culture?*, University of New England, Armidale, N.S.W., 1969
R. Sale. *Modern Heroism: Essays on D.H. Lawrence, William Empson, and J.R.R. Tolkien*, University of California Press, Berkeley, CA, 1973
—. *Fairy Tales and After: From Snow White to E.B. White*, Harvard University Press, Cambridge, MA, 1978
K. Salen & E. Zimmerman, eds. *Rules of Play: Game Design Fundamentals*, MIT Press, Cambridge, MA, 2004
M. Salu & R.T. Farrell, eds. *J.R.R. Tolkien, Scholar and Storyteller: Essays In Memoriam*, Cornell University Press, Ithaca, NY, 1979
T. Schindler, ed. *Concerning Hobbits and Other Matters: Tolkien Across the Disciplines*, University of St. Thomas, 2001
C. Scull & W. Hammond, *J.R.R. Tolkien: Artist and Illustrator*, HarperCollins, London, 1998
M. Sendak. *Caldecott & Co.: Notes on Books and Pictures*, Reinhardt, Viking, 1988
T. Shippey. *The Road to Middle-earth*, Allen & Unwin, 1982
—. *et al*, eds. *Leaves From the Tree: J.R.R. Tolkien's Shorter Fiction*, 4th Tolkien Society Workshop, The Tolkien Society, London, 1991
—. ed. *Essays and Studies 1990: Fictional Space: Essays On Contemporary Science Fiction*,

Oxford University Press, Oxford, 1991
—. *J.R.R. Tolkien: Author of the Century*, HarperCollins, London, 2000
R. Shorto. *J.R.R. Tolkien: Man of Fantasy*, Kipling Press, New York, NY, 1988
B. Sibley. *The Lord of the Rings: Official Movie Guide*, HarperCollins, London, 2001
M.E. Smith. *Tolkien's Ordinary Virtues: Exploring the Spiritual Themes of The Lord of the Rings*, InterVarsity, 2002
A. Smol. ""Oh... Oh... Frodo!": Readings of Male Intimacy in *The Lord of the Rings*", *Modern Fiction Studies*, 50, 4, 2004
J.D. Stahl, ed. *The Lion and the Unicorn*, 19, 1, June, 1995
M. Stanton. *Hobbits, Elves and Wizards: Exploring the Wonders and Worlds of J.R.R. Tolkien's The Lord of the Rings*, Palgrave Macmillan, New York, NY, 2001
D. & C.D. Stevens. *J.R.R. Tolkien*, Borgo Press, San Bernadino, 1993
C.R. Stimpson. *J.R.R. Tolkien*, Columbia Essays on Modern Writers, no. 41, Columbia University Press, New York, NY, 1969
B. Strachey. *Journeys of Frodo: An Atlas of J.R.R. Tolkien's The Lord of the Rings*, Unwin Paperbacks, Allen & Unwin, London, 1981
R. Sturch. *Four Christian Fantasists. A study of the fantastic writings of George MacDonald, Charles Williams, C.S. Lewis and J.R.R. Tolkien*, Zurich, 2001
Martin Sutton. *The Sin-Complex: A Critical Study of English Versions of the Grimms' Kinder- und Hausmärchen in the Nineteenth Century*, Schriften der Brüder Grimm-Gesellschaft, Kassel, 1996
D. Swann. *The Road Goes Ever On: A Song Cycle*, Allen & Unwin, London, 1967
J. Thomas. *Inside the Wolf's Belly: Aspects of the Fairy Tale*, Sheffield Academic Press, Sheffield, 1989
C. Tolkien. *The Silmarillion by J.R.R. Tolkien: A brief account of the book and its making*, Houghton Mifflin, Boston, MA, 1977
J. & P. Tolkien. *The Tolkien Family Album*, HarperCollins, London, 1992
Tolkien's World: Pictures of Middle-earth, HarperCollins, London, 1992
M. Torre. "The Portrait of Evil in *The Lord of the Rings*: Reflections Personal, Literary, and Theological", *Logos: A Journal of Catholic Thought and Culture*, 5, 4, Fall, 2002
J.E.A. Tyler. *The New Tolkien Companion*, Macmillan, London, 1979
—. *The Tolkien Companion*, Gramercy, New York NY, 2000
R. Unwin. *The Making of The Lord of the Rings*, Willem A. Meeuws, Oxford, 1992
—. *George Allen & Unwin: A Remembrancer*, Merlin Unwin Books, Ludlow, 1999
G. Urang. *Shadows of Heaven: Religion and Fantasy in the Writing of C.S. Lewis, Charles Williams, and J.R.R. Tolkien*, SCM Press, London, 1971
J. Vanhecke *et al. De Mijnen van Moria: Essays over J.R.R. Tolkien*, EXA, Uitgave, 1983
—. *J.R.R. Tolkien 1892-1992*, Stadsbibliothek en het Archief en Museum voor het Vlaamse Culturleven, Antwerp, 1992
R. van Rossenberg, ed. *Motieven in Midden-aarde: Essays over Tolkien en Fantasy, Lembas-extra*, 1988, Een Unquendor uitgave, Tolkien Winkel, 1988
—. ed. *Elrond's Holy Round Table: Essays on Tolkien, Sayers and the Arthur Saga, Lembas Extra 1990*, An Unquendor Publication, Tolkienwinkel, The Netherlands, 1990
—. *Hobbits in Holland. Leven en Werk van J.R.R. Tolkien (1892-1973)*, Koninklijke Bibliothek, Den Haag, 1992
R. Vink *et al. Tolkien: Herdenkingsnummer van LEMBAS*, Uitgeverij Sirius en Siderius, Den Haag, 1983
—. ed. *Tolkien and the Spirit of the Age*, Tolkien Genootschap "Unquendor", Leiden, 1987
S. van der Weide, ed. *Proceedings of Unquendor's Third Lustrum Conference*, Lembas-Extra, Unquendor, Leiden, 1998
Orson Welles, in *Orson Welles: Interviews*, ed. M. Estrin, University of Mississippi Press, Jackson, 2002.
R.C. West. *Tolkien Criticism: An Annotated Checklist*, Kent State University Press, 1991
M. White. *Tolkien: A Biography*, Abacus, London, 2002
C. Wilson. *Tree by Tolkien*, Village Press, London, 1974
I. Wojcik-Andrews, ed. *The Lion and the Unicorn, Children's Films* issue, 20, 1, June, 1997
J. Wyatt. *A Middle-Earth Album: Paintings by Joan Wyatt Inspired by J.R.R. Tolkien's The Lord of the Rings*, Thames & Hudson, London, 1979
J. Zipes. *Breaking the Spell: Radical Theories of Folk and Fairy Tales*, Heinemann, London, 1978
—. *Fairy Tales and the Art of Subversion: The Classical Genre for Children and the Process of*

Civilization, Heinemann, London, 1983

—. *Trials and Tribulations of Little Red Riding Hood: Versions of the Tale in Socio-Cultural Context*, Heinemann, London, 1983

—. *Don't Bet on the Prince: Contemporary Feminist Fairy Tales in North America and England*, Methuen, New York, NY, 1986

—. *The Brothers Grimm: From Enchanted Forests to the Modern World*, Routledge, New York, NY, 1989

—. *Breaking the Spell: Radical Theories of Folk and Fairy Tales*, University of Kentucky Press, Lexington, 2002a

—. *Sticks and Stones: The Troublesome Success of Children's Literature From Slovenly Peter to Harry Potter*, Routledge, London, 2002

Jeremy Robinson has written many critical studies, including *Arthur Rimbaud*, *The Sacred Cinema of Andrei Tarkovsky*, and *Steven Spielberg: God-Light*, plus literary monographs on: Shakespeare; Samuel Beckett; Thomas Hardy; André Gide; Robert Graves; Lawrence Durrell; and John Cowper Powys.

It's amazing for me to see my work treated with such passion and respect. There is nothing resembling it here in relation to my work.

Andrea Dworkin (on *Andrea Dworkin*)

This model monograph – it is an exemplary job, and I'm very proud that he has accorded me a couple of mentions… The subject matter of his book is beautifully organised and dead on beam.

Lawrence Durrell (on *The Light Eternal: A Study of J.M.W. Turner*)

Jeremy Robinson's poetry is certainly jammed with ideas, and I find it very interesting for that reason. It's certainly a strong imprint of his personality.

Colin Wilson

Sex-Magic-Poetry-Cornwall is a very rich essay… It is a very good piece… vastly stimulating and insightful.

Peter Redgrove

ARTS, PAINTING, SCULPTURE

web: www.crmoon.com • e-mail: cresmopub@yahoo.co.uk

The Art of Andy Goldsworthy
Andy Goldsworthy: Touching Nature
Andy Goldsworthy in Close-Up
Andy Goldsworthy: Pocket Guide
Andy Goldsworthy In America

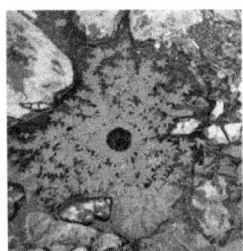

Land Art: A Complete Guide
The Art of Richard Long
Richard Long: Pocket Guide
Land Art In Great Britain
Land Art in Close-Up
Land Art In the U.S.A.
Land Art: Pocket Guide
Installation Art in Close-Up
Minimal Art and Artists In the 1960s and After
Colourfield Painting

Land Art DVD, TV documentary
Andy Goldsworthy DVD, TV documentary
The Erotic Object: Sexuality in Sculpture From Prehistory to the Present Day
Sex in Art: Pornography and Pleasure in Painting and Sculpture
Postwar Art
Sacred Gardens: The Garden in Myth, Religion and Art
Glorification: Religious Abstraction in Renaissance and 20th Century Art
Early Netherlandish Painting
Jasper Johns
Brice MardenLeonardo da Vinci
Piero della Francesca
Giovanni Bellini

Fra Angelico: Art and Religion in the Renaissance
Mark Rothko: The Art of Transcendence
Frank Stella: American Abstract Artist
Alison Wilding: The Embrace of Sculpture
Vincent van Gogh: Visionary Landscapes
Eric Gill: Nuptials of God
Constantin Brancusi: Sculpting the Essence of Things
Max Beckmann
Gustave Moreau
Caravaggio

Egon Schiele: Sex and Death In Purple Stockings
Delizioso Fotografico Fervore: Works In Process I
Sacro Cuore: Works In Process 2
The Light Eternal: J.M.W. Turner
The Madonna Glorified: Karen Arthurs

LITERATURE

J.R.R. Tolkien: The Books, The Films, The Whole Cultural Phenomenon
J.R.R. Tolkien: Pocket Guide
Beauties, Beasts and Enchantment: Classic French Fairy Tales
Tolkien's Heroic Quest
Brothers Grimm: German Popular Stories
Sexing Hardy: Thomas Hardy and Feminism
Thomas Hardy's *Tess of the d'Urbervilles*
Thomas Hardy's *Jude the Obscure*
Thomas Hardy: The Tragic Novels
Love and Tragedy: Thomas Hardy
The Poetry of Landscape in Hardy
Wessex Revisited: Thomas Hardy and John Cowper Powys
Wolfgang Iser: Essays and Interviews
Petrarch, Dante and the Troubadours
Maurice Sendak and the Art of Children's Book Illustration
Andrea Dworkin
Cixous, Irigaray, Kristeva: The *Jouissance* of French Feminism
Julia Kristeva: Art, Love, Melancholy, Philosophy, Semiotics and Psychoanalysis
Hélene Cixous I Love You: The *Jouissance* of Writing
Luce Irigaray: Lips, Kissing, and the Politics of Sexual Difference
Peter Redgrove: Here Comes the Flood
Peter Redgrove: Sex-Magic-Poetry-Cornwall
Lawrence Durrell: Between Love and Death, East and West
Love, Culture & Poetry: Lawrence Durrell
Cavafy: Anatomy of a Soul
German Romantic Poetry: Goethe, Novalis, Heine, Hölderlin
Novalis: *Hymns To the Night*
Feminism and Shakespeare
Shakespeare: *The Sonnets*
Shakespeare: Love, Poetry & Magic
The Passion of D.H. Lawrence
D.H. Lawrence: Symbolic Landscapes
D.H. Lawrence: Infinite Sensual Violence
The Ecstasies of John Cowper Powys
Sensualism and Mythology: The Wessex Novels of John Cowper Powys
Amorous Life: John Cowper Powys (H.W. Fawkner)
Postmodern Powys: New Essays on John Cowper Powys (Joe Boulter)
Rethinking Powys: Critical Essays on John Cowper Powys
Paul Bowles & Bernardo Bertolucci
Rainer Maria Rilke
Joseph Conrad: *Heart of Darkness*
In the Dim Void: Samuel Beckett
Samuel Beckett Goes into the Silence
André Gide: Fiction and Fervour
Jackie Collins and the Blockbuster Novel
Blinded By Her Light: The Love-Poetry of Robert Graves

POETRY

Ursula Le Guin: *Walking In Cornwall*
Peter Redgrove: Here Comes The Flood
Peter Redgrove: Sex-Magic-Poetry-Cornwall
Dante: Selections From the *Vita Nuova*
Petrarch, Dante and the Troubadours
William Shakespeare: *The Sonnets*
William Shakespeare: Complete Poems
Blinded By Her Light: The Love-Poetry of Robert Graves

Emily Dickinson: Selected Poems
Emily Brontë: Poems
Thomas Hardy: Selected Poems
Percy Bysshe Shelley: Poems
John Keats: Selected Poems
John Keats: Poems of 1820
D.H. Lawrence: Selected Poems
Edmund Spenser: Poems
Edmund Spenser: *Amoretti*
John Donne: Poems
Henry Vaughan: Poems
Sir Thomas Wyatt: Poems
Robert Herrick: Selected Poems

Rilke: Space, Essence and Angels in the Poetry of Rainer Maria Rilke
Rainer Maria Rilke: Selected Poems
Friedrich Hölderlin: Selected Poems
Arseny Tarkovsky: Selected Poems
Paul Verlaine: Selected Poems
Novalis: *Hymns To the Night*
Arthur Rimbaud: Selected Poems
Arthur Rimbaud: *A Season in Hell*
Arthur Rimbaud and the Magic of Poetry

D.J. Enright: By-Blows
Jeremy Reed: *Brigitte's Blue Heart*
Jeremy Reed: *Claudia Schiffer's Red Shoes*
Gorgeous Little Orpheus
Radiance: New Poems
Crescent Moon Book of Nature Poetry
Crescent Moon Book of Love Poetry
Crescent Moon Book of Mystical Poetry
Crescent Moon Book of Elizabethan Love Poetry
Crescent Moon Book of Metaphysical Poetry
Crescent Moon Book of Romantic Poetry
Pagan America: New American Poetry

MEDIA, CINEMA, FEMINISM and CULTURAL STUDIES

J.R.R. Tolkien: The Books, The Films, The Whole Cultural Phenomenon
J.R.R. Tolkien: Pocket Guide
The *Lord of the Rings* Movies: Pocket Guide
The Ghost Dance: The Origins of Religion
The Cinema of Hayao Miyazaki
Hayao Miyazaki: *Princess Mononoke*: Pocket Movie Guide
Hayao Miyazaki: *Spirited Away*: Pocket Movie Guide
The Peyote Cult
HomeGround: The Kate Bush Anthology
Tim Burton : Hallowe'en For Hollywood
Ken Russell
Cixous, Irigaray, Kristeva: The *Jouissance* of French Feminism
Julia Kristeva: Art, Love, Melancholy, Philosophy, Semiotics and Psychoanalysis
Luce Irigaray: Lips, Kissing, and the Politics of Sexual Difference
Hélene Cixous I Love You: The *Jouissance* of Writing
Andrea Dworkin
'Cosmo Woman': The World of Women's Magazines
Women in Pop Music
Discovering the Goddess (Geoffrey Ashe)
The Poetry of Cinema
The Sacred Cinema of Andrei Tarkovsky
Andrei Tarkovsky: Pocket Guide
Andrei Tarkovsky: *Mirror*: Pocket Movie Guide
Walerian Borowczyk: Cinema of Erotic Dreams
Jean-Luc Godard: The Passion of Cinema
Jean-Luc Godard: Pocket Guide
John Hughes and Eighties Cinema
Ferris Buller's Day Off: Pocket Movie Guide
The Cinema of Richard Linklater
Liv Tyler: Star In Ascendance
Blade Runner and the Films of Philip K. Dick
Paul Bowles and Bernardo Bertolucci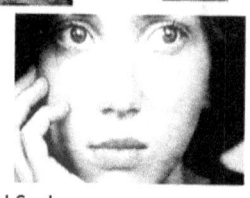
Media Hell: Radio, TV and the Press
Detonation Britain: Nuclear War in the UK
Feminism and Shakespeare
Wild Zones: Pornography, Art and Feminism
Sex in Art: Pornography and Pleasure in Painting and Sculpture
Sexing Hardy: Thomas Hardy and Feminism

The *Light Eternal* is a model monograph, an exemplary job. The subject matter of the book is
beautifully organised and dead on beam. (Lawrence Durrell)
It is amazing for me to see my work treated with such passion and respect. (Andrea Dworkin)
Sex-Magic-Poetry-Cornwall *is a very rich essay... It is like a brightly-lighted box.* (Peter Redgrove)

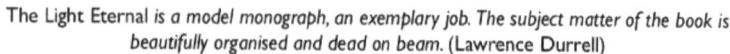

CRESCENT MOON PUBLISHING   P.O. Box 1312, Maidstone, Kent, ME14 5XU, Great Britain
0044-1622-729593   cresmopub@yahoo.co.uk   www.crmoon.com